MONUMENT

MONUMENT

IAN GRAHAM

An Ace Book
Published by The Berkley Publishing Group
A division of Penguin Group (USA) Inc.
375 Hudson Street
New York, New York 10014

Cover art by Jerry Vanderstelt.
Cover design by Rita Frangie.

PRINTING HISTORY
Orbit Books hardcover edition / October 2002
Ace trade paperback edition / April 2004

Library of Congress Cataloging-in-Publication Data

Graham, Ian, 1971–
Monument / Ian Graham—Ace trade pbk. ed.
p. cm.
ISBN 0-441-01135-7
1. Tramps—Fiction. 2. Thieves—Fiction. 3. Relics—Fiction.
I. Title

PR6107.R345M66 2004
823'.92—dc22

2003063667

PRINTED IN THE UNITED STATES OF AMERICA

10 9 8 7 6 5 4 3 2 1

For my mother and father

Acknowledgements

My colleagues in the bookshop, who have endured my professional shortfailings with remarkable patience: Katherine, Paula, Gilly, Suzanne, Alison, Sarah, Janet, Cat, Daniel, Andy, Anthony and Julian.

Rob Bowker, for placing order #1.

Mike Rowley at *Enigma* magazine, for his enthusiasm.

Dave Gemmell, for his advice, encouragement and unfaltering support.

Tim Holman, my editor, for his guidance and immeasurable patience.

Howard Morhaim and Abner Stein, my agents, for their hard work and insight.

Richard Stockley, for things technological.

Ben Svensson, for fifteen years of friendship and intoxication – may many years of similar lie ahead.

Rachel Graham, who has inflicted upon me all manner of pain and ridicule, yet remains the finest of all imaginable sisters.

And to Claire, for understanding – and apple trees and brightness.

Chapter 1

Thus it commenced, on a cloudless night,
A clothes-maker of the south
Of Meahavin
Received the word of the creator-god
And vowed to do His bidding.
Abandoning all worldly goods, he left
His home and became a Most Holy Pilgrim . . .

Extracted from the unexpurgated, forbidden account
of the Pilgrims by Mascali, the Ninth Witness

It was a foolish fashion, thought the big man. A mixture of vanity, bluster and juvenile stupidity.

Across the common room, a group of stonemasons sat at a long table. They were young men, sinuously muscled from long hours of labour. White dust caked their skin, hair, eyelashes – they seemed much less men than phantoms granted flesh. They were drinking ale, jesting, and waiting for the whores to arrive. The big man objected to none of these things. Alcohol, laughter and women were sensible pursuits. But he found absurd the manner in which the stonemasons wore their purses.

Each purse hung from its owner's belt on a two-inch braided leather strip. Some strips were brightly coloured, reds interwoven with greens and blues. Others were darker: a sombre plaiting of blacks, browns, and dried-blood ochre. The purses dangled from these strips as vulnerable, and as tempting, as ripe apples. The most cack-handed thief could've snatched one.

And that, supposed the big man, was precisely the point.

Like any young men with hot red blood in their veins, the stonemasons wished to appear confident, strong, dangerous . . . exactly the type of men who could fearlessly expose their valuables to theft. For no one would dare steal them. It would be akin to snatching food from a lion's jaws: an act of suicidal lunacy.

The big man lifted a wine flagon to his lips.

Since mid-morning, he had been in the tavern. He had scarcely budged from his corner table – except to use the pissing yard and purchase fresh drinks at the bar. He had imbibed enough alcohol to float a warship. Whisky, gin, rum, ale, wine . . . all had sluiced into his stomach. He had drunk enough to make most men fall violently sick. Enough, perhaps, even to kill those of an under-developed constitution. But the big man was immeasurably resilient. Effortlessly, he could drink ten times as much as most men.

And *looked* like he could.

Drink had bloated him. Over his belt sagged an ale gut – a flaccid drum of flesh, straining against his tunic. His face was swollen. And never a handsome man, he now resembled a boar. His nose had been broken so frequently in drunken brawls that it had crumpled to a snout. His beard – thick, tangled, lice-thronged – was the dull black of a tusker's pelt. His slightly hunched shoulders, barrel chest and lumbering movements added to his porcine appearance. Only his eyes looked fully human. Set in watery, bloodshot whites, the green irises were sharp, attentive. They glittered insolently.

The big man's name was Ballas.

It was time, he decided, to get himself some money.

He dropped his wine flagon deliberately and watched it shatter on the floor.

Startled by the sudden noise, the stonemasons glanced over.

'Clumsy bastard,' shouted one – a red-haired youth, his skin still blemished by childhood freckles. His brown eyes were cold and cruel; they burned with a type of habitual resentment. He gazed intently at Ballas. 'Look at the state of him,' he urged his friends, pointing. 'There is dried vomit on his shirt. His hair bristles with lice. I'd wager piss stains daub his breeches. Tell me, fat man: when did you last take a bath?'

Ballas shrugged.

'You seem untroubled by your own filth,' said the youth. 'And by your stench. Do you go whoring, eh?'

Ballas nodded.

'I take it the girls hold their breath? I take it they struggle to keep down their gorges? For you're more likely to provoke nausea than desire.'

Ballas shrugged once more.

'You have no self-respect, fat man,' said the youth. 'If I ever hit low times and live as you do, I'll kill myself. Sweet grief, I'd slit my throat. I'd slice off my balls. I'd do anything to bring about my death. No matter how painful, no matter how degrading.' He turned to the other stonemasons. 'Promise that one of you'll butcher me, if ever I take on the fat man's aspect. Go on: we are all loyal to one another. I'd do the same for you. It'd be a true act of friendship. A mercy killing. Surely you wouldn't deny me?'

The red-haired youth's purse dangled from a plain black strip. Its burden of coins strained against the fabric. Ballas eyed it for a moment like a snake eyeing a mongoose.

He stooped to pick up a shard of flagon glass.

'No, wait,' came a voice.

A serving girl hurried over. 'I shall do that. You'll only cut yourself, and then I'll have to mop up blood as well as wine.'

Kneeling, she used a short-handled brush to sweep the shards into a heap.

'You have been here since we opened,' she said, glancing up. 'It is a rare thing, to see someone drink as much as you. You have guzzled a river, sir. You are not going to turn foul, are you?'

'Foul?' murmured Ballas.

'You know: *rowdy*. This is a peaceful tavern, more or less. We don't want trouble.'

'You'd reckon it best if I left?' asked Ballas. His deep voice rolled with a Hearthfall burr.

'No,' said the girl quickly.

'A serving girl doesn't ask a man if he's going to go rotten,' said Ballas. 'Not if she wants him to stay, and keep drinking. I've spent a purseful here—'

'You misunderstand me,' interrupted the serving girl.

'I misunderstand *nothing*,' said the big man, rising. 'I'm not welcome here, right? So I'll just piss off, then. There're finer places in Soriterath – places where a man can drink, *and* be well treated.'

Edging around the table, Ballas swayed. The floor seemed to tilt like the deck of a tide-shaken ship. Gripping the table's edge, Ballas steadied himself. He was drunker than he had expected. Taking a deep breath, he started towards the doors.

He took ten paces, tripped – and crashed into the red-haired stonemason. The stonemason fumbled his tankard; the vessel clanked on to the table, and an ale pool spread over the surface. With an angry shout, the stonemason sprang to his feet.

'You bloody *oaf*!' he snapped, his eyes blazing. 'Can't you even walk properly? Look what you have done!' He pointed furiously at the spilled ale.

'Accident,' mumbled Ballas. 'I'm drunk. Every step is an adventure. Forgive me.'

The stonemason wrinkled his nose. 'Close to, your stink is even fiercer than I imagined. You reek worse than a tanner's shop!' He pushed Ballas away.

Surprised by the youth's abrupt move, Ballas stumbled over a stool and fell to the floor.

The stonemason stood over him. 'You owe me a tankard of ale.'

'I've got no money,' said Ballas, slowly. 'I've got . . . nothing.'

'No man without money can get as drunk as you are . . .'

'No man as drunk as I am,' replied Ballas, struggling to his feet, 'can possibly have any money *left*. I've supped enough to bankrupt a Blessed Master. To settle his account, he'd have to pawn the Sacros.'

'Do not lie to me,' said the stonemason. He advanced on Ballas.

'Aiy!' The serving girl glared at them from across the room. 'Do you want me to summon the tavern-master? He has a wolfhound as big and ill-tempered as a bull: would you like him to turn it loose on you?' She looked sharply at Ballas. 'Go on: do as you promised – *leave*. The first time I saw you, I knew you were bad.'

'Is that so? Then you're smarter than you look,' said Ballas. He glanced at the stonemason. He considered insulting the youth. He knew exactly what to say. The youth was embarrassed by his freckles. In every other aspect he was a man, full-grown and strong. Yet he still bore the faint leopard-markings of a child. Alternatively, Ballas could ridicule his acne: it sprawled over his chin, each spot a sore red hue, and pus-laden.

Ballas said nothing. It was wisest by far simply to leave. Turning, he shambled outdoors.

It was mid-afternoon. Bright autumnal light fell from a clear blue sky. The big man stood in a thoroughfare of half-frozen mud. On either side, there were taverns constructed from pale grey stone. Many appeared to be half-derelict: the wooden eaves were rotting, mosses and moulds blotched the brickwork, and paint had long since peeled from the doors. Ballas had been in Soriterath for only a few days, yet this particular area was one of the shabbiest he had encountered – not only in this city, he reflected, but in all of Druine. Soriterath was the Holy City, the city where the Pilgrim Church leaders dwelled. But it was not a place of splendour. In the opulent areas, there were grand buildings, true enough; but mainly the city was like many in Druine: a place of creeping squalor, of houses, taverns and shops constructed from tired stone and mouldering wood, packed tightly together, as if to confine as many souls as possible to the smallest space. And, like many such cities, it had a distinctive smell: a combination of decaying vegetation and decomposing flesh. The greengrocers dumped their unsold produce in the streets, and when any of the city's feral animals – a rabble of rats, cats and dogs – died, their carcasses were left to rot where they lay. A similar fate awaited many human corpses; others, weighted with rocks, were dumped in the Gastallen River. In an effort to control the diseases emanating from such corpses, the Pilgrim Church had erected communal pyres throughout the city. During times of plague and famine, Ballas had heard, the air over Soriterath grew black with the smoke of burning flesh.

Soriterath might have been the Holy City, but it frequently had a hellish aspect.

And when common room pessimists spoke of the country's decline, of Druine's gradual slide into moral ruin, they often held up Soriterath as an example.

When Ballas arrived here, he had felt instantly at home.

An icy breeze swirled along the thoroughfare, stinging his cold-cracked skin.

He shivered. Then he grinned.

'Let me see what I have here,' he said, unfurling the fingers of his left hand. Upon his palm crouched the stonemason's purse. It had been easily stolen. When Ballas had tripped – deliberately – into the young man, he had cut the purse from its strip with the shard of flagon glass. He had performed the operation with a conjuror's dexterity.

The purse was full.

'When night falls,' murmured Ballas, 'I shan't be dossing on the streets.'

Then he noticed that the purse felt light. *Too* light, for a purse burdened with coins.

Frowning, he rubbed it. He felt what he had previously observed: coins' hard edges, straining against the fabric.

Yet the lightness persisted.

Was the wine playing a trick on him? Could it make heavy objects seem near-weightless – just as it made ugly women appear beautiful?

He emptied the purse on to his palm. And cursed as a dozen discs of plain wood tumbled out.

He hurled them to the ground.

'Pissing eunuch,' said Ballas, as if the stonemason was present. 'Freckled, pimple-crusted eunuch. I ought to castrate you, and complete the effect.'

A door slammed open. Echoes raced along the thoroughfare.

The stonemason stepped from the tavern. Two others stood beside him.

'You idiot,' said the red-haired youth, pacing toward Ballas. His fingers probed the strip, dangling purseless from his belt. 'Did you imagine I wouldn't notice? Did you suppose that, like you, I am so insensible that I can suffer an indignity without realising?'

'What are you talking about?' said Ballas, lamely.

'Oh, come now – don't feign innocence. You stand with my purse in your hand, my coins spread about your feet. You know fully what I speak of.'

'It was a jest, nothing more—'

'As is this, my friend.' Springing forward, the stonemason swung a flagon against Ballas's head. Dazed, Ballas staggered. A second blow landed on his cheekbone. Then the stonemason kicked him in the crotch.

There was a heartbeat of terrible expectation – then a choking pain surged from Ballas's testicles to his throat.

Sinking to his knees, Ballas vomited. The stonemason ran forward and kicked him in the face. The impact knocked Ballas on to his back.

Kneeling beside him, the stonemason punched him in the mouth. Then he brought down the flagon on Ballas's head – again and again, until the vessel shattered.

Then the real violence began.

The stonemason's friends kicked Ballas in the chest, legs and stomach. They used their fists, too, and delivered blow after muscle-jarring blow. Ballas felt like a fox set upon by hounds. His body jerked this way and that. The stonemason struck him repeatedly in the face, as if determined to disfigure him . . .

Eventually, exhausted, the three men grew still.

Silence fell.

Then came a splashing noise. Something showered on to Ballas's face.

Grimacing, he cracked open his swollen eyes.

The stonemason was urinating on him.

'Is it not apt that one who belongs in a sewer should be wetted by liquid destined for a sewer? Is this fluid not your true habitat? Aren't you as at ease in piss as a fish is in water?'

The stonemason laughed; his companions laughed, too.

'A warning, fat man. If I ever set eyes on you again, or catch your stench, you are dead. Understand? I've been merciful. But next time, I'll drag down lightning, and blast you from this world into the next.' He spat at Ballas. Then, turning, he walked away.

His friends followed him, vanishing back into the tavern.

Ballas sat upright. Over his body, bruises blossomed: his skin throbbed as blood spread beneath it. Tiny spasms rippled through his muscles. Lifting his fingers, he touched his nose – and gasped: it had been broken yet again. Right now it felt like nothing more than a plug of bloody gristle.

'Bastards,' he grunted. 'Pissing bastards . . . But now, let me see.' He gave a blood-clogged laugh. 'Maybe it is not all bad news.'

Within his left hand nestled a second purse. This one also belonged – *had* belonged – to the stonemason. Like the first it was stuffed full. Unlike the first it felt heavy.

Ballas upended it. Out on to his palm tumbled twelve copper pennies. A week's wage for an apprentice stonemason.

'Well, young man,' he said, 'the purse hanging from your belt was a cheat. But this one . . . Ha! Little boys have much to learn. Treat this as a lesson.'

Getting to his feet, Ballas limped away along the thoroughfare.

Several hours later, Ballas clambered from a pallet-bed and pulled on his leggings.

From the purse he rummaged two pennies, tossing them to the plump whore beneath the blankets.

He had visited a different tavern – he could not recall its name – immediately after the beating. He had drunk a flagon of Keltuskan red. Then, his ardour roused, he had purchased a few hours of the whore's time and taken her upstairs.

She had expressed surprise that someone so recently beaten could possess carnal inclinations. In her experience, they flowed away with a victim's blood. Ballas insisted that, in his case, that was not so. The whore had believed him.

To her credit, she had treated him gently. She had performed the more strenuous motions of coupling, allowing Ballas to remain immobile, grunting like a pig happy at the trough. Contrary to the stonemason's expectations, his sweat-odour had not offended her: on the windowsill a bowl of herbs smouldered, their fragrance filling the room and masking any other smell.

Ballas put on his shirt and boots.

Opening the shutters, he observed the night-cloaked Soriterath streets. He felt drunk, satisfied, tired – and thirsty. He was a stranger in the city. But he recalled that, a few streets away, there was a tavern that sold a sweet white wine, which would provide a gentle end to a trying but satisfactory day.

He left the chamber and went down a flight of steps into the common room. There was noise here: every table was occupied, and laughter shook the rafters. Ballas crossed the floor and stepped out into the night.

Reaching back, his gaze on the darkened street, he tried to shut the tavern door. It moved a few inches – then halted.

Grunting, he tugged harder but it would not budge.

He glanced back.

And exhaled.

In the doorway stood a tall, thin figure. He had small dark eyes, a pimple-spattered chin – and freckles.

He gripped a cudgel in his right hand.

'We have hunted you all evening,' he said, very quietly. 'Your persistence amazes me. You steal from us once, and get beaten. Then you steal from us again. Truly, I believe drink has destroyed your mind. The Four preached abstinence. I always thought that it was over-pious nonsense . . . But now, I see the hazards of the bottle.'

The stonemason's friends appeared.

Ballas opened his mouth. But the stonemason said, 'Do not speak. At the moment of his death, a man ought to tell the truth. And you utter only lies.' Leaping forward, he slammed the cudgel against Ballas's cheekbone. The big man fell. Before he could move, the stonemasons were once more upon him.

Chapter 2

On the eastern coast, in Saltbrake town,
A Chandler received the creator-god's word
And became a Pilgrim, and upon a road
Of Suffering and Enlightenment, he would learn
The true natures of Good and Evil . . .

'Will he live?'

'Oh – he might.'

'You sound uncertain . . .'

'Years ago, I tended a farmer who had been stampeded by a herd of bulls, and I doubt strongly he would have traded his injuries for this fellow's.' The voice, that of an old man, paused thoughtfully.

There was a long sigh.

'Look at him,' the voice continued. 'There is scarcely a square inch of flesh unbruised. From head to toe, he is caked in dried blood. I dare say many of his bones are broken – and the Four only know what more, ah, *subtle* damage has been done.'

'Subtle damage?' echoed the other voice – that of a much younger man. He spoke softly, but with great urgency. As if fearful a moment's laxity would exact a terrible cost. 'What do you mean, Calden?'

'Damage to his innards,' replied the old man. 'To his lungs, heart, liver. They are fragile things. It isn't always obvious when they are injured. They may bleed, and no one – neither patient nor physician – will know. And there are other maladies that do not loudly proclaim their presence. A blood-taint, for instance, kills as readily as any poison. Yet it will not be detected until it strikes.'

'But you *will* treat him – as best you can?'

'Of course. But Brethrien, observe him closely. It may be necessary – despite my ministrations – to give him the Final Blessing.'

Ballas lay perfectly still. He had already attempted to open his eyes. But the surrounding flesh was too swollen. His body felt at once strange and familiar. Strange, because the beating had covered it with contusions – and, as the old man had suggested, many bones were probably broken. Familiar, for Ballas had been beaten many times. He had grown accustomed to the terrible foreignness of how his body felt when freshly thrashed.

He wondered where he was. He tried opening his mouth so that he might ask. But his lips too were swollen, and stuck together with blood.

'His Blessing,' said the younger man, 'has already been administered. I delivered it in error. I came upon him in the street, covered in blood – and *frost*: I found him at dawn, and he had been outdoors overnight. I presumed he was dead.'

'An understandable mistake,' said the old man.

'When the Papal Wardens tried to load him upon a cart, so that he might be taken to the city's pyres, his wounds bled afresh.'

'So his heart was still beating . . .'

'I could scarcely believe it. I sent for you straight away.'

Something splashed into a bowl of water.

'Well, his wounds are clean,' said the old man. 'As for the blood covering the rest of him, we shall leave it be. It will do no harm.'

There was a wet grinding noise, slow and rhythmic. A pestle pulverising something in a mortar.

'Knitbone?' queried the young man.

'Yes, and a fine thing I brought plenty of it. A meadow's-worth would be hardly sufficient.' The grinding paused.

Ballas sensed the old man leaning close.

'He has been drinking. From his breath, it seems he has downed a lively mixture: whisky, ale, wine, rum . . . He has varied tastes.'

'I found him on Vintner's Row,' explained the young man. 'A place of taverns, gambling rooms and . . . ah . . .'

'Brothels,' finished the old man. As if the younger man would have problems speaking the word. 'I know of Vintner's Row. And that urges me to ask: what do *you* know of your patient?'

'Know of him? Well, nothing. I merely found him, in a poor state. It was my duty to help him. I have sworn an oath. I cannot ignore a distressed soul.'

The old man muttered something.

'Pardon?'

'Be wary,' repeated the old man, loudly. 'No decent-minded man takes his pleasures on Vintner's Row.' The grinding noises stopped. 'Unroll that bandage, will you? My thanks.' A squelching noise followed. As of a paste being smeared.

'I will grant him the benefit of the doubt.'

The old man laughed. 'The doubt? What is there to be doubted? You find him in one of Soriterath's most disreputable quarters, stinking of liquor, beaten halfway to the Eltheryn Forest . . .'

'I must grant him shelter,' said the younger man firmly.

'For how long?'

'Until he heals. Assuming such an event . . .'

'. . . Such a minor miracle . . .'

'. . . Occurs,' finished the young man.

The squelching stopped. Something cool and sticky was draped over Ballas's chest. A poultice. For a heartbeat the sensation was nearly pleasurable. The unguent numbed Ballas's flesh, and cooled it.

Then a gentle pressure was applied, to fix the poultice.

Pain swept through Ballas's body. He felt as if a lightning bolt had struck him. He imagined white heat crackling from rib to rib, then erupting from his pores. Every sinew tightened. Every muscle clenched.

He gasped.

'Ah, a response – did you see it?' In the old man's voice there was a note of surprise. 'That is encouraging.'

If the old man spoke again, Ballas did not hear. Garish scribbles of light sizzled behind his eyes. The pain steadily increased, until Ballas thought he would burst into flame.

Then: a swirling numbness. A delicious resignation engulfed him. He found himself spinning gratefully into warm black oblivion.

After a few days – because he was constantly slipping in and out of consciousness, he was unsure how many – Ballas opened his eyes. He found himself in a small white-walled room that had a single shuttered window and a fire blazing in the grate. The floor was bare stone, and there was a table laden with an array of medicinal items: bandages, swabs, yarn and needles for stitching wounds, herbs that could be ground into poultices.

The young man was a priest. No older than twenty-five years, he glowed with pious devotion. His fair hair was short-cropped into something resembling a monk's cut. His dark blue robes hung loosely on a slender frame. This, coupled with his pale skin, lent him the appearance of someone recovering from a serious ailment.

Yet he was animated by holy urgency.

Even the smallest tasks – the bringing of food and water, the examination of Ballas's wounds – seemed of the utmost spiritual importance.

Often, while changing Ballas's dressings, he asked, *Who are you? Where are you from? Will anyone be worried about you – ought I tell someone where you are?*

Ballas never replied.

The questions irritated him; his life was his own business, not some tender-hearted priest's.

But if he *had* answered, he would have revealed only that he was a vagrant and so hailed from everywhere and nowhere. No one in Druine would be concerned about him. Not the tavern-masters who sold him wine, ale, whisky. Not the whores who caught his mouldering seed.

The small room depressed Ballas. The persistent fire-smoke, the colourless walls and unguent-scent made him restless. He wanted to breathe clean, cold air. He needed to experience sensations other than warmth.

More than anything, he needed a drink. The priest had administered many medicines – except for those he craved most strongly.

One afternoon, Ballas felt strong enough to rise. Swinging his feet from the pallet-bed, he stood. A constricting pain seized his chest. As if an iron band was bolted tightly around it. Swearing softly, he waited for the discomfort to pass.

He was naked, he realised. Except for dried blood. It covered his body like a second skin. Grunting, he flexed his left arm. Where the flesh creased, blood-flakes cracked loose, drifting to the floor. Where had the blood come from? he wondered. A stab wound? A bottle-slash? It did not seem so. Inspecting his body, he found no sharp-edge injuries. Only jagged tears, where blunt objects had struck forcefully enough to split his skin.

Bruises covered his chest; they had ripened from black to a mix of metallic greens and golds. Murmuring, he touched his face. A nose shattered still further, a grotesquely swollen jaw, lips split open like sausages left too long upon the grill – these were the things his fingertips encountered.

Grunting, Ballas spat on the floor. A gobbet of red-tinged saliva quivered on the stone.

A heap of clothes lay in the corner. A brown tunic, soft cotton vest and black leggings . . . They were not Ballas's clothes. Yet they were intended for his use. Ballas tugged on the leggings. They were a comfortable fit. But the vest was slightly too tight. And the tunic couldn't easily accommodate Ballas's ale gut, which stretched the fabric almost to breaking point.

The boots were exactly the correct size. As they should have been: for they were Ballas's own, scrubbed clean of blood and vomit. The ripped stitching had been repaired, too.

'Holy man,' murmured Ballas, 'what are you, eh? A conscientious soul? Or a meddling toe-rag?'

Ballas left the room, stepping into a long corridor. At the far end stood a door, half ajar. Beyond, there was a kitchen. On a shelf rested wooden cups and bowls. There was a fire enclave but the stacked logs were unlit.

The priest Brethrien sat at a table.

Writing on a parchment, he wore an expression of rapt concentration. An illuminated edition of *The Book of the Pilgrims* lay open in front of him. Around his neck, he wore an elongated brass triangle: a miniature of Scarrendestin, the holy mountain.

'These are not my clothes,' said Ballas, entering the kitchen. His voice was naturally loud, with a growling note.

The priest jerked, startled. A blob of ink dripped from his quill-tip, splattering the parchment. Turning his face to Ballas, he blinked.

'These are not my clothes,' repeated the big man. 'Where are the clothes you found me in? I want them back.'

'You walk very quietly,' stammered the priest. Nervously, he fingered his Scarrendestin pendant – as if it were a protective amulet. 'I did not hear your footfalls . . .'

'For the last time, where are my clothes?'

'They had to be burned,' replied the priest.

'Burned?' asked Ballas darkly.

'They were infested,' explained Brethrien. 'Every manner of crawling thing inhabited them. They were, ah, *unhealthy*: unless one were a blood-feasting parasite – a louse or a grip-worm, say. They were threadbare, too. I suspect only the wildlife held them together.' He gestured to Ballas's new apparel. 'I apologise if I have taken a liberty. But, truly, your old clothes could not be saved. And those that you presently wear – they are of better quality. The wool is soft, yes? As soft as when it lay upon the sheep's back. Your old tunic was as coarse as a hair shirt.' He laughed uneasily. 'Saint Derethine suffered many self-imposed tortures. But I dare say even he would have shrunk from your tunic.'

Ballas stared balefully at Brethrien.

'I, ah . . . Do you hunger?'

'For days, I've eaten piss-all but soup,' grunted Ballas. 'Of course I hunger.' His gaze alighted on a shelf of wine flagons. 'But my thirst troubles me more.' Grasping a flagon, he started tugging out the cork.

Alarmed, the priest sprang to his feet. 'No!'

He seized the flagon, trying to wrest it from Ballas. 'Please – you cannot drink that! It is forbidden!'

'Why so?' Ballas lifted the flagon to the window. 'What's inside, holy man? I reckoned this to be wine. But perhaps it's something else. The piss of a martyr, perhaps? Better still, that of a Blessed Master?'

'Holy wine,' said Brethrien. 'You are holding holy wine. The Brandister monks made it; and the Masters bless it in accordance with the strictest rituals – rituals transcribed by the Pilgrims . . . by the Four: may they lead me safely to the Eltheryn Forest . . .' He faltered. 'Holy wine can be imbibed only as part of a church service. Morning, noon, eveningfall – it matters not *which* service; but the wine can be drunk then, and *only* then. To do otherwise is sinful, and will bring only misfortune. Please – give me the flagon.'

'D'you have any wine I *can* drink?' Ballas allowed Brethrien to take the flagon. '*Un*holy wine, perhaps?'

The priest shook his head.

Ballas scowled. It was typical of his ill luck that he should be in the care of such a man.

Brethrien cradled the flagon as if it were a baby. Then he set it gently upon the shelf.

'What do you have to eat?' demanded Ballas.

'Many good things,' said Brethrien. 'Porridge oats, potatoes, carrots—'

'What about meat? Beef, pork, venison . . .'

'The Four forbade the consumption of animal flesh,' said Brethrien. 'So I abstain from anything that has eye, ear or mouth. My larder is bare of all except the soil's produce.'

On the table rested a linen-draped cheese block. Drawing back the covering, Ballas lifted the morsel to his mouth – and bit down. His lip wounds reopened, streaking blood over the cheese. He chewed carefully, wary of shattered teeth. The stuff was watery, tasteless.

'Pathetic,' muttered Ballas, tossing it back on to the table.

The priest stared, his blue eyes glinting anxiously.

'A problem, holy man?' asked Ballas.

'I—' Brethrien faltered, as if his true feelings were difficult to utter. He sighed. 'If you crave meat, you may purchase some from the market.'

Ballas laughed – an ill-humoured snort. 'Do you reckon I'm a man of money? I haven't got a penny to my name.'

From within his robe, Brethrien produced a purse. 'Two pennies ought to be enough,' he said, proffering the coins.

Ballas gazed at the copper discs nestling in Brethrien's palm. Then he glanced at the priest.

'Go on,' said the holy man. 'Take them, if you truly crave meat.'

Shrugging, Ballas did as he was told. You're a trusting soul, he thought, eyeing the priest. Or a stupid one.

'You are bleeding,' said the priest, gesturing at Ballas's tunic. Blood soaked the sleeve. Scarlet drops pattered from the cuff. 'Are you certain you are well enough to visit the market?'

'I'll find out soon enough,' said Ballas.

'Yes, I suppose you will.' Brethrien blinked rapidly. 'I was, ah, wondering if you might do me a favour. It is but a small thing—'

'Have you tended my injuries,' said Ballas, 'so you might use me as an errand boy?'

'Of course not!' exclaimed Brethrien, fiddling with his triangular pendant. 'I nursed you because . . . because you were injured and I am a priest, wishing only to do the Four's work. That is all. I was not trying to . . .' he groped for words '. . . strike a contract with you. Far from it.'

The holy man's edginess irritated Ballas. Every gesture – every blink, every anxious touch of his pendant – scraped upon the big man's nerves. The holy man was as timid as a dormouse. It was understandable that he should harbour a certain unease: he had, in his home, a bruised, bloodied stranger whose temperament inclined towards surliness and who, even after a period of abstinence, still smelled of alcohol.

Yet the priest's response seemed excessively nervous. He had the demeanour of someone almost fearful for their life.

It wouldn't remain a problem for long. Already, Ballas had decided to leave the priest-home. He did not belong in such places. Not even as a guest. Only brothels and taverns brought him pleasure. Better not to linger in the stale air of Brethrien's abode.

'W-will you perform my errand?' Brethrien rummaged again in his purse. 'It is, as I said, only a small thing.' He plucked out three more pennies. 'There is a man, Calden, who applied the first poultices, and who taught me how to look after you. He is a fine soul. Sharp-witted, yet compassionate: he has not cultivated his mind at the expense of his heart. It will be—'

'What do you want me to do?'

The priest faltered.

'Come on!'

'He supplied many things that aided your healing,' blurted Brethrien. 'Herbs, physician's tools . . . I must repay him. He is not a wealthy man.'

'You are mistaken,' said Ballas sourly. 'I've yet to meet an impoverished physician. Like their leeches, they are parasites. One sucks blood, the other money. What does a physician leave behind? Just a healthy bankrupt. They get fat and happy on our suffering.'

'Calden is not a physician,' explained Brethrien. 'Rather, he is the curator of the museum on Half-moon Street. Go now, and you will find him there. I expect he will be pleased to see you. And surprised: he did not believe you would recover, let alone so quickly. You have a strong constitution. He—'

'I'll do as you ask,' interrupted Ballas, taking the coins.

'You know the way to Half-moon Street?'

'Are there taverns close by?'

'I believe so.'

'Then I'll know Half-moon Street.'

Five pennies – he felt them in his palm. Enough for an evening of wine. Of ale. Of whores.

If only all thefts were so simply done, thought Ballas. What an easy world it'd be, if every man were as gullible as this priest.

'Give Calden my best wishes,' said Brethrien.

But Ballas had already crossed the kitchen and was leaving the priest-home.

Ballas walked slowly through Soriterath. After the priest-home's warmth, the outdoor chill bit him deeply. He had half-forgotten that winter was approaching. Soon, a layer of crackling frost would cover Druine. Snow would fall. The land would be blizzard-struck; and the streets, where Ballas slept, would be heaped with frozen white.

For twenty of his forty-five years, Ballas had lived as a vagrant. He was painfully well acquainted with the bitter cold of autumn and winter. If asked, he could describe times of exceptional suffering. On Kranstin Moor, he had slept in a ditch; the nocturnal cold had been so profound that when he woke he found himself bonded to the ditch soil. His clothes were stiff, as if carved from thin wood; his fingers' skin stuck to blades of grass. Once, in Genhallin Town, after a night's drinking, he fell into a pond; and for the next two weeks his wet clothes glinted with ice shards. And on the road from Coarthe to Falrannan, wind and hail-blasted, he had near perished from exposure. A passing merchant had saved him. He gave Ballas fresh clothes, and food, and whisky; he stacked wood and lit a campfire, and rubbed warmth back into the big man's limbs. The gesture surprised Ballas. Not enough, though, to stop him robbing the merchant at first light, knocking him out with a lump of firewood for good measure.

Ballas couldn't clearly recall how badly, during those times, the cold had hurt. But he knew that he was uncomfortable now. The chill seemed to originate *inside* himself: it spread out through his flesh, as if radiating from his bones. He did not believe that the cold itself was notably severe. He simply felt it keenly. Perhaps the priest-home had softened him. Maybe his damaged body had become suddenly sensitive to a lack of heat.

More likely, Ballas was underdressed for the weather. The holy man had not given him a cape. Leggings, vest, tunic – *they* had been provided. But a warm woollen cape, with a fur-lined hood? The priest's generosity had limits, it seemed.

Scowling, Ballas moved onwards.

He wandered through the narrow streets, thinking of the coins in his pocket, scarcely caring where his footsteps took him. After a while, he found himself in familiar surroundings. He had last been here . . . how many nights ago? It did not matter. Everything had been cloaked in darkness but even now, in daylight, the taverns remained familiar. One in particular had a place in his memory. Over the doorway hung a sign: a stumpy, rivulet-encrusted candle burning with a red flame – an indication that the tavern also contained a brothel. Ballas briefly recalled his time there, and the whore he had rutted with in a room on the second floor. He smiled at the memory of her warm, fleshy limbs. And the ginger-and-cinnamon scent of her hair.

Then his gaze lowered to the thoroughfare. His smile faded.

This was where he had been beaten. What name had the priest given this place? *Vintner's Row.*

Ballas halted, shuffling uneasily from foot to foot.

He did not want another encounter with the stonemasons. He fleetingly imagined their surprise at setting eyes upon him; and discovering that despite their best efforts, he was still alive. This surprise would quickly darken to anger – as if Ballas had insulted them by staying in the world of the living. They would want to rectify matters. They would want desperately to finish, for once, a job that they had begun . . .

Ballas hastily went down a side-street, and walked westwards until he emerged into a large city square.

It was market day. The square was crowded with wooden stalls, and Ballas walked amongst them, his eyes open for anything he might spend the priest's money on. Most items did not appeal to him. He had no desire to buy jars of herbs and spices, or jewellery carved clumsily from oak and mahogany. Similarly, he had no use for cooking pots and cutlery. Or for religious tokens, such as verses from *The Book of the Pilgrims*, etched into beech wood, or quilled upon scrolls of fine parchment.

He passed through a cluster of fishmongers' stalls. Their outspread wares, a jumble of cod, salmon and rainbow trout, glinted as if fashioned from silver. He walked by the butchers' stalls, offering ragged cuts of pork, beef, venison and gammon, all oozing in their own bright juices.

Only when he reached a cooked meat stall did he stop. He ravenously eyed minted lamb cutlets, roast pork encased in a thick layer of crackling, grilled steak awash with gravy . . . The big man deliberated for a few moments, before choosing a honey-glazed chicken. It had been roasted that morning, and though it was now stone-cold, this did not bother Ballas. He ate the chicken greedily, swallowing mouthful after mouthful, until only the pale bones remained.

Wiping his hands on his leggings, he wandered to a stall selling spirits and wines. It was a cold morning, and he felt in the mood for whisky. He bought the cheapest flagon he could find, caring less for its taste than its potency. Leaving the market, he began to walk further across the square.

After a few steps, he realised precisely *which* city square this was.

There was an oak tree at the far side of the square. A huge oak tree, its trunk was twice as broad as that of any other oak he had ever seen. Its hue was so dark brown as to be almost black; and its branches groped outwards, like a mass of thick black serpents.

There were human heads nailed to those branches. Three, all counted. They were too far away for their features to be clearly seen. To Ballas's eyes, they were scarcely more than dark lumps, hanging there like baubles. Curious, the big man strolled over, uncorking the whisky flagon as he went.

Gradually, the heads became clearer. One belonged to an old man. His tiny green eyes were stretched wide, his mouth open as if he were in shock. On another branch, there was the head of an adolescent boy. His eyes were bright blue in colour, and his skin was pale, delicate. Between his eyebrows, the stub of a nail glittered; underneath it, dried trickles of blood marked his nose and cheeks. Against the youth's pallor, it seemed as garish as a cheap whore's lip-daub.

Ballas took a sip of whisky. The hot fluid swirled down his throat. He gasped, feeling a pain that was both pleasurable and reassuring.

His gaze drifted to the lowest branch.

The head of a young woman was nailed there. Her eyes were deep brown, her hair auburn and curling. She was pretty in a vulgar, peasant-like fashion. Ballas looked at where her neck ended; where the skin and muscle terminated and there was nothing except empty air, and he found himself wondering what her body had been like. Probably, it had been voluptuous; a thing of softness and warmth, a treat to hold. Exactly the sort of body Ballas savoured the most.

What had been her crime? he wondered. Witchcraft? Seership?

The details were not important, Ballas realised. She had been nailed to the Penance Oak: that meant her crimes had been unholy. She had not offended her fellow man. Rather she had, in some way, defied the Pilgrim Church. Perhaps her crime *had* involved magick. For those who practised the forbidden arts were often found upon the Oak. It did not matter whether their skills were used benignly, or with genuinely wicked intent. Magick was outlawed as contrary to the Four's teachings and as such, those who used it had to be punished.

But those who did not practise magick also found their heads nailed upon the Oak's dark branches. Those who blasphemed in a holy place;

those who spouted heresies; those who sought the services of a magicker . . . All of these people offended the Church. And all of these people warranted retribution.

A crow flapped down on to the young woman's head. It loitered there for a moment; then, hopping lower, it set its spindly-toed talons around her bottom jaw and, perching there, started to jab its beak into her left eye, attempting to prize it out as if it were a pearl inside an oyster.

Murmuring, Ballas raised the flagon to his lips.

Then someone called: 'Dare you drink so near to the Oak?'

Ballas ignored the voice.

'Citizen,' it cried again, 'do you not understand that the Oak is holy, and your actions are a blasphemy?'

Your actions are a blasphemy. The words' formality disturbed Ballas. They were not like those used by the common folk. He turned round.

Two Papal Wardens approached. The Realm's keepers-of-law, the foot soldiers of holy justice. They wore jet-black tunics, each with a narrow blue triangle stitched into the chest. Each man bore a sheathed sword and a dagger. Their helms were polished black iron. Beneath these hung chain-mail ventails.

A young Warden put out his hand. 'Give me the flagon,' he said. 'It is forbidden to drink in Papal Square.'

'I am not drinking,' said Ballas easily.

The Warden's gaze hardened. 'The flagon holds whisky – I can smell it from here. And you are pouring it down your throat. So you're drinking, citizen. Now stop this nonsense and give me the flagon.'

'It's whisky, true enough,' said Ballas. 'But I drink it as a *medicine*.'

'A medicine?'

'It stops me freezing to death.'

'I have no time for such games,' said the Warden, tightly. A tawny fringe poked out under his helm. He was twenty-five years old. Certainly no older, thought Ballas. Who was this pup, to confiscate his whisky?

'Give me the whisky,' the Warden repeated.

'What if I refused? Would you nail me to the Oak? Would you claim that the Four – the virtuous, forgiving Four, who love every living soul – those Pilgrims, who traipsed this wondrous land, so we might be forgiven – will you say they demand my execution, for drinking a little liquor?'

Ballas realised he was slightly drunk. He had drunk the whisky flagon half-empty.

'We'll make a bargain,' he continued. 'I'll keep my whisky. I'll find a doorway, somewhere or other, and finish it off. Then we'll both be happy, aye? I'll be warm and drunk. And you . . . you'll have restored order to the Square.'

Turning, he ducked under the Oak's lowest branches.

'Halt! Stay right where you are!'

Ballas ignored the command.

A hand grasped his shoulder. The grip was relatively gentle, meant only to restrain. But it sent pain flaring through Ballas's bruised flesh.

Crying out, Ballas spun round – and reflexively lashed out at the Warden. The movement was clumsy. The big man's open hand struck the Warden's cheek – a blow that was neither punch nor slap. The Warden stumbled, surprised. Then he sprang at Ballas, slamming a fist into his face.

The impact burst open Ballas's lips.

Stepping closer, the Warden doubled-punched Ballas's chest. Gasping, Ballas felt rib grate against cracked rib. Another punch drove into his stomach. Ballas groaned and sank to his knees.

The Warden moved closer. But the second Warden restrained him.

'At ease, Janner,' he said. He was much older than the first Warden and sported a grey moustache. On his tunic's shoulder he bore the two red stripes of a Warden Commander.

'He struck me!' shouted the younger Warden.

'This is holy ground,' said the Commander. 'If he were in an alleyway, you could treat him however you liked. But not here. Not so near the Oak. Not so near the Sacros.'

At the northern edge of Papal Square there was a wall of white, faintly gleaming marble, thirty feet tall. It was so neatly constructed that the individual bricks could not be seen; instead, it looked as if it had been sculpted from a single, enormous block. It encircled a large, pyramidal building, fashioned from scarlet stone. Its height was almost dizzying; two, perhaps three hundred feet tall, it loomed over the Square, and the marketplace, like a blood-coloured mountain. It seemed scarcely possible that it had been erected by human hands; rather, its scale gave the impression that it was the work of the creator-god Himself. There were windows set into the brickwork, arched and shadowed; their frames were crafted from some bright golden metal, possibly brass, but in all likelihood, gold. The walls were traversed by narrow ledges of black stone, upon which a scattering of crows roosted.

Around the main building, there were four towers, each five hundred feet tall. Each of these towers, Ballas knew, represented one of the four Pilgrims. Upon every tower's red-tiled spire, there fluttered a flag symbolising the occupation of a Pilgrim: a loom for the clothes-maker Pilgrim, a ship's sail for the sailor, a candle for the chandler and a flensing knife for the tanner. In the day's strong light, the towers spread weak shadows across Papal Square.

The Warden Commander gestured toward the building. 'We have to be careful,' he told the younger Warden. 'If we misbehave, and we are seen . . .' His voice trailed off. He had no need to say anything else, realised Ballas. The edifice beyond the marble wall – the Esklarion Sacros – was home to the Blessed Masters. The seven highest-ranking clergymen in Druine; the seven men who, garbed in scarlet robes, governed the Pilgrim Church.

And because there was no power in Druine *except* the Pilgrim Church, they governed Druine itself: every acre of forest and farmland, every mountain and every pool and every river, was under their control. And the life of every living thing.

'Should we drag him to an alleyway?' asked the younger Warden. 'Then we could—'

'We will leave him be,' said the Commander. 'He has learned his lesson. Do you live in this city?' he asked, turning his gaze on Ballas.

'That is not your business,' replied the big man.

'Vagrancy is a crime,' replied the Commander.

'I *had* lodgings,' muttered Ballas. 'But I've abandoned them. As I shall abandon this city. It's brought me only ill luck.'

'We have all endured bad fortune,' said the Commander, with unexpected sympathy. 'From your condition' – he gestured towards Ballas's blood-sodden garb – 'you have suffered more than most. Perhaps it was warranted. Perhaps it was not. But I will offer you a few words of advice. Return to your lodgings. Do not leave the city. Vagrancy is vagrancy, whether here or on the road to somewhere else. Wardens can distinguish between a traveller and a tramp. You will be arrested. Besides, you are in no fit state to travel. Winter is almost here. You will freeze.'

'Not if I have whisky,' said Ballas.

The Commander took the flagon from him. Ballas was in too much pain to resist.

'Watch your step,' said the Commander.

Turning, he strode away, followed by the young Warden.

'Bastards,' muttered Ballas.

Grunting, he tried to stand. Nerve-splitting pain surged through his body. With a yelp, Ballas sagged against the Penance Oak. He coughed up a splash of bile. A breeze swept over him. He began shivering – as if the gust had blown unabated from the Frozen North. He had never felt so sick. So frail. So vulnerable.

This feeling – painful, unfamiliar – appalled him.

Growling, he grasped the Oak and dragged himself upright. His legs buckled. He dropped once more to his knees, heavily.

A few passers-by stared. A courting couple, a gang of children, an aged, stern-eyed woman . . . they watched him, half disgusted, half amused.

'What do you want?' shouted Ballas. *'What do you want?!'*

This outburst hurt his ribs again. He groaned. The children laughed. Angry, Ballas thrust out a hand at them. They sprang back, as nimble as squirrels, elusive. Ballas overbalanced, falling on to all fours.

He lifted his head slowly, like a wounded animal.

'You should follow the Commander's advice,' said the aged woman. 'Gaze upon yourself, and you will see he has spoken sense. You are a wretch. You are drunk, injured, incapable—'

'Shut up!' shouted Ballas. 'Let me alone. All of you – be gone!'

Yet there was something in the old woman's words, Ballas conceded.

Leaning against the Oak, feeling nauseous, he realised that he was not strong enough to leave Father Brethrien's care. A single night on the streets could kill him. He might freeze to death. Or his open wounds, exposed to disease-infested vermin – the rats, dogs and cats that wandered the city – might get infected with a blood-taint.

The holy man's fluttering manners annoyed Ballas. But if he were to stay alive, he had to remain in the priest-home a little longer.

And that meant performing his errand.

Leaving Papal Square, Ballas shuffled to Half-moon Street. Several times he paused to catch his breath, or to vomit. When he arrived at the museum, his ribs were throbbing and bile blotched his tunic front.

Stooping through a set of arched doors, he found himself in a large, high-ceilinged chamber of oaken display cases. Ballas scarcely glanced at the exhibits. Out of the corner of his eye he saw pottery, clothing, weaponry, carved idols – each item either from the past or from some region far beyond Druine – or both. But he took no proper notice. History was a futile passion, a bloodless sifting of bones and dust. Only the present mattered. For only in the present did fleshly joys exist. A whore's rutting room was more beguiling than an ancient queen's bedchamber. Common-room gossip more fascinating than intrigues of court. A cockfight more exhilarating than an account of a long-forgotten war.

Ballas passed through the chamber. Then another. In the third, he heard voices – they came from a small doorway in the wall to Ballas's left.

Stooping through the doorway, Ballas found himself at the top of a flight of steps. He followed them down, halting a few steps from the bottom.

Ahead stretched a long candlelit vault. Dark stone slabs paved the floor. From the walls shelves jutted. Upon some, animals' skulls rested. There were deer, bull, wolf and ram skulls, each one white and criss-crossed with faint fracture lines. But there were also skulls of unrecognisable origin. A snout bone extended from one; from another's pate jutted a curving, sharp-tipped horn, surrounded by inch-long spikes. Another skull had an absurdly heavy and protuberant jaw. Another had only a single eye socket, staring emptily from the forehead. Jumbled bones were heaped beside the skulls: a pale mound of fibulas, tibias, ribs, vertebrae.

Other shelves held ancient vases, statuettes, graven images . . . objects like those exhibited in the chambers above.

An old grey-robed man stood in the vault's centre. Alongside him was a second man, of middle years and with a crumpled, wind-scoured face.

'So,' asked the old man, 'how are things at the Academy? The institution – it is thriving, hm?'

'It is thriving,' said the second man. 'As far as anything can thrive with the Church's boot planted on its throat.'

'The Blessed Masters are proving troublesome?' It was the voice Ballas had heard in the priest-home, when his injuries were first tended. 'They are interfering, yes?'

'Every day, they place tighter limits on what we may study. They are suspicious of certain disciplines. They mistrust Linguistics, believing it may expose as counterfeit the testimonies of the Nine Witnesses. I do not understand how it could do so – the testimonies' authenticity is beyond doubt. Yet the Church remains wary. And wary, too, of history: our historians are permitted to teach only a single Church-approved version of the past: one that acknowledges the Four's existence, but does not delve deeply into Their lives – or even the age in which They lived.'

'Including the Red War?'

'From the blood spilled during our conflict with the Lectivins,' said the other man, 'Druine, and the Church's power grew. There must be no reappraisal of that time. The foundations must be seen to be secure. The Church thinks it wisest to blindfold those scholars who would look closely.'

'What do they fear, I wonder?' said Calden, softly.

'Fear? I do not believe the Masters *fear* anything: for there is nothing of substance *to* fear. There are hundreds, *thousands* of accounts of our conflict with the Lectivins. From the arrival of the Lectivin ships upon our shores, to our obliteration of the Pale Race, everything has been transcribed innumerable times. There is nothing new to be discovered.' He sighed. 'I think the Church worries that if people study the Lectivins, the Lectivins will cease to seem . . .' He paused.

'Extraordinary?'

'Extraordinary,' agreed the other man. 'In our hearts, the Lectivins were demons, djinns, *cohkaris* – we know this is not so, but our hearts believe it nonetheless. However, our hearts will grow sceptical if our minds insist often enough that, in truth, the Lectivins were merely a different species. And in that, they were no more extraordinary than dogs, birds or fish. Or ourselves. The Church cannot permit this.' He grew quiet. Then, as if uttering a dangerous secret, he said, 'Have you heard about the archaeological dig in the Galdirran hills?'

'A few rumours have floated my way.' The old curator nodded. 'Lectivin relics were unearthed, were they not? Then the Church closed down the excavations.'

'You would imagine the relics were of a great and terrible nature. A nature that could shake the Church to its core . . .'

'But they were not?'

'The archaeologists unearthed bowls, spoons, eating daggers – that is all. Simple objects, in design similar to our own. And therein lies the problem. The Lectivins were not hugely unlike ourselves. Our appearances differed. But, like us, they prayed, crafted churches . . . and ate with cutlery.' He laughed softly. 'Such tiny details destroy any air of mystery. It is hard to imagine a real demon using a spoon. To preserve the Lectivins' traditional image, the excavation was, as you said, terminated. The relics were confiscated, the ground filled in.'

'And the archaeologists?'

'I do not know for certain. But they have not returned to the Academy. Perhaps, when the site was earthed over, they too were buried. This is a dangerous era in which to be a thinker.'

The two men were silent for a long time.

Eventually Calden asked, 'I take it *your* subject has not been forbidden?'

'The Masters have yet to find geology objectionable,' replied the other man. 'I suspect they actually approve of it: they have a taste for fine, glittering objects, mined from the soil.'

'I have something that may interest you,' said Calden, moving towards a shelf.

Muttering to himself under his breath, bored by the two men's talk, Ballas almost descended the final steps into the vault. Yet he paused. Something had changed in Calden's manner. Drawing out a wooden casket, the old man seemed excited. And infused with pride – as if he was about to amaze the geologist with something clever. Or unexpected.

Maybe the casket contained nothing of interest. A pottery fragment. A famous warrior's rusted dagger handle. A quill used by a revered philosopher. Any article that, despite its drabness, would thrill a scholar.

But maybe it held something better.

Ballas stepped back into the gloom at the stairwell's base.

Calden placed the casket on a wooden desk, then opened it with a key strung around his neck.

'This is why I sent for you,' he said, taking out a black iron disc, about four inches across. In the centre nestled a blue gemstone, measuring an inch from side to side. Near the disc's edge, four more stones – blood red, this time – were inset at the cardinal compass points.

'What do you think?' asked Calden, passing it to the geologist.

'It is pretty,' said the other man. 'What is it?'

'I have yet to deduce its function. Perhaps it is a mere ornament. Or maybe a talisman of some description. Several weeks ago, a scholar of some eminence passed away. He bequeathed me a collection of items, of which this was one. I believe its origins were as unknown to him as they are to me. Now,' he moved slightly closer, peering himself at the disc, 'tell me what the gemstones are.'

'Those on the outside appear to be rubies.' The geologist touched a fingertip to them. 'Yes – rubies.'

'And the gemstone in the centre?'

'Opal,' replied the geologist. 'No, wait. It is too dark. Diamond, perhaps. Stones of a similar shade have been brought from Gohavi.'

'It is not a diamond.'

'How can you be so certain?'

'Hold it to a candle flame,' said Calden, 'and tell me if any diamond in history has behaved like this gemstone.'

Crossing the floor, the geologist lifted the disc to a candle burning in a niche. From his position on the steps, Ballas could not see the effect of the flame's light on the gemstone itself. But what he could see surprised him. Startled him, even.

A wash of blue light poured from the gemstone, illuminating the geologist's face. The light was strong; blinking, the geologist tilted his head. Then he frowned.

'Calden,' he whispered, 'I have never seen such a thing.'

'A marvel, is it not?'

'Never have I witnessed such a play of light within a gemstone's depths. It does not merely glitter; it . . . it . . .' Words failed him briefly. 'Those flecks, drifting and falling, like sparks in a furnace . . . each flaring like a fragment of gold . . . like sunlight in a rock pool's shallows . . . You said it was left to you, by a scholar of note. Where did *he* obtain it?'

'I do not know. He travelled widely, within Druine and beyond. He could have found it anywhere. I have consulted the major texts. Bahane's *Catalogue of the Earth-Bright*, Tharkannan's *Minerales Universalis* . . . Of such a stone, there is no mention. Perhaps—'

'—It is unique?' finished the geologist.

Calden nodded.

'Perhaps it is indeed one of a kind,' said the geologist thoughtfully.

'If you wish to study it properly,' said Calden, a touch hesitantly, 'you may borrow it. If you promise that, in your hands, it will be safe.'

The geologist lowered the disc. The candle flame no longer lit the gemstone. The blue light vanished.

'It will not be safe,' said the geologist plainly.

'You fear the Church might confiscate it?'

'The frame-piece has a primitive look; the Church might believe it was a religious item, from the age before the Melding. They will not permit such items to circulate. And my students – they are interested less in scholarship than in drinking and whoring. Such pastimes are not inexpensive. Every now and then, a few items are stolen from the storage rooms. Such a piece as this,' he touched the disc, 'might prove a great temptation. It is best not to place shining things within the sight of magpies. Now, Calden, I must go; I have to deliver a lecture on Catharrian emeralds. In themselves, they are truly beautiful. But compared to that gemstone? Ha! They might as well be lumps of coal. Fare you well, Calden.' Turning, he walked towards the door.

Spinning on his heel, Ballas jogged noiselessly up the steps, unseen by the geologist and the curator.

Ballas returned to the priest-home. In the kitchen, a fire blazed. Warm air curled over the big man as he stepped inside.

Father Brethrien was kneeling at the hearth, prodding the fire with a brass poker. 'Did you pay Calden?' he asked, glancing up.

'Aye,' replied Ballas truthfully.

'Was he happy to see you? You are, in part, a testament to his skills as a physician. He must have found it gratifying to—'

'We did not speak. I merely paid him and went.'

The curator had wanted to talk. When Ballas gave him the coins, he had asked some question about the big man's health. Uninterested, Ballas had ignored him.

Now he treated the priest the same way. Striding past him, Ballas went to his sleeping-room. He uncorked a whisky flagon, stolen from the cart of a market-stall owner. Taking a long swallow, he thought of the iron disc. Of the four glinting rubies. Of the blue gemstone.

He remembered the geologist's awe. He heard again the talk of drifting golden sparks . . . of uniqueness . . .

'What am I,' murmured Ballas, 'but a magpie? Enjoy your bauble while you can, curator. Soon it will be gone.'

Chapter 3

Amidst the western hills of Banderine
A tanner heard the creator-god's word
And, thus blessed, forsook his trade for
The vestments of a Pilgrim;
And he too would gaze into the heart
Of Good and Evil . . .

Slowly, Ballas's body healed. The bruises faded and his skin grew fish-pale. The lacerations closed over, leaving thin pink scars. His cracked ribs – though still sore – no longer ached intolerably at the mildest touch.

During this time, the big man's days passed monotonously. The priest gave him two pennies a day, to be spent on food. Sometimes the money *did* find its way into a butcher's hand: Ballas purchased all manner of treats that, as a vagrant, he had been denied: herb-sprinkled pork cutlets, venison sausages, honey-roasted duck and – just once, for the portions were minuscule – a pair of lark's wings. Other times, he spent the money on alcohol. He would settle in a tavern for a whole afternoon and imbibe ale and wine. When he hungered, he would visit the market and *steal* what he craved. Market-place meats were not as fine as those found in butcher shops – there were no lark wings or duck – but the pilfered morsels were enough to fill his stomach. Naturally, he carried out such thefts with caution. He rarely visited the same stall two days in a row; often, he would walk the extra half-mile to a different market.

In the evenings, he would sit in his sleeping-room, drinking. The priest seldom troubled him. Perhaps he accepted the big man's silences. And if he detected liquor upon his breath, he never mentioned it. The holy man was content for Ballas to indulge himself.

Ballas thought often of the iron disc. Of the gemstone. And the thought aided his recovery. After fourteen days, Ballas felt well enough to leave the priest-home.

The day had passed like any other.

Ballas had risen at noon. Taking a small amount of meat-money from the priest, he had settled in a tavern and grown moderately drunk. At the market, he stole a slab of cooked steak, which he ate greedily; then – as if Mistress Fortune was favouring him – he found upon the ground a dropped purse: it contained coppers enough for a flagon of whisky. When the light began to fade, and the early nocturnal chill seeped through the streets, Ballas returned to the priest-home and went to his sleeping-room.

As full darkness settled on Soriterath, he heard the priest-home's front door creak open – then close softly. Cracking open his window shutters, he peered out.

Fifty yards away stood Brethrien's church: an oval flat-roofed building of dark brick, with a five-foot-tall iron Scarrendestin image mounted over the doorway and a bell tower at the rear. A dozen people waited outside.

Squinting, Ballas saw Father Brethrien walking towards them, ready to deliver his evening sermon. Something gleamed dully in his right hand. A flagon of holy wine, Ballas realised.

'Good idea, priest,' he said softly, closing the shutters.

He went into the kitchen. From the shelf he took a wine flagon.

'Let us see,' he muttered, tugging out the cork, 'how good those monks are at winemaking.'

He took a long swallow. Then he grimaced. The liquid was coarse – it scorched his throat like vinegar.

'Pilgrims' blood! Is this what pious folk drink? Seems they want to suffer like the Four did.' Shrugging, he took another swig. This time it tasted no worse than any tavern wine.

He looked around the kitchen.

In the corner stood a sack of vegetables. Ballas nodded to himself: the sack would prove useful later. On the table rested a heap of parchments, a bowl of ink and the knife Brethrien used for sharpening his quills. Taking the knife, and a wooden fork from the shelf, Ballas returned to his sleeping-room.

Sitting upon the pallet-bed, Ballas whittled at the fork. Offcut curls of wood tumbled to the floor. The resinous tang of a carpentry shop pervaded the room, mingling with the scents of the fire. Ballas worked carefully, and for a time was oblivious to anything except his carving. He pared the fork down to a long strip, then fashioned one end into a series of grooves and ridges. He rubbed his thumb over them. Then he peered at them with the intense scrutiny of a master craftsman. Grunting, he deepened a groove by a fraction.

Nodding contentedly, he laid the piece upon the bed.

Then he realised that the wine flagon was still half full. Downing it in one gulp, he returned to the kitchen. He put the knife back upon the table, and the empty flagon on the shelf. Then – after a heartbeat's hesitation – he took two more flagons from the shelf.

He went back into his room.

After some time, the church bell tolled: the evening sermon had finished.

Opening the shutters, Ballas saw the congregation filing into the street. A short while later, Father Brethrien emerged from the holy building. He walked back towards the priest-home.

Closing the shutters, Ballas listened intently.

He heard the priest-home door open, then shut. He heard Brethrien placing a metal cover over the fire, dousing it. He heard the priest's footsteps treading softly along the corridor, to the holy man's own sleeping-room. A door closed. A bolt was near-noiselessly slid home.

Ballas waited.

As he did so, he uncorked the third wine flagon. He had grown accustomed to its sharp taste. It was – surprisingly – a potent concoction, and a warm numbness crept through his body. He felt ready. The big man tingled with anticipation.

He didn't have an eye for beautiful things. Of course, he could tell a beautiful *woman* from an ugly one. But that was an inborn talent. His pulse would race, his child-maker stiffen – all without his volition. It was reflexive, he supposed.

Inanimate objects had no such effect on him. A silken shirt didn't seem more elegant than a sackcloth tunic. A pebble no finer than a diamond.

But he *did* understand what others found appealing. What they would spend money to acquire.

Ballas left the sleeping-room. He listened at Brethrien's doors. The priest's breaths were faintly audible – soft, regular, they belonged to a man asleep.

He went into the kitchen.

With dull surprise, he found he was still grasping the third flagon. Such an object would be an encumbrance. So he drank it empty, then put it on the table.

Kneeling, he emptied the vegetable sack on to the floor. Carrots, potatoes, peas – the stuff of Brethrien's meals – tumbled out. Bundling the sack under his arm, Ballas opened the door and stepped outside.

A few stars shone. The moon glowed; it almost formed a perfect circle. Silver light illuminated the muddy street. A cold wind made Ballas shiver. He shut the priest-home door. Then he walked towards the church.

Moonlight glimmered on the Scarrendestin image over the door. Kneeling, Ballas untucked the whittled-down fork from his belt. He inserted its grooved, ridged end into the keyhole. Delicately, he twisted it back and forth. He felt inside the inner structure of the lock. Something was wrong, he realised.

Straightening up, he twisted the ring-handle. The door creaked open. The lock-pick had not been needed. The door wasn't locked.

' "Bar not the doors of your churches," ' he murmured, reciting a passage from *The Book of the Pilgrims*, ' "for no man is a trespasser in a House of the Four".' Ballas suspected he'd learned it during childhood. Now it swirled up into his mind, like a gas bubble from a swamp. 'Holy man,' he muttered, 'you take things too literally.'

He slipped through the door into an ante-room. Moonlight illuminated it inside. Ballas found a lantern hooked on the wall. Taking it, he fumbled for a flint and steel – then realised it would not be necessary.

Opening a second door, he moved into the worship hall.

At the far end, on a white altar, a candle burned. Its light was not sufficient to fill the hall: shadows clung to the walls, and to the rafters overhead. Following the aisle, Ballas approached the candle and used its flame to light his lantern.

Yellow radiance spread outwards. Stone pews grew visible as the gloom retreated. The rafters' outlines became clear; the cobwebs strung among them – too high to be reached – glittered like threads of fire. Upon them dark blots trembled, then fled.

Ballas swept his gaze through the worship hall.

The Pilgrim Church preached frugality. Thus the pews were uncushioned, the floor bare. There were no windows – as if natural light were something decadent.

The walls, though, were hung with tapestries. Each one depicted a part of every Pilgrim's journey to the holy mountain, Scarrendestin. The tale was a simple one. Four ordinary men – a clothes-maker, a chandler, a tanner and a sailor – were visited, in dreams, by the creator-god. He ordered them to travel across the land and, through suffering and hardship, learn the difference between good and evil. After many trials and virtuous acts, they met on top of the holy mountain, where – in reward for their holy labours – the creator-god joined them into a single divine entity. And this entity became the gatekeeper of the Eltheryn Forest, through which dead souls had to travel to reach heaven. Good souls were shown the way. Bad souls had to stumble through the oak-crowded darkness, suffering all manner of torment, until their souls were purged.

Ballas glanced at the tapestries. Then he turned to the altar.

Upon it rested a Blessing Bowl of finely etched bronze; a model of Scarrendestin, fashioned from brass; and a goblet from which holy wine was drunk. Ballas unrolled the empty vegetable sack and dropped the first two items inside. Lifting the goblet, he found that an inch of holy wine remained in it. He gulped the liquid down, then put the goblet too in the sack.

Around the worship hall, unlit candles perched upon ledges. Each nestled inside a short brass holder. They would not be worth much: a ha'penny each. But a reflex, ingrained by years of rough living, demanded that Ballas take them: it was foolish to ignore an easy theft. He tossed the candleholders into the sack. Giving the hall a final glance, he walked towards the ante-room and left the church.

He took his bearings.

The museum stood on Half-moon Street – almost a full mile away. But he could halve that distance by cutting across Papal Square.

Ballas set off at an easy pace. Dawn was seven or eight hours away; there was no reason to rush.

Yet a kind of excited urgency crept into his steps. He found himself striding out, and grinning . . . grinning like a child on Winterturn's Eve, eager to unwrap its linen-swaddled gifts: toys, sweetmeats and sugared apples.

A single thought revolved in his skull: Soon I will be rich, soon I will be rich . . .

He thought again of the whores he would enjoy. And the sort of lodgings he would take: a comfortable room, in a decent tavern, with a soft bed and clean blankets. He thought about the amounts of wine he would consume. No more would he run out of money before he was sated. He'd be able to drink until his stomach burst.

He laughed breathlessly.

'They reckon that money changes a man,' he murmured, emerging on to Papal Square. 'That wealth bends him into another shape. That it casts a spell, turning him into a different man. Well, it's not going to happen to me.'

He approached the Penance Oak.

Three heads were nailed to the branches.

Moonlight glinted on their eyes . . . eyes as lifeless as those of hooked fishes.

Ballas's gaze flitted towards the Esklarion Sacros. By the dark wooden gates half a dozen Wardens stood sentry. A brazier burned, the hot coal-light glimmering on their helms.

'No one'll say, "Money has twisted Ballas". If they speak of me at all, they'll just say, "Money has let him be Ballas more *vigorously* – just as a falcon can act more like a falcon, when it is cut from its traces and permitted to fly free." '

Ballas passed the Penance Oak, then left Papal Square. Within fifty heartbeats he had reached the museum.

He looked up and down Half-moon Street. There was no one in sight.

Kneeling, he pushed his lock-pick into the keyhole – and found that, unlike the priest, Calden, the old man, was a wise soul: the door was locked.

Ballas turned the lock-pick carefully. Its stem grated as it met the mechanism's tumblers. Then there was a muted click.

The door opened.

Still carrying the church lantern, Ballas entered the first chamber.

Light flashed upon the display cases' glass panels. Ballas's image was reflected in them, dark and ghostly. He walked through the first and second chambers and on into the third.

The vault doorway was locked.

Ballas produced the lock-pick – then hurled it away. Taking a step backwards, he kicked open the door. There was no point in being stealthy here.

Ballas went down the steps into the vault.

It was precisely as he remembered.

Upon the shelves stood an assortment of relics: skulls and bones, antique pottery, statuettes, and figurines crafted from glass, ivory and polished stone. Setting down the lantern, Ballas moved to the shelf from which, two weeks ago, the old man had taken the wooden casket that held the iron disc.

He froze.

The casket was not there – only a heap of moth-eaten silk. Reaching out, he touched the material, then tugged it from the shelf. He expected to find the casket behind it.

There was nothing.

'What have you done with it, old man?' he asked softly. 'Where have you put it?'

Stepping back, he surveyed the shelves.

His gaze flicked over the assembled items. The lantern swung slightly in his hand. Shadows swam in a goat skull's eye sockets. Glints flared on a green glass goblet. Cursing softly, Ballas shook his head.

'Old man, are you taking the piss, hm?'

He clenched his jaw. The walk to Half-moon Street had made him sweat. His woollen clothes rasped against his skin. His heart thudded. The taste of holy wine lay sour on his tongue.

On a shelf lay a chess set. The board was of chequered red and black glass. The pieces, also glass, were coloured blue and yellow. Was the casket secreted behind this game that sparkled in the lantern light?

Ballas kneeled, intending to take a look. Yet his patience snapped.

'Pilgrims' blood,' he muttered and, hooking his fingers around the board's edge, he swept it from the shelf. It hurtled across the vault. Striking the far wall, it shattered in a small explosion of red and black. Shards bounced upon the floor, then grew still. The chess pieces lay scattered, some broken, some intact.

Ballas peered at the shelf. The casket wasn't there.

His face reddened as the blood surged under his skin. He swung his arm along another shelf. A cluster of animal skulls flew through the vault. A lion's skull exploded against the wall; white fragments pattered down like hail. Ballas stepped back. His heel pulverised a field mouse's skull. He stared accusingly at the empty shelf. There was still no sign of the casket.

His hands shook. He closed his eyes, slowly. 'Where is it? Where, in this hoard of useless, pointless shit . . . where is it?' His eyes flicked open. '*Where is it?*' he shouted, his temper breaking. '*Where* is *it?*'

A red mist clouded his vision. It seemed to seep from the brickwork, from the shelves and from the relics themselves.

Snarling, Ballas lashed out with his fist, clearing a shelf of glass statuettes: the tiny, delicate figures of warriors, politicians and philosophers shattered upon the stones.

Again, there was no sign of the casket. His snarl turning to a growl, the big man swept his forearm through another clutch of animal skulls. Then a row of pottery, decorated by fine Eastern brushwork. The bone- and pot-fragments mingled on the floor: a crunching brown-and-white jumble. Tapestries were heaped on another shelf. Centuries old, and fragile, some tore as Ballas hurled them aside. Others disintegrated into powder. A battalion of carved ivory soldiers – each one no larger than Ballas's thumb – occupied a further shelf. Ballas's hand felled them like a lightning bolt.

He looked furiously from shelf to shelf.

Sweat trickled down his face. The sharp edges of a smashed relic – Ballas did not know which – had cut open his palm. As he drove his hand through a group of ornamental cups, an arc of blood streaked the wall. His wounded hand stung slightly. The pain was somehow pleasurable. The noise of destruction – the breaking glass and shattering earthenware – also pleased him. It filled his ears, as loud as the drumming of his heart.

He moved like a tornado through the vault. Soon, every shelf was bare.

Ballas sagged against the wall.

Under his feet, there was a scree of shattered pieces. Glass splinters winking in the lantern light. Fragments of dull pottery. Glossy slivers of porcelain. Pale bits of bone . . . all were blood-splashed: his life-juice pulsed from his injury. It blotched his leggings, dripped on to his boots. Lifting his lacerated hand to his mouth, Ballas suckled upon the wound.

He took deep breaths.

'If it isn't here, it must be elsewhere.'

It was a foolish, obvious comment. Yet it gave Ballas hope.

'Where will it be? Where would the old man have put it? Surely . . . surely he wouldn't be stupid enough to *exhibit* it? To place it where anyone might see?'

Ballas did not know where else it could be. Snatching up the lantern, he climbed the steps into the third chamber.

He moved among the display cases. Each one contained stuffed animals. There were birds, their chests puffed with horsehair packing: ospreys, eagles, hawks, crows, sparrows, magpies . . . As Ballas raised the lantern, their glass-bead eyes winked. The bottom of one display case was strewn with leaves, twigs, logs; on this replica forest floor lurked rats, mice, beetles, squirrels – even a deer foal. Some cases held spiders, long-legged and shadow-fringed. Others had in them bears, lions, elks . . .

But there was no iron disc. No gemstone.

Ballas explored the second chamber. Here, the display cases held relics from lost civilisations: artefacts of the harsh-featured, slant-eyed Lectivins from the distant west; of the Vokarian tribes of the south; of the Schabrines from the equatorial regions . . .

Again, Ballas could not see the iron disc.

Cursing, he half-ran into the first chamber. He found himself surrounded by items from still existent but far-flung civilisations: the Distant East, with its white linen robes and shawls, its hook-bladed swords and knives; the thick furs and spears of the seal-hunting Daskeri, a tribe from the snow-locked Far North . . .

Once more, there was no hint of the disc.

Ballas swore. His rage blazed sun-hot. He shook his head, disgusted.

Springing forward, he slammed his boot into a display case. Smashed glass spun glimmering into shadow. Ballas stared. He felt his hopes shrinking away. The prospects he had contemplated with near-feverish joy . . . the pretty whores, unlimited wine, comfortable lodging rooms . . . they all fizzled out like a warming campfire in heavy rain.

Shouting out, he kicked the display case again, his boot kicking its now-glassless frame. It teetered, then toppled. A jumble of knives and furs spilled out.

Ballas stared fiercely at them. Then he glanced beyond the case, at the wall twenty yards away.

He blinked.

A dark shape stood at the edge of the lantern-glow. Ballas thought at first it was a man: a small, oddly hunched man.

His nerves sparked – then grew calm.

It was not a man at all, but a doorway.

Ballas rushed over. He grasped the ring-handle and twisted. Locked. Lowering his right shoulder, he bull-charged the door, springing its lock and forcing it back off its hinges. Taking a breath, he stepped through.

The room was very small. In the centre stood a tiny desk. The walls were covered with shelves, each one stacked with parchments. The air was very dry.

Ballas looked around. And swore. The room contained nothing except the desk – and parchments.

The big man muttered a profanity. Then fell silent. On the desk was a book. Gilt lettering flickered on its spine in the faint light: *Catalogue of the Earth-Bright.*

The old man had told the geologist of his attempts to identify the blue gemstone. Perhaps he was *still* trying to discover what the gemstone was . . . and doing so here, in this parchment-heaped room?

The light wavered. The lantern's flame was guttering.

Cursing, Ballas snatched up a candle. He lit it from the last flaring of the lantern. Then he placed it back on the desk.

A huge impatience seized him. He grasped a parchment stack and pulled it off the shelf. The stack broke apart; dry sheaves fell to the floor. Ballas had hoped to find the casket, or the disc, hidden behind the pile. But there was nothing.

Ballas repeated the action further along the shelf – and more parchments, as dry as autumn leaves, floated to the ground. His frustration worsened. His temper blossomed into a red fury. Grabbing handful after handful of parchments, he threw them around the room, until every shelf was bare.

He stepped back, gasping.

'Damn it!' he shouted. 'Damn everything!'

Turning, he kicked over the desk. The *Catalogue of the Earth-Bright* thudded to the floor. The lit candle fell on to the scattered parchments.

Ballas moved towards the door – then hesitated.

In the corner, rising waist-high, was a tower of parchments. Preoccupied with the shelves, Ballas had not noticed it before. Stooping, he toppled it with his forearm – and found, tucked behind it, the black wooden casket he had seen before . . . the casket that had contained the iron disc.

Grinning, Ballas took the casket in his arms. It felt heavy; he shook it, gently: something bumped inside.

He tried to lift the lid. But it was locked. He reached for his lock-pick, then remembered that he had thrown it away upstairs, in the third chamber. It did not matter: he would simply have to use more brutal methods to open the casket. Turning, he hurled it against the wall. It struck the brickwork corner first and the lid sprang open.

The iron disc fell to the floor.

Ballas laughed – a loud throat-scraping burst of joy . . . and relief.

He snatched up the disc. He clutched it as tightly as a drowning man might grasp a floating wooden spar.

The disc was unmarked: it bore no ornamentation, no etchings: it was, to Ballas's inexpert eye, crude, ugly, primitive. But the rubies . . . he recognised that they *must* be worth a purseful of gold. And the blue gemstone – the true reason he had lusted after the disc – how much would *that* be worth? The old man had said it was unique, so it could have no fixed price. But such items, Ballas knew, fetched colossal amounts. He stroked his thumb over its surface. It was as smooth as ice. He looked at its blueness . . . its rich, rock-pool blue . . .

'A candle,' he muttered. 'Let's see what dazzled the geologist, shall we?'

Only then did Ballas notice that the candle was lying on the parchments – which were starting to burn. Their edges glowed orange-red, then curled, blackening. Smoke trickled upward.

Ballas paused before making his next move.

Grunting, he picked up the candle and moved the disc towards its flame.

The stone grew bluer, its light almost dazzling. Within its depths golden sparks drifted: they rose and fell as if propelled by a gentle tide. They sparkled, star-bright. Ballas became transfixed.

'What man, when offered such a thing, could refuse?' he murmured.

He coughed as smoke drifted into his mouth. The fire crackled merrily as it consumed the parchments. The flames danced knee-high. Now they were spreading quickly. Streamers of ash floated across the room.

Rising, Ballas looked at the flames. Then he looked at the disc.

'Whores, drink, a warm room . . .' Lifting the disc to his lips, he kissed the gemstone.

He glanced at the fire one last time. Then, turning, he hurried from the museum, and stepped out into a night in which stars shone elegantly down from a cold night sky.

Ballas took shelter in a stable adjoining a tavern.

In the darkness, surrounded by the comforting scent and warmth of horses, the big man curled up in the corner. He lay on a covering of straw damp with horse piss; yet he took pleasure in the squalor of his circumstances, for he knew that it would soon end.

At this hour, on the morrow, he would be in a better place.

A common room, perhaps – laughing loudly, his face liquor-flushed.

Or a brothel, rutting earnestly with a dark-eyed whore.

Ballas pillowed his head on his forearm. He gripped the sack of stolen goods to his chest. He felt the jagged jumble of church oddments, and the smooth edge of the disc.

Smiling faintly, he fell asleep.

Chapter 4

In the south-west ports of Calcarin,
A sailor too received the creator-god's Blessing.
Refusing the ocean, he took a land journey
Of divine torment, as a Pilgrim,
To gaze upon Good and Evil . . .

An hour after dawn, Ballas stood in the workshop of Jasreith Logos, a crafter of cheap jewellery.

The stolen church oddments were spread on a workbench. By chance or design, Logos had arranged them in the same order as upon the altar. The candleholders were clustered at the edge, their brass surfaces reflecting the pulsing glow of Logos's furnace.

Logos was a squat man in his fiftieth year. His face was heat-flushed, and faintly tanned. White hairs curled from his nostrils and ears.

He picked up a candleholder. He turned it over, weighing it in his palm.

'Brass,' said Ballas flatly. 'It's made from brass.'

'I do not require your help,' said Logos, his voice thin and dry, 'in identifying what it's made of.' He set it back down upon the workbench. 'The hue, lustre and texture all cry "brass". And if they did not . . . well, all the Pilgrim Church's ceremonial pieces are fashioned from brass. Except for those used in the grand cathedrals. Those are wrought from gold.' He looked Ballas up and down. His grey eyes were as attentive as a cat's. 'Of course, such cathedrals are guarded by Wardens. To burgle such a place, one must be a brave man. And I sense that you, my friend, are of frailer mettle.'

He picked up the model of Scarrendestin. Furnace light glinted upon it.

'Five pennies,' said Logos.

'For the model alone?' asked Ballas, surprised.

'For everything.' Logos laughed sardonically – as if Ballas were a foolish child. 'For *everything*,' he repeated.

Ballas had slept well, amid the horses and stable straw. He had woken feeling strong, healthy – and optimistic. Soon he would be rich. For the first time in many years, he'd greeted the dawn in a fair mood. And that mood persisted. Even Logos's attitude – his rasping laugh, his condescension – failed to irritate the big man. Ballas felt as though he was, slowly but surely, entering a new phase of his life. A phase in which he'd no longer be a scavenger, a creature hurtling from one desperate deed to another.

Because of the iron disc, and its stones, he'd live like a caliph of the Distant East.

Yet he wanted a fair price for the oddments. It was a matter of principle, he supposed.

'These pieces are worth ten pennies,' Ballas told Logos. 'This is church brass, aye? It's of good quality. Melt it down, and you can make it into the finest jewellery—'

'That is true,' Logos interrupted briskly. 'But church brass is cursed.'

'Cursed?'

'It brings ill fortune on the bearer.'

Logos cracked open a window shutter. A cold breeze swept in. The furnace coals glowed.

'Do you suppose the Pilgrim Church authorities are *happy* to have their belongings taken? Do you imagine they consider their loss no loss at all – more like a charitable donation?' His thin laugh returned. 'They are not charitable people. Nor are they forgiving. Cross them, and they will seize you, and do with you as they wish.'

He turned to Ballas.

'I wish to sleep easily at night. I do not want to lie with an ear cocked for Wardens.' He spread his hands and shrugged resignedly. 'These pieces in themselves are, indeed, worth ten pennies. But if I were to purchase them, I would also be purchasing a death sentence. Such thefts carry a man to the gallows. I doubt that a hemp collar would suit me.'

'So you won't take them?'

'For ten pennies, no. But five . . . five would be a different matter. Say five, and our bargain is struck.'

'You're a strange man,' said Ballas quietly. 'It seems that you value your life at five pennies.' He sighed loudly. 'But I shan't argue. All right. I accept. Five pennies it is – and some information.'

Logos's eyes narrowed. 'What type of information?'

'There's something else I'm going to sell. A beautiful object. The experts reckon it's unique. I need to find a buyer . . .'

'Show it to me,' demanded Logos, curiosity evident in his tone.

Ballas shook his head. 'It's beyond your means. Any man who wrangles over five pennies can't afford it.'

'This object – it is of dubious provenance?' asked Logos.

'Maybe,' replied Ballas vaguely. 'Its buyer has to be wealthy. And uninterested in its origins. You know of such a man?'

'This is Soriterath,' said Logos. 'Druine's holiest city. Of course there are men who will be interested.'

'Name some.'

'Masser Helkirrith, Jorath Kette, Carrande Black—'

'That last one sounds familiar,' interrupted Ballas. 'Reckon I heard it mentioned in a tavern.'

'That is most probable,' agreed Logos. 'Black owns a number of taverns. They are but one of his interests, among many.'

'Where can Black be found?'

'He can be approached only through his agents,' said Logos. 'Are you familiar with Red Street? Black's taverns are there: the Broken Moon, the Opened Eye and the Weary Blacksmith.'

'I know them,' said Ballas.

'His agents conduct much of their business in the common rooms,' said the jewelsmith. 'Find one, and see what can be done.'

From his purse Logos took five pennies. He held them out to Ballas. But as the big man reached for them, Logos snatched back his hand.

'Do not tell Carrande Black I sent you,' he said, suddenly serious.

'He is a cruel man?' asked Ballas, tilting his head.

'He is a *rich* man,' said Logos. 'And no man grows rich by being sweet-tempered.'

He dropped the coins into Ballas's outstretched palm. Then he picked up the model of Scarrendestin.

'Go,' he told Ballas. 'I have work to do.'

Logos placed the model on a metal tray, which he slid into the furnace. The miniature began to glow.

The jewelsmith glanced at Ballas. With a nod, the big man left.

Ballas arrived at the Broken Moon at noon – just in time to place a bet on a cockfight.

A chalk circle had been sketched on the common-room floor. A film of blood already greased the boards. Stray feathers lay here and there, blowing in a draught. Through the odours of fire- and pipe-smoke, Ballas smelled the harsh, strangely *unnatural* odour of offal.

He pushed through the crowds to the serving bar.

After purchasing a flagon of Keltuskan red, he moved close to the chalk circle.

A thin excitement prickled in Ballas's gut. Two cockerels were being prepared. The first had a metal spike, as sharp-tipped as a dagger, fastened to its beak. The second had thin metal spurs tied to its legs, each as keen-edged as a flensing knife.

Ballas pondered the birds' physical condition.

Some of the first one's feathers were missing, exposing patches of freshly wounded skin. The second, however, didn't seem to have fought before. It was well fed, glossy-feathered, and bore no noticeable scars.

'Care to place a wager, eh?' A brown-garbed man edged close. His black hair stuck up in spikes, and his green eyes glittered. His ears were like a rat's: pink, translucent, shot through with vivid red veins. A coin pouch was belted around his waist. On his middle finger an emerald ring sparkled. The large jewel caught Ballas's eye.

'What are the odds?' asked Ballas, looking at the man curiously.

'He's the favourite,' said the man, gesturing to the cockerel wearing the beak-spike. 'He looks battle-torn, true. But he fights fiercely. I'd give you three to one.'

'And the other?'

'Untried,' shrugged the man. 'Let's say four to one, because of his inexperience.'

'A penny on the first bird,' said Ballas, handing the coin to the man who nodded, then moved off into the crowd.

The cockfight began.

The bout was bloody and protracted. The beak-spike bird jabbed ferociously at its rival, ripping out an eye and puncturing its throat. The other repeatedly sprang upon its opponent's back, its spurs slicing through feathers and flesh. Blood oozed from the wounds. After twenty minutes, the killing blow came: a spur slashed open the beak-spike bird's stomach. Blue-green intestines poked out. The bird collapsed, its talons clawing the floor spasmodically.

The audience cheered.

The bird's owner retrieved his ward and inspected its wounds, wondering whether they could be stitched so the bird could fight again.

Having lost his bet, Ballas settled at a corner table.

Gambling was a foolish, wasteful habit. It gave a brief flash of pleasure – then came disappointment. In his time, Ballas had lost money on wagers of all kinds. Not just on cockfights, but on dog-baitings and bare-knuckle brawls. And on less exciting events: coin tossing, dice rolls, frog races . . . Always, he left poorer than he'd been when he'd arrived. And, always, he didn't hesitate to gamble again.

He had lost a penny – what of it? Soon he would be rich.

The big man licked his lips and sipped at his wine.

In the corner, the man with the emerald ring was paying out to those who had gambled well: those who had been fortunate or wise enough to bet on the spur-garbed cockerel.

Yet he was also selling something from a drawstring bag. Ballas squinted, attentive. From the bag the man extracted a twisted brown root, no larger than an infant's thumb. A gambler handed him a few pennies. Then, grinning, he went away with the root.

Ballas frowned.

'You,' he said to a serving girl who was scrubbing cockerel's blood from the floorboards. 'Come here.'

Rising, the girl approached. She was an unimpressive creature. Her skin was pale. A cold sore glistened at the corner of her mouth. She was incredibly thin. She moved slowly, as if gripped by profound lethargy. Her eyes were only half focused.

Ballas gestured to the man with the emerald ring. 'What is he selling?'

The girl glanced over. 'You do not know?'

'Wouldn't have asked if I did,' retorted Ballas, scowling.

The girl stared at Ballas. Her pupils were enlarged, as if submerged in darkness. She swayed slightly. 'I thought it strange . . .' she began.

'Thought *what* strange?'

'That you didn't . . . that you do not know what Gramiche is selling. You look as if you have suffered hard times; and many beleaguered souls find Gramiche's wares helpful . . . He is selling many things, all bundled into one. Sunshine, happiness, enlightenment – one can converse with the Four, and with spirits, and with ancient scribes and learned men.' She blinked dreamily. 'It is marvellous. You ought to try it yourself. You can see everything, from the moments of creation – the rains that formed the sea and the suns that bared the land – right up to the end of time. And there are other things, *unimaginable* things. The hidden scripture of Nature becomes clear. The meaning of a butterfly's wingbeat, of a sand dune's shape . . . they can be understood. In such things there is language, and a truth.'

Ballas began to understand. 'He is peddling visionary's root?'

The girl nodded. 'Are you going to buy some?'

'Perhaps,' lied Ballas, carefully. 'The man who sells it – where does he get it from?'

The girl gestured vaguely. 'The Distant East. It grows wild there. Any man with a sickle may harvest it . . . and in doing so he will garner dreams and knowledge and all good things.' A trickle of brown-tinged saliva crept from the side of her mouth. She wiped it away with her finger.

The girl's eyes grew hazy. She swallowed. 'The East – that is where all the root comes from.'

'And Gramiche travels there himself?' asked Ballas.

The girl frowned. 'I do not think so. His master hires merchants – and adventurers – to smuggle it in.'

'And his master's name?'

The girl hesitated. 'Carrande Black.'

'Tell me about him,' said Ballas flatly.

'He owns this tavern, and others,' said the girl. 'And he does not merely import goods – he exports, too.' In her eyes unease flickered. 'I ought not to speak of such matters.'

Ballas took a penny from his purse. 'Talk honestly,' he said, 'and you will be paid. What is a penny to you, hm? Half a day's wage?'

She looked at the penny warily. Then she plucked it from Ballas's palm. 'Black exports whores,' she said, half whispering.

'And you consider that bad?'

'He sends them to the East,' she said. 'Often, the girls are willing. They have heard fine tales of harems. They believe they will be pampered, well fed . . . and, if they prove their worth, their owners will wed them. But often, the girls Black sends have no wish to leave. Some are whores who, for all its ugliness, are content to stay in Soriterath. And others . . . they are not whores at all.' She chewed her lip. 'They are ordinary girls. Bakers' daughters, carpenters' sisters . . . In the East, pale skins are prized, for they are rare. But a pale-skinned virgin – she is truly valued. But how many virgins labour as whores? None, of course. So Black must find them in different ways. Sometimes, he sends men to the provinces. There, where poverty reigns, some parents are willing to trade their children for money, for food. But, more often, Black just kidnaps them. He snatches them from the streets. And that is that.' The girl faltered. 'He took my sister.'

Ballas gazed evenly at her. 'Yet still you buy root from him? Still you make him rich?'

The girl blinked, confused – as if Ballas's question was unfathomable. 'There is no one else in Soriterath who sells it,' she said eventually. 'And besides, my sister vanished a long time ago – yes: a long time ago.'

Ballas was silent for a moment. 'And Carrande Black has grown rich through such dealings?'

'He is one of the wealthiest merchants in Soriterath,' replied the girl, nodding.

Ballas took a gulp from his flagon. 'Go,' he told the serving girl.

White-fleshed, gaunt, she drifted like a spectre to the chalk circle. Kneeling, she scrubbed the blood-wet boards. The cockerels' blood marked her hands.

Ballas drained his flagon. Rising, he walked over to Gramiche's table.

He stood at the back of the queue, watching the rat-eared man sell twist after twist of root. Gramiche's hands were small, stubby-fingered. And ochre-tinted from handling the drug. They moved dexterously, taking root from the bag and dropping coins into his pouch. There was a calm, confident air about him. Ballas thought this strange: if he was caught peddling root, his head would be nailed to the Penance Oak. As the serving girl had said, root gave its user certain insights, certain flashes of arcane knowledge. Ballas was uncertain precisely what the Church objected to in this. Perhaps they *did* fear that the people would become too aware, and be seduced by their root-inspired understanding away from the Four's teachings.

But Ballas did not think so.

Maybe the Blessed Masters wanted Druine's inhabitants to suffer, and turn to the Church as a balm. Maybe they objected to any release from pain.

Ballas shrugged inwardly. Such details were of no concern to him.

Nonetheless, Gramiche's easygoing manner surprised him. Perhaps he had grown complacent. Perhaps he believed that since the Wardens had not previously arrested him, they would never do so.

The queue inched forwards.

Eventually, Ballas found himself at the table.

'You lost the wager, did you not?' said Gramiche, glancing up. 'You placed a penny on the beak-spike cockerel.'

'That is true,' said Ballas.

'Then you are after some root, hm?' Gramiche's green eyes glimmered. A faint smile quirked his lips. 'If you hurt, in body or soul, it will soothe you. And if you are ignorant, it will bring enlightenment.' He spoke the words with wry cynicism. Root was a sham, an indulgence of fools. And he knew it. He knew also that those who used it were helpless to do otherwise. It was fiercely addictive.

'I want you to arrange a meeting for me with Carrande Black,' said Ballas bluntly.

Gramiche blinked. Then he glanced at two heavy-set, broad-shouldered men sitting beside him. Ballas had noticed them before. They were part of the reason Gramiche could wear the emerald ring without fear.

'Who are you?' he asked, leaning forward slightly.

'My name doesn't matter,' replied Ballas. 'What matters is that your master is wealthy, and has an eye for beautiful things.'

'Why should that concern you?'

'I own *the* most beautiful thing,' said Ballas. 'A gemstone that outshines every other in Druine – a unique piece that I am willing to sell.'

'A gemstone,' murmured Gramiche. 'What would *you* know of

gemstones – and beauty? Your expertise, I think, does not extend beyond drinking. And sleeping rough. I speak as one who recognises such things.' He gestured towards Ballas. 'You are filthy. You stink. And recently,' he peered at Ballas's face, 'you have been beaten. These are not the characteristics of someone acquainted with beauty. A gemstone of merit? My friend, you wouldn't know frozen piss from citrine quartz.'

Ballas felt his temper rising. Not because Gramiche had spoken falsely: every word he'd uttered was true. But because he'd had the audacity to say such things at all. Gramiche was a small man, Ballas noticed. Yet, nestling between the two bigger men, who were clearly in his service, he was safe. There was a species of tropical fly that behaved in a similar fashion. It alighted upon the head of a *galskiros* – a savage, marsh-dwelling creature – and, once there, remained safe from the birds and rats that normally preyed upon it. Ballas wondered idly if it was part of the natural order, that the weak should exploit the strong.

'The gemstone's been looked at by a geologist from the Academy,' said Ballas.

'Ah! You are a friend of scholars, are you?'

'*I* am not,' said Ballas. 'But the gemstone's previous owner was. The geologist reckoned it was unique. But you don't need to be a scholar to know that. A halfwit could tell from a single glance. I hear your master likes sparkling things. Things that are unusual – and valuable. Let me meet with him, and I'll offer up the gemstone. Of course, my price'll be high. But fine things don't come cheap.'

Gramiche sighed. 'A persistent fellow, isn't he?' he said, glancing at one of the big men. 'And brisk of tongue. It is often the case with vagrants. They rarely stop talking – if only to themselves. You often find them in ditches, muttering. Or on street corners, rocking back and forth, jabbering like prophets of the East. It is a form of lunacy, I think.'

He stared closely at Ballas.

'But that is by the by. Even one who dwells in a midden may find a treasure. Who is to say what strange circumstances may lead a worthless soul to a thing of value? Show me this gemstone, vagrant.'

'I haven't brought it with me,' said Ballas. 'I thought it wise to leave it somewhere safe.' Ballas had taken lodgings in the Scarlet Star – a tavern half a mile from the Broken Moon. At this moment, the iron disc nestled under the floorboards of his room. In his mind's eye, Ballas could see it there, amid dust, cobwebs and spiders' carcasses.

Gramiche laughed. 'You cannot show me this gemstone – yet you would have me take you to Carrande Black? A man whose time is scarce? And whose patience is short?'

'If you don't,' said Ballas heavily, 'I'll find a different buyer. And he'll be boastful, of course. He'll tell others about the gemstone. Its reputation will spread, and your master'll hear of it – then he'll want to know why he doesn't have it. Why it isn't his to be boastful about. When you, little Gramiche, say it's your fault – and, believe me, I'll tell the buyer that you turned it down, so your master *will* find out – how'll Carrande Black respond? With gratitude? I don't think so. He's a ruthless man, isn't he? He doesn't care for other folks' suffering. He'll slice your balls off.'

Ballas leaned close to Gramiche. The little man wore a fragrance – lavender, it seemed.

'But if your master owned the gemstone, wouldn't he be happy? Wouldn't his reputation soar up, like a bloody lark? Wouldn't he love you like a brother? Wouldn't he give you a little extra in your wages – and leave your balls where they hang?'

Gramiche touched a finger to his lips. 'What if this gemstone is merely coloured glass or a sparkling pebble, plucked from a stream bed? You might be lying about its uniqueness.'

'Then your master needn't buy it,' said Ballas. 'As you said, he's an impatient man. If anyone'll get punished, it'll be me – for wasting his time. You can say you had no reason to mistrust me. Which you haven't. After all, didn't you just say that people like me sometimes come across beautiful things?'

Gramiche grew thoughtful. Ballas watched him, trying to assess his mood.

Gramiche lifted the ring to his lips, sucking absently on its emerald.

'If you are deceiving me,' he said eventually, 'you will be killed. Either by my master – or by me. For I too am short-tempered, and not fond of wasting my time.'

'Your master won't be disappointed,' said Ballas easily.

'Very well. Do you know the warehouse on Scimitar Street?'

'I'll find it.'

'Go there at eveningfall. We will see if this gemstone is all you claim.'

Ballas returned to his lodgings at the Scarlet Star.

In his room, he prised up the floorboards. The iron disc nestled safely beneath them. He brushed away the dust and a clinging tangle of cobwebs.

Sitting upon his bed, he watched the daylight fade.

As the sky darkened, he hid the disc inside the sack, left the tavern and headed off in the direction of Scimitar Street. After half an hour of walking, he found the warehouse Gramiche had spoken of. Ducking inside, he was greeted by the man with the emerald ring.

'I trust that, this time, you have brought the gemstone?' asked Black's assistant, leading Ballas up a flight of wooden steps. 'I trust, too, that its beauty hasn't tarnished since we last spoke? For what I said still stands: waste my master's time and either he or I will punish you.'

They halted upon a landing, outside a black-painted door. Gramiche rapped upon it. After a pause, he showed Ballas through.

Carrande Black's office was large. And elaborately furnished. Deep blue rugs, edged with gold thread, covered the floor. On the walls hung tapestries, many from the Distant East. In red-silver stitching, there were depictions of caliphs' pleasures: couples rutting in bathing pools, and under palm trees; men on horseback hunting sand deer, desert bulls and triple-horned *mohjariks*; others gambling in lantern-lit hallways, winning and losing diamonds on the roll of carved bone dice.

A bookcase stood by a curtained window. It held no ordinary volumes: the spine letterings were picked out in finely cut gemstones, and were done in a strange, looping script. Ballas guessed that the books, like the tapestries, originated in the East. Gold ornaments rested on shelves, glittering in the candlelight. There were finely crafted boxes, inset with black diamonds, ornamental daggers with quartz-encrusted hilts – and a statuette of a naked woman surging up from a pool: every water droplet trickling over her body was a fragment of polished opal.

Carrande Black sat behind a mahogany desk. His grey-white hair was fastened in a ponytail. Although his garb was plain – merely black trousers and leggings – it was made from the finest wools and silks. Two gold rings gleamed on his fingers. In each, the stones were tiny and pale, yet they flickered brilliantly. Ballas sensed that, despite their small size, they were immeasurably valuable.

Black's face was narrow, his jaw sharp-tipped. His lips were thin; his eyes, capped by jet-black brows, were cold and dark. Yet they glowed: the irises might have been crafted from obsidian.

The merchant was writing upon a square of parchment. Gramiche gestured for Ballas to be seated. The big man settled himself upon a bare wooden chair in front of the desk.

For a while, nothing happened. Carrande Black continued writing as if Ballas were not present. The big man fidgeted. Black's quill rasped back and forth. The noise irritated Ballas: it echoed in his ears like the chattering of a solitary locust.

Suddenly, Black stopped writing. Signing the parchment, he laid down his quill.

'Gramiche tells me you have an item of interest,' he said, looking up. His gaze was predatory: the calculating stare of a hawk, hover-hanging over a wheatfield. 'A gemstone, yes?'

Ballas nodded. 'A gemstone of great beauty,' he said.

'Then let me see it,' said Black, spreading his hands wide.

Ballas took the iron disc from the sack. He set it on Black's desk.

The merchant glanced at it, then looked at Ballas. 'There are *five* stones there – the blue one in the centre and' – he picked up the disc – 'four rubies around the outside.'

Ballas glanced at Gramiche. The little man sat perched upon a divan pushed up against the office's wall.

'I did not mention the rubies,' explained the big man, 'for, although they are in themselves fine, they cannot be compared with the blue gemstone.'

Carrande Black turned the disc over. He rubbed his fingertips over the gemstone. Then over the rubies. 'How did you come by this piece?'

'It doesn't matter,' said Ballas. 'I own it, and that is all that counts. Except, of course, whether *you* want it for yourself.'

Black peered at the blue gemstone. 'A university scholar claims that this is unique, you say?'

'Yes,' replied Ballas.

'He is mistaken,' replied Black flatly, a faint smile touching his lips. 'The wise, educated man is wrong. This –' he tapped the gemstone '– is diamond. I have seen similar before. I will give you two gold pieces for it, and for the rubies.'

Ballas smiled. 'You make the same error as the scholar.'

Black lifted his chin. 'Explain yourself.'

'Hold the gemstone to a candle flame.'

Black glanced curiously at Gramiche, as if the man with the emerald ring knew what to expect.

The little man shrugged.

'Do as I suggest,' said Ballas, 'and you'll see it is no diamond. You'll find it's like nothing else in Druine.'

'It is not for you to give my master instructions,' said Gramiche sharply.

'Be silent,' replied Black, quietly. 'If he offends me, he shall know it soon enough.' His gaze lingered on Ballas for a moment. Then he tilted the iron disc towards a candle on the desk.

Blue light streamed over Black's face. From where he was sitting, Ballas couldn't see the sparks in the stone. Yet their reflections were visible upon the merchant's skin: a cluster of pale yellow-blue flickers, slowly swirling.

Black's expression remained unimpressed. This was a pretence, Ballas knew. In Black's neck a pulse fluttered. On his forehead a vein swelled. His hands trembled.

For a few seconds Black gazed into the gemstone. 'It *is* pretty, I grant you that. I'll give you three gold pieces for it.'

'You jest,' said Ballas quietly. 'You offered two before you held it to the candle. I've seen what happens when light strikes it. I know it's worth more than an extra gold coin. Pilgrims' wounds, each ruby is worth two in gold. Perhaps four. They're of decent quality. You know they are, Carrande Black.'

Black plucked a velvet purse from his belt and took three gold coins from it. He placed them upon the table where they glimmered in the candlelight.

'Three gold coins,' said the merchant softly. 'Have you ever seen so much money? I suspect you are a self-indulgent man. What pleasures do you favour? Women? Drink? Visionary's root? Whatever. With these coins –' Black touched them lightly '– you can create a private heaven on earth. How many people have such an opportunity? Think carefully about what you will be abandoning if you refuse my offer.'

The uppermost coin reflected a candle flame's light. The tight bud of brightness swayed back and forth. It mesmerised Ballas: he watched it, dully hypnotised, feeling an increasing desire to accept Black's offer. He scratched his head. Then he grunted.

'I'll take nothing less than *fifteen* gold pieces.' He watched Black for a reaction.

The merchant remained impassive. Except for a faint arching of his eyebrows. A slow blink.

'Now it is *you* who jest,' said Black, a strangely equable note in his voice.

'I've spent my life dirt-poor,' said Ballas. 'I find little in money to laugh about.'

Black touched a knuckle to his lips. 'Five gold pieces,' he said softly.

'Merchant, are you deaf? I asked for fifteen—'

'And I have offered *five*,' said Black, his eyes shining darkly. 'Do not imagine that, if you persist, I shall propose more: I will not. The piece is pretty, the gemstone sparkles – but it is still a mere bauble: a toy, a glinting nothingness. Can you not be content with what I am offering? *Five gold pieces*. How often can someone of your nature expect to gain such a sum?'

'What do you mean by my "nature"?' asked Ballas, scowling.

'Every creature has its habitat,' said Black. 'Fishes dwell in water, scorpions inhabit the desert. Why? Because they have no choice. Their nature demands it of them; they belong nowhere else. So it is with men. Some belong in mansions. Others in the gutter. You, my friend, are of the latter sort. Your habitat is that of the rat. Of the stray dog. Do not fight against it. You can change it no more than an eagle can shun the sky.'

'You insult me,' said Ballas.

'I merely state the truth,' replied the merchant evenly.

'The truth?' Ballas's temper flared. The merchant had pushed him too far. For some perverse reason, Black had chosen to taunt him. 'The truth?' repeated Ballas. 'I'll give *you* a truth.'

Surging to his feet, he drew back his fist. In his rage, he wanted to punch Black. To smash his skull into shards, as he had smashed the animals' skulls in the museum.

Black sprang out of his chair, unsheathing a knife as he did so. The long curved blade flashed. Ballas hesitated. Gramiche rose from the divan, clutching a short-bladed dagger.

'It is wisest,' said Black softly, 'if you leave.' The merchant looked at Ballas calmly. 'Go – and take the bauble with you.'

Ballas snatched up the disc. 'You are a fool,' he said. 'I shall offer this to someone else. The loss is yours, merchant.'

Turning, he strode from the room.

Carrande Black's office door slammed shut. The merchant heard loud bootsteps, accompanied by muttered curses, descending the stairs to the warehouse floor.

'Follow him,' he said, sheathing his knife.

'Master?' Gramiche asked, uncertain what Black intended.

'I honestly believed he would have settled for five gold pieces.' Black moved to the window. 'Perhaps he would have done – if he had been more calm. Perhaps he would not.' He shrugged. 'Who can tell? With every passing day, I grow more amazed at the greed of man. And it is most pronounced in the lazy, the squalid . . . the unworthy. Did you see the gemstone sparkle?'

'I did,' said Gramiche. 'Its beauty surprised me. Where do you suppose he found it?'

'That is hardly important,' said Black, opening the curtains. 'Only its future is of relevance. I would like to have that gemstone, Gramiche. He claimed that it was unique. And though he was mistaken, I still desire it . . . Find out where he has taken lodgings. Or, at least, where he is dossing for the night. I will summon Lukas and Ragrialle.'

Gramiche moved to the door. 'Master, you could have easily afforded fifteen gold pieces. Yet you refused to pay . . .'

'Such a sum, in the hands of such a man, would arouse suspicion – particularly from the Papal Wardens. They would grow curious: has he robbed a clergyman? A mendicant? A merchant, even? When they extracted the truth from him, things might have become dangerous for me.'

'The man has clearly stolen the disc,' said Gramiche, frowning. 'And, true, it is thought criminal to buy stolen goods. But you are a friend of the Blessed Masters. Surely a blind eye would be turned.'

'Maybe,' murmured Black. 'Maybe not. It is not wise to leave such things to chance. The Masters expect discretion from me. If I grow careless, if I draw attention to myself . . .' He shook his head. 'We shall not take any chances.'

He fell silent. Boots stamped along the paving slabs below. A thick-shouldered bearlike figure shambled down the street.

'He is walking northwards,' said Black. 'Do not lose him. And do not let him see you. We shall take the disc from him; then we shall take his life. It is safer for us that way. Perhaps that is our age's hallmark: the cleanest transaction, the bargain least likely to incriminate, is not that which passes between one merchant and another – but the one between the killer and the killed. Now go.'

With a bow, Gramiche vanished through the door.

Carrande Black exhaled. Then he closed the curtains.

In his lodging room in the Scarlet Star, Ballas sat upon his pallet-bed, a wine flagon in his hand.

Except for moonlight seeping around the shutters' edges, the room was pitch dark. This did not trouble the big man. If a thousand candles burned and the shutters were flung open, he would still see only what he presently saw: Carrande Black's office, furnished with riches.

And the merchant himself: his thin, dark-eyed face floated in Ballas's vision like a vile apparition. In his mind's ear the merchant's spiteful, pretentious talk of the habitats of man rang out, over and over. *Your habitat is that of the rat. Of the stray dog.*

He recalled Black's quick, agile movements when Ballas had threatened to strike him. The merchant had been supremely self-assured. He had acted with the calm urgency of a man avoiding a threat no fiercer than that of a garden wasp. That too, thought Ballas, had been meant as an insult.

'Years ago,' murmured the big man, 'I'd have slaughtered you. I'd have slit your throat before you'd had a chance to scream.' He drank deeply from the flagon.

On his lap rested the disc. He traced his fingers over the gemstone and the rubies.

'Five gold pieces. Did you truly believe I would accept *that*?'

Of course, Black *had* believed it. Ballas suddenly understood why. Black, who had enough gold to outshine the sun, was not dazzled by such meagre amounts. But he reckoned Ballas – a man compelled by his nature to scavenge and grub – would be. Black had expected the coins, glinting on the desk, to act upon Ballas like a candle flame on a moth: first, to glare-deaden his wits; then, to draw him inexorably closer . . .

Would every rich man behave the same way? Would they all expect him to be beguiled by the tiniest scattering of gold?

If they did, then they would be disappointed.

Yet maybe things would be more fruitful if he guarded against it. And against *himself*: for, in truth, the five gold coins *had* tempted him. A mild ache had seized his ribcage. His mouth had gone dry. He had been only a quivering of will-power away from taking the money. From selling the disc too cheaply.

He drained the wine flagon, then uncorked another.

As long as the rubies and the gemstone were fixed within the iron frame, he would have no choice but to sell them as a piece. Thus it was easier, by far, for people like Black to offer what seemed a reasonable amount, when they were in truth deceiving him. Black had offered five gold coins – yet it was worth fifteen . . . *at least*. For who could tell what a ruby, taken alone, might bring?

'Isn't it true,' said Ballas, slurring, 'that a man buying a *number* of precious things expects some sort of reduction, because he is giving out such a large amount of his money? Yet, if each stone were sold alone, more money could be made? Some like the easiness of selling all at a stroke. I don't, though. For all I have is time. From these stones,' he got clumsily to his feet, 'I shall squeeze every drop of gold . . . just as a winemaker tramples every bit of juice from his grapes.'

He groped for a candle.

Unable to find one, he opened the window shutters. Moonlight flooded the room, making visible the pallet-bed, a table and a few empty flagons.

Ballas reached for his knife – then grunted. He did not have a blade right now. Church Law forbade the bearing of weapons in Soriterath.

Scowling, he went down to the common room. He bought another flagon of wine. And a piece of mustard-coated beef, with which the tavern master supplied an eating dagger.

Back in his lodging room, Ballas ate the steak. Then he moved to the window. As he did so, moonlight flashed upon the blue gemstone. Inside, the golden sparks flickered silver – then faded back to gold.

'A pretty effect,' muttered Ballas.

He braced the disc against his stomach. Then he jammed the dagger-tip between a ruby and the edge of the socket in which it nestled. Levering the blade back and forth, he tried to prise out the stone.

After a few moments he stopped. And swore.

The stone would not budge. Clearly, the disc's maker had been a competent craftsman. In most baubles, the ruby would have popped out easily enough.

Now it seemed that Ballas had a struggle on his hands.

He tried a different ruby. Grunting, he rocked the knife back and forth. His face reddened with effort. Suddenly, moonlight struck the blue gemstone again. The gold sparks glared silver once more. And a shaft of blue-white light shot up from the gemstone.

Or seemed to.

It lasted only a heartbeat. Startled, Ballas jolted, shifting the gemstone out of the moonlight. The blue-white light had been bright – so bright that blotches drifted now across Ballas's vision, as if he'd gazed into a lantern and then looked away abruptly.

Scowling, he blinked and rubbed his eyes.

He thought about the light-shaft. Then he shook his head.

'Tired,' he murmured. 'I'm as tired as a bloody pack mule.' His gaze lit on the empty flagons. 'Tired, and drunk on Keltuskan Red. Pilgrims' wounds, that stuff is poisonous. It's as vile as serpents' piss. It does my head no good – or my guts. When I'm rich, I'll sup finer wines. Wines that're just as potent – but kinder.'

His gaze returned to the disc.

He tapped his dagger-tip upon it, thinking. He decided to try getting the blue gemstone out. The rubies were fine. He could get a good amount of gold if he sold them. But only the blue gemstone would make him truly *wealthy*. Better by far if he expended some effort getting that one out of its socket. The rubies he'd deal with later. Or perhaps, once rich, he would *hire* a jewelsmith to remove them.

Ballas worked the dagger-tip in between gemstone and socket rim. He pressed the dagger sideways, working it against the jewel. The gemstone stayed socket-locked. Cursing, he applied greater pressure. The blade began to bend.

'Pilgrims' blood,' he grunted, 'come free, won't you? For the Forest's sake—!'

The blade continued to bend. Adjusting his grip, Ballas tried sliding the dagger deeper. He tilted the disc fractionally –

– And blue-silver light speared up from the gemstone.

It flooded the lodging with brilliance. Everything acquired a shadow. Not just the table and the wine flagons, but tiny things as well. Dust heaps on the floor. A moth carcass by the skirting board. A spilled wine-drop. A cobweb in a corner.

Surprised, Ballas jumped once more. But not so much that the gemstone moved out of the moonlight.

He held the disc steady.

The light-shaft was changing.

It broadened, funnelling out into a cone shape. Its light was pure, crisp – a thousand times clearer than fire- or lantern-light. Clearer even than the sun. The cone widened, stretching upwards and outwards.

The light's texture altered. Somehow it tightened. Or, more accurately, *hardened*.

It seemed to grow almost solid.

Different shades of blue-silver seeped in. Some darker. Others lighter.

Gradually an image appeared.

It took Ballas several moments to take in everything he was now seeing.

There was a landscape. A desert, it seemed. The horizon was ridged with dunes. Yet these didn't seem to be made of sand. Somehow, Ballas sensed they were ash: a pale, blue-grey powder, like the remains of a campfire. In the distance a forest could be seen. In the sky there was neither sun nor moon. No stars shone, no clouds drifted. It was impossible to tell if it was night or day.

In the foreground there was a figure. It wore a pale robe of some glossy material. Silk, perhaps. It kept its back to Ballas. Only the back of a bony, hairless head was visible.

Slowly, the figure turned.

A Lectivin. The Pale Race had been extinct for centuries, obliterated during the Red War. They existed only in history books. In folk memories. And in church sermons.

Yet now Ballas gazed upon an inhabitant of Lectivae.

Its features were stark, angular. Like those of a primitive carving. Its eyes were slits, its mouth a lipless gash. Its cheekbones jutted sharply, as if trying to pierce the skin that covered them. Yet its nose hardly existed – a mere gristled ridge over two perforations. There was something insectile about the Lectivin. It reminded Ballas of a preying mantis.

Yet Lectivins were not of insect stock. They were – had been – intelligent creatures: more sharp-witted than humans. And fearsome fighters. During the Red War, they had proved themselves both disciplined and savage.

Ballas stared, numbly.

The Lectivin stared back.

The big man licked his lips.

'Strange,' he murmured. 'I've never seen anything like this before. How's it done? Magick? Or some trickery with lenses?'

It didn't matter. This image – this sculpture from moonlight – would increase the disc's value dramatically.

Carrande Black had offered five gold pieces. Now, Ballas was certain, he'd part with thirty, forty, *fifty*. What bored, wealthy man wouldn't crave such a piece?

You won't reckon it a bauble any longer, thought Ballas.

He drew a breath.

But it is too late, Black. You've missed your chance. You insulted me. So I'll find a different buyer.

The Lectivin's mouth twitched. It was speaking, Ballas realised. No sound came from the image. Ballas grunted, disappointed. If the Lectivin could be heard, the disc would be worth ten more gold pieces.

The Lectivin made a peculiar gesture. Its palm held outward, it touched the air in front of its chest. Then the air several inches lower. Then to the left. And the right. As if it were marking out the points of a cross.

Then it touched the imaginary cross's centre.

It lowered its hands.

Stooping, the Lectivin took a roll of fabric from the ground and unfurled it. It was made from shining, silvern cloth. Stitched upon it, in dark thread, were sixty or seventy sigils. Frowning, Ballas tried to read them. They were unfamiliar. He assumed they were in Lectivin script.

They transfixed him, though. Their darkness against the cloth's brightness held his gaze.

His head started to ache. A dull, tentative throbbing at his temples.

At first it didn't trouble him. But the pain grew stronger. Assuming the blue-silver light was to blame, he tried to lower the disc. To move it out of the moonlight, so that the image would disappear.

He could not do so.

His arms would not budge. Grunting, he strained – yet it seemed his muscles had locked solid.

He gazed at the sigils.

Gradually, the image brightened. The blue-silver light intensified, but Ballas was unable even to squint. The light poured through his wide-open eyes. It seared his brain like engraver's acid. Then it spread through his body. Every nerve end flared. Ballas tried to cry out. Tried to summon help. Yet his mouth wouldn't work. He managed only a faint groan.

The light grew brighter. And brighter.

Ballas shifted his gaze.

The Lectivin watched him dispassionately –

– And suddenly Ballas could move.

Shouting out, he slumped to the floor. The disc spun from his fingers, rolling like a coin over the boards. The image shrank back, vanishing.

Moaning, Ballas clutched his head. His skull pulsed, his brain felt like a clod of charred flesh. He tasted blood – he had bitten through his lips.

He tumbled sideways, curling into a ball. Slowly, he sank into blackness.

Ballas opened his eyes.

The lodging room was dark. Sweat plastered the big man's body. His flesh felt like it was on fire – yet he was shivering. He felt as if he were suffering from a fever.

Muttering, he pushed himself into a sitting position.

He was in pain.

Yet he was aware that a greater pain – the worst he'd ever felt – had passed.

He opened his mouth to swear. To condemn profanely whatever had caused the pain.

Yet he couldn't remember.

Blinking, he rubbed his face. His gaze fell upon the iron disc, at rest upon the floorboards. Somehow, it had been to blame. Of that, he was certain.

But *how* had it hurt him?

Ballas thought hard. The last thing he could recall was trying to prise out the blue gemstone. He had been over by the shutters . . . there had been moonlight . . . yes – somehow, moonlight was important . . .

Grunting, he picked up the disc. He took two paces towards the shutters – then halted.

'Don't be a bloody fool,' he told himself. 'I'm not going to go through it again, whatever it was, just to satisfy my curiosity.' He tossed the disc on to his pallet-bed. He drank a few mouthfuls of wine. Then a floorboard creaked outside the lodging-room door.

Ballas's hackles stirred.

There was a dull scraping sound. Slowly, the door began to open.

Ballas shrank into the corner, hiding in the shadows and clasping the wine flagon to him as if for comfort. Through the window, he saw a man in the street below, mounted on a black horse. Darkness hid his features. But a ponytail was visible, foam-white in the moonlight.

Carrande Black, thought Ballas.

The door swung open. Two broad-shouldered men charged in. Each wore a knife at his hip. Ballas recognised them from the Broken Moon. He recognised too the shorter figure that followed.

Gramiche.

Ballas drew back further into the corner.

Gramiche moved to the pallet-bed. 'We are in luck,' he said, picking up the disc. 'This is what our master seeks.' He peered closely at it. His lips worked silently. 'Strange,' he murmured. 'Very strange. The rubies . . . they have lost—'

'Sir,' interrupted one of the broad-shouldered men.

Gramiche glanced at him. 'What?'

The man pointed into the corner where Ballas was huddling.

'A silent one, isn't he?' said the little man, thoughtfully. Then, loudly: 'We almost didn't realise you were there. In a past life, were you a church mouse, hm?'

Ballas did not move. He stood stock-still, wondering what would happen next.

'Kill him,' Gramiche told the two bruisers. 'Make sure he stays quiet for keeps.'

Unsheathing a dagger, the first man sprang at Ballas. The move did not startle him. He had half expected it.

Stepping to his right, Ballas smacked the wine flagon against his attacker's head. The vessel did not shatter; it merely gave out a dull *boom*. The man stumbled, dazed. Then his knees buckled. Ballas kicked him hard in the face. He jerked backwards. Blood gouted from his nose.

The second man looked stunned. He hadn't expected his companion to fall. Swearing, Ballas crunched a left hook into his cheek. He fell on to the pallet-bed.

Gramiche drew a short-bladed dagger.

A part of Ballas wanted to punch the little man. Another part wanted to retrieve the disc. But the flagon-struck thug had got up, his eyes blazing with pain and fury. Gripping his dagger, he came forward.

Drawing back his arm, Ballas hurled the flagon at him. His aim was poor. The flagon flew past the man, shattering against the wall.

Cursing, Ballas ran from the lodging room.

He sprinted along a short landing. The stairway to the common room was pitch dark. Ballas slowed down, treading cautiously on the wooden steps. Then he heard footfalls on the landing above.

'You bastard!' shouted someone – the first bruiser, thought Ballas. 'I'll cut your bloody balls off!'

Ballas started to run down the stairs.

Half drunk, moving in total darkness, he quickly lost his footing. He fell heavily on to the steps, and rolled the remaining distance to the common room.

The fire had burned itself out. But a few embers still glowed in the hearth.

Ballas ran to the door. Then struggled to find the latch. His fingers touched cold metal—

—And then he felt a blow in the small of his back.

Groaning, he sagged against the door.

He wondered if he had been stabbed or punched. From past experience, he knew that the two sensations were, initially at any rate, practically identical: each started as a dull, throbbing ache. He pushed himself sideways, and a second blow whistled past his head. He heard knuckles slam against the door.

One of the thugs swore.

Struggling upright, Ballas groped through the gloom. His fingertips brushed fabric. He grasped the thug's tunic front. Then he jammed a hand between his legs. He felt the cloth-clad weight of the bruiser's testicles. Grunting, Ballas squeezed.

The man sucked in a breath. Then he made a choking noise.

Seizing his belt, Ballas dragged him towards the fireplace. Five paces closer, he tripped him. The man pitched face first into the embers.

Sparks swirled up. The thug howled.

Ballas fumbled open the door and plunged outside.

Turning to his left, he broke into a run. He was already exhausted. The fight had sapped his energy. And the pain of the blow – whether stab or punch – had weakened him.

Yet the energy of desperation drove him on. He jogged flat-footedly alone the paved street.

Suddenly, hooves scraped on stone.

Ballas stumbled, surprised.

He glanced back. On his dark horse, Carrande Black cantered toward him. Ballas cursed. He had forgotten about the merchant.

He started to run. But a few seconds later, Black had caught up with him. Something struck Ballas's skull. The world tilted. He dropped to the ground.

The hoofbeats halted.

Slowly, Ballas looked up. Ten paces away Carrande Black was slipping a cudgel back into a velvet sheath.

Grunting, Ballas pushed himself up on to all fours. He touched his head where the blow had fallen. His hair was sticky with blood.

'Did I not say that you belong in the gutter?' asked Carrande Black. 'Look: you even have the posture of a rat.' He paused. 'I heard screams from the tavern. It seems you have been fortunate. You have escaped Lukas and Ragrialle. Maybe a vermin-god is watching over you, eh?' He glanced past Ballas.

The big man looked in the same direction.

Gramiche had emerged from the tavern. He ran over, a knife in his hand.

'I have the disc, master,' he said, drawing closer. 'But some strangeness has befallen it. The outer stones—'

'Later, later,' said Black mildly. 'Our business with our friend remains unfinished.'

'I will tend to it,' said Gramiche, approaching Ballas.

Grasping Ballas's hair, Gramiche jerked back the big man's head. Then he pressed the knife against the skin of his throat.

'I shall butcher you,' explained Gramiche, 'as those in the Distant East butcher their cattle. Yours will be a holy death. Or perhaps . . . perhaps it will not be. For was not the vile rebel Cal'Briden killed in such a fashion? Was his throat not slit? Ah – it does not matter. The job will be done, and you will be dead. That is—'

Ballas grasped the little man's wrist. Pulling down on it and simultaneously rising swiftly, he crashed the top of his head into Gramiche's face. Black's henchman gave a muted cry. Spinning, Ballas drove a right hook into his jaw. Gramiche dropped, sprawling upon the ground.

Carrande Black spurred his mount towards Ballas.

As he drew close he halted. He jerked the reins, and the horse reared up. The creature's black form blotted out the stars. Its hooves flailed, and solid steel cracked against Ballas's forehead.

Pain shot through Ballas's skull.

Stumbling against the wall, he vomited. Blood poured into his eyes. Wiping it away with his sleeve, he saw Carrande Black dismount.

Whipping open his cape, the merchant approached.

'You have had a run of good luck,' he said, unsheathing a long-bladed dagger. 'Perhaps I am partly responsible. Ragrialle and Lukas are slow-witted. I ought to have sent better men. As for Gramiche – for all his virtues, he is not, and never will be, a killer.'

Seizing Ballas's jaw, Black slammed the big man's head back against the wall.

'Pray to your vermin-god, my friend. Let us hope it pities you.' Black lifted the knife – then footsteps echoed along the thoroughfare. His dark gaze flickered sideways.

Ballas saw his opportunity. Grasping the back of Black's neck, he slammed his forehead into the merchant's nose. Black gave a grunt of pain. Ballas grabbed his wrist, dragging down his hand. Slowly, he wrenched the point of the blade round towards Black's own stomach. The merchant squirmed, his eyes panic-lit.

'Release me,' he said, scarcely able to breathe.

Blood was still seeping into Ballas's eyes. He could no longer see Black. Yet he gripped him tightly . . . so tightly that Black could not move. The dagger inched closer to the merchant's belly.

'Please,' said Black, his tone suddenly desperate. 'I have money . . .'

Ballas forced the dagger into Black's stomach and, angling it up towards his heart, kept on pushing. The merchant gave a rasping gurgle. Warm blood trickled over Ballas's hand. Black grew limp, then slid to the ground.

The footsteps that had distracted Black came closer. Ballas wiped the blood from his eyes. Three Papal Wardens ran over. One held a blazing torch.

'He tried to murder me,' said Ballas, pointing at Carrande Black.

A Warden punched Ballas in the face. Then another hit him – hard – in the gut.

'Wait! You must understand—' Out of the corner of his eye Ballas saw Gramiche scrambling to his feet. The little man ran off into the darkness. A Warden gave chase.

'Yes, capture *him*! He's the—' A skull-jarring punch to the head. Dizziness flooded over Ballas. His knees sagged. For the second time that evening he spun into unconsciousness.

When Ballas awoke, he was being dragged towards a long, low building of black brick.

His hoof-split forehead had stopped bleeding. Dried blood caked his face. His limbs felt heavy. He didn't think that, even if the Wardens released him, he would be able to stand. Vomit soaked his beard. His vision swam in and out of focus.

They halted at a small arched portal. A grey-eyed Warden rapped sharply on the door.

'What is this place?' Ballas asked groggily.

'You cannot guess?' The Warden laughed. It was a humourless, cruel sound. 'You have murdered a man; his blood stains your hands – and you cannot guess where we, the Wardens, are taking you?'

'*What?* I've murdered no one! The bastard tried to kill me. I didn't bloody murder him – just defended myself.'

'There are many jails in Soriterath,' continued the Warden. 'Some are less pleasant than others. This is one of the worst.'

The door swung open. The Wardens manhandled Ballas along a gloomy corridor.

'But do not be downhearted: you may not be here long. The courts of Soriterath are the briskest in Druine. It is said that a murderer can be convicted before his victim's corpse has cooled.'

'I am *not* a murderer,' hissed Ballas. 'A killer, maybe – but only because I had to be. I was *attacked*. Don't you understand? Carrande Black was trying to kill *me*. Must a man stand still and let another butcher him? I ain't cattle. I ain't a pig in a charnel house—'

'Save such protests for your trial,' said the Warden gruffly.

They bundled Ballas into a small cell. The ceiling was low, the floor wet with the previous occupant's urine. A stench of faeces assailed Ballas's nostrils. The big man's gorge rose. 'Sweet grief,' he muttered.

The Wardens fastened manacles around his wrists and ankles. Then they left the cell. The door slammed shut. A heavy bolt grated across.

Ballas stood in the darkness.

'I'm not a murderer!' he shouted. 'Do you hear? The knife I used on Black was his own – and he would've used it on me. Is that too complicated for you? Listen to me!' He jerked on his manacles. The chains rattled taut, tugging against the wall in which they were secured. 'I saved my own life – that's all I did. That is not a crime! *That is not a crime!*'

Ballas sagged back against the wall, then slid to the floor. His wounded head bled again. He pointed to the torn flesh. There was no one to see him do so – yet he jabbed a thick finger towards the wound. 'Isn't this evidence enough?' Thick syrupy blood oozed down his face. It seeped through his beard on to his lips and felt like it was scalding him.

He felt unutterably tired. He lay down on the slick stones. He closed his eyes. A jumble of images swarmed through his mind. He saw the iron disc. And he glimpsed moonlight . . . a vague blue-silver shape . . . that flickered in his mind's eye, then vanished.

Then Ballas saw Carrande Black. He felt the dagger sinking into the merchant's guts. It had been a good feeling. The best feeling. The sudden ease of movement, as the blade pierced through the feeble resistance of the outer flesh – it had thrilled Ballas, almost as much as shooting his seed into a whore's joxy.

Yet it had also damned him.

Chapter 5

And these four Pilgrims wandering, knowing not
Of one another, yet each servant
To the same master, each suffering
Horrors of fire and hail, and the wickedness
Of unbelievers . . .

Using a golden-handled knife, Blessed Master Godwin Muirthan cut through the ribbon that bound together the sheaf of parchments.

In the autumnal sunlight that poured through the window of his chamber high in the Esklarion Sacros, Muirthan spread the documents over his desk.

In his fifty-seventh year, he was the youngest of the Blessed Masters. In some ways he seemed youthful for his age. His hair, falling to the nape of his neck, was obsidian-black – expect for grey patches at the temples. He was very tall, very solid of shoulder. His physique was that of a farm labourer, not a clergyman.

In other ways, though, his true age was apparent. His face was jowly and his expression severe. His mouth was perpetually downturned – as if everything inspired distaste.

He was not garbed in a priest's blue robes. He wore the blood scarlet befitting his status as a Blessed Master.

Around Muirthan's neck hung a Scarrendestin pendant. This too differed from those of ordinary priests. Theirs were triangles of brass. The Masters' pendants were fashioned from red gold.

Muirthan scanned the documents.

Each bore news from a different part of Druine. Each was tediously predictable. Long ago Muirthan had learned that, contrary to holy teachings, man was not a species of infinite variety. It was said that the creator-god had distanced man from the animals by making every human soul unique. This was untrue. Its falsity was evident in the documents, in the repetitious events they described. In the famine-struck eastern provinces, citizens had rioted, demanding grain. In the northern regions, where plague had struck, women – both elderly and young – had been imprisoned by their fellows and burned alive, for the populace believed witchcraft had created the sickness. In a western village, a spate of birth deformities – probably caused by fouled river water – had frightened the locals into feverish piety: they thronged the church, petitioning the Four for help . . .

Such responses were predictable.

Riots, scapegoating, grovelling to deities – they had occurred countless times before, for exactly the same reasons. Plunge a man into particular circumstances, and he would behave in a manner almost identical to that of his fellows. Life, Muirthan believed, was but a recycling of the same events, over and over. Only in repetition was man infinite.

The last parchment detailed events in Soriterath. It described every happening of ecclesiastical significance: the deaths of priests and theologians, alleged miracles, outbreaks of heresy . . .

Muirthan's gaze alighted on a particular entry. He read it once. Paused. Read it again.

Then he rang the small bronze bell on the corner of his desk.

The door opened. A boy in a servant's garb entered.

'Blessed Master,' he said, bowing. 'How may I serve you?'

'Find the other Masters,' said Muirthan flatly. 'They must convene in the Ninth Hall before the turning of this hourglass.' He indicated the item concerned where it stood on the desk. Both its glass bulbs at present held the same amount of fine sand. 'It is a matter of prime importance.'

The servant nodded, then left the chamber.

Half an hour later, Godwin Muirthan strode into the Ninth Hall. On the wall hung tapestries of the customary religious sort: woven in glittering blue and gold threads, they depicted the Trials of the Pilgrims, and their melding upon Scarrendestin. Dark blue carpets covered the floor. Around a long oval table of richly polished mahogany sat the other Blessed Masters.

Muirthan's gaze flicked over them.

Some were half sunken in infirmity. Skeletal, thin-fleshed, they belonged wholly to neither life nor death. They existed in a type of breathing limbo. Yet their physical frailty did not affect their mental strength. They were sharp-minded, Muirthan knew. And competent. Many had been Masters for several decades. The Church's business, and that of Druine, were for them reflexive matters.

Other Masters, like Muirthan, were younger. Yet there was not a callow man among them. They held dominion over every citizen's spirit – and over the physical world in which he or she lived.

Such power – absolute, unwavering – hardened the heart, and mind, of every Master.

Within a year of his appointment, a fresh Master would grow jaded. Wonderment, mystery . . . they perished quickly. Only understanding remained: cold, bare, hard-edged understanding. Muirthan recognised this as true for himself. He believed it was true for the others.

Yet today he felt a pang of unease.

He strode to a table alongside an arched window. He poured himself a goblet of water. Then he gazed beyond the Sacros's outer wall, to the Penance Oak.

'Why have you gathered us, Godwin?' asked a Blessed Master.

Muirthan turned.

It was Hengriste who had spoken. Of all the Masters, he was the oldest. His pate was hairless and liver-spotted. Above his white beard, his cheeks were hollow. 'Is there trouble in Druine? A dilemma that needs resolving . . . a wound that needs caring for?'

'A dilemma, a wound – yes, both are true,' said Muirthan. 'Carrande Black has been murdered.'

A Master murmured, 'Carrande Black?'

'He is a merchant,' said Hengriste sharply. 'He is also a tavern-owner and a whoremonger. And he imports visionary's root, for which we have a use. He sells it to us cheaply. In return, we grant him immunity from prosecution and tax him only lightly.' He looked to Muirthan. 'Has the killer been caught?'

Muirthan nodded. 'As we speak, he is in the prison on Shackle Row. He killed Black outside the Scarlet Star – a tavern half a mile across the city. Our Wardens heard the sounds of violence, and captured him. But only after he had slain the merchant. It is not yet known why he killed Black. A Warden says he claims it was self-defence . . .'

'Are there witnesses?' asked Hengriste.

'The tavern-master of the Star said he heard fighting in the lodging room of Black's killer. But he did not investigate. Perhaps he was fearful for his own safety; I don't know.

'There was certainly at least one other man involved. When the Wardens arrived, he fled. As yet, he has not been caught. It isn't known whether he was Black's ally or the killer's. If any others had a hand in the deed, there is no trace of them.'

He sipped at his water.

'Our predicament is clear. Carrande Black was not our sole supplier of visionary's root. He was not even one of the largest. But if we fail to deal properly with his death, other root bringers may get nervous.'

'You are saying, Godwin,' began Hengriste, tilting his head, 'that if we deal too gently with his killer – if, for instance, he is found innocent of the crime; or, if convicted of it, he is granted an easy death – they will feel we are not committed to their well-being?'

'By nature, root smugglers are cautious,' said Muirthan. 'They are instinctively suspicious and mistrustful. If they believe their loyalty to us is not reciprocated, they will be reluctant to trade with us. We must make it appear that we consider Black's death a serious matter.' He shrugged. 'If we do so, not only will we prevent doubts creeping into their minds but we may also consolidate our alliance. If a man of their own sort is killed, for whatever reasons, they will perceive the murderer's punishment – if it is extreme – as a gesture of good faith. Their allegiance to us will thus be strengthened.' He drew a breath. 'And that would not be a bad thing. The caliphs of the East are patrolling their waters, seeking western vessels laden with the root. For root bringers, these are dangerous times. We must treat them carefully. I need not remind you how much we need visionary's root.'

'And for this extreme punishment,' said Hengriste, 'you have something in mind?'

'When Carrande Black agreed to import root, we granted him Church Protection. His murder, therefore, may be interpreted as a holy crime.'

'You would put his killer upon the Oak?'

'The other root bringers would understand that he was upon the branches *not* because he was, in any meaningful sense, guilty of a holy crime. They would look upon his death simply as fearful retribution for an act that we, the Blessed Masters, treat seriously. From this, they would take reassurance.'

Blessed Master Hengriste nodded. 'You talk sense, Godwin. I will consent to such an action. In theory, we ought to put this killer in front of a Papal Court. That is, we ought to try him ourselves. But I do not believe that is necessary. Whether his crime was justifiable or not, he must be condemned as guilty. For the sake of the Church, the verdict is preordained. By nightfall, his head will be nailed to the Oak. Our root bringers will be happy. And of course, Nu'khterin will continue to be of use to us.' The old Master raised a finger. 'However, the man must be interrogated. We must learn fully of his connection with Black. Did he truly slay the merchant in self-defence? If so, why was Black pursuing him? It may be of no significance. Then again . . .'

'Are we unanimous, then,' said Muirthan, 'that the killer – whether he has killed with good cause or not – should be put upon the Oak?'

The Blessed Masters all agreed.

All night, Ballas had remained in the cell. Despite his fatigue, he had scarcely slept.

At first, rage had kept him wakeful. He wanted to revenge himself upon Carrande Black. It was the merchant's fault that Ballas was manacled in a tiny stone box that stank of other men's terror. If Black hadn't tried to steal the disc, he would still be alive – and Ballas would be free.

For this, the merchant deserved punishment. Over and over again. Black was dead; his corpse probably lay in a Chapel of Rest somewhere. Yet Ballas was filled by a frustrating urge to kill him again. And again. And again. In his mind, he recalled the easy entry of the dagger into Black's guts. He wished now that he had thrust the blade in more slowly. That he had driven it in far higher, behind the merchant's ribs. That the merchant hadn't died so quickly . . . that he'd lain on the ground for a long time, writhing like a damaged insect.

Eventually, Ballas's rage faded. He felt weak, tired. He considered his own future. He would be tried for murder. If found innocent, he would be set free. If declared guilty, he would be put to death. He considered briefly the different modes of execution. He might be hauled on to a gallows platform, in front of Soriterath's citizens, and hanged. Or set face down on a wooden block, so that a red-masked executioner could drive an axe blade through his neck. He could even be locked in a cage elemental: a circular metal cage, dangling on a chain by the city gates, where slow starvation and exposure to wind, rain, hail and frost would gradually but inexorably kill him.

A bolt grated and the cell door was opened. A group of Papal Wardens dragged Ballas out of the prison building, into hard noon light. After hours in blackness, the light seemed to sear the membrane from his eyes.

Grimacing, he was loaded on to a cart, then driven across Soriterath to Papal Square.

The cart rattled towards the Esklarion Sacros. The vast building, salamander red, sparkled in the sharp light. The four huge towers thrust skywards.

'You are taking me to the Sacros?' asked Ballas, confused.

'Yes,' replied a Warden – a brown-haired man, with a chill-pinkened nose.

'Then you're making a mistake. I'm a murderer . . . that is, I am to be *tried* for murder. I'm not a heretic. And when I killed, I used a knife. Not a bloody magical charm.'

'You have committed a holy crime,' the Warden said. He touched a scroll, tucked into his belt. 'Your Document of Accusation,' he explained. 'I presented it to the prison-keeper, to secure your transfer to the Sacros's cells. You are no longer to be investigated for murder. Rather, your crime is far more grievous. It is Divine Slaughter. Are you familiar with the term?'

Ballas shook his head.

'Black was a Servant of the Church,' said the Warden. 'I do not know *how* such a man could be employed by the Masters, but they consider his murder a terrible deed nonetheless. As bad as the killing of a priest. Worse, perhaps.' He shrugged. 'If your guilt is proven, my friend, *that* is your destiny.'

He pointed across the Square. Ballas looked toward the Penance Oak. Three crow-pecked heads were nailed to the branches.

'It is an agonising death,' said the Warden. 'In this world of fragile flesh, there are a million tortures a man can suffer. But the Oak is the fiercest of all. It is rumoured that after the head is cut away, the condemned man's soul is torn from his body . . .'

'Torn? How?'

'I know not,' said the Warden. 'The crows, perhaps.' He laughed mockingly. '*You* will know, soon enough.'

They neared the Sacros. The heavy black gates swung open. The cart passed through, entering a paved courtyard. The Wardens hauled Ballas from the back of the cart, then led him along a shadowed cloister and down a flight of stone steps, until they arrived at a sparsely furnished chamber.

There were a few wooden chairs. A desk of unvarnished wood. Candles burned in niches.

Ballas was shoved into a chair. The Wardens watched him warily, their hands upon their dagger hilts.

For what seemed a long time, nothing happened. Ballas sat silently, listening to candle flames guttering on their wicks. To the trickling of molten wax. To his own heart beating: to the succession of dull, sullen thuds.

Then the door opened.

A man stepped inside. For the first time in a long while, Ballas felt a touch of *true* fear.

The Blessed Master was tall, broad-shouldered. His hair was black, but grey-dusted at the temples.

The Master gazed at Ballas. Ballas gazed back – then looked quickly away. As if to look upon a Master were a dangerously insolent act.

A defiant part of Ballas said: *Do not fear him; he is but a man . . .*

But that was untrue.

Absolute power raised Masters beyond such a meagre status. They were arbiters of Druine's fate. Of the fate of every individual. At their bidding, men were tortured and murdered – or beatified and blessed. Druine nestled in their cupped hands. No earthly power could oppose them. Such men,

Ballas knew, were answerable to no one. What could compel them to treat a man benignly? Nothing. What could urge them to favour justice over expedience?

Nothing.

For an hour Godwin Muirthan interrogated the prisoner.

On first seeing the big man, certain instincts had prickled within the Master. He knew instantly that the fellow wasn't to be trusted. Mercenariness glinted in his eyes. He had the ever-hungry, ever-alert gaze of a thief. Certainly, it was diluted by fear – but that was to be expected: what man wouldn't be perturbed when he was to be questioned by a Master?

There was something dangerous about him, too. Muirthan tried to identify the source of this impression. Perhaps it was his size. The prisoner was as tall as Muirthan, and broader. The Master seldom encountered people as well built as himself. Maybe the novelty of this experience unsettled him. Or maybe it was the prisoner's battered looks. His face was bruised. A deep, crescent-shaped wound pulsed in his forehead. Blood flakes crusted his skin and beard.

Of course, Muirthan had seen such things before. But on most people, they seemed unnatural, a deviation from the proper order of things.

On the prisoner they appeared wholly appropriate. As if, in some perplexing fashion, he had been *designed* for injury. As if it was his rightful state to bear bruises and wounds.

The prisoner spoke calmly.

In a deep, careful voice, he recounted the details of Black's death. When he had finished, Muirthan ordered the Wardens to imprison him in the cells far beneath the Sacros.

'Blessed Master,' said the big man, 'you believe me, don't you? You understand I'm innocent? That I'm not a murderer? I wouldn't ever kill a Servant of the Church. Not knowingly. Not unless it were his life or mine.'

Muirthan did not reply. Leaving the chamber, he walked through the Sacros, seeking Hengriste.

He found the old Master in the library. He was seated at a table, poring over a parchment. A lantern burned, sinking his eyes into deeper shadow. As Muirthan approached, the old man looked up.

'You have spoken with him?' he asked.

Muirthan nodded. 'He is a liar, of that I am convinced.'

Hengriste smiled faintly. 'All men are liars, Godwin. Every twentieth phrase, whether uttered by saint or sinner, is a deceit of some description.'

His voice grew soft. 'Every living thing thrives upon untruths. A fox moves stealthily, so that its prey will not know it is close by. Is that not dishonest? Certain butterflies bear markings that make them appear something they are not: they seem to be just a bit of tree bark, or a delicate leaf. Such ruses prevent birds from eating them. But, nonetheless, that too is a type of dishonesty.'

He interlaced his fingers.

'The question is not whether our prisoner lies. But what the nature – and extent – of those lies are. What did he tell you, Godwin?'

'Yesterday, he tried to sell an ornament to Carrande Black . . .'

'An ornament?' Hengriste frowned.

'A metal disc, set with gemstones. He says it is a beautiful, valuable piece. The man is a vagrant; he admitted as much. When I asked how he came to possess the ornament, he said it was payment for a good deed.'

Hengriste laughed. 'He is painting himself as a pious man, is he?'

'He says that, on the road outside Soriterath, he found a vintner whose cart had broken a wheel. The vintner was frightened, fearing that if he did not reach the city quickly, he would be set upon by bandits. Our prisoner claims he repaired the cart. In return, the vintner gave him the ornament. I asked him the vintner's name; he said he did not know.'

Pulling up a chair, Muirthan sat down.

'He offered the ornament to Carrande Black. The merchant refused, claiming the price was too high. Then, during the evening, Black sent his men to steal the ornament. A fight followed, of course – and Black was killed. The prisoner says Black had three accomplices. One of them was a man the prisoner named as Gramiche: he said that as soon as the Wardens arrived, this Gramiche fled. That tallies with the Wardens' account.'

'This man, Gramiche – he was apprehended?' asked Hengriste.

'No. The Wardens are still seeking him.'

'Do you suppose the prisoner has misled us? That, in fact, the man whom the Wardens chased was *his* accomplice – not Black's?'

'It is possible.' Muirthan nodded. 'Though men in the prisoner's circumstances seldom lie. They want to strike a bargain. They want to help us, and so save their skin. Often, this involves betraying their companions.'

He laid one hand flat on the table.

'As I said, the prisoner has lied to us. But these lies are trivial things. Maybe he did not help a stranded vintner; maybe he stole the disc. Maybe he even took it from Black himself. But he has no deeper connection with the merchant. Nor is he involved with the importing of visionary's root. He is a tramp, a treader of the road. He is also a drunk and a petty thief. He could not be trusted. None of Black's rivals would be foolish enough to employ him. His path crossed with Black's by mischance – nothing more. I am convinced of it.'

'Good,' said Hengriste. 'He shall be put upon the Oak this evening, yes?'

'I shall supervise it myself,' replied Muirthan.

The Wardens led Ballas down several flights of stone steps, into the belly of the Esklarion Sacros. They shut him in a large, echo-haunted cell. In the instant before the door closed and all light vanished, he glimpsed a figure slouching against the far wall.

The door shut. He heard laboured breathing.

For a moment Ballas did not speak. He took stock of his own situation. He felt curiously numb, as if there were too much to absorb. If, at this hour on the previous day, his present circumstances had been described to him – if, for instance, a fortune-teller had predicted he'd stand accused of a holy crime and be imprisoned beneath the Sacros – he would have reacted with disbelief. Yet here he was.

Speaking in the direction of the figure, he said, 'Who are you?'

'A dead man,' came the reply. 'A man living posthumously.'

Ballas licked his lips. 'What is your name?'

'It hardly matters . . .'

'Tell me,' said Ballas flatly.

'It is Gerack,' sighed the man. 'Is there anything else you wish to know? For it is distracting to face questions when one is but hours from the Penance Oak.' The man paused. 'I am frightened. I would happily spend eternity in this cell, rather than be put upon the Oak. I hear that it is an extraordinary way to perish. The pain is colossal . . . that of a thousand deaths.'

'You have committed a holy crime?'

'A holy crime, yes – but also a humane one. I have a daughter; she is in her seventh year and, like myself, she suffers an illness of the lungs. Often, she wakes at night, gasping, unable to draw proper breaths. She weeps and claws her throat . . . It is an awful thing, to see one's child suffocating. To watch her eyes glaze, her body contort.'

Ballas sensed that the other prisoner was looking towards him. He felt the man's eyes probing vainly through the dark.

'Do you have children?' asked Gerack.

'No,' Ballas replied.

'Then you cannot understand. You will think me foolish . . . But, in desperation, I sought the help of a healer. He promised that, by the use of magic, he would cure her. His fee was high. I am not a wealthy man, and I had to pawn the few valuable things I owned. When I had enough money, I hired the magicker and he tended to my daughter. Of course –' bitterness crept into his tone '– his spells had no effect. His rituals, his chanting, his laying-on of hands . . . they were futile. He might as well have recited a nursery rhyme.

'When, a fortnight later, I found his head nailed to the Oak I felt pleased. He was a fraud. A charlatan. He grew wealthy from others' wretchedness. He deserved to suffer.

'But then . . . then I felt afraid. For it is a holy crime not merely to be a magicker, but to enlist their services. It matters not whether the magicker is genuine or false. Whether his spells are potent, or mere stirrings of air – it makes no odds to the Pilgrim Church.

'Fearing that the magicker had kept a list of those he had tended, and that this list might be in the Church's hands, I gathered up what belongings I could and, with my wife and daughter, tried to leave Soriterath.

'We were stopped at the city gates. The Wardens were suspicious. Perhaps they can instinctively spot wrongdoers . . . As I feared, the magicker *had* made a list. And the Church had seized it.

'I was arrested and tried. And now . . . now I sit here, knowing that tomorrow my wife and daughter will be escorted by the Wardens to Papal Square and forced to look at my head, nailed to the Oak. It will be a holy lesson. A divine education. They will see the fate of all sinners. In my features, they will discern my death agonies. The Church's work will be done.' Gerack was silent for a heartbeat. Then he added, 'What was *your* crime?'

'I killed a Servant of the Church,' said Ballas.

'Ha!' The other man's laugh was joyless. 'Did he suffer?'

'Not as much as I'd have liked.'

'And now you are to face the Oak for it . . .'

'I've been tried,' said Ballas, 'but no verdict's been passed. I killed to preserve my own life. And I didn't know I was fighting one of the Masters' men. I can't be found guilty. It's not possible.'

'It *is* possible,' said the other prisoner, 'and it has happened.'

'What're you talking about?'

'Do you suppose you would be here if the Masters thought you innocent? A verdict *has* been passed – you merely haven't been informed.'

'Horseshit,' said Ballas sharply.

'It is the *truth*,' retorted Gerack. 'When I was brought here, a Warden referred to this cell as "Gatarix's Cave". Are you a reader of the holy book? Know you the tale of Gatarix? He was the seaman who tried to murder the Four. Of course, he failed. For his crime, he was imprisoned in a cave near the holy mountain – then he was decapitated and his head was nailed to an oak. When you are taken from here, it will be to the Penance Oak. Do not delude yourself. You have been questioned by a Master?'

'I have.'

'By the time you gave your last answer, he would have decided upon your guilt. If he thought you innocent, you would have been released immediately. But here you are, as doomed as me.'

Ballas was quiet a long time.

'A man is only doomed,' he said at last, 'if he accepts his fate. And I don't. I shan't perish. Not upon the Oak. Not by the Pilgrim Church's hand.'

'What do you propose?' The other prisoner laughed despairingly. 'Do not say you intend to escape—'

'It is that, or die,' said Ballas.

Groping through the darkness, he placed his hands on the door. He pressed against it. It did not budge. He hadn't expected it to.

Yet he had to do *something*.

'If you want to live,' said Ballas, 'you must do as I say.'

'It is futile,' said Gerack, 'to fight death, when death is assured. Let us accept it, as placidly as we can. For us, there shall be no escape.'

Ballas's anger flared. He charged through the dark to where he guessed the other prisoner was seated. Reaching out a hand, he grasped the man's shirt-front.

'Death is *not* assured!' Ballas dragged Gerack to his feet. 'Do you hear me?'

The man seized Ballas's wrist. 'Let me go! You are being foolish!'

'And you reckon it's *wise* to go meekly to the Oak?'

'I will have no part of this! I want to sit quietly. I want to think of my wife. And of my daughter. They are all that I have. All that I shall leave behind. If I carry them in my heart, maybe the Oak won't prove so bad.'

Ballas slapped Gerack around the head. The man yelped.

'You pissing halfwit! You needn't leave them behind. There *has* to be a way out. Always, there's some way to escape.'

'Escape? Where would we escape *to*?' The other man spoke quietly. 'Have you no inkling of the Church's power? There is not a square inch of ground unwatched by the Masters' men. There are not merely Wardens to contend with, but agents – ordinary people, employed by the Church to spy upon their fellows . . .'

Ballas stood very still. 'D'you want to live? Or die?'

'You speak as if we truly have a choice.'

Ballas did not reply.

Gerack exhaled. 'What must we do?'

Ballas thought for a moment. 'When the Wardens come, we'll surprise them. As soon as the door opens, we'll fight.'

'That is hardly subtle,' said the other prisoner softly.

'Piss on subtlety. Violence'll serve us better than anything else. Now: are you hurt? Do you have any injuries?'

'My head aches where you struck me. Otherwise, no. But I warn you, I am not a fighter. I am not strong of limb. Or spirit.'

'That doesn't matter,' said Ballas. 'We're not fighting a duel. It won't be honourable combat. We have to kill – that's all. Or injure. It's not that difficult. Go for their eyes, their throats – and their balls. Use your wits, too. Take their weapons, if you can – and *use* them. More than anything, be ruthless. For your own sake. And your family's.'

'You speak as if you have experience of such things,' said Gerack.

'My life hasn't been easy,' replied Ballas, after a pause.

They waited.

Ballas had been brought to the Sacros at noon. He estimated it was now mid-afternoon, or thereabouts. Every midnight, a curfew was placed upon Papal Square, so heads could be nailed unobserved to the Oak. Nine hours or so would pass before the Wardens came for him.

He sat down on the floor.

Time trickled slowly by.

Ballas and Gerack hardly spoke. They maintained a heavy, brooding silence. The other prisoner was thinking of his wife, Ballas supposed. And of his daughter. What he would have to do if they were all to remain safe – assuming he *did* manage to escape.

It seemed that the Wardens would never arrive. But, after a seeming eternity, footsteps echoed outside the door.

Ballas got to his feet.

'Get ready,' he said.

Heart pounding, Ballas waited a few seconds. The bolt slid back and the door swung open into the cell. Outside stood six Wardens. Springing forward, Ballas raised his fist –

– Then staggered back, as a Warden crashed the torch he was carrying into the big man's face. Momentarily blinded, Ballas gave a startled cry. Someone punched him in the stomach. Then something hard cracked against the side of his head. Blow after blow struck Ballas. Fists, feet and knees pounded his body. He dropped to the floor. The attack lasted ten, maybe fifteen seconds. It was crushingly savage. The Wardens were well-trained fighters. They knew precisely how to splinter bones and snap gristle. When they'd finished, blood was pouring over Ballas's face. A dull buzzing filled his ears. His bones and muscles ached.

Groaning, he opened his eyes.

A moment of residual blindness. Then the cell grew clear to his vision.

The Wardens gazed down at him.

They were breathing heavily. They seemed amused, satisfied. The other prisoner sagged against the wall.

In the light from the torch Ballas saw that Gerack was a thin man, with a short beard. His hair was black, and unevenly cropped. His arms were folded protectively across his chest. He shivered violently. His wheezing breaths were very loud.

'On your feet,' the torch-bearing Warden told Ballas. 'I wish to show you something.'

Slowly, Ballas got up. Another Warden grasped Ballas's wrist, forcing his arm up behind his back. The big man grunted.

'See this?' asked the torch-bearing Warden, casting light on the cell wall.

Near the ceiling, there was a hole the size of Ballas's fist in the brickwork.

'Despite their flair for the beautiful,' said the Warden, 'the architects of the Sacros were practical men. This cell has been designed to create echoes; and these echoes pass through that opening, and travel along a pipe to a chamber nearby. Every utterance can be clearly heard.' The Warden smiled. 'In the Sacros, a condemned man has no secrets. If he takes a piss, the splashing sounds as loud as a waterfall. If he farts, it roars like thunder.'

The other Wardens laughed.

'If he plots an escape, however crude, that too will be heard. Now: it is midnight. The Oak's branches have been stripped bare. And Nu'hkterin hungers.'

'Nu'hkterin,' murmured Ballas. 'Who . . . what is Nu'hkterin?' He wondered if it was an animal of some sort. Something that would feast upon him in the moments before his death.

'Be patient,' said the Warden. 'In time, your curiosity will be sated.'

The Wardens took Ballas and Gerack from the cell. They led them out into the courtyard. The gates were opened, and they stepped out on to Papal Square.

It was a clear, calm night. Stars shone. Moonlight illuminated the Penance Oak. Eight hundred paces away, it was a spindly silhouette: an upthrust of jagged blackness. Ballas's stomach tightened. He felt a faint touch of panic. A part of him wondered how many men's heads had been nailed to the Oak. How many had made the final walk across the Square.

He shook his head. It did not matter. *He* was destined for the Oak. That was the vital truth.

He struggled tentatively against the Warden's grip. If he could break free . . . if he could run from the Square, into a side alley . . .

The Warden jerked his arm higher up his back.

Tendons stretched. Ballas gasped.

It did not take long to reach the Oak.

Gerack, who had been weeping, grew hysterical. He gave a plaintive half-bestial scream. It soared above the Square and drowned out every other noise: the crackling torch flame, the creaking of the breeze-stirred Oak's branches. It was as heart-freezing as a wolf's cry. It was a noise of utter loneliness.

'Be quiet.' Stepping forward, the torch-bearing Warden punched Gerack in the stomach. He bent at the waist. Sinking to his knees, he struggled desperately for breath. Ballas recalled how, in the dark placidity of the cell, the other prisoner's breathing had been strained. Now it was savagely laboured. He gulped air frantically, like a landed fish. Bright tears started from his eyes.

Footsteps sounded.

Restrained by the Warden, Ballas couldn't turn to see their source. He simply listened as they drew closer.

The Wardens straightened and drew back their shoulders.

'Blessed Master,' the torch-bearer said as he bowed.

The Master who had interrogated Ballas appeared. At his side stood a far shorter figure, wearing a robe of brown wool. A deep hood was pulled up, concealing its features.

A monk? wondered Ballas. A priest of some sort?

The Blessed Master pulled a dark cape tightly around himself. 'It is a cool evening,' he said, glancing at the Wardens. 'Let us begin, yes? I have no wish to freeze to death.' He produced a scroll. Unfurling it, he read, 'On this, the eleventh day of the eleventh month, nine hundred and ninety-six years after the Melding of the Four, it is my duty to initiate the execution of two men who, in accordance with scriptural imperative, have been tried, and have been found guilty of holy crimes. Gerack Galkarris, of the holy city of Soriterath, you hired a magicker's service – when it is against the Four's teaching to practise or benefit from magick.

'Anhaga Ballas, of no permanent lodgings, you murdered in cold blood a Servant of the Church – when it is decreed that those who pledge loyalty to the Four, and to the institutions that represent them, must not be harmed by mortal agency.' His gaze flicked between Gerack and Ballas. 'You are each sentenced to die a redemptive death upon the Penance Oak.'

Turning, he nodded towards the robed figure.

The figure drew back its hood. Its flesh was bone-pale, wrapped tightly around a protuberant skull. Its eyes were down-slanting slits, its nose two tiny holes. It had a thin incision for a mouth. Its pate was hairless.

The figure was a Lectivin.

Ballas gaped. Lectivins were extinct. They had been annihilated during the Red War.

He stared intently at the creature.

Its face had a heavy solidity. The brow jutted, an overhang of thick bone. Its lips quivered, skinning back from short sharp-tipped teeth. As if it were a hunting dog. Closing its mouth, it chewed slowly. Brown saliva bubbled on to its lips. Ballas smelled visionary's root.

Suddenly, a faint memory stirred. Hadn't some Lectivins been born blind? Hadn't they gained sight through visionary's root?

Ballas looked at its eyes. There were no whites, no irises. Only glossy scarlet flesh. Yet in them there was a glitter of intelligence. Or of brutish awareness, at least. Its gaze was not locked on Ballas. Somehow, though, it was *seeing* him.

Gerack's hysteria had subsided. Now he shivered, and murmured something over and over.

'They do not exist, they do not exist . . .'

'At will, Nu'hkterin,' said the Blessed Master.

The Lectivin approached Gerack. The Wardens forced the prisoner down on to his knees. The Lectivin placed a slender-fingered hand upon his head.

'*Gavis covaris ectin,*' it said – its voice halfway between a growl and a rasp. '*Elterrev suvin movarin, Cohlarin edris uvarite* . . .' The words were foreign, unintelligible. Ballas presumed they were in the Lectivin language. Yet the Lectivin itself seemed to be struggling with them. As if it found speech difficult. '*Cuarav malavic sovari, Kalac kristiv hovarite* . . .'

The Wardens stepped back from Gerack. At that instant, he arched backwards. And shrieked.

His eyes rolled white, his body spasmed.

'*Malverne cujaris espive,*' continued the Lectivin. '*Mantari saluvi somnalis* . . .'

For a short time, the incantation continued. Then the Lectivin gestured briefly to the Wardens. Grasping Gerack's hair, they jerked back his head.

The Lectivin reached inside its robe and pulled out a hooked blade of some white material – ivory, perhaps. Angular sigils marked its surface.

The Lectivin moved behind Gerack. Then it pressed the blade's inside edge against his throat. Slowly, it pulled the blade through the man's neck. Ballas realised, feeling faintly ill, that the blade must have been indescribably sharp. The Lectivin did not saw it back and forth to pierce the flesh. Nor did its alien features betray any exertion. The blade split Gerack's throat as if it were insubstantial – a piece of silk, maybe. Or a cobweb strand. The cutting edge sank through skin, flesh and muscle. There was a muted squeak as it rubbed against vertebrae. Then it emerged blood-wet from the back of Gerack's neck. His body slumped to the ground. His heart was still beating; gushes of dark blood pulsed from the gory stump that protruded from the top of his now headless torso.

The Lectivin held up Gerack's sliced-off head by the hair. Turning, it handed the grisly thing to a Warden. The Warden braced it against a low branch. From a hip bag, another Warden took out a mallet and a long nail. He pressed the nail's tip between Gerack's eyes. Then he slammed the mallet against the stub-end, sinking the nail an inch deep into his skull.

Gerack's severed head shrieked silently. The mouth jerked open – yet, with no lungs to supply air, not a sound emerged. In Gerack's eyes, the irises rolled down; the head stared wildly at the Warden.

The Warden struck the nail again. It slid another inch deeper. In Gerack's face every muscle quivered. The mute screaming continued.

The Warden hit the nail again and again until only the stub-end was visible. It looked like the tail of some brain-devouring worm burrowing into Gerack's head.

The Lectivin approached.

'*Elkiros marra skivon*,' it said. '*Calvarris cunjarik makaros . . .*'

A blue light appeared under Gerack's neck-stump. Gradually it took shape. It shifted, and then it resolved into a vague, ever-fluctuating outline of Gerack's body.

Gerack stopped screaming.

A look of nervous terror touched his features. As if he was now expecting something worse, far worse than he had suffered so far. As if he was waiting for an even greater pain – and willing it never to arrive.

The Lectivin raised the blade. A blue light, the same hue as the outline of Gerack's body, glowed from it. Slowly, the Lectivin dragged the blade through the outline.

Gerack shrieked. No sound erupted from his mouth – nor did it need to. His agonised expression was more telling than any noise. His jaw hinged fully open, stretching more than was naturally possible. His eyes bulged, threatening to burst from their sockets. His nostrils flared as blood seeped from his nose.

Like a surgeon, the Lectivin probed around with the knife inside the outline.

The creature smiled raggedly. As if tasting rapture, it half-closed its eyes. Its lips quivering, it seemed to sniff the air.

This continued for some time. Then it withdrew the knife.

The blue outline shrank back inside Gerack's neck-stump.

The prisoner's head shook wildly. It seemed as though it would dislodge itself from the Oak. But suddenly it grew still. The neck muscles slackened. The eyes grew blank.

'What have you done to him?' breathed Ballas.

The Lectivin did not reply.

'*What have you done?*' snapped the big man. He had known Gerack for only a few hours. But he felt a sudden kinship with him. It was a self-serving kinship, Ballas knew. It was said that death was the most solitary experience. And Ballas, about to die himself, did not wish to be alone.

'It has tortured the sinner's soul,' said the Blessed Master.

Ballas looked sharply at him.

'It is a talent of certain Lectivins,' explained the Master. 'To have one's soul devoured is the highest pain. So much so that the human form – that is, the physical being to which the soul is attached – cannot adequately express the agony of it. We cannot scream loudly enough; our muscles cannot clench tightly enough. It is pain beyond all that we are designed to suffer. It is pain from another world.' He looked evenly at Ballas. 'I do not exaggerate. Nor do I conjecture.' He smiled – a fleeting quirk of the lips. 'This you will discover for yourself.' Turning, he nodded to the Lectivin.

A Warden punched Ballas in the stomach. The big man was thrust down on to his knees.

The Lectivin approached. Its pale hand settled on Ballas's head. Ballas tried to squirm free, but a Warden looped an arm around his throat. Two other Wardens tightened their grip on his arms.

The Lectivin applied a gentle pressure. Ballas felt its fingertips hard against his scalp. '*Gavis covaris ectin,*' it began. '*Elterrev suvin movarin, Cohlarin edris uvarite . . .*'

Numbness crept into Ballas's legs. It was a familiar feeling – that of a muscle locking solid.

He tried shifting his leg. It would not budge. The stiffness increased around his knees – and it hurt: it felt as if the muscle was trying to burst the joint from its socket.

Soon he could not move. The Wardens backed away.

Pain ripped through Ballas's body. His spine warped backwards. Every atom of flesh seemed to burst into flame.

The Lectivin's incantation continued. With every rasped word, Ballas's pain increased. Ballas tried to howl, to scream for help – or mercy.

Suddenly the Lectivin jolted. Its incantation faltered. The creature took a step back – as if perturbed.

Ballas did not know what troubled the Lectivin.

He knew only that the numbness had left his body. Crying out, he sprang to his feet. Spinning round, he punched the first Warden in the face. The second he struck in the throat with the edge of his hand. Both men fell. Whirling back, Ballas drove his balled fist into the Lectivin's face. He felt smooth, parchment-thin skin against his knuckles. And bone.

The entity staggered, the curved blade slipping from its fingers.

A third Warden approached. Ballas swung a booted foot into his crotch. The Warden pitched forward, slumping on to his knees. Ballas hit the Lectivin a second time. The creature swayed, then fell. With full force, Ballas kicked it in the face. His boot struck it under its jaw. Its head shot back and it sprawled on the ground.

Out of the corner of his eye, Ballas glimpsed a figure approaching.

The Blessed Master ran at him, unsheathing a silver-hilted dagger. Stooping, Ballas swept up the Lectivin's knife. In his hands it was light, easy to handle.

The Blessed Master faltered, hesitating as though Ballas had done something extraordinary.

Ballas sprinted towards him. As he swung the Lectivin blade, the Master raised a defensive hand. The weapon sliced straight through his fingers. The bloodied digits pattered to the ground. The blade continued on, shearing through the right side of the Master's face. A blood-wet clod of hacked-off flesh fell at the holy man's feet. His exposed eyeball quivered in a red socket. A slab of bloodied muscle trembled, laid open to the air.

The Blessed Master drew a creaking breath. Then he fell to the ground.

Ballas dropped the hooked knife. Turning, he sprinted across Papal Square, heading for a shadowed alleyway.

Two Wardens blocked his path. As he approached, they turned around, hearing his footsteps.

Within seconds, Ballas was upon them. Leaping feet first at one Warden, he slammed his boots hard into the man's chest. He toppled, gasping. Landing heavily, Ballas snatched the fallen Warden's dagger. Rising, he drove it down through the other Warden's collarbone. Then, wrenching it out, he watched the second Warden slither to the ground.

Ballas glanced across Papal Square.

Then he ran off into the night.

Chapter 6

And these four Pilgrims knew not
Of a fifth, from beyond the water,
Serving no master but itself,
Bowing to no will but its own . . .

Ballas awoke.

He lay in the ruins of a dwelling place, in a northern part of Soriterath. Frost glittered upon tumbled bricks. Through the raftered but unthatched ceiling he saw a hard dawn sky.

He wondered, briefly, how drunk he must've been to doss down in such a cold, unsheltered place. He wondered how much he had imbibed. For certain, it had been a heavy night—

A succession of images flashed in front of his mind's eye.

The Penance Oak. A Lectivin. A head freshly nailed to an oak branch. A Blessed Master, half his face sliced away.

Ballas jerked upright. Sweat glued his clothes to his body. He was trembling. 'Pilgrims' blood! Sweet bloody grief!'

He struck the underside of his fist against the wall. Then he raked his fingers back through his hair. Waves of alarm surged through him. He had not merely been sentenced to the Oak, but he had escaped. He had not merely escaped, but he had mutilated – possibly killed – a Blessed Master in the process. The scale of his misdeeds chilled him. He lay motionless for a few long moments, absorbing his situation.

He had to leave Soriterath. A man hunted by the Church – for, surely, the Masters would be seeking him – ought not linger in Druine's holiest city. There were more Wardens in Soriterath than there were anywhere else. And all, Ballas was certain, would be eager to arrest him.

Ballas got to his feet. Cautiously, he peered out of the ruined dwelling place. The thoroughfare outside was empty. Licking his lips, the big man contemplated his next move. Across the street there was another derelict building. A spike of broken glass, stabbing up from the window frame, held his reflection. Ballas moved closer and the image grew clearer.

He looked at the reflection of his face. His hair was long, his beard matted. His nose was skewed to one side, visibly recently broken. Bruise circles ringed both eyes. His lips were split and swollen. On his forehead, the skin was frazzled pink where the Warden had crashed the torch against it. In the centre was an ugly semicircular scar, made by the hoof of Carrande Black's horse.

Such injuries, even in a violent place like Soriterath, were unusually severe – and eye-catching. Wherever Ballas went, he would draw attention to himself. If he was to survive, he had to remain unnoticed.

He rubbed his jaw, thinking.

Footsteps sounded along the thoroughfare. Nerves jangling, Ballas looked around. A youngish man, tall and lean, was walking towards him. Under his arm he carried a loaf. And, folded but not wholly concealed in dark cloth, a portion of what looked like uncooked ribs. There was a small market place half a mile northwards, Ballas recalled.

As he approached, the man's gaze fell on Ballas who watched his expression for any flicker of unease. Or of wary recognition.

Nothing.

Ballas lifted a hand in greeting. 'My friend,' he said, 'I take it the market is open?'

The man smiled – a genuine, unsuspecting smile. 'It is, it is.'

'Good,' said Ballas. 'I am not well. I need cod liver oil – and bull's blood.'

'You look awful.' Halting, the man looked Ballas up and down. 'You *have* been in the wars. What, in mercy's name, happened to you? You look as if an avalanche has rolled over you . . .' He winced. 'I am sorry: forgive my bluntness. Tact is something I have yet to master.'

Ballas thought quickly. 'My tale is not a pleasant one,' he said. 'By trade, I'm a Papal Warden . . .' At this, the man straightened up. Now a blend of edginess and undue respect touched his features. 'Oh – be at ease,' said Ballas, smiling amiably. 'I hold no grudge against you – unless you were with those who beat me. Which I know you weren't. For they were familiar to me. I arrested them yesterday morning, for some petty crime. I treated them leniently, demanding only that they pay a fine. Yet it damaged their pride, I reckon. And made them vengeful. Last night, as I was leaving a tavern, they set about me. I'm not a small man – as you can see – but there's only so much even I can do. So – ah – they gave me a thrashing.'

'A thrashing?' The man's eyebrows shot up. 'They have done more than that. I'd wager they were trying to kill you.'

'Perhaps,' said Ballas, nodding. 'Nonetheless: I have to report the attack to my fellow Wardens. We've got to keep our eyes open, understand?' He paused. 'You've come from the market, yes?'

The man nodded.

'Were any Wardens there?'

'Usually there are but two or three. But today there have to be a dozen. To be truthful, it makes me uneasy. Something is happening . . . something serious. But I do not know what. I spoke to a friend who lives near Papal Square. There are many Wardens there, too. And throughout the city. What—' He hesitated. 'What is going on? Can you tell me?'

'I fear I cannot,' said Ballas quietly.

'Church business?'

Ballas nodded. 'I will, however, compliment you on your cape. The wool is soft,' he said, lightly gripping the garment. 'I reckon it must keep the cold out and the heat in.'

'It was a gift,' said the man, 'from my wife. She fears winter will be harsh, and I may fr—'

Ballas head-butted the man – a single, skull-jolting blow. Knocked unconscious, he fell to the ground. Ballas unfastened the cape, then drew it on. Glancing up and down the thoroughfare, he dragged the man into the dwelling place. Then, pulling up the cape's hood, he returned outdoors.

'The Wardens are out in droves,' he muttered. 'They are wolves, and I am their prey. But that is no surprise.' He fingered the hood's wool. His face was partially concealed – that was something. But he could not hide his size. For the first time in years, he was conscious of his bulk. He was six spans taller than most men. He stood out like a mountain among hillocks. He stooped slightly, as if his height *could* be disguised. Then he straightened up. Such an unnatural posture would draw attention. Safer by far to walk as he usually did.

He moved slowly along the thoroughfare.

Soriterath was a walled city. There were four entrance gates, one at each cardinal compass point. If Ballas were to leave, he would have to choose between the north, south, east or west gates. He thought hard.

Where, in Druine, would I be safest? he wondered. North of Soriterath? Or south . . .

For a time, he pondered the matter. Then he realised there was scant point in doing so. *Nowhere* in the Realm would be safe. He recalled the prisoner Gerack's words: *There is not a square inch of ground unwatched by the Masters' men.*

From west to east, Druine measured one thousand miles. From south to north, seven hundred and fifty. Yet at this moment it seemed as confining as the cell under the Sacros.

Nonetheless, Ballas had to leave Soriterath. He continued walking, and found himself heading eastwards.

He kept to backstreets and alleyways seldom trodden. He stayed well away from Papal Square. And he fought steadily rising feelings of unease. He glanced at every passing face, seeking some hint that he had been recognised. He kept his hood drawn up, and he frequently looked backwards, ensuring no one was following him. He was seized by an urge to run – to simply sprint from the city. Yet he fought it down, maintaining a brisk but unexceptional pace.

Eventually he reached the city gates.

The portcullis was raised. A slow stream of carts trundled into the city. Many belonged to merchants: their wares were heaped on the backs of the vehicles, covered by leather tarpaulins. As they entered, the cart drivers were directed to an inspection point twenty yards away, where Wardens checked for forbidden materials: prohibited scrolls and books, implements associated with magickers' work, visionary's root . . .

Ballas grimaced.

There were roughly thirty Wardens on the gates. And they were scrutinising not only those entering the city – but those who were leaving. That, Ballas knew, was unusual. And entirely predictable: a Blessed Master had been attacked, and his assailant was still at large.

Ballas swore. He had to leave Soriterath. Yet he couldn't simply walk out through the gates.

He thought for a moment. Then he caught the smell of burning coal. He looked past the inspection point. There was a blacksmith's shop – Ballas made out dirt-thick smoke floating towards the sky.

He licked his lips.

'Maybe it will work,' he murmured, 'maybe it will not . . .'

Keeping close to building-fronts, he edged around the open area in front of the gates, then ducked behind the inspection point. He swept his gaze around the assembled carts. He swiftly noted the goods heaped on them: pots, meats, fish, silks . . . all bound for Soriterath's markets. Turning, he approached the blacksmith's shop. It was an open-fronted building; under a low roof, a furnace glowed, and a hammer rested upon an anvil. A row of tools dangled from wall hooks. The blacksmith, his face soot-blackened, was some yards away, shoeing a merchant's horse. He was engrossed in his task. The merchant stood close by; but he was poring over a scroll – an inventory, perhaps, or a contract.

Ballas exhaled.

Treading silently, he ducked into the smithy. Taking a pair of tongs from a hook, he plucked a coal from the furnace: it glowed softly in the metal grips. Then he snatched a jar of oil from a shelf, and went quietly back outside. Neither blacksmith nor merchant saw him.

He returned to the inspection point. He crept behind a cart, put down the jar and, with the hand thus freed, peeled back the tarpaulin. Rolls of silk lay beneath. Ballas glanced up at the cart's owner. Deep in conversation with another merchant, he had not noticed Ballas. Carefully, Ballas picked up the oil jar and emptied its contents over the silk. Then he tucked the burning coal deep within the lustrous fabric.

He stepped back, waiting.

For a short time, nothing seemed to happen.

Then thin streamers of smoke began to twist up from the silk. An instant later, small flickering flames appeared. They crawled slowly up the rolls – then, reaching an oil-sodden portion, erupted with a yellow-orange flash. Fire swiftly rampaged over the silks. Within heartbeats, the back of the cart was burning vigorously.

The cart's owner glanced around.

'My silks!' he shouted. 'The Four have mercy! What has happened!' He ran towards the cart. Nearing the flames, he halted. He looked wildly around. 'Water! Somebody bring water! Oh please – I am going to lose *everything*!'

A chestnut gelding was harnessed to the cart. Something startled it. Ballas didn't know whether it sensed the flames dancing close to its rump or whether the merchant's frantic cries provoked it to panic. In truth, he did not care. *Something* had the desired effect. Terrified, the horse broke into a crazed gallop. The cart's owner dived out of the way, but a wheel rolled over his ankle. Bones cracked; the cart's owner howled. The cart crashed through the inspection point. Like some fierce contagion, panic spread among the other carthorses. Whinnying crazily, they too launched into fear-spurred gallops. Some veered towards the city gates; a grey mare thundered into a cluster of Wardens. The rest scattered in all directions, careening through the crowds.

Wardens rushed to halt the horses. They snatched out at bridle straps. Some sprang on to the carts' driving benches and took up the reins.

The city gates were unguarded. Walking briskly, Ballas cut across the inspection point and passed through the gates.

Ahead lay an expanse of moorland. A hoof-churned mud path crossed the dull grass and frost-browned bracken.

A rider approached the city gates. As he drew closer, he dismounted, as Papal Law decreed.

Ballas moved toward him.

The rider – a middle-aged man, with steel-grey hair – frowned. 'Trouble, is there?' he said, indicating the gates.

Ballas glanced back. The blaze had spread from the silks. Many other carts were aflame; even from so far away, he could hear burning wood cracking and popping. Smoke curled over the city wall.

'Some accident or other.' Ballas shrugged – then he punched the rider in the stomach. The grey-haired man dropped to the mud, gasping.

Ballas climbed upon the rider's horse – a firm-muscled white mare. Gripping the reins lightly, he turned the horse. Then, jabbing his heels into its flanks, he urged the animal into a canter.

Ballas rode out on to the moorland, leaving Soriterath behind.

Chapter 7

Its lineaments were not those of a man.
They had the sharpness
Of shattered stone.
Its skin lacked the hues of blood,
Shining palely, as if carved from
Living bone . . .
. . . And it bore knowledge permitted
Only to the creator-god . . .

Until late afternoon, Ballas rode eastwards. He kept clear of the road, preferring the secluded, sheltered dips between hills. In a matter of hours, the day's autumnal clarity – the crisp, near-painful brightness of sky and sun – vanished, and everything slid into dull overcast. A grey sky hung low over the moorland. Drizzle slanted down, prickling Ballas's skin. A cold breeze swirled from the north. Yet Ballas, garbed only in tunic, vest and leggings, was sweltering. A sort of angry, fearful disorientation warmed him. The world had grown unfamiliar. The anonymity that Ballas had previously enjoyed had, in a day and a night, been shattered. The Wardens were already seeking him. Soon every Servant of the Church would be doing the same, as would every clergyman.

Ballas swore.

He wondered if the Masters would reveal the reasons why he had to be captured. Would they speak of the killing of Carrande Black? And – more importantly – of the mutilation, possibly murder, of one of their own? Or would they concoct fictional crimes of which he would be accused?

It did not matter. Such things were mere details. The Masters would strain every sinew, torture every nerve to track him down.

Cursing softly to himself, Ballas directed his mount towards a brook that bubbled between two rowan trees.

Dismounting, he kneeled on the bank and drank the cold water. Then he rinsed his face. As he did so, his fingers brushed his beard. Pausing, he touched his hair – black, greasy, shoulder-length.

He would have to remove both beard and hair. If the Masters were circulating his description, those features were bound to be part of it.

Rising, he unbuckled the stolen mare's saddlebags. He hoped to find a traveller's grooming tools: soap, a razor . . . Yet the bags were empty, except for a few copper pennies rolling loose in the bottom.

Ballas sat on a rock, thinking.

How rapidly would news of his crime spread? How much time would pass before people became watchful?

Ballas could not be certain. But he knew that, for the time being, he was reasonably safe: the Wardens might be pursuing him, but ordinary folk were not. In a few days, all might have changed. But for now, he had nothing . . . well, *little* to fear from towns and cities – apart from Soriterath.

Remounting, Ballas continued towards the east.

As nightfall approached, Ballas arrived at Crendlestake, a large town crouching on the banks of Merefed River. Before he reached the settlement's edge, it occurred to him that the man whose horse he had stolen might have ridden from this town. Swinging from the mount, he slapped the creature's rump hard; giving a surprised whinny, the animal cantered off over the moorland.

His stolen cape's hood pulled low, Ballas walked into Crendlestake. It was faintly familiar to him: after all, he had been a vagrant for fifteen years. Maybe twenty. It was entirely possible that he had been here before. Or perhaps he had not – in Druine, one town pretty much resembled another. The buildings were constructed from either dark slatted wood or grey stone. The thoroughfares were usually of bare earth – mud in wet weather. Only in wealthier districts were paving stones laid.

Ballas walked quickly through the gathering dusk. After a short time, he found the Black Bull: a small, cheap tavern, in which he used the saddlebag pennies to purchase a lodging room, two flagons of whisky, some bread and cheese, and the temporary use of shaving implements. A serving girl brought a bowl of warm water, a razor and a block of tallow soap to Ballas's room. She also loaned him a shard of mirror-glass. She offered to cut his hair for an extra penny, but Ballas refused.

In the lodging room, candles glowed. Ballas propped the mirror-glass against the wall. He looked intently at his reflection. The bruises only hinted at by the spike of window-pane that morning glowered thunderhead-black. The hoof-strike from Carrande Black's horse, the beating delivered by the Wardens – they had left their mark. Although Ballas had rinsed his face in the stream earlier, specks of dried blood still clung to his forehead. Taking the soap, he scrubbed his skin clean. Then he worked a lather into his beard.

He had not shaved for ten years. It was, he discovered, a painful process.

Half blunt, the razor tugged savagely at his beard. It seemed much less to cut than to scrape. Scowling, Ballas dragged the blade over his skin, again and again and again. Blood splashed into the foam-capped bowl.

After what seemed like a long time, his beard was completely gone.

Ballas stared.

His jaw was strong, but not in a handsome fashion. There was something bestial about it. Something mulish, perhaps.

It was also scar-scrawled. A thin stripe slashed across his chin. Another arced towards his cheekbone. The razor's touch had aggravated them. They burned livid pink, almost as if freshly made.

Ballas touched them. Gently.

For a heartbeat, it was no longer autumn. The lodging room grew warm. Out of the floorboards drifted the scents of sun-struck grass. Somewhere, a dragonfly's buzzing drone struck up. From the corner of his eye he glimpsed light flashing on tarn-water. There was laughter and then . . . then there came a distant scream.

Ballas jolted. Panic gripped him. Thrusting out his hand, he knocked the shard of mirror-glass from the wall. It flew spinning, flashing, across the lodging room – then, striking the floor, it shattered into tiny fragments. Breathing heavily, Ballas clenched his fist. Tighter and tighter. Until iciness seized the lodging room once more. Until he could smell nothing but candle smoke.

'How many years,' he panted, 'since last I thought of . . . of . . . Pilgrims' blood! It doesn't matter. The past is dead, and only crows should pick at corpses.'

He grasped the whisky flagon. With shaking hands, he pulled out the cork. Then he took four long swallows. The hot fluid coursed down his throat. He waited for the first hints of numbness to sweep over him. Nothing. Impatiently, he drank another mouthful. And another, until the flagon was half empty.

Then, at last, he found a hazy restfulness.

Half an hour before dawn, Ballas woke. Last night he had emptied both whisky flagons. When his eyes opened, he found himself sprawled on the lodging room floor, his head throbbing.

Sitting up, Ballas rubbed his jaw. His palm rasped over bristle. He swept a hand over his head. The previous night, intoxicated and lacking a mirror, he had cut his hair. He suspected it wasn't a neat crop. But at least it was short.

Getting to his feet, Ballas quenched his thirst from a water jug in the room corner. Then he stepped out on to the landing and went downstairs.

The common room was empty. From behind the serving bar, Ballas stole a whisky flagon, then left the tavern.

The sky was a rich dark blue. On the horizon, above the rooftops, the blue lightened at the slow lifting of the sun. The morning was cold; frost sparkled on the ground. The brittle chill refreshed Ballas. And the pre-dawn silence was oddly comforting. The streets were empty. The only sound was Ballas's scuffing tread. He felt isolated, alone – as if he were the only man in Druine. It seemed impossible that in Soriterath the Blessed Masters were plotting his demise. That, in all likelihood, Wardens were travelling under the same dawn sky as himself, observing the same blueness as himself – intent on capturing or killing him.

Then the silence broke.

A distant voice sounded, echoing among the buildings. Laughter followed and something heavy knocked against something hollow.

Ballas paused, frowning. Then he looked far to his right. The Merefed River flowed gently past.

'Of course,' he muttered. 'This is a dock town . . .'

It would be far safer to travel by water than land. The Merefed River cut through empty moorland and was seldom patrolled by Wardens. And, if Ballas was part of a group, perhaps he would be less conspicuous. Certainly, a lone rider drew more attention than a dozen bargemen.

Ballas followed the sounds and passed between wooden storehouses on to the jetty. A barge was moored fifty paces away. It was a crudely fashioned, unpainted, inexpensive-looking vessel. The rowing benches were bare, uncushioned wood, and the craft lacked a frame over which a canopy might be strung to shelter oarsmen from the rain. The only adornment was a rusted nameplate, nailed to the port side: *The Otter.*

The barge was being loaded with crates and barrels. A gang of men carried them from a storehouse, then passed them down through a deck hatch. A stocky, black-bearded man watched them closely. He had a broad, flat face and lively blue eyes. Leaning against the bulwark, one hand resting on the tiller, he exuded both authority and comradeship. Yet, in the past, he had clearly upset *someone*: a scar ran from his left cheekbone over his eye socket and across his forehead. A permanent squint folded the scar-traversed eyelids.

Ballas watched him for a moment. Then he approached. As he drew close, the man looked him over.

'Fair morning,' he said, scratching his arm. 'A fresh one, isn't it?'

'Aye,' replied Ballas. He halted at the barge. Under the jetty, water lapped against the props. Ballas gestured to the cargo vessel. 'This yours?'

'It is,' said the man, nodding. 'Every rotting joist and leaking join and bright-eyed hull rat – they all belong to me.'

'How far are you going?'

'This load,' the barge-master waved a hand towards the hatch, 'is destined for Redreathe.' Redreathe was a town a hundred miles to the east. This pleased Ballas: if he could secure a place on the barge, he would be relatively safe for several days – the time it would take to reach Redreathe. The black-bearded man tilted his head. 'You look thoughtful, my friend,' he said, peering at Ballas.

Ballas blinked. 'These are trying times,' he said quietly.

'Oh?'

'I've had some poor news,' said Ballas, shrugging. He looked sharply at the barge-master. 'Yesterday evening, I found out that my sister has fallen ill. Some blood taint or other; I don't know exactly what. And if I did, it would make no difference, for I'm not a physician, merely someone who loves his sister and wants to be at her side when she perishes . . . and perish she will. From what I've been told, her malady can't be cured. She is feverish, all night she is tormented by appalling visions – demons, phantoms, the undead. She suffers fits, too. And it is all anyone can do to stop her from biting off her own tongue . . .'

'It sounds as if she's got spindlebrack,' said the barge-master, 'or maybe red-sleeper. They both show the symptoms you described, and neither can be treated. All a physician can do is lessen the victim's pain. They say such illnesses provide the worst ways of dying . . .' He grimaced. 'Forgive me. I am speaking tactlessly.'

'Barge-master,' said Ballas plainly, 'my sister dwells twenty miles outside Redreathe. Please, grant me a place upon your barge.' As he said this, the barge-master winced, as if suddenly uncomfortable. 'I ask only so that I may be with her. And I wouldn't be an idle passenger. I'll take the oars like every other man. I'm broad of shoulder and, in truth, a little heavy labour will help take my mind off my worries . . .'

'My friend,' interrupted the barge-master, 'I pity you. Truly, were it possible, I would not merely offer you a place upon a rowing bench but would order my men to work at double-speed, so that you could be with your sister in good time. But every bench is taken. I have already promised places to a dozen men. Forgive me,' he said, his hands spread wide in a gesture of helplessness, 'but I am a man of my word. I cannot withdraw my promise. And many of my oarsmen have to provide for their families. These are lean times; winter is coming, and a ha'penny may be the difference between hunger and a warm meal.'

'I am desperate,' said Ballas. 'If there is anything I can do to—'

'I am sorry,' the barge-master broke in. 'I can suggest only that you wait for another barge to pass through.'

Ballas sighed. 'Very well. That is what I'll do. I hope that one comes quickly, that's all.'

Turning, he walked back between the storehouses. He could not wait for a second barge to moor at the docks. Dawn was breaking; he did not wish to be seen in broad daylight by more people than was necessary. He scowled. He had no choice but to travel overland. He would have to steal another horse. Once more, he'd need to follow the clandestine routes that led away from Soriterath. Moving quickly, he started back toward the Black Bull. A stable adjoined the tavern. From there, he would pilfer a mount. Then he would ride—

He halted.

Brisk footsteps rang out. A young man, wearing a thick leather coat, was half running, half walking towards the jetty. For a moment Ballas hesitated. Then he trotted towards him.

'Begging your pardon,' he said, drawing close 'but do you row upon *The Otter*?'

Slowing, the man looked at Ballas suspiciously. 'Yes, I do,' he said, nodding. 'What of it?'

Ballas did not say anything more. Instead, he drove his fist into the oarsman's face, hard. The oarsman stumbled backwards – then fell as two brisk punches knocked his head first left, then right. He lay upon his back, gazing sightlessly at the sky. Stooping, Ballas grasped his ankles and dragged him into an empty storehouse. He found a short coil of rope and tied the man's wrists and ankles together. Then he rooted through his pockets and found four copper pennies. He slipped them into his own pocket.

A short time later, Ballas returned to the jetty. He sat at the water's edge, fifty paces from *The Otter*. He uncorked his whisky flagon and stared sorrowfully into the river. Eventually, the barge-master walked over.

'Good whisky, is it?' he asked.

'Foul,' said Ballas. 'Liquid horseshit. But so what? I'm not interested in its taste. It brings numbness – and *that* is all I ask of it.'

'It also supplies warmth,' said the barge-master. 'Which is not to be sneered it. As I said before, the morning is fresh. So I will strike a bargain with you. Share the whisky, and you may have a place upon my barge.'

'Truly?' said Ballas, in mock surprise.

'I am a man of my word, as I said,' replied the barge-master. 'But it seems that others are not. One who swore he would work for me has not arrived. Perhaps he got a little too drunk last night. Maybe he has abandoned his profession. Pah! It does not matter. I can wait no longer. There is a place for you, if you want it.'

Getting to his feet, Ballas proffered the whisky flagon. The barge-master took a deep gulp. Then he shuddered. 'By the Four's balls, that is as bad as you claimed. Still,' he pressed the flagon back into Ballas's hand, 'take a mouthful yourself, and I'll consider our contract sealed.'

Ballas did as he was asked.

'There,' said the barge-master. 'Now you are one of the crew. My name is Culgrogan.' He proffered his hand. Ballas shook it: Culgrogan's grip was firm. 'What is your name, my friend?'

Ballas hesitated. 'Gadner,' he said at last.

'Ha! A religious man, are you?'

Ballas frowned. 'What do you mean?'

'Gadner – wasn't that the first name of Gatarix, who tried to slay the Four?'

It was. Walking towards the barge, Ballas thought it an appropriate name. Like Gatarix, he had attacked a holy figure. Like Gatarix, there would be those who sought his death.

Yet the name was well chosen in a different way. A way Ballas did not – could not – suspect.

All day, pausing only at noon, they rowed along Merefed River. The water-course wound through some of the wildest moorland in Druine. Much of it was uninhabited; and this suited Ballas. If Wardens were to appear, he would see them long before they spotted him. And if they *did* recognise him, he would need only to leap from the barge and swim to the opposite side of the river to avoid them.

Ballas worked hard at the oars. He was unaccustomed to such physical exertion. Yet he found it strangely gratifying. Lulled by the rhythm of each stroke, and the soft lapping of water against the hull, he sank into a contented daze. The other oarsmen spoke among themselves. Their chatter was trivial; they talked of whores, and drinking, and the bets they had placed the previous evening on a series of bare-knuckle fights.

Only when night fell and they moored at the small village of Barrelhand did Ballas start to feel pain. As he rose from the rowing bench, he noticed that his back ached. His backside too throbbed; and fluid-fat blisters covered his palms. He cursed softly.

'A problem?' asked the barge-master.

'I've worked too hard,' muttered the big man.

'From such infirmities,' said Culgrogan, gazing at Ballas's blisters, 'springs healthy pride.' He clapped Ballas on the shoulder. 'And thirst. You are a drinker, yes?'

'What true man is not?'

'There is a fine tavern up this way,' said the barge-master, pointing along a lane. 'They serve the worst of all whiskies; wine that bears the flavour of the grape-treader's feet; and ale that might've been ladled from a pisspot. But after a long day, each tastes as fine as nectar.' He climbed on to the jetty. 'There are whores, too. Nice plump village girls. The air here is clean and the women grow strong and happy. Isn't that right, lads?'

The oarsmen responded with laughter.

Ballas stepped from the barge. 'I thought you claimed these were family men.'

'They are,' said Culgrogan. 'But when a fellow weds and brings children into the world, do his bollocks shrivel, hm? Does he cease to be a man? Of course not. His urges persist. Thus he does the virtuous thing: he ruts with a whore.'

Ballas was intrigued. 'Whoring is virtuous?'

The barge-master nodded keenly. 'For two reasons. Firstly, a man may hump a whore – but he will not fall in love with her. He knows she is unsavoury. And besides: she has already revealed her secrets to him. So he is not interested in romancing her. He merely lies with her, then returns home to his wife.

'Secondly – and for every man in Druine this is vital – if he is lying with a whore, he is not lying with another man's wife. Thus we may all trust each other . . . we may look upon one another not as rivals, but as brothers.' Throwing back his head, Culgrogan cackled. 'A strange world, is it not, when men act peaceably towards one another *not* because of the Pilgrim Church's teachings but thanks to the merits of whores?'

A *click-click* of footsteps echoed along the lane. The barge-master grew suddenly still. He tilted his head, listening. Then a broad grin wreathed his face.

'Ha! Is it not the greatest thing, to have no *need* of a whore's services? That is, to have a lady who will perform a whore's role – yet demand no payment? Isn't *that* the best arrangement? Here she is, my boys: the Red Flower of Barrelhand.'

A woman stepped out of the shadows. She wore a long white skirt, and a blouse of tight-clinging linen. Her eyes were deep, dark, and glinted in the moonlight. Dusk's mystery pooled under her high cheekbones. She had a wide mouth, her lips blood red with lip-daub. Her black hair billowed outwards in a gypsyish frizz. A scarlet-petalled flower nestled behind her ear. 'Culgrogan,' she said, approaching the barge-master, 'you must keep your voice down! I am not some plaything to be flaunted in front of your companions.'

Yet her broad smile suggested she enjoyed such attention.

'But, my love, I am a proud man!' Culgrogan protested. 'Ought a fellow to conceal the source of his joy? Is it proper for a horseman to keep stabled his finest filly? Must a falconer keep his best bird cooped up?'

'Must *you* liken me to animals?' asked Red Flower, looping her arm around his waist.

'But if our pleasure is animal,' began Culgrogan, 'if tonight we become a two-backed beast . . .' He left the sentence unfinished. Smiling broadly, he turned to the oarsmen. 'Have a fine evening, my friends. I will see you at the break of dawn. Assuming my lady does not, in the fashion of desert-dwelling spiders, devour my head after—'

'Be silent!' said Red Flower, covering his mouth with her hand.

They disappeared back along the lane. Behind Ballas, an oarsman said, 'It is a pleasant thing to see husband and wife so devoted.'

'It is,' said another. 'One day, I hope to witness it.'

'You mean—'

'She is Culgrogan's mistress.' A pained tone was to be heard in this third oarsman's voice. 'The Four know how he manages it but in every dock there is some ripe lady awaiting him. Of course, they are already wed – but that does not trouble Culgrogan. He thinks of himself as a schoolboy, robbing apples from an orchard. Or a poacher, lifting trout from a stream.'

'Yet he gave that talk about the virtues of whores . . . how they prevent men stealing others' wives.'

'Once I mentioned that to him,' said the third oarsman. 'In this, as in all things, he was pragmatic. If no man ever lay with another's wife, no man would fear being cuckolded. Thus there would be no need for whores. But what would become of those girls who, pretty but frail-minded, could find no other profession? They would starve. So Culgrogan makes mistresses of many, and cuckolds of the same number, and a few young women can live comfortably. Did the Four not teach that even minorities must be protected? Culgrogan is a holy adulterer. His fornication is an act of devotion.'

The other oarsmen laughed.

'He is a sophist,' said one.

'What man is not,' replied another, 'when seeking to justify unjustifiable pleasures?'

They followed the lane to a small black-fronted tavern. In a crowded common room, they found a long table and settled down at it. The tavern-master brought whisky, wine and ale. The men drank, gossiped and laughed; crude jokes were told, and every oarsman soon sank into happy, raucous drunkenness. A few whores drifted in. For a time, they conversed with the oarsmen. They spoke slyly, as if flirting: yet, unlike true flirts, *their* approaches ended with honest copulation. Oarsman after oarsman stumbled upstairs with a girl on his arm.

Ballas, however, abstained. He was tired and his body was sore. He wanted merely to drink, and relax. Seated apart from the others, at the table-end, his sipped first at wine, then whisky.

After a while, the barge-master returned. The oarsmen cheered.

'How was she?' asked one.

Culgrogan grinned. 'A delight, as always.' Stretching out his arms, as if waking from a long sleep, he slumped tiredly into a chair. 'A magnificent girl, is Red Flower. I could almost fall in love with her.' He poured himself a cup of wine. 'Yet I doubt I could manage too many nights of such savage passion. Her bedroom manners are those of a whirlwind. She seizes and shakes and slaps a fellow; he finds himself flung this way and that. I swear I can feel bruises rising.' He drained his cup, then replenished it. 'But, in small bursts, such violence is invigorating. To Red Flower,' he said, raising the cup.

For a time, Culgrogan made small talk with the oarsmen. Then the tavern door slammed open. Cold air gusted inside.

What happened next happened quickly.

A broad, blond-bearded man appeared on the threshold, flanked by two companions. He swept the room with a predatory pale-blue-eyed gaze. His stare locked on Culgrogan. The newcomer's face reddened. Oblivious, Culgrogan continued drinking – until the blond-bearded man strode over, seized the barge-master's tunic collar and yanked him from his stool. Culgrogan struck the sawdust-strewn floor with a yelp. The blond-bearded man kicked his head, hard. Once, twice, three times. Then he hauled Culgrogan up on to his feet. He punched him twice in the face.

Culgrogan swayed. 'What . . . ?' he mumbled through blood-slick lips.

'You piece of horseshit,' said the blond-bearded man.

'Who are you?' stammered Culgrogan. 'I don't understand—'

'You are the man from the barge,' shouted his assailant. 'The one who's been fornicating with Felishia! Do not deny it. She has confessed *everything*!'

'You are mistaken,' began Culgrogan.

'A man knows when his wife is deceiving him,' snapped the other man. 'He knows, too, when she has been pleasured.' He unsheathed a short-bladed dagger. 'I have seen it before – *many times*. She has become a habit, has she? Well, if you cannot temper your lusts . . .' Drawing back his hand, he thrust the dagger forward, aiming at Culgrogan's crotch. The barge-master pranced backwards, terrified.

'Sweet grief! Be reasonable!'

'The hour for that has passed,' began the enraged man – then he staggered as a wine flagon hurled by Ballas struck his head.

Ballas rose to his feet. The blond-bearded man whirled, his eyes blazing. 'You would defend this maker of cuckolds?'

Ballas did not reply. He was not inclined to argue with strangers. Springing forward, he struck the man's nose savagely. It burst open in a spray of blood. The cuckolded man stumbled back, but quickly regained his balance. Slashing his dagger back and forth, he came forward. He lunged, jabbing the blade towards Ballas's throat. Catching his antagonist's wrist, Ballas rammed his forehead against the cuckold's already damaged nose. Then he delivered two bone-crushing blows to the man's jaw. The cuckold sagged, but Ballas did not relinquish the grip on his wrist. Slowly, he twisted the blond-bearded man's arm. Tendons popped. The man howled—

—Then one of his companions ran at Ballas. As he came close, Ballas swung up his right boot, connecting perfectly with his attacker's crotch. The man pitched sideways, wheezing; Ballas smashed a fist into his cheek-bone.

The angry cuckold's second companion took a step forward. Then he halted as Ballas shot him a dangerous glance.

Ballas returned his attention to the injured cuckold. And finished the work he had started. Very slowly, he twisted the man's arm. More tendons snapped, some cracking as loud as whip-strikes. Only when the limb felt utterly loose did Ballas let go.

The man lay sprawled on the sawdust, his arm flopping at an obscene angle. Tiny convulsions shook his body.

The tavern-master stepped forward. 'Enough, enough,' he said – even though the fight had clearly finished. He was tough-looking, tall, with steel-grey hair. Yet he turned pale at the sight of the blond-bearded man's arm. 'Sweet mercy,' he breathed. 'You two.' He gestured sharply at the man's companions. 'Take him out of here. Find someone to tend his injuries.' He looked at Ballas. 'And you: can you be trusted?'

'If no one else attacks my mates,' said Ballas, breathing heavily.

The tavern-master laughed humourlessly. 'I do not believe that is likely.'

The injured man's friends carried him from the tavern. Ballas returned to the table. The barge-master sat beside him, dabbing at his split lips with a dishrag provided by the tavern-master.

'You fight well,' he said, slurring slightly. 'What is your trade? Soldier? Pugilist?'

'I've had many trades,' Ballas answered, shrugging. 'I drift from one to the next.'

'Well, I am in your debt, my friend.'

'Nah, you're not,' said Ballas. 'I am relying upon you to take me to Redreathe. If he . . . if Red Flower's husband had killed you, I'd be at a loss.'

'Even so,' murmured the barge-master. He rubbed his split lips cautiously. Then he winced. 'Ah, that hurts. I tell you, if he had expended as much passion upon Red Flower as he did upon me, she would not have strayed. She would be a very happy woman.'

Ballas looked across the common room. He found himself staring at a brown-eyed whore. Her hair was copper-coloured. A faint flush tinted her cheeks.

Ballas no longer felt tired. Or sore. The fight had filled him with restless energy. His hands shook. His heart hammered.

'Do you want her?' asked the barge-master.

Ballas glanced at him.

'She is yours.' The barge-master pressed a penny into Ballas's palm. 'No matter what you say, I *am* in your debt. So look upon her as a down payment, yes? Go on. Take her upstairs. You have earned her.'

Closing his fingers around the penny, Ballas got to his feet.

'He rutted with Felishia,' said Bradburn. 'He rutted with my wife. And when I went to the tavern to have my vengeance, this other man – this bloody *animal* – got up and . . . Aah!'

'Be quiet!' snapped Cobaris, a fat man in his middle sixties. He was bald, except for a white clump of hair over each ear. Upon his pate, sweat glistened. He disliked tending injuries. He was not a physician, neither by trade nor inclination. Yet he was the only man in the village capable of repairing – or, at least, *trying* to repair – such a wound.

Bradburn lay upon the table in Cobaris's kitchen. His face was deathly pale. His skin twitched, as if every muscle underneath it were quivering.

Cobaris sighed. He did not hold out much hope for Bradburn's arm. Not a single shoulder tendon remained whole. In itself, this was amazing: whoever had inflicted the wound was a man of considerable strength. The consequences for Bradburn would be unpleasant. Cobaris intended to bandage the limb flat against Bradburn's side. Maybe – *maybe* – the tendons would heal. But he doubted it: the damage to them was too extreme. Realistically, one of two fates awaited Bradburn's arm. It might, over time, grow rotten: the flesh would blacken, the blood turn poisonous, and Bradburn would die. Or the arm might stay untainted – but utterly useless: just a flopping tube of flesh, dangling from his body.

Cobaris lifted a cup of brandy to Bradburn's lips. 'Drink,' he said. 'It will ease the pain. And calm you down a little.'

'I have no wish to be *calm*,' snapped Bradburn. 'I want only to be avenged.' Yet he drank the brandy gratefully.

Bradburn's arm lay draped across his chest. Cobaris lightly took hold of his wrist, in order to move it to his side. Bradburn howled. Cobaris recoiled, as if the damaged limb had turned into a serpent.

'More brandy,' groaned Bradburn. 'Please – I want to feel nothing, absolutely *nothing*.'

'Very well,' murmured Cobaris. 'I dare say I shall not be able to treat you while you are sober in any case, for you are as hysterical as a girl.'

'It hurts, damn you!'

'I dare say that it does,' sighed Cobaris, picking up a brandy flagon. The fluid inside was twenty years old. It was a rare, expensive brandy; it caressed the tongue like some divine fire. Yet here he was, wasting it on a man ill placed to appreciate it. He filled the cup, watching the dark liquid glint in the candlelight. He fed a sip to Bradburn.

The injured man swallowed, then coughed. 'Curse them. Curse every whoreson bargeman that visits this village! They are all of a kind. They are lazy, irresponsible . . . they care nothing for the people they meet or the places they stop at on their journeys. They are water rats, and nothing more.'

'I take it, then, that it was a bargeman who made a dishonest woman of your wife?'

'It was,' muttered Bradburn. 'And a bargeman who defended him. As I said, he was an animal – a pig-faced, ale-bellied *animal*. Still, it looked as though *he* had recently taken a beating. His face was bruised, and cut; it is a pity that whoever fought him did not kill him. More brandy, Cobaris.'

Cobaris retrieved the flagon.

'The man was a barbarian,' said Bradburn. 'Worse than that, he was a *peasant* – in the ugliest sense. His clothes were soiled, and blood-speckled. He stank of sweat . . . But then, he did hail from Hearthfall – a land of unwashed rustics and cider-supping—'

'Hearthfall?' said Cobaris, pausing.

'Yes, Hearthfall,' repeated Bradburn. 'Hurry up with the brandy. I am in—'

'How do you know he is from Hearthfall?' asked Cobaris, his voice quavering. 'Did he tell you?'

'Oh yes,' said Bradburn sarcastically. 'We had a pleasant chat before we tried to kill one another.'

'I am being serious,' snapped Cobaris, grasping Bradburn's wrist. The injured man screamed.

'What in Druine's name are you doing? Let me go!'

'Answer my question,' said Cobaris impatiently.

'He spoke with a Hearthfall accent,' gasped Bradburn. 'You must have heard it: that burr which rolls along like Hearthfall's green hills and makes the speaker seem a halfwit.'

Cobaris released Bradburn's wrist. 'You said he was a big man?'

'A forearm's length taller than me, and as broad as a barn door.'

'And he was bruised, you say, as if he had taken a recent thrashing?'

'Must I repeat everything I've already told you? Yes, yes and yes again – he is all those things. Now, for pity's sake: more brandy!'

Cobaris wasn't listening. Snatching up his cape, he hurried from his home and half ran through Barrelhand's dark lanes to the tavern. He ducked into the common room and went straight to the serving bar.

The tavern-master looked up. 'What will it be, Father—'

'Silence,' interrupted Cobaris.

The tavern-master blinked.

'Just give me a cup of Baskirian Red,' muttered the fat man, wiping a hand over his bare scalp. He looked furtively around the tavern. 'Tell me,' he said, as the tavern-master poured the wine, 'there was a fight here but a half-hour ago. Bradburn lost – his friends brought him to me, his arm wrenched . . .'

'I saw the entire thing,' said the tavern-master, nodding. 'Will he recover?'

'That hardly matters,' muttered Cobaris, snatching up the cup. 'Where is the man he fought?' His gaze swept around the common room. He could discern no man matching the description given by Bradburn.

'He went upstairs, with a—' began the tavern-master, then fell silent. He tapped Cobaris's forearm lightly, then pointed to a flight of wooden stairs.

A tall, broad, preposterously ugly man was treading down the stairs into the common room. Bruises clouded his features. By his side walked a copper-haired whore.

Cobaris stared hard at the man. Then, draining his cup in a single gulp, he turned to go.

'A ha'penny,' called the tavern-master. 'You haven't paid—'

'Later!' replied Cobaris, waddling briskly from the tavern.

He returned home. Bradburn still lay upon the kitchen table. Only now he clutched the brandy bottle, and was suckling upon it like a baby at its mother's teat. Yet this waste of fine brandy did not trouble Cobaris. He rushed upstairs to his study. Taking a tiny square of whisper-fine parchment, he quilled a note. In his haste, his writing skirled wildly; the ink blobbed, and the quill-tip pierced the parchment. Swearing, Cobaris tried again. Slowly, this time.

He turned to a metal birdcage in a corner of the room. Inside, a pigeon rested upon a perch. Only this morning, it had appeared outside his window, rapping its beak upon the glass. A message had been tied around its leg; an item of serious yet exciting news, from the Blessed Masters themselves. A fugitive was being sought. His crime, though undisclosed, was clearly one of enormity. If any holy man were to set eyes upon him – or someone who *might* be him – they had to send word to the Sacros . . . *without delay*.

Father Cobaris opened the cage and attached the rolled-up square of parchment to the pigeon's leg. Then he opened the study's window.

The bird flapped out, got its bearings and then swerved westwards, towards Soriterath.

Father Cobaris of the Pilgrim Church felt quite breathless. Excitement gripped him – and optimism. Maybe, if he led the Masters to the fugitive, he would be moved to a better parish. One in a city somewhere. Not in a dreary village, beside a river of sour water.

He cursed; it was a shame that Barrelhand was so insignificant that no Wardens were posted there.

But it did not matter.

The Wardens would arrive soon enough. And then—

There came a shattering of glass. Then a lung-ripping howl.

'Bradburn,' muttered the priest.

Chapter 8

And this pilgrim suffered
The justice of men who believed him
Evil – yet he cast retribution upon them
And they perished . . .

At first light, Ballas and the oarsmen left the tavern. They went to the dock where *The Otter* was moored. Many of the oarsmen were hung-over. They shuffled along the lane, on to the jetty, drag-footed and sore-headed. A few vomited, upchucking lurid gutfuls of half-digested ale. Others bore their pains in cringing silence. Under his bruises, the barge-master's skin was green-tinted. Well accustomed to liquid excess, Ballas alone seemed unaffected. He drew deep breaths of cold morning air. And remembered with pleasure the previous night's whore.

The oarsmen clambered on to the barge. The barge-master untied the mooring ropes and, very slowly, the vessel moved away from the jetty. Every dip, draw and lift of the oars extracted groans from some oarsman or other. Those who had made the walk from the tavern without upset, yet nonetheless had uncertain stomachs, found the sudden exertion fiercely emetic. Leaning over the side, they threw up into the Merefed's clear waters. The barge moved sluggishly onwards. Fleetingly, it seemed to Ballas a craft of the dead: a boat manned by reanimated corpses.

At noon, things had grown a little better. The barge-master called a halt and handed out a sparse lunch of bread, cheese and – for those who believed an extra dose of poison relieved that same poison's effects – whisky. Ballas ate greedily, and swallowed large mouthfuls of whisky. Then he gazed into the water. A few rainbow trout slid by, glinting under the surface.

'Wishing you'd brought a fishing rod?' asked the barge-master, settling cross-legged close by.

Ballas did not reply.

'Sometimes I trail a line as we move onward,' said the barge-master, smiling. 'Every fish in the Merefed is strong-fleshed – and fine-tasting. There's trout, roach, barbel, carp . . . and pike. You ever eaten pike?'

'Once or twice,' said Ballas vaguely.

'It is surprisingly delicious, if properly cooked,' said the barge-master. 'Most people would no sooner eat a freshwater wolf than its land-dwelling namesake. And that is a shame. They deprive themselves not merely of its flavour but also of the joys of capture. Hook a pike – and the battle has only just begun. It is said that, in the south, where the waters are warmer, they grow as large as sharks. Venture into a lake or a river and they will rip a lump out of you. They have been known to devour dogs, even deer. Can you imagine such a thing?'

Ballas did not speak. He simply watched the trout moving past the barge.

'You are not a talkative soul, are you? Even in your cups, you uttered scarcely a word,' commented the barge-master.

'My sister is ailing,' said Ballas simply, remembering the fiction he had woven to obtain a place on the barge. 'When I get home, perhaps she'll be dead. Such thoughts are distracting.'

The barge-master sighed. 'Forgive me,' he said. 'I had, for a moment, forgotten your unhappy circumstances. I will leave you in peace.' Rising, he walked to the prow, then sat down with the other oarsmen.

Ballas chewed on a lump of cheese. He thought of Redreathe – of what he would do once he arrived there. He wondered whether he could any longer live safely as a vagrant; was it the wisest course, to wander from town to town, city to city, for the rest of his life? Would such constant movement make it harder for the Pilgrim Church to track him down? Or would it create difficulties of its own? Wherever he went, he would be a stranger; people would mistrust him, perhaps suspecting that he was a fugitive.

Would it be best if he settled down? Somewhere remote. Somewhere the Pilgrim Church's influence was weaker.

He realised there was no such place. As Gerack, his fellow prisoner under the Sacros had said, the Church's resources were limitless: they employed not only priests but Wardens and agents of various types.

Ballas rubbed his jaw.

'Perhaps I'm doomed,' he murmured, glancing at the sky. 'And perhaps – perhaps it doesn't matter.'

The barge-master returned to the tiller and gave orders to resume rowing. Ballas gripped an oar's shaft in a blistered palm, and the barge inched steadily forwards. Once more, he allowed the slow rhythms of travel to put him in a half-trance.

The afternoon was darkening towards evening. The barge slipped into a narrow channel. On the bank to Ballas's right silver-black willows grew, trailing their branch-tips in the water. Drawing back on the oars, Ballas felt the air suddenly hum. Something black streaked past his face. The air hummed again – and the screaming began.

Ballas's gaze whipped to the bank.

Half a dozen Wardens emerged from the willows. Already, they were nocking fresh arrows to their bowstrings. On the barge, several men had been hit. A black shaft jutted from an oarsman's throat; another was lodged in a different oarsman's eye socket. Ballas threw himself face down on the deck. Six more arrows hurtled towards the barge. One slammed into an oarsman's gut, pitching him into the water. Another plunged into a shouting oarsman's open mouth; the arrowhead tore its way through the back of his neck.

Ballas swore.

On the bank every Warden nocked another arrow. Except for one. In his palm nestled a glass sphere; a dark liquid sloshed around inside it. A wick stuck out from its topmost curve, burning with a flickering flame. Drawing back his arm, the Warden lobbed the sphere on to the barge. As it struck the deck slats, it shattered, spilling the liquid – which burst into fire. Within seconds the deck was ablaze. An oarsman, standing close to the burning fluid, found his legs engulfed in flames. Shrieking, he stumbled towards the edge of the boat, intending to leap into the water. But an arrow pierced his lower back. Crying out, he arched backwards – then fell silent when another arrow skewered the back of his head.

Ballas crawled across the deck. Glancing at the bank, he saw that the Wardens were drawing more arrows from their quivers. Momentarily safe, he dragged himself over the side of the barge and into the river.

Gasping, he splashed into ice-cold water. For a half-instant he was submerged; water rushed into his mouth, and panic gripped him. He kicked furiously and rose to the surface. Reaching out, he grasped the barge's hull and wedged his fingertips into a join between the wooden planks. Suddenly, a brown-haired oarsman crashed into the water beside him. A moment later another oarsman joined them. Ballas looked at him. He was a scrawny, sharp-boned man: from the night before, in the tavern, Ballas recalled that his nickname was something bird-related . . . Sparrow: the man was known as Sparrow. He clawed frantically at the hull, trying to find a grip, and sank momentarily under the water. Then he surfaced, gasping.

'Sweet grief,' he said, finding a fingerhold on the hull, 'what is happening? Why are the Wardens attacking us?' He looked wildly at Ballas. 'They are trying to kill us . . . I do not want to die!' He shivered as if fever-gripped. On the deck, men were screaming. A stink of burning flesh drifted down. Sparrow sniffed – then groaned. 'I don't want to die,' he repeated.

Ballas thought hard. 'Do as I say, and you'll live. You can swim?'

Sparrow nodded.

'And you carry a knife?'

Sparrow nodded again. Then his eyes widened further. 'What are you planning? Do you . . . do you want to *fight* them?'

'We haven't got much choice,' said Ballas.

'You are mad,' said Sparrow, his voice quavering. 'They do not merely outnumber us – they are *Wardens*. Do you suppose you can treat them like you treated . . . treated that man in the tavern last night?' He blew out a long breath. Shaking his head, he said, 'We must beg for mercy. Why . . . What have we done wrong? They . . .' He grimaced, trying to find the correct words.

'Beg if you wish,' said Ballas. 'But they'll take no notice. They mean to slaughter us.' He licked his lips. 'I don't know why, but that is their mission.' He turned to the brown-haired oarsman. 'What's your name?'

'Garrullon,' he replied.

'Are you carrying any weapons?'

'Only a knife – short-bladed, blunt-edged . . . but all right for killing, if killing is necessary.' Closing his eyes momentarily, he shook his head. 'I can scarcely believe my own words.'

'It's our blood or theirs,' said Ballas flatly. He gestured at the river bank, across the water from where the Wardens stood. The ground was clear: there were no willows to hide behind. He pointed along the river, towards an arched bridge twenty paces away. 'As soon as we are on dry land, they'll cross over and attack us. We must be prepared. The bridge is narrow; if we meet them upon it, they'll only be able to come at us two at a time. The odds will be more favourable, I reckon.'

'Even so . . .' said Sparrow uncertainly.

Ballas glanced at Garrullon. 'Are you ready?'

The brown-haired oarsman nodded.

'And you?' said Ballas, turning to Sparrow.

Sparrow's eyes were shut and his lips were moving noiselessly. He was praying, Ballas realised. The Papal Wardens, who served the Pilgrim Church, were about to slaughter him. Yet still he petitioned the Pilgrim Church's divine beings; still he asked the Four for aid, absolution, mercy . . .

Sparrows eyes flicked open. 'I am ready.'

'Then let us go,' said Ballas. 'Swim to the bank, and climb straight out.' He looked from Sparrow to Garrullon. 'Then fight like dogs, yes?'

The two men nodded.

Pushing themselves off, they swam to the far bank. There they each seized hanks of grass, ready to drag themselves ashore. For a moment they paused. They looked at each other. In Sparrow's eyes, Ballas saw fear: the man was not accustomed to such adventures. Garrullon also seemed nervous. Yet self-control gave his eyes a hard glitter.

In seconds, Ballas knew, both men would be dead. And their deaths were necessary, if Ballas himself was to escape.

'On my third count,' said the big man. 'One, two, three . . .'

Sparrow and Garrullon heaved themselves on to the bank. Remaining in the water, Ballas glanced at the bow-clutching Wardens. Already they were drawing back their bowstrings. In an instant, they had taken aim. Then they released their black arrows, which sped across the river, cutting through the fire and smoke pouring from the barge. A shaft slammed into Sparrow's neck and another thudded into his lower back. He shrieked. Then Garrullon gave a muffled grunt as an arrow struck him between his shoulders. Another drove into the back of his head. Both men fell to the ground. His body spreadeagled over the bank, Sparrow slid slowly down into the water.

Momentarily safe – the Wardens hadn't yet nocked fresh arrows to their bowstrings – Ballas scrambled on to the bank. Then he sprinted towards the bridge. As he drew close, an arrow whizzed past his face. Diving flat on to the ground, he felt a second arrow tear through the flesh covering his shoulder blade. Grunting, he struggled to his feet. Then he hesitated.

Three Wardens raced over the bridge. As they approached, they drew their swords – each weapon flat-bladed and heavy. Ten yards from Ballas, they slowed.

'This is the one,' said the nearest Warden. He had small green eyes, and a heavy brow. He gazed at Ballas, then laughed – an oddly innocent sound. 'Sweet grief, it *is* – he matches the description, no question.' He glanced at the burning barge, drifting on the Merefed's current. 'It is said that when the Day of Reckoning arrives and a great conflagration incinerates the world, only cockroaches and the pure-hearted will emerge unharmed from the ash. Which do you suppose he is: cockroach, or saint?'

'He does not seem the pious sort,' said another Warden.

'That is true,' murmured the green-eyed Warden. Springing forward, he kicked Ballas in the stomach. Ballas sank to his knees. 'Tell me: what was your crime? Every Warden in Druine is hunting you. So what did you do, hm? Piss in the font at some Soriterath chapel? Bugger a Blessed Master?'

Ballas's gaze flicked from Warden to Warden. He did not speak.

'Oh, come now,' said the Warden who'd kicked Ballas. 'Speak freely. What have you got to lose? Soon you will be dead. Unburden yourself.'

Ballas stayed silent.

'Very well,' sighed the same Warden. 'It doesn't matter, anyway. I am sure that we shall learn what you did soon enough. Perhaps, when we deliver your head to the Blessed Masters, we shall be let in on the secret.' He raised his sword high, preparing for a neck-cleaving stroke.

'I attacked a Blessed Master,' said Ballas suddenly.

The Warden paused, his sword still raised. 'You did what?'

'I slashed a Master's face in half,' said Ballas, quietly. 'A single swipe of a sharp blade . . . I don't know if I killed him or not. I imagine the Church uses Druine's best physicians. So perhaps he hasn't yet entered the Eltheryn Forest.'

The Warden lowered his sword until its tip rested on the ground. '*When* did this happen? Describe it to me.'

'It's a simple story,' said Ballas. 'Several nights ago, I was due to be nailed to the Penance Oak. This didn't seem like a good idea. When the Blessed Master tried to stop me escaping, what choice did I have but to lash out?'

'Small wonder that the Masters crave your death,' said the Warden, visibly impressed. 'No one knows that a Master has been wounded – or killed.'

'There're other things the Church would like to hide,' said Ballas.

'Such as?' The Warden was genuinely curious.

'The Masters have a tame Lectivin. He assists them at the Penance Oak. He uses a strange magick to torture the victim's soul . . .'

The Warden gaped. 'This cannot be—'

Leaping to his feet, Ballas whipped a dagger from his belt and rammed it into the green-eyed Warden's guts. Snatching up the fallen man's sword, he advanced on the two remaining Wardens. The men backed away, shocked. Then they held their ground.

Ballas looked from man to man.

The Warden on Ballas's right side charged, his sword raised aloft. The blade sliced down – but Ballas lifted the stabbed Warden's sword, deflecting the blow. He kicked the oncoming Warden in the stomach. Then he swung the sword sideways into his neck. The man fell instantly, his neck half-severed.

Ballas glanced across the river. On the far bank, the three remaining Wardens had raised their bows and were taking aim.

Ballas looked at the last standing Warden on his side of the Merefed. The Warden stared back at him. Then he flung down his sword and turned to run away. Ballas dived forwards, tackling him to the ground.

He jumped back to his feet and kicked the fallen Warden hard in the crotch. Grasping the man's dropped sword, he hacked through the Warden's right hand. Blood gouted from the stump. The Warden screamed. Dragging him to his feet, Ballas curled his forearm around his throat. Then he unsheathed the Warden's dagger and touched the blade-tip to his eye socket.

'You,' he grunted, 'will be my shield.' Ballas glanced at the other Wardens, their bows poised. 'Do not struggle, and I promise I will spare you. Understand?'

'Y-yes,' stammered the injured Warden.

Slowly, Ballas crossed the bridge to the far bank. The bow-wielding Wardens watched him uneasily. Two of them lowered their weapons. The third shifted his aim slightly, until the arrowhead pointed directly at Ballas's face.

'Don't be stupid, Haren!' shouted the Warden whom Ballas held. 'Don't be an idiot!'

'I always aim true,' said the other Warden. 'I can hit him easily from here!'

'More likely you will hit *me*!'

'There is no danger,' said the arrow-aiming Warden. 'No danger at—'

Ballas sank his dagger into his human shield's eye socket, then dived sideways. The mutilated Warden staggered, howling. In panic, the Warden called Haren released his arrow. It sank into the half-blinded Warden's ribs.

The other two Wardens stared. Moments ago, they had been the aggressors. Now Ballas sensed their fear. Three of their colleagues were dead. They felt their own vulnerability – and their mortality – coursing through their souls.

The three surviving Wardens hesitated – then they ran towards their horses, tied to a rowan tree fifty paces away.

Ballas's gaze followed them. Then it alighted on a previously unseen figure: a fat, bald-headed priest, seated upon a black mare. Frowning, Ballas realised he had seen him before. It took him a moment to remember where.

The tavern, he thought. He failed to settle his bill; the tavern-master called to him . . .

The priest glanced at the retreating Wardens. Then he jabbed his heels into his mare's flanks. Turning, he started out across the moorland.

Moving quickly, Ballas unsheathed the sword of the last Warden killed in the skirmish. Taking a few steps, he hurled the weapon through the air. The flat of the blade struck the back of the fleeing holy man's head. He toppled from the saddle, landing awkwardly on the ground.

Ballas approached.

The priest lay upon his back. As he drew closer, Ballas noticed an unnatural stillness in the holy man's posture. He was not dead: his chest rose and fell and, staring at the sky, he blinked furiously. Yet he stayed strangely immobile.

Ballas halted at the priest's side.

'Help me,' pleaded the holy man. 'Please – you must help me. My arms, my legs . . . they are numb! I can feel nothing! Nor can I move.'

'Help you?' asked Ballas. 'Were you not here to witness my death?'

The priest winced. 'Whatever your crime, I will arrange a pardon. Help me, and you need no longer fear the Church.'

'You're a clergyman of influence?' asked Ballas.

'Yes, *yes*! Many think that one day I shall be invested as a Master.'

'Liar,' said Ballas flatly. Picking up the sword, he thrust its blade through the holy man's neck. The priest's eyes glazed. His expression slackened.

Kneeling, Ballas unfastened a coin pouch from the priest's belt. Inside nestled a couple of gold pieces. Attaching the pouch to his own belt, Ballas strode back to the river bank.

He was part-way through looting the body of the Warden he'd stabbed in the eye when there came the noise of splashing water.

A stocky, black-bearded figure clambered out of the Merefed. The barge-master.

Ballas paused, staring.

The barge-master shook drops of water from his fingertips – a bizarre gesture for one already soaked to the skin. He spat on the grass. Then he looked up.

He blinked.

'You're alive,' he said flatly. Then he looked at the slain Wardens. 'And many others are not.' He glanced at the barge, drifting steadily down the Merefed. Flames capered upon the deck. It resembled a pagan funeral craft, Ballas thought.

'Why . . . why were the Wardens attacking us?' asked the barge-master.

'I don't know,' said Ballas and shrugged.

'My cargo is legal. I transport only silks, wine, a few items of jewellery . . . Nothing forbidden by Papal Law. Damn everything, but why did they murder my oarsmen, and burn my boat? I cannot see why— Look out!'

Ballas spun round. The half-blinded Warden lunged at him. By some miracle of resilience, he had not perished. Wrong-footed, Ballas slipped on the wet grass. The Warden slashed left-handed with his retrieved dagger at Ballas's face – then he toppled backwards as the barge-master hurtled into him. The Warden sprawled on the ground. Wrestling the dagger from his hand, the barge-master drove the blade hilt-deep into his throat. The Warden spasmed. Then, finally, grew still.

The barge-master stood. 'A strong fellow,' he said, eyeing the Warden's injuries. 'A knife in his eye, one hand chopped off, an arrow in his chest – and still he does not die.' The barge-master helped Ballas to his feet and said, 'A mistake or not, for certain the Wardens now have *real* cause to arrest me – and *you*, my friend.' He gestured to the corpses. 'This has been a black day for the Church. Oh – ha! And it gets blacker still.' He pointed across the moors. 'A dead priest. Is that not the maggot in the rotten meat?'

Suddenly, thunder boomed. Lightning bolts flashed along the horizon.

The barge-master laughed. 'We have angered the creator-god,' he said, shaking his head. 'Worse, we have angered the Church. Where are we to go?'

Ballas stared broodingly at him. 'I don't crave company.'

'Nor do I,' said the barge-master. 'But, like it or not, our fates are now intertwined. It is safer, for both of us, if we travel together. Besides, you are bleeding. What is it, your shoulder blade? Let me look.' He moved behind Ballas. 'That is deep – very deep. I can see bone through that gash in your flesh.'

'It'll heal,' said Ballas.

'Only if it is stitched,' replied the barge-master. 'And it is in too awkward a position for you to reach. Look: the hour is late, a storm is upon us – it would be sensible to find shelter, somewhere that I can tend your wound. Then we could discuss what to do next.'

Ballas inwardly conceded that, yes, that would be sensible. His wound needed closing up . . . and, if the Wardens returned, it would be far better if he were not alone.

Ballas glanced to the opposite river bank, where Garrullon lay. A short distance away, Sparrow floated face down, arrows sticking from his neck and back.

Ballas and the barge-master took what coin the fallen Wardens possessed, retrieved their horses, and rode northwards through the thickening storm. As night fell, and lightning bolts provided the only illumination, they found a deserted barn beside an untenanted farmhouse. First they inspected the farmhouse, expecting it to provide good shelter. But there was no roofing thatch and every room was exposed to the sky. So the two men took themselves and their horses into the barn.

From a small store in the farmhouse, Ballas gathered a bundle of firewood. In the middle of the barn floor, within a ring of stones, he started a fire.

They found medical provisions in a Warden's saddlebag: a needle, thread, and powdered herbs that, when mixed with water, would become a wound-disinfecting paste.

The barge-master heated the needle in the fire. Then he stitched Ballas's arrow-scored shoulder blade. Once the treatment was finished they took from the saddlebags a couple of pieces of dried beef, which they ate seated at the fire's edge.

Also in the saddlebag was a map of Druine. Ballas gazed at it in the firelight.

'Making plans, hm?' asked the barge-master.

Ballas glanced at him. 'My sister is still sick,' he said. 'I've got to travel to Redreathe. That much has not changed.'

'I don't know what I am going to do,' said the barge-master. 'Until this afternoon, I had my own set of plans. I would work the barge for another five years. Then I would retire. I have a little money put aside – not enough to live on but sufficient to help sustain me if I invested it wisely. I intended to find myself a young wife, who would give me six strong, healthy children. Now, though . . .' He sighed. 'I have killed a Warden. Everything is different.'

'No one except me saw you take his life.'

'True,' nodded the barge-master. 'Yet I still do not know *why* we were attacked. What if the Church is hunting me? I will not lie to you: I have led a sinful life. I have fornicated; in my wake, there are a hundred . . . a thousand cuckolded men. What if one was a friend of a priest of influence? Or a Servant of the Church? Might they not persuade the Church to exact revenge upon me?'

'I doubt it,' said Ballas quietly. 'Your sins are minor. They don't threaten the Church's power.'

The barge-master's shoulders sagged.

Ballas looked at the map again. His gaze wandered from the northern mountains to the southern coast; from moorland tracts to marshland swamps. He knew he couldn't run for ever. The Wardens would pursue him until he was captured – or killed. If he remained in Druine they would eventually find him.

He glanced up. The barge-master stared at him.

'A problem?' asked Ballas.

'No,' said the barge-master. 'I am tired, that is all. It has been a trying day . . .' He yawned. 'I must sleep.'

Ballas too felt oppressively tired. Sitting back against the barn wall, he closed his eyes. He began to drowse – then a flash of blue-silver light flared in his mind's eye. Ballas jerked wide awake. He looked around the shadowed, firelit barn. Then he sighed.

'Lightning,' he murmured. 'That is all.' Tiredness swept over him. He shut his eyes, and drifted off to sleep.

The following morning dawn light woke Ballas. Sitting upright, he rubbed his face and felt the stitches in his shoulder blade tug tight. He grunted. Then he glanced across the barn. The barge-master slept curled up in the corner, his head pillowed on his arm. Muttering, Ballas got to his feet. He had slept right through the night. Yet he felt groggy, as if he had not slumbered at all. He realised that he had been dreaming. He could not recall the dream itself, although he knew somehow that it had been strange, and troublesome. Frowning, he tried hard to remember. He felt it floating just beneath the surface of his memory – and its presence irritated him: he *wanted* to know what the dream had been.

Yet it remained elusive.

Scowling, Ballas walked towards the barn door, intending to step outside and urinate. Yet movement caught his eye. The day's fresh light seeped through gaps between the wooden wall-planks – and this light had been blocked fleetingly by a dark shape. Cursing softly, Ballas peered through a gap. Two of the Wardens who had escaped the previous day stood outside. They had exchanged their short-bows for lethal-looking crossbows.

Ballas hurried to the barge-master. Clamping a hand over his mouth, he shook him awake.

The barge-master's eyes flicked open.

'They've found us,' said Ballas, removing his hand.

'The Wardens?'

'Two of those who fled yesterday,' said Ballas, nodding. 'Clearly they don't want to go back empty-handed to the Masters.'

'What do we do?'

'Fight,' replied Ballas, shrugging.

'That's easy for you,' said the barge-master. 'You are as broad and heavy as a bull. But me? My talents lie elsewhere.' He gazed through a gap in the planks. 'Sweet grief, they have crossbows. I have seen such weapons in use. They are fearsome contraptions: once I witnessed a bolt slam clean through a full-grown boar's head. I thought such devices were outlawed by the Blessed Masters.'

'They are,' said Ballas, casting around for something – anything – he could use as a weapon. He found a pitchfork propped upright in the corner. The prongs were rusty but sharp-tipped. He tested its weight in his palm. It would have to do. 'Find yourself something to fight with,' he told the barge-master.

The barge-master did not move from the gap. 'What can we do?' he asked softly. 'We are even in numbers – but mismatched in weaponry. What are our tactics to be, big man?' There was an odd note in his voice.

'I'll think of something,' said Ballas.

The barge-master moved away from the wall and crept cautiously through the barn, seeking a makeshift weapon. Ballas stared through the gap. The Wardens were discussing how best to attack. But Ballas had a plan of his own. The Wardens were nervous. Even now, their crossbows were aimed at the barn door. Ballas suspected that as soon as the door opened at least one Warden would release a bolt. To ensure that the remaining bolt was dispatched effectively, the second Warden would need a proper target – an enemy to aim at.

Ballas glanced at the barge-master. He had found a plank that, split lengthwise, would make a useful cudgel.

'Will this do?' asked the barge-master, raising the plank.

'Aye,' replied Ballas – knowing the barge-master would have no opportunity to use it.

The barn was freezing cold. Yet sweat glistened on the barge-master's face. 'Are the Wardens still out there? Where are they standing?'

Ballas looked out through the gap. 'They haven't budged,' he began – then toppled sideways as something slammed into the side of his head.

The barge-master stood over him.

'What—' began Ballas.

The barge-master smashed the plank-edge into Ballas's forehead. The impact rolled the big man on to his back.

'You are not to be trusted,' said the barge-master. 'That was Garrullon and Sparrow's mistake. They believed you were helping them escape –' another blow, this one across Ballas's cheekbone '– yet, in truth, they were merely arrow fodder. Their deaths provided you with a few seconds of safety. The Wardens' arrows had been loosed; they needed time to reload. From the water, I witnessed everything. And I think you have been plotting to use me in a similar fashion. Well, my friend, it shall not happen.' He swung the plank once more – this time, it struck between Ballas's legs.

Dropping the plank, the barge-master moved to the door.

'What are you doing?' groaned Ballas.

'I am going out there,' said the barge-master mildly.

'Don't be a fool,' retorted Ballas. 'Last night, you whined you didn't know why the Wardens attacked the barge. You wondered if they were hunting you . . .'

'I spoke those words,' agreed the barge-master. 'But I fear that, as is my tendency, I was being insincere. I heard you tell the Wardens of your sin. I confess its magnitude impressed me. You attacked a Master: few men can make an equal boast. And that talk of a Lectivin, in the Church's employ . . . That is intriguing. But it is none of my business. It matters only that I live. And if my life depends on betrayal . . .' He shrugged. Slowly, he half-opened the barn door. Then he thrust out his empty hands so the Wardens could see he was unarmed. He shouted to them: 'I am surrendering. Allow me to come out: I am not the man you seek. He is in here, and incapacitated. Act quickly, and he will not trouble you.'

The barge-master slipped outdoors. Ballas listened for the dull *thunk* of a crossbow bolt sinking into a living body. Yet it seemed the Wardens had believed the barge-master. Groaning, Ballas got on to all fours. He looked through the gap. The barge-master was talking with the Wardens, pointing towards the barn.

The Wardens glanced at each other. Then they grinned.

Cursing, Ballas got unsteadily to his feet. The barge-master's blows to his head had dazed him. The barn seemed to roll and tilt like a seashell tumbled by an ocean current. Stooping, he seized the pitchfork. His hands were blood-greased. He wiped the dark fluid on his tunic. Then he gripped the haft, holding the pitchfork horizontal. Leaning heavily against a pillar, he waited.

Both Wardens entered at the same moment.

An instant later the pitchfork plunged into the nearest Warden's chest. He gazed at the implement, a look of bemused confusion on his face. He touched the pitchfork with quivering fingertips and looked at Ballas, perplexed. Then he sank to the floor, next to the crossbow he'd dropped. As he did so, Ballas sprinted forward, wrenched out the pitchfork and stabbed the prongs into the second Warden's throat. His crossbow clattered from his hands. Ballas withdrew the pitchfork, and plunged it deep into the Warden's guts. He dropped, sprawling lifelessly across his colleague.

Panting, Ballas glanced to his right.

The barge-master was watching him through the barn door. His lips were working noiselessly. His eyes were glazed; his stare was that of a man who knows he is already dead. He looked at the Wardens. Then he turned and ran.

Moving unhurriedly, Ballas picked up one of the crossbows. A black-fletched bolt nestled in the loosing gully. Ballas stepped casually outdoors.

The barge-master was fifty yards away, sprinting over the moors. Lifting the crossbow, Ballas squinted, taking a careful aim. Then, very slowly, he pulled the trigger.

A heartbeat later the barge-master fell. Blinking, Ballas walked over to him.

A bolt stuck out from the back of the barge-master's knee-joint. He writhed, his stubby-fingered hand clutching at moor-grass.

'Oh, sweet grief,' he said, his voice cracking. 'Please, please . . . Be merciful! Let me help you. I have friends in the north: they will be of great use . . .'

'Of great use?' sighed Ballas, sounding both bored and weary. Kneeling, he gripped the bolt, then wrenched it from the barge-master's leg. The barge-master howled. Ballas snapped the blood-slick quarrel into the crossbow and swiftly pulled the weapon's cord tight again to reset it, ready to fire once more. Using the toe of his boot, he rolled the barge-master on to his back.

'I can help you get to Belthirran!' screamed the barge-master, his gaze fixed on the arrowhead.

Ballas squinted. 'Belthirran?' he asked, uncertain if he had heard correctly.

'Belthirran,' echoed the barge-master. 'The Land Beyond the Mountains. That is what you want, is it not? All last night, you were muttering its name in your sleep.'

From deep in Ballas's memory, his dream floated up – momentarily as bright and vivid as a freshly woven tapestry.

He had been seated on a stone ledge shot through with red-tinged copper veins. A green valley sprawled below. There were farmhouses and cattle fields. In the far distance, figures moved. Though he couldn't discern their features, he sensed they were happy. And contented. Those feelings washed over Ballas. Upon his high ledge, he felt at ease. He was gazing upon Belthirran – and it soothed him.

Belthirran.

The name spun through Ballas's mind. A place untroubled by Wardens. Or blue-robed priests. A place where no sermons were intoned, no Scarrendestin effigies gleamed.

He looked intently at the barge-master.

'Spare me,' said the wounded man, 'and I will prove of some use. I swear it!'

'You know the way to Belthirran?'

'No,' replied the barge-master, 'but I know of men who do. Years ago, I traded in forbidden texts. Documents outlawed by the Church. Treatises on magic, astrology, mathematics . . . Back then, this profession could make a man rich. Among scholars there was a hunger for such things. Some of the texts concerned Belthirran. Some were descriptions of the Land Beyond the Mountains. Others had maps showing routes over the mountains. A few of these may still exist. There is a man in Keltherimyn who'll know where they are.'

'What's his name?'

The barge-master stared meaningfully at the bolt. 'Please . . .'

Grunting, Ballas lowered the crossbow.

'He is called Lugen Crask. Like myself, he was a smuggler. But he was far more deeply involved than I was.'

'Lugen Crask,' repeated Ballas softly.

'He is well known in Keltherimyn. He was captured by the Church once – but they spared him. Most smugglers were sent to the gallows. But Crask merely served a prison sentence. He spent two decades in a cell in Salworth.'

Ballas peered at the barge-master. And decided that he was telling the truth. The man trembled and every muscle in his face was taut. He was too frightened to weave such an elaborate lie.

'Lugen Crask, at Keltherimyn,' said Ballas, lodging the names in his memory.

The barge-master nodded.

Ballas raised the crossbow, aiming at the mid-point between the barge-master's brows.

'What?' The barge-master stared uncomprehendingly. 'You promised—'

'I promised nothing.'

'Bastard,' breathed the barge-master. Bitterness crept into his voice. 'I hope you die, you bastard. I hope the Wardens find you and kill you, and your death is a torment.' Suddenly he laughed – a half-hysterical sound. 'Sooner or later you *will* be caught. For there is nowhere you can escape to. Belthirran is a myth, a rumour. True, some men *claim* to have been there. But they are not to be trusted. They are madmen, liars, fantasists.' He swallowed hard. 'Abandon dreams of Belthirran. The Wardens won't rest till your blood is on their knives. You will be ripped apart.'

'Perhaps,' agreed Ballas. Then he squeezed the crossbow's trigger.

Chapter 9

And across the land, this pale pilgrim
Moved, caring nothing for good
But following the path of evil, and seeking
The place of power where the true Pilgrims
Were to coincide . . .

For three days Ballas rode northwards, with a stealth that was rapidly becoming habitual. He avoided the wheel-rutted roadways as far as he could. The lightly trampled paths, cutting through the green-yellow moorland grass, were less dangerous because they were less frequently ridden upon. Yet Ballas again chose caution, riding where he could through hills or beside rivers. His only company was the black mare on which he sat, stolen from a slain Warden outside the deserted barn. And the creatures that dwelled on the windswept, rain-blasted moors. Pheasants, deer, badgers – even those free-wandering grey wolves that, for the time being, had escaped extermination by the Pilgrim Church.

At night, Ballas bedded down in places that provided meagre comfort. Caves, forests, the gaps between tall lichen-blotched limestone blocks – they all gave shelter of a kind. In the moments before sleep – and as he rode, through grey, drizzly daylight – he thought of Belthirran: the Land Beyond the Mountains.

Ballas suspected it was a heathen land. A place unsullied by the Pilgrim Church. Whenever he thought of Belthirran, he saw his dream. He saw fields, cattle, far-off cook-fire smoke. A place of ease, of rest.

Small wonder that he should think so often of Belthirran. That it should glimmer in his mind's eye when he woke at dawn. That it should come to life when he settled to sleep at dusk.

Yet Ballas did not know what Belthirran truly was. He felt a near-overwhelming urge to gallop northwards to the mountains. Yet he acted with restraint. It was unwise, he thought, to behave as if he knew for certain that Belthirran existed. The Land Beyond the Mountains was a rumour. A thing of speculation . . . of dreams. It might not exist. Or might not exist as he imagined it. Beyond the Garsbrack Mountains there might be nothing save ocean water. Or dry, dead soil, unable to support life. Or a wilderness, wolf-prowled, boar-haunted – a place too fierce for man to dwell within.

Ballas hungered for Belthirran. Yet he had to be certain it would serve his purposes.

After three days Ballas reached Keltherimyn. The home of Lugen Crask.

Keltherimyn hunkered on the edge of a north-eastern bend of the Merefed River. It resembled any small dock-town in the Realm. The buildings were made from grey stone and were topped with thatch. The roads were largely unpaved, a lattice-work of frost-toughened mud. Ballas arrived in the late afternoon. Already, autumnal gloom was settling. His hood pulled up, he rode through the town, wondering how best to locate Lugen Crask.

Where could a former smuggler of forbidden texts be found?

In Ballas's experience, a man who had once employed his talents illegally often, once his taste for danger had vanished, practised them in a perfectly lawful manner. Maybe Lugen Crask was an archivist. A librarian. Or a tutor to a wealthy merchant's children.

There were no archives in Keltherimyn. No library. Nor was there any suggestion that, in this impoverished place, there was anyone who could afford a tutor for their offspring. Scowling, Ballas rode along every lane, street and ginnel, finding only taverns, butcher shops, barber-surgeons – and, to the north, a market square that, at this late hour, was shutting down.

Muttering to himself, Ballas decided he ought to find lodgings. Or, for safety's sake, a warm, inconspicuous place: a stable, again – or maybe the leaf-sheltered roots of a hedge where he could doss down and sleep unnoticed.

It would be a cold night, though. Already, he was shivering. His clothes were damp and he needed something to warm him.

Riding along a lane, he saw a cart travelling the opposite way. A young man with curling brown hair was on foot, leading the horse by its bridle. On the back of the cart nestled a dozen whisky flagons, and various other spirits. Ballas touched the purse tucked behind his belt. His fingertips met hard-rimmed coins – four copper pennies, stolen from the dead Wardens, and the two gold pieces taken from the priest.

That was good. He could at least pay for his drink. He would not need to rob the young man.

'You there,' called Ballas, drawing closer. 'That whisky, is it for sale?'

The young man slowed. 'Two pennies for a flagon. I brewed it myself; it is fine stuff.'

Remaining in his saddle, Ballas proffered two copper coins. Reaching up, the young man took them.

'Your face is not familiar, my friend,' said the young man, walking to the back of the cart.

'I'm from the south,' replied Ballas, thinking quickly. 'I'm on an errand that irks me.'

'Few visit Keltherimyn for the fun of it,' said the young man, picking up a flagon. 'Always, they are driven by need. Why have you come here?'

Ballas hesitated. 'I'm looking for my uncle.'

'What is his name?'

'Lugen Crask.'

The young man paused. 'Crask?' He held the flagon, standing motionless. Then, as if a spell had broken, he held the container out to Ballas. 'Here,' he said.

'You seem surprised,' observed Ballas, taking the flagon.

'I did not know Crask had any family – except for his daughter. And she is an odd piece.'

'Odd?'

'Withdrawn. Too wise for her years. She looks at people as if they are beasts . . . as if they are eels . . . Ha! I should watch my tongue. For I am speaking of your cousin, am I not?'

Ballas shrugged. 'Speak freely. Me and Crask are bound by blood – not by loyalty. And as for his daughter? We've never met. Our family unravelled long ago, not that it was ever tightly stitched.' He slipped the flagon into his saddlebag. 'I'm here to tell him it's unravelled even further – and irreparably.'

'A death?' said the young man, understanding immediately.

'Crask's brother – my father.'

'I am sorry to hear it. It is a terrible thing, to lose a parent.'

'Where can I find my uncle?'

The young man pointed northwards. 'That direction.'

'What's the street name?'

'Street name? Truly, you haven't spoken with your uncle for some time. He does not live on a street; unless every channel among the reeds counts as one.' The young man smiled. 'He has a cottage out in the marsh. If you'd been here a half-hour earlier, you would have found him in the market. He trades here—'

'Trades? *What* does he trade?' For a moment, Ballas wondered if Crask still smuggled forbidden texts.

'Eels,' said the young man. 'He plucks them from the marsh. And, though I have no love for him, I confess they are the finest in Druine. White-Tooth, Red-eye, Mottled Spider-Crop – he captures them all. Including those commonly thought uncatchable: Skull-Walker, Slender-Alice . . . He has a rare knack. You will find a gate at the marsh's edge. Pass through and tread northwards. Eventually, after a half-mile, you will find your uncle's home.'

With a nod of thanks, Ballas rode through the streets of Keltherimyn to the gate.

Beyond a low fence, the marsh spread out – a rush- and reed-clutched expanse of sodden earth. Pools of water bubbled softly, releasing a pale vapour that lay like gauze upon everything. The day's weak light scarcely pierced it. Instead, it seemed to linger within it, illuminating it from the inside. A strong odour of decay drifted from the marsh. It was a place where everything that lived also rotted. Slimes of decomposition slicked the vegetation.

There was no path into the marsh. No neat line of stones, nor any stretch of raised dry ground. Grunting, Ballas realised the black mare would not walk placidly over the sinking ground and through clinging undergrowth. Dismounting, he stepped out into the swamp.

His leg plunged calf-deep into the waterlogged ground. Muddy liquid surged over his boots, flooding them. The big man swore, loudly. Still cursing, he trudged on a few paces. And noticed a deadening of his words: within the mist, his profanities – though loudly voiced – scarcely sounded. He paused, listening. Every other noise was also muted. Somewhere, a crow croaked; branches creaked; the water glooped – and each sound, usually clear, was weak and brief.

The mist prickled Ballas's skin.

He continued walking. After a time, he glanced back. The gatepost had vanished from view. He took a few more steps, and found it increasingly difficult to lift his feet. Water-dwelling weeds ensnared his ankles. Dragging free a foot, he found black leeches – half a dozen, glossy and gently pulsing – stuck to his boots. He stared. Then he noticed other bits of wildlife upon him. On his breeches, pale-bodied spiders crawled. A long centipede slinked along his sleeve; Ballas knocked it away – then found three beetles, their carapaces a swirling metallic purple, creeping up his tunic front. These too he flicked away.

The creatures did not bother him. Years of sleeping rough had accustomed him to such things. Even before then, as a child living upon a farm, he had been comfortably familiar with all kinds of parasite and insect.

The marsh's fauna did not worry him.

Until something large and heavy bumped against his shin.

He glanced down. Something briefly broke the water's surface. In the mist-cloaked light, it was scarcely discernible: just a sleek glistening flash, there for an instant, then gone, slipping underwater.

An eel. A large one, true enough. As heavy as a small child, perhaps. But just an eel, nonetheless.

For some time, Ballas moved onwards.

Then something coiled tightly around his ankle. He stumbled. Pitching forwards, he swept out his right hand, grasping a willow branch. Reflexively, he thrust out his left hand to balance himself and to break his fall if his grip on the branch failed. His hand splashed wrist-deep into the marsh. Cold swamp-water swept over his skin. Then a sharp pain coursed up his arm.

'Pilgrims' blood!' barked the big man, jerking out his hand.

He peered closely at it. In the thick flesh at the base of his thumb there were four small marks. Each was a neat puncture, made by something needle-sharp. At first they were hardly visible. Only when they started bleeding did Ballas see them properly.

'Bastard,' he muttered. 'Pissing whoreson bastard . . .'

Blood dripped into the water. Below the surface something stirred. An eel's head emerged, as smooth as a ripened plum. Its mouth open, it surged forwards, drinking the blood-drops. Then it sank away.

Scowling, Ballas sucked the bite wound. He drew his sleeve over it so that the cuff absorbed the blood.

He walked quicker now. As he went he concentrated on what he would say to Lugen Crask. He could not tell him the truth. He could not reveal that he had attacked a Blessed Master. That the Church was hunting him. And that the only sanctuary was Belthirran. He needed to construct a lie. But what?

Something else brushed against his shin. Ballas faltered – then he tripped as an eel curled around both ankles. Swearing, he fell face first into the water. He tried to rise but a great weight now lay upon his back.

Eels squirmed around him. Not just one or two. But dozens. He *felt* them. They wrapped themselves around his limbs like shackles. Their smooth-scaled sides slithered against his face. Their muscled flanks nudged him.

Amid so many creatures – amid the ugly smothering horde – he felt a claustrophobia unlike anything he had experienced before. The strong, elastic-bodied eels choked him. Panicking, he twisted, jerked, thrashed out – anything to break their imprisoning hold.

They were strong. Too strong for Ballas.

Yet they suddenly released him.

He scrambled to his feet. A few lingering eels dropped from him. They tumbled reluctantly from his shoulders, arms, legs. One clung doggedly to his wrist. Ballas tore it free and flung it far across the marsh.

He looked down.

Around his legs the water was motionless. Vapour bubbles popped on the surface – but nothing else disturbed the calm.

Ballas wiped water from his eyes. Then he gasped as his fingertips brushed some wound in his forehead. His hand came away wet with blood.

His tunic sleeves were bloodied. His leggings were bloodied. From the wound in his forehead, blood seeped into his eyes.

Ballas suddenly felt weak. The weakness was not the soft feebleness that follows panic. It was infinitely more exhausting. And irresistible.

Grunting, Ballas tugged back his sleeve. He saw exactly what he expected: bite marks. Two sets of four perforations.

He swore.

Lifting his head, he strode forwards. He did not know what type of venom eels carried. Whether it killed. Or paralysed. He did not even know what species of eel had attacked him. More than one kind, he knew. Most had been black-skinned. But others had been scarlet, some deep green.

He had to reach Lugen Crask's home. The eel-catcher – the one-time smuggler of forbidden texts – would have an antidote.

Blinking, Ballas tried to keep his eyes open. Yet he felt too tired. Stumbling, he sank to his knees.

'Come on, damn it,' he urged himself. 'Get a grip . . .' He struggled to his feet – then his legs buckled.

Once more, he lay face down in marsh water. Now, though, he did not attempt to rise. There was no strength left in his arms, his legs. Every tendon might as well have been servered, every muscle cut away.

Water swirled into his mouth. Ballas realised he was drowning. Again, panic surged through him – yet there was nothing he could do.

Darkness crowded in on the edge of his vision. A thick purplish gloom, slowly clouding his sight. The world seemed to spin from under him; he was falling.

The water seethed as the eels returned. Glint-fanged jaws gnawed at Ballas. In the depths of his numbing fatigue, only the pain had clarity.

But that too passed.

The darkness thickened. And, suddenly, there was nothing.

Chapter 10

At every step, the pale pilgrim
Like a phantom shocked each living thing.
The bears and wolves fled the woodlands
As he passed through, as if they saw
Into his soul . . .

Ballas awoke to the smell of decay. Before he opened his eyes, he recognised it as the marsh-stench: the odour of rotting vegetation. In his mind's eye he glimpsed eels. Once more he saw the tubular creatures, locking themselves around him. As if his nerve ends held sensory echoes, he felt again their teeth clamping upon his flesh, their scaly sides brushing against him.

He opened his eyes.

His last memory had been of drowning in marsh water. Yet he was no longer outdoors. He was propped upright on a pallet-bed, in a sparsely furnished room. The floor and walls were made from bare wooden slats. Atop a crude rib-work of rafters, the roof was thatched. Ballas had no inkling how he had arrived there. It didn't trouble him, though. He was growing accustomed to missing patches of memory, whether through violence or too much drink.

But it troubled him when he tried to move and found he could not. The paralysing eel-venom – had it damaged him permanently? Was he now a cripple?

His stomach heaved. In panic, he opened his mouth to shout – and then he realised his immobility had a less worrying cause.

Thick rope bound his arms to his sides. His legs were tied together at the ankles and knees. Another rope crossed his chest, tying him to the pallet-bed.

He struggled against the ropes. They refused to loosen.

At that moment a door opened. A man somewhere in his sixth decade stepped through. His grey-white hair was close-cropped; he sported a pepper-hued beard. His face was heavily lined, yet there was a brisk fluidity to his movements – as if every gesture had to be made quickly. In some men, such indicated nervousness. But this fellow seemed utterly calm. He glanced at Ballas. Then he looked quickly away. Murmuring, he closed the door.

'You are awake,' he said, looking again at the big man.

'Untie me,' said Ballas flatly.

Smiling, the bearded man said, 'You must be thirsty. You drank gutfuls of marsh water, true; but for a day and a night, nothing has passed your lips – except for anti-venom.'

'Old man,' said Ballas thickly, 'do as I tell you: *untie me*.'

As if Ballas had not spoken, the man lifted a cup to his lips. 'Drink,' he said. The fluid inside smelled sweet – like the mingled juices of a dozen fruits. Ballas *was* thirsty but he ignored the offering. Sighing, the other man moved away.

'At first,' he said, 'the ropes were for your benefit. In your blood, there were half a dozen strains of eel venom. Each acts in roughly the same fashion. They relax certain muscles. Namely, those that are useful in self-defence and escape: the arms, legs, and so on. The lungs and heart, however, remain unaffected. The eels in this marsh prefer to dine on *living* flesh, you see. So they render you incapable, while preserving your life. If a man somehow avoids being consumed, and is given an anti-venom, his recovery will be attended by violence. The paralysed muscles spasm. Limbs thrash out, the head snaps back and forth – if the patient is poorly attended, he may kill himself. Or, however unwillingly, damage those very people who seek to help him. You will understand, therefore, that the ropes were necessary.'

'But now I am cured?'

'You are,' said the man, nodding.

'Then untie me.'

The man shook his head. 'Now you are trussed up for *my* benefit. Out here, in the marshes, I have few . . . I have *no* visitors. That pleases me. In Keltherimyn, I am not well liked. There are many who would be pleased by my death. I am tolerated, of course: for who else can catch eels as well as I? There are breeds that only a few people in Druine can lure into their traps. These are in great demand. Their skin is turned into fine leather; their meat, if properly cooked, is a delicacy. In the market place, I sell these eels – for a pittance. The denizens of Keltherimyn then trade them on in Branhurst City, or Ganbrait, or wherever, for colossal profits. Thus I am spared. Thus I am granted peace. Naturally, I cannot dwell among these people. Who would live happily alongside those who despise him? So I live out here, in the marsh. And the eels help me in another way. Some men employ guard dogs to maintain their safety. I, however, have the eels. People rarely even *attempt* to reach me. Which is why,' he looked closely at Ballas, 'you puzzle me.'

'Are you Lugen Crask?'

'That is no secret,' replied the man.

Ballas spoke softly. 'It is said you trade in forbidden texts. Documents outlawed by the Pilgrim Church.'

For a long time, Crask did not speak. 'That is untrue,' he said eventually.

'I have been told—'

'Years ago,' interrupted Crask, with a note of irritation, 'I *did* trade in such documents. I was not alone. There were many of us, throughout Druine. Some were scholars, hungry for "the truth" – whatever that is. Others were merchants, interested only in growing rich. For a while, we thrived. The Church had no inkling of our activities. Arrogant and happy, we basked in the sunlight of freedom; and the shadow of holy justice did not trouble us.' He shrugged. 'Then, one day, we woke to darkness. The Church had grown wise. Many of us were arrested. Our texts were destroyed – or confiscated. And we each paid a high price. Some of us were executed. Myself, I was incarcerated in the prison at Salworth. For twenty years I ate stale bread and drank fouled water. I spoke to no other living soul, except the warder who brought my food. The only light came from a feeble candle on a high ledge. For two decades, I smelled nothing but my own filth and the wet stones of the cell wall.' He lifted his chin. 'Such circumstances force one to reappraise one's philosophy. In that cell, I discovered that money and learning are worthless. *Liberty* is the most valuable thing in life. Upon my release, I vowed never again to jeopardise my freedom.'

He stared hard at Ballas.

'The people of Keltherimyn do not understand this. I am more law-abiding than any of them. Yet they still regard me as a criminal – a defiler of Holy Law.'

'That is why they shun you?'

'Look around you,' said Lugen Crask, as if Ballas had not spoken. 'There are no forbidden texts here. Whatever you want from me – whatever kind of document you require – I cannot assist you.'

Ballas gazed levelly at him. 'I do not seek documents. I seek *knowledge*. Which were you, Crask: merchant or scholar?'

'The true question,' said Crask, 'is what are *you*? A Papal Warden, hm – here to entrap me? Or have the townsfolk sent you to discover evidence that I am *still* a criminal?'

'I am neither of those things,' replied Ballas. 'I have no love for the Wardens. Nor for the townsfolk: a whisky merchant sent me here, without warning me about the eels. My condition,' he glimpsed a bite-mark on his forearm, 'is his doing.'

Crask released a long breath. Then he proffered the cup again. 'Drink this,' he said. 'It will purify your blood. As well as slake your thirst.'

This time Ballas did not refuse. Crask lifted the cup to his lips. Ballas gulped the liquid; it was sweet-tasting, and refreshing.

'Night is falling,' said Crask, moving to the door. 'I must tend my eel traps.'

'You're going to leave me here, tied up like this?'

'As I said, I do not trust you. On the morrow, I shall send for the Wardens. They will remove you from this place.'

'Release me,' said Ballas, alarmed at the prospect of Wardens, 'and I will go of my own accord.'

'You have visited me for a reason,' said Crask sharply. 'Will you abandon your purpose the moment I untie you? I do not think so.'

'If I state my purpose,' said Ballas, 'will you consider it?'

Crask grew very still. A flicker of curiosity crept into his eyes. Touching a knuckle to his lips, he said, 'Very well.'

'I have to know about Belthirran.'

'The Land Beyond the Mountains,' murmured Crask, frowning. 'The fountainhead of rumour, and dreams, and futile speculation. Why does it interest you?'

'My motives are not your concern,' said Ballas. 'But Belthirran – it exists?'

'There is *something* on the other side of the Garsbracks. But what, I cannot say.'

'Some of the forbidden texts must have concerned Belthirran.'

'Many of them did,' agreed Crask. 'But how is one to sift truth from lies? Many of the texts, on all matters, were forgeries – concoctions intended to make unscrupulous merchants rich. If they had no true documents, they quilled false ones. These were circulated throughout Druine, gradually attaining the lustre of truth.' He smiled thinly. 'When the Church arrested me, I had only such fraudulent tracts. That, I think, saved my life. For if I had had *genuine* texts, I would have been hanged.'

'Did you know of anyone who crossed the Garsbracks?'

'Some men claimed to have done so.' Crask shrugged. 'But such accounts cannot be trusted. One contradicts another – and none provides evidence. Some contained maps of supposedly safe routes over the mountains. If anyone followed them, they did not return. Which, I suppose, may indicate either success or failure.'

Ballas licked his lips. 'Where can I find such maps?'

'Most will be in the Church's hands – or they will have been destroyed. A few may be scattered throughout Druine. But I don't know where.' He opened the door. 'Now, I must go to my traps.'

'You said you would release me . . .'

'I said I would *consider* it.' Crask gazed evenly at Ballas. 'You are seeking forbidden knowledge. It would be unwise of me to have such a criminal roaming freely about my home.'

Lugen Crask left the room, closing the door behind him.

Crask entered the next-door room. In an iron bowl, coals burned, warming the air. A young woman sat cross-legged upon a rug close by. She was tying her red hair into a ponytail. She looked up as Crask came in. Her face was slim and delicately featured. She had high cheekbones and a broad mouth, and even though her skin was pale she did not look unhealthy. She finished tying her ponytail, then lowered her hands to her lap. She watched Crask attentively, her hazel eyes reflecting light from the glowing coals.

'You were eavesdropping,' said Crask plainly.

'Of course, father,' she replied, smiling faintly. 'The stranger is as much my concern as yours. After all, it was I who saved him.'

Crask nodded.

'Why won't you help him?' she asked simply.

'He is a fugitive,' replied Crask, taking a stitched leather coat from a chair back. 'When I mentioned the Wardens, he reacted strangely. A look of alarm crossed his face.'

'I am surprised it could be discerned through the bruises,' said his daughter.

'It was in his eyes,' said Crask, indicating his own. 'It was visible even though they were bloodshot.'

'And it proves nothing,' said his daughter, folding her arms. 'Wardens are not always the most wholesome of people. A certain wariness is understandable. Look at Jaspar Grethinne. He is a drunk, a gambler, his justice is arbitrary – and in the performance of his duties, he is corrupt.'

'That is true,' murmured Crask. 'I doubt whether he will remove our guest without payment of some sort. Let us hope we have a good harvest tonight. We can pay him in eels, yes? Now, are you coming?'

Rising, the young woman drew on her own coat and they stepped outside.

Heresh followed Lugen Crask through the marsh. In her right hand she held a lantern. Its light, yellow and sickly, reached out only yards before the mist absorbed it. But, like her father, she knew the marsh well. They had dwelled there, amid vapours, rushes and eels, for ten years. In daylight every clump of vegetation – every reed-patch and tussock – was familiar to her. And in darkness, she read through her boot soles the character of the ground. She recognised every submerged stone, every root-tangle and dip and rise of the swamp. This was her home.

She gazed at her father's back. A furled net was draped over his shoulder. Under his arm he held a small leather sack. He walked quickly, his boots splashing in the water.

Sunk in the marsh were ruins. An ancient building, too tumbledown to be identified, had been swallowed by the yielding ground. Here and there, sections of masonry still protruded. It was this, in part, that enabled Crask to catch eels normally considered elusive.

They halted at a channel of white rock. Heresh supposed it was a drainage duct of some sort: it was simply a long trench of pale stonework terminating in a wall. Glancing over, her father tossed the net to her. Then he upended the sack into the channel.

A tangle of cow-guts tumbled out. Sniffing, Crask stepped back.

There was nothing to do now except wait.

After a time, there was a far-off splashing noise. And a busy rustling of reeds, as if a strong breeze was blowing though them. Gradually, the noises grew louder. In the moonlight, distant rush-tips quivered. Thin ripples spread over the water's surface. Heresh stepped back from the channel.

'They are coming,' she said.

'I hear them,' replied her father, softly.

A moment later, eels surged into the channel. The slick-bodied creatures seethed, each one intercoiling with its neighbours. They rushed towards the cow-guts, their bulbous heads rising from the water. Heresh knew that many of them had exotically coloured skins – blues, pinks, oranges – yet, in the moonlight, they all appeared black. The first eels reached the bait; their maws opened, exposing needle-fine teeth. Over the seething water rose munching sounds.

Crask draped the net over the channel, fastening it to pegs driven into the masonry. One end of the net was weighted with stones. Grasping it, Heresh walked to the point where the channel met the marsh. She dropped the net, trapping the eels in the channel.

Within moments, the cow-guts were devoured. The eels turned around and started to swim back to the marsh – only to find that the net blocked their way. They surged against it, then swam mindlessly back and forth along the channel.

By dawn, they would be dead. These eels – rare, brightly coloured – thrived only in hot climes. They survived Druine's cold by staying near warm-water vents in the marsh-bed. When tempted by food, though, they would venture into cold water, returning once they had eaten. Now, trapped in the channel, where the water was icy, they would perish. Heresh would come back at first light and collect them. Only in such a fashion could these venomous species be harvested safely.

The residents of Keltherimyn wondered how the eels were caught. Some believed knowledge from forbidden texts was used. Magical rituals from the Distant East. Eel-slaughtering spells from the tropics. Heresh smiled. How would they respond if they knew the truth? If they were told of the simple net-and-cold-water trick devised by her father?

Heresh watched the eels.

'Come,' said her father, touching her shoulder. 'The night is cold, and I am tired.'

'What if the stranger proves troublesome?' asked Heresh, as they trod back toward the cottage.

'Troublesome?'

'He is trussed up,' said Heresh, 'in an uncomfortable fashion. In truth, he is our prisoner. From the looks of him, I doubt he's very happy about it.'

'He will not stir all night. I fed him a mix of galbore and falcharon . . .'

'A sedative?'

'I told him it was a blood-purifier.' Crask smiled faintly. 'I promised it would aid recovery.' He sighed. 'It was not so great a lie, my girl. It may not help him, but it will assist us. And it is more vaccine than remedy for it will prevent a plague of violence befalling us. He will snooze like an exhausted child, and disturb us not at all.'

'And in the morning, when he wakes? He will know he has been poisoned. His skull will ache from the galbore and falcharon. He may even grow mildly feverish.'

'What of it? When he wakes, he will be the Wardens' problem. Let Jaspar Grethinne deal with him.'

The day had started badly for Jaspar Grethinne.

At dawn a cacophony of magpies had roused him. Perched on his windowsill, they had *shreck-shreck*ed so loudly that it had seemed his skull, made brittle by a hangover, would shatter. Cracking open his eyes, the Warden Commander had found himself sprawled upon his living-room floor.

He had groaned – a deep, heartfelt noise of pain.

A man could gauge his drunkenness in different ways. The degree to which his speech slurred or his footsteps reeled were decent indicators. So too was the number of arm-wrestling bouts he initiated. And the women he endeavoured – clumsily, humiliatingly – to seduce.

The most reliable, in Grethinne's experience, was far simpler. A *tipsy* man always found his way to his bed. But a truly drunken man – a man savagely, almost suicidally soused – slept where he collapsed. It did not matter where. On a road, in a ditch, or in the middle of a wheat field – a truly ale-frazzled man was equally content.

The previous night, Grethinne had been ale-frazzled.

He had been gambling, too. A huge mistake, for a drunken man. Yet one a drunken man often made.

Struggling upright, Grethinne's gaze focused on a table close to the hearth. Two wooden dice rested upon it. He winced, recalling the extent of his losses. With a bellyful of ale, he had grown preposterously self-confident. Mistress Fortune guided his hand – he had been certain of it. Thus he had bet a month's wages on a single throw. When he lost, he presumed it had been an aberration – that Mistress Fortune had blinked. So, on the next throw, he had staked his Commander's dagger with its ruby-decorated hilt: a weapon, part ceremonial, part practical, bestowed by the Church on all Commanders. For ten years it had been his prized possession. Like his red shoulder-stripes, it represented his sole achievement in life. He had worn it, hip-sheathed, with deep pride. He kept it well polished, so that when light struck it – when the pale iron flashed and the rubies sparkled – others would be reminded exactly what he was.

And Grethinne too would be reminded.

Perhaps he lived in Keltherimyn – a festering town, peopled by idiots. But he was a *Warden Commander*. A man of power. Of influence. Every slack-jawed, dull-witted denizen knew it. Few men respected Grethinne. But all feared him. And he found that immensely gratifying.

Yet, at the gambling table, all men were equal. There was no special dispensation in tournaments of luck for Warden Commanders. He had lost his wages. And his dagger.

As Grethinne washed and then got dressed in his Scarrendestin-blazoned tunic, he brooded upon these matters.

He sensed that, as his day had started poorly, it would continue in a similar fashion.

He was mistaken.

The marsh-dwelling former convict, Lugen Crask, was waiting at the guardhouse. He brought incredible news. News that Grethinne, convinced of his own ill luck, scarcely dared believe.

Crask had a stranger imprisoned in his home and, fearing that he might be violent – and a lawbreaker – requested that the man should be removed by Wardens. In return, Crask offered Grethinne a bribe: a basketful of rare eels.

In itself, this was good news. Grethinne could sell the eels for a small fortune. Enough to pay off his gambling debts. Enough, more importantly, to buy back his dagger with its jewelled hilt.

When Crask described the stranger, however, Grethinne's heart leaped. Crask spoke graphically of the man's appearance: very tall, very broad, very ugly. A face and body covered with scars, old and new. And an accent from a rustic corner of Druine: Hernshire, Crask suggested – or Hearthfall.

Hearthfall.

On hearing this, fireworks went off in Grethinne's mind. Several days ago, he – like every other Warden Commander – had received an urgent edict from the Blessed Masters, stating that a dangerous fugitive was at large who, if encountered, should be exterminated. They did not disclose the fugitive's crime – but for such an edict to be issued, it was clearly serious. How serious had been apparent from the sweat-lathered state of the horse on which the courier who'd delivered the message had ridden into Keltherimyn. While his mount was being fed and watered, the courier had told Grethinne that similar alerts were going out all over Druine by whatever means were fastest: messenger pigeons, elite horseback riders, even the semaphore and heliograph towers used only in times of national emergency to get news to the remotest parts of the country. The fugitive's name was Anhaga Ballas. And his description matched exactly that given by Lugen Crask.

Grethinne's sour mood evaporated. Not only was the fugitive in Crask's home, but he was trussed up – and *drugged*. Crask had fed him a powerful sedative; at present he was slumbering happily, like a baby.

Gathering four of his best men, Grethinne ordered Crask to take him to his cottage.

Soon the Warden Commander was trudging through marshland. His leggings were mud-splashed. Under his tunic he sweated fiercely.

Everything was dark water, rotting plant life, mist . . . and eels. Grethinne hadn't seen any of the creatures. Yet he sensed them, drifting under the surface. They were watching him – for they watched *all* things in the marsh. The marsh was their universe. And every human was an intruder. They worried Grethinne. Even the dead specimens, on Crask's market stalls, made him uneasy. He could not quite say why. Perhaps it was their tiny bubble-curved eyes. Or their unearthly sleekness. Maybe it was their sheer *number*: a solitary eel was not a fearsome thing. But they always moved in writhing hordes . . . a slithering infinity of glossy, limbless forms.

'Crask,' said Grethinne, 'are you certain we are safe?'

'Of course,' replied the eel-catcher, several paces ahead. 'Tread where I tread, and all will be well.'

Grethinne glanced at the other Wardens. They too seemed uneasy. The Commander spat into the water.

'Crask,' he called out, 'this is a foul place. How can you live here?'

'I don't have much choice,' replied Crask. 'As well you know.' Halting, he pointed at a few dark rocks sticking up from the water. 'Walk on them,' he said. 'Stay out of the water.'

'Why?'

'If you don't,' said Crask, 'you will die. The more venomous eels live around here. A single bite will paralyse you. The man you are to take from my home did not use the stepping stones. He paid dearly.'

The Warden Commander got on to the stepping stones. Like a tightrope walker, he moved forward carefully, his arms outstretched for balance. He kept his gaze fixed on the rocks. Yet still he glimpsed the occasional elongated dark shape below the surface. Eels, perhaps? Or tree branches, rotting on the marsh bed?

Grethinne swallowed.

'Crask,' he said, 'these eels you are to give me – are there many of them?'

'There will be a full basket, as I said before,' replied Crask, striding casually over the stones. 'Enough to bring a couple of gold coins, if they are sold for a fair price.'

Grethinne smiled thinly. 'They will be,' he replied.

The stepping stones ended. Lugen Crask guided the Wardens another quarter-mile into the marsh. Then they halted at the eel-catcher's cottage: a well-constructed wooden dwelling, perched on stilts above the water level. They clambered up a flight of steps on to a porch.

Lugen Crask drew a knife.

His move startled Grethinne. Had the old man lured them into a trap of some sort? Reflexively, Grethinne reached for his precious dagger – and found the sheath empty.

He cursed.

Crask gave a mirthless laugh. 'Settle your nerves, Commander,' he said, a touch of irony in his voice. 'This blade is not a weapon, just a cleansing device.' He waved the knife at Grethinne's boots. Looking down, the Commander saw leeches, at least a dozen fastened to each boot. Their tiny mouths probed the leather.

Grethinne cursed again.

Stooping, Crask began prising the creatures from his own boots. Taking another Warden's knife, Grethinne copied the eel-catcher, sliding the blade beneath each slick body and wrenching it off. His hands were shaking and, too often, the knife sliced a leech open. Trickles of blood ran down his boots.

Eventually, the cleansing was over.

Lugen Crask led Grethinne into his home. Gesturing at a closed door, he said, 'Through there.'

Grethinne looked at the other Wardens. Noiselessly, they drew their knives. This seemed to surprise the eel-catcher.

'Is that really necessary?' he asked.

Crask did not know about the Masters' edict. He hadn't the faintest inkling that the stranger in his home might, in truth, be the most wanted man in Druine. Grethinne had decided not to enlighten him. There were a few things he needed to think through.

'Crask, I am Warden Commander, you are an eel-catcher,' said Grethinne. 'I do not pretend to understand your profession. You should not claim expertise in mine.'

'I was merely implying that this is my home, and I would prefer there to be no bloodshed.'

'Your preferences,' replied Grethinne, 'are not my concern.' Turning the door handle, Grethinne stepped through.

The fugitive lay bound on a pallet-bed. He was as Crask had said. Tall, broad-shouldered, and ugly. Bruises covered his face – yet his features were still discernible. A strong, mulish jaw. An oft-broken stub of a nose. A heavy brow and wide solid forehead. All these had been mentioned in the edict.

Alongside Grethinne a Warden whispered, 'It is him.'

Grethinne nodded.

'Crask,' he said, turning to the eel-catcher. 'Not everyone in Druine is pleased to be woken by Wardens. Your guest may act violently. Much as I dislike you, it is my duty to ensure that you come to no harm. You must leave us alone, for the time being.'

'He is already tightly bound,' said Crask. 'What harm can he do?'

Grethinne did not reply. He merely stared hard at the eel-catcher. Spreading his hands in a gesture of resignation, Crask left the room.

'Things have turned out well for us, Commander,' said another Warden. 'Deliver up this fellow, and surely we shall receive some reward. The Masters, I understand, are generous in such matters.'

'Speak softly,' whispered Grethinne, placing a hand on the man's shoulder. 'We must not wake our prisoner too soon.' He glanced at the door, ensuring that it was shut. 'Besides, there are things that must be known only to us. Things Crask must not hear.'

'What do you mean?' asked the Warden.

Grethinne looked around at the gathered men. 'When we hand over the fugitive to the Masters we shall, as you said, get some reward. And it may well prove substantial. But should we not try for *more*?'

The Wardens listened attentively.

'What shall we tell the Masters? The truth? Ha – I do not think so. For it is hardly glorious, is it? "An old man captured him, then tied him up and drugged him – all we did was bring him out of the marsh and lock him in a prison-cell." ' Grethinne shook his head. 'No. For all its accuracy, that tale will serve us badly. We ought to devise a better yarn.'

'Such as?' asked a Warden, blinking.

'Simple,' replied Grethinne. 'We say that *we* captured him – and that it was a long, dangerous task. For days, we tracked him across moorland. The weather was foul and our prey was cunning. Against great odds, we caught up with him. Naturally, there was much violence at the moment of capture. We shall claim he fought like a madman. If needs be, we shall each present injuries as proof. Just bruises and shallow cuts – nothing too severe.' He rubbed his hands together. 'The Blessed Masters will appreciate our efforts. Perhaps we shall receive something *more* than money. Promotions, maybe. Or – and I pray this is so – perhaps they will grant any request for a transfer to a different town. I despise Keltherimyn. It must be the worst posting in Druine.'

'With respect, Commander,' said a Warden, 'you are overlooking something. Lugen Crask will know the truth. What is to prevent—'

'Lugen Crask,' said Grethinne mildly, 'will die.'

The Warden raised his eyebrows.

'Once he has led us beyond the swamp's dangerous areas, we shall kill him and throw his body to the eels.'

'And his daughter?'

'The same.' Grethinne shrugged. 'People will assume that they grew careless and tumbled into the eels' nest. No one will care too much. Crask and his daughter are hardly well liked. And if their corpses are dredged out and examined for marks of foul play – well, after the eels have sated their hunger there won't *be* any corpses: only bones. Now,' he went on, directing his gaze to Anhaga Ballas, 'let us ensure that, when this one wakes, he will not prove troublesome.'

The Commander moved towards the bed.

Ballas was woken up violently. A series of hard blows jolted his head this way and that. Opening his eyes, he found a Warden Commander at the bedside, delivering punch after punch. A thin man, it seemed that he had to work doubly hard to inflict harm. Exertion reddened his face and a snarl tightened his features. With a Warden's assistance, he rolled Ballas from the bed. The big man struck the floor heavily. Stepping back, the Commander kicked him in the ribs, then in the stomach. His wrists and knees bound, Ballas couldn't defend himself. He curled into a ball and took the thrashing.

Eventually it stopped.

'Is there no hangover remedy,' said the Commander, panting, 'as potent as brutality? Shotten herrings, hair of the dog – they are myths, not cures. Only a little fist- and knee-work can soothe an aching skull.' His boot-tip nudged Ballas's side. 'On your feet, Anhaga Ballas.'

Raising his head, Ballas looked at the Commander.

'Come on,' snapped the man. 'Get up!'

'I am not Anhaga Ballas,' rasped Ballas, tasting his own blood and feeling bruises spread across his flesh. 'You've got the wrong man.'

'Do not lie to me,' said the Commander. 'There is not a Warden in Druine who has not been alerted by now to your –' he gestured vaguely at Ballas's form '– *appearance*. You are a distinctive-looking man. That is unfortunate. How can a fugitive as large and ugly as yourself remain undetected? He cannot – no more than a walrus can lie unnoticed in an aviary.' He gestured peremptorily to two of the Wardens. Grasping Ballas's wrists, they hauled him to his feet. One of them kneeled swiftly and untied the big man's knees and ankles.

Ballas stood steadily for a moment. Then the room seemed to lurch. The big man staggered and if the Wardens had not seized him he would have fallen. Groaning, he spat out a mouthful of bile on to the floor. He felt sick. And it was a nausea different to that which usually followed a beating. Sweat seeped from his pores, yet he felt cold. His eyes burned, as if a coarse fabric had scraped them raw. And the dawn light creeping through the window shutters seemed unbearably bright.

He sagged in the Wardens' grip. The Commander watched him with interest.

'For a man so keenly sought,' he said, 'you seem unable to cope with even a minor beating. Think yourself fortunate: I treated you leniently. I could have inflicted much greater harm upon you.'

'I am . . . sick,' said Ballas hoarsely. 'I have been . . . poisoned. The old man fed me something, I am certain of it.'

'Oh yes – a sleeping draught,' said the Commander thoughtfully. 'He was afraid of you, Anhaga Ballas. He thought it wise to keep you subdued.' He squinted at Ballas. 'I am curious. Of all Druine's criminals, it is you the Masters wish most urgently to apprehend. Yet I cannot imagine what your crime is. You do not seem to be a forger, or a maker of counterfeit coin. Nor do you seem sharp-witted enough to be a Denouncer of the Church. Or even a magicker. Tell me: what is your crime?'

Ballas did not reply.

'Oh, come now – this is no time for modesty. What great, glittering misdeed has attracted the Masters' wrath?'

Again, Ballas did not speak.

The Commander stared intently at Ballas. Then he shrugged, sighing. 'It doesn't matter. I am certain that all will be told when I deliver you to the Masters.'

Ballas blinked. 'You're not going to kill me?'

'Not unless you force me to,' replied the Commander. 'The Masters *have* issued an edict demanding that you should be killed on sight. Then your head is to be sundered from your neck and sent to the Esklarion Sacros as proof of the deed. But I think the Masters would appreciate it more if their quarry was delivered *alive*. I am certain they have all manner of morbid reprisals that, if given the chance, they would wish to inflict upon you.' A smile flickered over his lips. 'In return, I will gain their favour. When I woke this morning, I saw only dark clouds. Now the sun blazes brightly. Strange, how one's fortunes can so suddenly change.' Glancing at the Wardens, he said, 'Come. Let us get on with it.'

They half dragged, half carried Ballas into the next room. Lugen Crask stood beside an unlit bowl of coals. Beside him was a young red-haired woman. Crask's daughter, Ballas knew. He had not seen her before – he'd only heard her voice through the wooden cottage walls.

The Wardens ushered Ballas out through the door and on to a long porch. For an instant he saw the marshland: the reeds and rushes, mist and water. Then sharp daylight seemed to explode inside his skull. Grimacing, he screwed his eyes shut.

Behind him he heard the Commander say, 'Crask, the sleeping draught has profound side effects. Look at him: he is as frail as a child.'

'He will have recovered by nightfall,' replied Crask.

'And in the meantime?'

'He will feel ill,' said Crask simply, 'as if fever-struck.'

Ballas squinted through slitted eyes. The light burned like a hot needle thrust into his brain. He wanted to shut his eyes again – yet he resisted the urge to do so. Painful sight was preferable to comfortable blindness. If he was to escape, he needed to remain alert. He gazed around the swamp, looking for anything that might help him. But he found nothing.

Then things got worse.

From a hipbag, the Commander took out a long silver chain, looped at one end. Approaching Ballas, he dropped the loop over the big man's head.

'A choker,' said the Commander, idly grasping the other end. 'Such devices tame the most ill-behaved curs. True, it is an ugly, brutal implement – yet remarkably effective. Not only on dogs –' he yanked the chain '– but humans, too.'

The loop slid tight around Ballas's neck. The sharp, hard links jerked against his throat-apple, squeezing it deeper into his neck. The pain was instant. Choking, Ballas coughed – then retched pale bile. Eyes watering furiously, he dropped to his knees. As if pleased by the effect, the Commander pulled the loop even tighter. Pitching on to his side, Ballas grasped the chain near the loop to prevent it tightening further.

The Commander glared balefully at him. 'Lower your hands,' he snapped. 'Release the chain.'

Ballas refused.

Snarling, the Commander swung his boot into Ballas's face. Ballas toppled on to his back. He looked involuntarily up at the sky. Though mist-obscured, it shone with dawn light – and this light lanced excruciatingly into his brain. Groaning, he shut his eyes again, embracing darkness once more.

On the porch floorboards, Ballas quivered. He felt the chain strung around his throat. He felt echoes of the light-sparked pain. He felt the after-effects of the sedative, swirling through his blood like an ague.

And he shivered. A hard, angry spasm.

He was naked, he realised – except for his leggings. Crask must have stripped off his marsh-wet clothing when he'd arrived at the cottage. Now Ballas was bare to the morning's frost. The cold slid over him like a sheet of ice. His teeth chattered, his bones ached.

He opened his eyes again, cautiously.

'Bring me something warm to wear,' he said, slowly.

The Commander laughed. 'You crave warmth? You crave a soft woollen tunic, a scarf and gloves? These are the privileges of *decent* citizens. Do you imagine that, when you are delivered to the Masters, you will experience comfort?' He spat on to the porch. 'I dare say you will then look fondly on your present misery. You will picture yourself as you are now and imagine yourself to have been a blessed soul, reclining on a river bank in the warmest region of heaven.'

'I shall freeze to death,' breathed Ballas. He noticed that the marsh water was half-frozen. The reeds protruded through thin plates of ice. The rush-tips glittered. 'You want the Masters to have me *alive*. Yet you do nothing to stop me dying.'

'Get on your feet,' snapped the Commander, 'and start walking. In case you do not know, fat man, exercise can keep the cold at bay.'

He tugged lightly on the chain. The loop slithered fractionally tighter. Gasping, Ballas struggled to his feet. Then he shivered even more fiercely than he had before.

'Wait,' said Crask's daughter, setting down the eel basket she'd been holding. Turning, she vanished into the cottage. She reappeared moments later, carrying a rough grey cape. She draped it over Ballas's shoulders, tying the lacings loosely around his neck. 'Not all of us,' she said, eyeing the Commander, 'are barbarians.'

'Your daughter has learned the virtue of compassion,' said the Commander, glancing at Crask. 'A pity she has not also learned to be discriminate. Save mercy for those who deserve it. And who have a long life ahead of them.

'Keep your muscles warm, and loose,' said Crask's daughter, ignoring the Commander's jibe.

Her words struck Ballas as strange. She was not urging him merely to stay warm – but to avoid growing stiff. Squinting, the big man turned his face to hers. In her eyes he saw – or thought he saw – nervousness. Even fear.

'Try to keep moving,' she said, quietly. Then, glancing at the Commander, she added loudly, 'That way, you will not freeze.'

She touched Ballas on the small of his back – a fleeting nudge with her fingertips. Was that significant? wondered Ballas. Or simply a casual gesture, something meant simply to comfort a condemned man?

Crask's daughter stooped for her eel basket.

The Commander snorted. 'A touching scene. Now, let us be moving.' He swept his gaze around the marshes. 'I am sick of this place already.'

They started southwards, toward Keltherimyn. Lugen Crask led the way. Behind him, the Commander held the chain, pulling Ballas steadily onward. Crask's daughter walked alongside the three Wardens.

No one spoke. The only noise came from boots crunching through ice. And from the Commander, whistling softly – and tunelessly, as if the quietness bothered him and he was trying to break it by any means.

They arrived at a long row of broad, flat stepping stones. Looking around, Ballas dimly recognised the area. It was the spot where the eels had attacked him. Grunting, he realised that if he had been more attentive he would have spotted the stepping stones on his way to Crask's home. Walking on them, he would have been beyond the eels' reach. And then – then he wouldn't have been poisoned. Crask would not have been able to tie him up. And Ballas would not, at this moment, be the Wardens' prisoner.

He swore under his breath.

They moved along the stepping stones. The Commander watched his footsteps carefully, scarcely glancing up. The other Wardens were also wary. Crask moved blithely over the frost-slick stones, as if heedless of the eels under the ice. And his daughter—

—His daughter halted suddenly.

'I have to rest,' she said, putting down the eel basket and hunkering down.

The Commander turned sharply. 'What?'

'I am tired,' replied the red-haired woman. 'I cannot go on. This basket is heavy. My arms are aching.'

'Do not be so weak.' The Commander gazed sourly at her. 'You can pause later, when we are in a –' he gestured at the marsh water '– safer place.'

'Commander,' said Crask's daughter, 'I am not stopping through *choice*. I cannot manage another step – not yet. Give me a few moments—'

'Warden,' said the Commander to one of his men, 'Carry the woman's load for her.'

'Sir?' asked the Warden, who was young and green-eyed.

'Carry the basket,' replied the Commander.

'The damn things stink,' said the Warden, approaching Crask's daughter. 'I don't want to spend the day reeking of dead eels.'

When he was a few paces away, Crask's daughter slid her hand into the basket. An instant later, she sprang upright, clutching a thin-bladed filleting knife. The Warden blinked – then reeled, as the cruel blade pierced the underside of his jaw. Losing his footing, he slipped from the stepping stone and sprawled upon the marsh. The ice was thinner here. It creaked briefly, then shattered like sugar glass. The Warden sank into a half-foot-deep stretch of marsh water. Blood splashed a few ice shards, then trickled into the water.

Ballas did not know why Crask's daughter had attacked the Warden. Yet one thing was clear: he had to act quickly. Sprinting at the Commander, he kicked him hard in the stomach. The Commander wheezed, bending forward at the waist. Ballas slammed a knee into his face. The Commander arched backwards, and crashed from the stepping stone into the water. Even when he fell, he still held on to the chain. The loop rattled tight around Ballas's throat. Choking, the big man felt himself pulled into the marsh. He struck the ice face down, smashing though it instantly. Cold, dark water swirled over him. Something sleek brushed his cheekbone.

An eel.

Scrambling to his feet, Ballas grasped the chain and wrenched it free of the Commander's grip. Loosening the loop, he drew it from round his neck, then leaped on to the stepping stone.

There was a moment in which time froze. A shocked stillness settled on the marsh. The injured Warden was sitting upright in the water. The Commander was on his feet once more, his eyes wide. Lugen Crask gaped uncomprehendingly. The three remaining Wardens stood statue-still.

Crask's daughter broke the stillness. Spinning, she sank the filleting knife into a Warden's stomach. He stumbled, then fell; his limbs splayed, he stayed spreadeagled on the stepping stone. Drawing his sword, another Warden ran at Crask's daughter. Lifting the weapon, he aimed a skull-splitting blow at the young woman—

—But Ballas swung the chain at him, the end wrapping around the Warden's wrist. With a sharp tug, he jerked the man off his feet. As the Warden toppled, Ballas ran over, then stamped a boot down on his throat. Snatching up the man's sword in an awkward two-handed grip, Ballas spun round and swept the blade-tip across the last Warden's throat. Blood spurted on to his tunic front. Growling, Ballas slammed the blade down into his head. The man's eyes rolled; he fell limply into a clump of reeds.

A cry shook the air.

Around the Warden who Crask's daughter had stabbed the marsh water seemed to slither and lurch. Dirty foam bubbled around the young man. His body jolted, as if seized by a fit. He tried to stand, yet something was restricting his movements. Shrieking, he struck at whatever was under the surface. Through the churning water Ballas glimpsed eels. He saw thick bodies. Variously coloured skins. Tiny swollen eyes. And teeth, sparkling like barbs of frost.

The Warden dropped backwards.

Screaming, the Commander tried to scramble up on to a stepping stone. But he couldn't find any purchase on its slippery surface. Turning, he ran in high wading strides through the water to a clump of tussocks. Clambering on to the raised patch of ground, he glanced back at Ballas.

Then he started off into the mist.

Swearing, Ballas wrenched the sword from the last Warden's head and hurled it clumsily towards the Commander. The blade spun murmuring through the air – and landed several yards to the Commander's left. Ballas cursed his poor aim. Then he fell silent. The Commander was slowing down. He stumbled from side to side, as if drunk. Then his knees buckled, and he collapsed.

Ballas walked unhurriedly over the stepping stones to the tussocks. The Commander lay on his side. His eyes rolled in their sockets and he breathed in short, sharp gasps.

Blood seeped from a tear in his leggings, just above his ankle. Ballas tugged the tattered cloth aside. Beneath it lay a circle of bite marks, oozing blood.

Ballas gazed evenly at the Commander.

'You should have killed me,' he said, grasping the Commander's wrist.

He dragged the law-keeper towards the marsh water. The man seemed to be trying to speak: his lips quivered and a thin rasping noise came from his throat. But Ballas ignored him.

At the edge of the tussocks, he paused. Then he rolled the Commander into the water. Within seconds, a hundred glossy, slender bodies were swarming over him. They coiled around his face and slithered into his mouth, devouring him from the inside out. The Commander's goggling eyes gazed helplessly at Ballas. The big man held his stare for a moment. Then he went back over the stones to Crask and his daughter.

Lugen Crask was frantic.

'Sweet grief,' he said, looking at the dead Wardens. 'Oh – sweet grief! There are not words—' He spun to face his daughter. 'What have you done? You stupid girl!'

'They meant to kill us,' explained the red-haired woman. 'When I was returning with the eels, I passed the window of the sleeping room and heard them talking. They wanted to tell the Masters that they alone had tracked and captured the fugitive. But they feared we would contradict this tale . . .'

Lugen Crask licked his lips. 'Why has this happened to me? To *us*? What have we done to warrant such—'

'Untie me,' interrupted Ballas, holding out his rope-bound hands.

Lugen Crask blinked.

'Come on!' snapped Ballas. 'Untie me!'

'You – you are a fugitive,' stammered Crask. 'I ought not—'

'We are *all* fugitives,' retorted Ballas, angry at the old man's hesitation. 'Your daughter and I have murdered Wardens. And you did nothing to stop us. *That* is a crime, old man.'

Crask did not move. Suddenly, his daughter leaned over the stepping stone and pulled the filleting knife from the second Warden's stomach. Striding to Ballas, she began sawing through his bonds.

'What are you doing?' shouted Crask, grasping her wrist.

'Did you not hear what he said? We are *all* fugitives!'

'I know what *my* crime is,' said Crask, dragging his daughter away. 'And I know what yours is. But this man's? He was a fugitive before he came here. We do not know what he has done. Although I suspect it was a violent deed. He seemed too easy with such . . .' His voice trailed off.

The filleting knife had sliced halfway through the rope. Now, clenching his fists and jerking them apart, Ballas snapped the remaining strands. The effort sent blood racing to his skull. A wave of nausea swept over him. For an instant, he felt dizzy. He swayed upon the stepping stone. Then he found his balance.

Breathing heavily, he said, 'Crask, you have seen how easily . . . how quickly a man's luck can turn sour. How fate can piss on him. Well, it pissed on me once by making me a first offender. Now it pisses on me again, making me a repeat criminal. Don't think I brought it on myself. I didn't.' He glanced around the marsh. 'We cannot stay here.'

Crask stared at him.

'The Wardens in Keltherimyn will soon wonder where their Commander is. This will be the first place they look.'

'You are mistaken,' said Crask firmly. 'If the Wardens intended to do as Heresh said . . . to pretend they, not I, captured you, they will have told no one they were coming here.'

'Crask, you forget what you are,' said Ballas.

Crask frowned. 'What are you talking about?'

'You smuggled forbidden texts. You have been a criminal. Consequently, in Keltherimyn you are mistrusted.' He scowled. 'When they realise their Commander is missing, the Wardens will seek you out. Your only choice is whether to remain here and face them – or to escape.'

Crask's mouth worked noiselessly.

'It is a choice,' said Ballas, 'that is truly no choice at all.'

They returned to the cottage, leaving behind the eel-gnawed corpses of the Wardens and their Commander. On the porch Crask's daughter, Heresh, prised leeches from her boots with the filleting knife, then passed the implement to her father. Crask did the same, flicking the fat-bodied parasites into the marsh. Then he held out the knife to Ballas. As Ballas took it, unease flickered in the old man's eyes. Stooping, Ballas cut the leeches from his own boots. Then, straightening, he grabbed Crask's tunic collar. 'Inside,' he said, shoving the man through the door. Seizing Heresh's upper arm, he jostled her through as well.

Ballas glanced across the marshes, as though wary of being watched. Yet there was no one else in this quiet, vapour-clogged place.

He stepped inside.

Crask and his daughter stared at him. A heavy silence hung in the room. Using the knife, Ballas gestured at Crask. 'Bring me my vest and tunic,' he said.

'I will get them,' said Heresh, moving towards a door in the far wall.

Ballas stepped in front of her, blocking her way. 'I told your father to bring them – and he will. Crask, do as I say.' He looked intently at Heresh. 'I do not trust you, woman.'

Crask disappeared through the door. Alone with Heresh, Ballas stood upright, swaying slightly. He felt sick to his guts. Freezing sweat trickled down his face. His eyes still burned. 'Your father said that by eveningfall I will have recovered from the sleeping draught. Is that true?'

Heresh did not respond.

'*Is that true*?' shouted Ballas, his voice filling the small room.

Heresh flinched, as though he'd slapped her. Her mouth slightly open in shock, she stayed silent. Yet this time her silence had a different reason, Ballas knew. Moments ago she'd been defiant, stubborn. Now she was simply too frightened to reply.

That was good, thought Ballas. If she feared him, she was less likely to cause trouble. Ballas stared intently at her, concentrating on her dark hazel eyes and her reddish hair, a few strands of which had escaped her pony-tail and hung loose.

'Why are you staring at me?' she asked quietly.

'I was thinking . . .'

'Thinking what?'

Ballas shrugged. 'You would make a good whore,' he replied. 'In Soriterath . . . in any city in Druine, men would pay a lot to lie with you. Perhaps we can reach an agreement later, hm? Your talents are wasted here, in the marshes. It would be more profitable to put a different type of eel into a different type of basket.'

Heresh fell silent once more – and this time she was mute with disgust.

Lugen Crask returned, carrying Ballas's clothes. Quickly, Ballas tugged on his vest and tunic. Then he drew the woollen cape around his shoulders. He felt no warmer for doing so.

'Yesterday,' he said, turning to Crask, 'we spoke of Belthirran. And you lied to me.'

'Lied?' stammered Crask.

'Yes, *lied*,' repeated Ballas. 'About one thing and another. You said no one knows what lies on the other side of the Garsbracks. You said every map that might lead a man over the mountains has vanished . . .'

'Every word I spoke is true,' retorted Crask.

'My friend,' said Ballas, 'I have spent much time among liars. I know their habits, their manners. And you are a liar.'

'If a truth displeases you, it is a lie – is that your logic?'

Ballas grew very still. With the knife-tip, he gestured to the front door. 'You,' he said, to Heresh, 'go outside.'

The young woman frowned. 'What – what for?'

'*Go outside!*' Grasping her forearm, Ballas pulled her through the door and out on to the porch. 'Stay there. Budge a half-inch and I swear I'll kill your father. Then I will kill you.'

Returning to the cottage, Ballas slammed the door shut. Grabbing Crask's shoulder, the big man pushed him across the room to the far corner, away from the window shutters. He did not want Heresh eavesdropping; it was vital that she did not hear a single word of what was to follow.

Standing a pace away from Crask, he said, 'What does your daughter know about your past?'

'My past?' said Crask, uncertainly.

'She knows you smuggled forbidden texts?' asked Ballas.

'Of course.' Crask nodded, puzzled.

'She knows about your time in prison – your twenty years of darkness, loneliness and despair?'

'Yes,' said Crask. 'She and I have no secrets.'

'Does she look upon you as any daughter does her father?'

'I do not understand . . .'

'Does she think you're an honest, loyal, decent-souled man?'

'Yes, yes, yes,' said Crask impatiently.

'Even though you are not?'

Crask frowned.

'Even though you are a betrayer? Even though, to save your own skin, you told the Church who your accomplices were – those men who helped you smuggle forbidden texts?'

Crask grew utterly motionless. The blood drained from his face. His eyes flickered nervously, a thin tremulous gleam inside each pupil; in his neck, a vein throbbed. Only these faint movements indicated he was a living man, not a waxen figure.

'Yesterday,' whispered Ballas, 'as I lay upon the bed, bound at wrist, ankle and knee, you told me you had escaped execution because the forbidden documents you possessed were *false*.'

'That is what happened.'

'Horseshit,' said Ballas gently. 'Lie to me again, Crask, and I'll cut your pissing throat.' He raised the filleting knife, touching its edge to Crask's skin. 'It wouldn't matter to the Church whether your texts were false or genuine. They do not care about such distinctions. To them, it'd matter only if you were on their side, or against them.' He licked his lips. 'You struck a bargain, didn't you?'

'No . . .'

'Do not lie,' breathed Ballas, moving the knife slightly. 'To save yourself, you told the Church all they wanted to know. "Who do you smuggle parchments with? Where do these parchments come from? Who buys them?" All these questions, you answered readily – for you feared the Penance Oak. Better to spend twenty years in a cell, than perish upon that tree.'

'You don't know . . .'

'But I *am* right, hm?'

Exhaling, Crask closed his eyes.

Ballas took the knife away from the old man's throat. 'I hear it is an awful thing, for a daughter to learn that her father is a coward. A son can understand it, for if he has ever felt afraid himself he knows how fear can overwhelm a man . . . how it can make him piss himself, how it can rob him of dignity, of pride. But a girl? A woman? They are foolish animals. They reckon men don't feel fear. Or if they do, then they have some knack for fighting it down. A man may lie, cheat, steal; he may torture, he may kill – and a woman will forgive him. But if he proves himself a coward?' Ballas shook his head. 'She will hate him for ever. More so, if he has touted himself as brave. More so,' he drew back his shoulders, 'if that man, that coward, is her father. A father, unlike a husband, must be perfect. He is his daughter's god. But to discover he is a false idol . . .'

'She will not believe you,' said Crask, breathing heavily. 'Never in a thousand years. How could she? You are a stranger, a fugitive – she will dismiss every word as a lie.'

'At first, perhaps,' nodded Ballas. 'But later? She will begin to grow curious, to ponder things – and then to doubt. Remember, Crask, one way or another you will be leaving this marsh. Perhaps your girl knows little about the way the Church works. But, soon enough, she will learn. And she'll recognise they are ruthless. That they seldom let their enemies live – unless, of course, their enemies have changed allegiance. Have become friends. *Informers.*'

Crask fell silent. Dragging a palm over his sweat-sparkled forehead, he said, 'Do you intend to tell her the truth?'

'Not if you do as I say,' replied Ballas.

'What do you want of me?'

'What lies beyond the Garsbracks?'

'I do not know – that is the truth: I swear it. The accounts *do* differ: some speak of a pagan land; others claim there is nothing but wilderness.'

'And the maps? Are they to be trusted? Do any still exist?'

'Again, I do not know—'

'You are beginning to bore me, Crask,' said Ballas, dangerously.

'—But there is a man who might have some inkling – some frail grasp of the truth.' Crask lowered his gaze. 'Many of the forbidden texts were copies. A scribe named Jonas Elsefar produced them. He was a quill-master of great repute. He could reproduce, to the finest detail, even the most convoluted map or design – and with the greatest speed. He certainly copied maps of the Garsbrack Range.' He looked up at Ballas. 'He may be able to help you. If he is still alive – I never met him but I understand he was much older than I, and never in the soundest health.'

'Where can he be found?'

'Granthaven, the last I heard,' replied the old man. 'It is a town, eight miles—'

'I know where it is,' interrupted Ballas. 'Now, you and your daughter must gather your things. Bring only what you will need for the journey.'

'Journey?'

'You are to travel with me.'

'Why?'

'You will introduce me to this quill-master,' said Ballas. 'You will ensure he trusts me, and does my bidding.'

'Have you not been listening? I never met him. He does not know me from Martyr Cadris!'

'You were labourers in the same trade,' said Ballas. 'That will count for something.'

Leaving Crask and his daughter to gather what they needed, Ballas stepped outside, settling upon the porch. He gazed at the marsh – at the bubbles bursting on the surface, each one a tiny gasp of vapour. And he listened to the voices inside the cottage. To the old man and Heresh discussing the forthcoming journey.

'We ought to do as he asks,' said Crask. 'He may look like some forest beast, but he has spoken sensibly. The Wardens are hunting us; when we are found, what can *we* do to escape capture? Fight? Not you and I, my girl. You killed a Warden, that is true: but only because you surprised him. We are safer in his company. That is all there is to it.'

'So, father, we are to remain with him for *ever*? I do not believe what threatens us will be over soon. Are we to employ him, then, as our private guardian?'

'Of course not,' said Crask tiredly. 'There are places where you and I will be safe. Your uncle, my brother – he will assist us. His home is in a far-off, seldom visited region. He will take us in. He will ensure all is well. Once we are there, we shall bid farewell to . . . to the fugitive.'

'Maybe we will never have the opportunity,' protested Heresh. 'Maybe we will have no need of a safe house, for we shall already be dead.'

'What are you talking about?'

'What is to say he will not kill us, once we have served his purpose? Once we have taken him to Jonas Elsefar?'

'What is to say he will?' retorted Crask.

'Oh, father – that is so weak—'

'I am merely saying we have no choice. What will happen, do you think, if we refuse to help him? Besides,' Crask sighed, 'I do not believe he will kill us – not unless we give him good cause. It pains me to say it, but I do not believe he is without honour.'

'*Him*? *Honour*?' Heresh sounded startled.

'It seems incredible, I know,' said Crask, 'but when I was a smuggler, I learned much about honour. As I acquired it myself, I grew able to discern it in others. And he has it – to a degree . . .'

Despite his fever sweats and light-stricken eyes, Ballas found himself grinning. 'You have the truth upside down,' he said to himself. 'You don't have any honour, Crask – you have confessed as much. And it is that lack you see in others – in *me*.'

He spat into the water: a blood-tinted splash of phlegm.

The cottage door opened. Lugen Crask stepped out, his daughter following him. He wore a long cape, the hood slung back. A rucksack was strapped to his back.

'We are ready,' he said, eyeing Ballas doubtfully.

'Good,' said Ballas, rising.

Chapter 11

A hundred miles from Scarrendestin,
The four true Pilgrims met, and found
They shared a common purpose, and their
Fortunes were intertwined. They rejoiced
At their trials overcome, and rejoiced
At their destiny . . .

They moved northwards, emerging from the swamp on to a stretch of bare moorland. Then they readjusted their steps, heading north-east over the yellow, frost-killed grasses. The sky was steel-grey – a sharp overcast that might or might not unleash drizzle or rain at any instant.

A cold wind blew from the east. It troubled Crask, forcing him to lift his hood, and to stoop, like a slave accepting a whipping from his master. Yet this same wind pleased Ballas. It bit at his face, threatening to crack open his skin; it pierced the cape given to him by Heresh, chilling him bone-deep. But it also *refreshed* him. Each gust blew away a little of the sleeping draught's ague-imitating after-effects. He felt himself growing stronger. And more alert. The light hurt his eyes less and less. His nausea ebbed, and when he shivered, it was the healthy shaking of a cold – not feverish – man.

Yet it would not be wise to travel on foot the eighty miles to Granthaven. If Ballas could have managed it, Crask could not.

After a few hours of silent walking, Ballas said, 'Are there any farms close by?'

'There is one, about ten miles that way,' said Crask, pointing eastwards. 'Why do you ask? You do not intend to seek lodgings, do you? For it is best, I think, if we leave as faint a trail as possible. We ought not be seen if—'

'We'll make our own lodgings,' interrupted Ballas.

'We shall sleep in the open?'

'Aye.' The big man nodded, glancing at the sky.

Crask muttered something. 'Then why such interest in the farm?'

'We need horses,' said Ballas, plainly. 'There's enough for us there, yes?'

Under his hood, Crask nodded. 'But I have no coin to purchase—'

'We won't be buying them.'

They continued walking. Ballas scanned the horizon. The view was desolate – an unbroken curve of moorland, bare except for the odd rowan tree that struggled up out of the damp earth. Even the sky was empty: no birds passed overhead – no crows or rooks, no ravens or hawks. Except for Crask and his daughter, the moors held no other living thing. Such barrenness gave Ballas a sudden sense of comfort. Where there existed no life, there existed no enemy. True, he couldn't count Crask and Heresh as allies: but for the time being, they were too wary to trouble him.

He looked to Crask.

'Have you brought anything to drink?'

'There is a river close by,' replied the eel-catcher.

'I wasn't talking of water,' grunted the big man. 'You got any whisky? Brandy?'

'No,' said Crask, shaking his head. 'Heresh and I – we seldom drink. Out in the marshes, it is wise to remain sober. A misplaced footfall can—'

'What food've you brought?' interrupted Ballas.

'None,' said Crask.

Ballas glared balefully at him. 'I told you to gather what you'd need for the journey. Did you reckon we'd eat nothing but air?'

'Our larder is empty,' replied Crask, a touch testily. 'I had intended to visit the market this morning – but certain events rendered it unwise. In my rucksack, I have a fishing line and a hook-pouch, though I was never much of an angler. Eels I can catch, because the marsh makes it easy. In their hunger, those dim-witted creatures follow their first impulse: to chase the scent of blood. It is—'

'I will fish,' said Ballas, weary of the eel-catcher's prattle.

As light seeped from the sky, the grey thickening to black, they camped at a small limestone cave, in a dip by the river. Crask built a fire from rowan branches, and lit it from a tub of dried moss kindling that he had had the foresight to pack in his rucksack. From two forked branches, and a straight one whittled sharp at the end, Heresh constructed a spit. On the river bank, Ballas unrolled a bobbin of catgut and tied a barbed hook to the end of the line. Out of the soil he dug a plump worm, which he speared upon the hook.

He cast his line into the dark river.

It had been many years since he had fished. Yet he felt instantly comfortable, feeling the river currents tugging at his line and awaiting the firmer tell-tale jerk of a strike.

For a while, he gazed at the water – just a strip of darkness, glinting occasionally where the fire's light touched it. Then he glanced over his shoulder, towards the camp. Crask was sleeping at the mouth of the cave; seated upright against a rock, he had not intended to drowse – overwhelmed by fatigue, he had merely dozed off. Near the fire, Heresh sat cross-legged. She stared at Ballas. But, in the uncertain light, Ballas couldn't tell if she was looking *at* him – or simply seeing something in her mind's eye. Her stare lasted for a long time. Eventually, she blinked.

'I am a killer,' she said, quietly. 'This morning, I took a man's life . . .'

'What of it?' grunted Ballas, returning his gaze to the river.

Heresh did not reply for many moments. 'I am a killer,' she repeated. 'In idle hours, I have imagined many things I might become. Many professions I might adopt, many ways in which I might one day live. Yet I never imagined I would be a murderer . . . a murder*ess*. It troubles me. I feel . . . guilty.'

'Guilt,' said Ballas, 'is a stupid habit – one you'd do well to break. The Wardens would've slaughtered you, and your father. You had to choose between life and death.' The big man shrugged. 'You'll never again be given such an easy choice. Don't feel guilty for wanting to live.'

Silence. The fire crackled, and river water lapped gently against the bank. Ballas thought he felt the line twitch tight. A cautious nip from a fish? Or just the current's touch?

'Do *you* feel anything . . . about the Wardens?' asked Heresh eventually.

'No.'

'But, soon enough, their mothers and fathers will grieve for them. Perhaps they even had families of their own. Wives, children—'

'Then they should've acted with more caution.'

'Caution?'

'The Wardens' families were the Wardens' concern. If they take up a trade that makes them risk their lives . . . if they act recklessly, then their families' grief is *their* doing – not mine. I didn't make them become Wardens. I didn't ask them to try and capture me, rather than kill me straight away. They behaved like fools. For that, they paid a high price. As have their families.'

'My father is right,' said Heresh, softly. 'You are too at ease with violence. Your crime – it *was* a violent one, wasn't it? The Church are hunting you for committing some brutal act . . .'

'So what?' snapped Ballas. 'Don't talk of brutal things as if they are special – as if they are dirty, or shameful, or wicked. Brutality is everywhere, woman. Every bird, animal, insect is violent. Killing is the most ordinary of deeds. To *not* kill – that is the *extra*ordinary action. To not kill

– that is *perverse*.' He spat into the river. Then he glimpsed something from the corner of his eye. A hawk hung hovering over a patch of moorland. The bird was a silhouette against the moon. 'Look,' said Ballas, pointing casually. 'Tell me what you see.'

'A hawk,' said Heresh, a puzzled note in her voice.

The hawk swooped, vanishing into blackness.

'Now,' said Ballas, after a pause, 'tell me what you're thinking of.'

'Of the bird's prey,' replied Heresh.

'Do you pity it?'

'Its guts are about to be ripped out – of course I do!'

'And the hawk?'

'I feel nothing for it.'

'This morning, what were you but the prey – and the Wardens the predators?'

'Oh, please: do not talk so . . . so predictably. It seems that every time an unintelligent man seeks to be wise, he points out something in Nature, and says, "That is how it is".'

'And you know better, woman?' asked Ballas, irritated.

'I know that men are not animals,' came the reply. 'At least, most men aren't.'

Ballas released a long breath. 'If your life depends upon another's death,' he said eventually, 'you must kill. Anything that comes after – any guilt or shame or feeling of dirtiness . . . well, that is nothing to worry about. Better to feel miserable for a short time than to be dead for all eternity.' He glanced back at her. 'If there is trouble coming – and there might be, for the Wardens are seeking us all – don't let your conscience slow your hand. Fight like you did in the marshes, and perhaps you will survive.'

The fishing line jerked in Ballas's hand. A long-dormant reflex made Ballas twist his wrist sharply, sinking the hook into the unseen fish's flesh. Pulling in the line hand over hand, he dragged the creature gently to the bank and lifted it from the water. In the firelight, it appeared to be a rainbow trout; Ballas discerned a faint pinkness to the silvern scales. Taking a stone, he struck the fish firmly upon its head. Its gills stopped pulsing; its body stopped contorting.

Muttering, Ballas tossed the fish to Heresh. Then he handed her the filleting knife.

'Cook it,' he said simply.

Heresh did as she was told.

She skewered the trout over the campfire. When it was cooked, she divided it into three portions. Ballas ate his third instantly; one moment it was in his fingers, the next it had vanished. When Heresh decided it was kinder to let her father sleep on, Ballas devoured Crask's share too. Then, hunkering in the cave mouth, the big man closed his eyes and fell asleep.

For a long time, Heresh stared.

How much of his talk had been truthful, she wondered. Did he really feel no guilt? No lingering soul-dirtying shame at killing? She supposed he had to feel *something* – a thin flicker of disquiet, perhaps. Surely, no one could perform such an act without it having some effect upon their emotions. To take a man's life was a colossal deed. It could not be ignored or shrugged off – could it?

A breeze stirred the campfire. Shadows crawled over the big man's face, mingling with the bruises and dried blood-splashes. Heresh gazed hard at his features. The thick bone-ridge of his brow. The heavy jaw, bristling with dark stubble. They disturbed her. She looked at his skin, coarsened by fierce weather – and fierce drinking. What had his profession been? Something dishonest: of that she was certain. Something that had brought him to the Pilgrim Church's attention . . . But what?

She realised it didn't matter.

Gazing at him, she realised his talk *had* been truthful. That morning, he had killed three men. Now, at eveningfall, he was sleeping peacefully, like a child.

She could not trust him. Once she and her father had served his purpose . . . once they had taken him to Granthaven . . . once they had introduced him to the quill-master Jonas Elsefar . . . he would kill them. He was being hunted, and would wish to leave as faint a trail as possible. Heresh sensed he trusted few people. So even if they swore an oath of silence, if they vowed to keep secret his location and his intent, it would make no difference. If they begged for leniency, for mercy – that too would have no effect: Heresh recalled the cold-hearted manner in which Ballas had dragged the paralysed Warden Commander into the eel-infested waters. Ballas was not disposed to compassion. Jaspar Grethinne had been a vile man, true; but his final moments had been unimaginably horrible, and she found herself pitying him.

She stared at Ballas. 'What choice do I have?' she murmured, taking up the filleting knife.

She rose silently. Then she walked around the campfire to the cave mouth.

Ballas slept on. His breaths were steady, rhythmic. Their depth, and hollowness, evoked something bestial. As if he were not a man at all, but some forest creature – a wolf, perhaps. Or a boar. Yes, a boar – how often, she wondered, had he been likened to such an animal? For in both appearance and habit, they might have been brothers.

Kneeling, she felt Ballas's body heat drifting over her leg. Soon he would be cold. As icy-blooded and lifeless as Jaspar Grethinne.

She lifted the knife.

It must be done, she told herself. Is it not what you advised, Ballas? Did you not say, 'If your life depends on another's death, you must kill'?

The blade quivered. A single throat-piercing strike would suffice. An unpleasant death, perhaps. But, to Heresh's mind, the safest. The most certain.

She drew a breath. Then brought down the knife.

The blade did not touch the big man's throat. Something obstructed Heresh's arm. Something made it jerk to a halt, the blade-tip several inches from its target.

She froze. A large hand gripped her wrist.

Ballas stared at her, his grey-green eyes glinting.

'Don't be a bloody fool,' he said.

His fingers tightened, bruising Heresh's flesh. She gasped. Ballas twisted her wrist slightly; the knife slipped from her fingers, landing noiselessly in the grass.

'I'm your only chance of survival,' said Ballas, maintaining his grip. 'Your father was right: I *am* a violent man, and if you are to live you will need my help.'

'How long will that help last? Soon you will have no use for us. What then?'

'Don't ask questions,' replied Ballas quietly. 'Be glad that I am here and that, for the time being, your life is worth something to me.' He released her. 'Go to sleep. We have a day of riding ahead. And –' he grasped Heresh's forearm; his fingers seemed to burn her skin '– if you get any more stupid ideas, I *will* kill you. Understand? I'll ram that bloody knife through *your* throat. Think how your father will feel when he finds you are dead.'

Again, Ballas released her. Heresh tried to think of something to say. Yet there was nothing – nothing at all. The big man left the knife in the grass, firelight dancing along the blade. He knew Heresh wouldn't dare touch it. He knew he was safe. Already, his eyes were closing, and he was drifting into a slumber.

Heresh bedded down at her father's side, and tried vainly to sleep.

Ballas woke an hour before dawn. Rising, he walked past the glowing campfire embers and, seizing the man's shoulder, shook Crask awake. The eel-catcher's eyes opened and, as if he had woken *into* a nightmare, he gave a startled gasp and cringed back against the rocks. Then he seemed to pull himself together. Breathing heavily, he wiped a night sweat from his forehead.

'You frightened me,' he said. 'You should not rouse people so roughly.'

'Wake your daughter,' grunted Ballas. 'We've got to be moving on.'

Crask woke Heresh and they left the cave mouth, traipsing north-east over the moors. As thin dawn light spread across the land, illuminating the frost-layered grasses and stones, the three travellers crested a low hill. A farmhouse lay ahead, surrounded by outbuildings. A large whitewashed stable adjoined a paddock.

'Come with me,' Ballas said to Heresh. Pointing at Crask, he added, 'You: stay here.'

The eel-catcher frowned. 'Where my daughter goes I go too.'

'Father,' interrupted the red-haired woman, 'let us not argue with him. I am certain he knows what he is doing. And is he not a man of honour? Is that not what you said yesterday, before we set out on this . . . errand?' There was something faintly sardonic about her tone. Something bitter, too. But Ballas couldn't tell whether these sentiments were aimed at her father or at himself.

Himself, probably. In his experience, women – unable to exact physical retribution – resorted to sharp words. Heresh had failed to kill him. Now, humiliated, she sought to lacerate him with insinuations.

Crask blinked uneasily. 'Take care of her,' he said, turning to Ballas.

'We're stealing horses,' replied the big man. 'That is all.'

They walked down the slope to the stable. Inside, they found three chestnut geldings, and a white mare roughly thirty spans tall. Ballas liked the look of the animal. Unhitching the tackle from a wall-hook, he saddled and bridled-up the mare, and instructed Heresh to do the same for two of the geldings. The young woman worked briskly, and the geldings were soon ready.

They led the horses from the stable, climbing the slope to the hill crest. Crask was waiting for them nervously. At his daughter's bidding, he clambered on to a gelding. His movements, as he swung into the saddle, were awkward. Once upon the creature he sat stiffly, like a wooden figurine.

'Many years have passed,' he said, holding the reins tightly, 'since I last rode. I was never a gifted horseman – that I readily admit. But I fear what skills I once had have now gone. I am not as supple as I once was. And it is said that, if you spend too long out of the saddle, your body's rhythms become stubbornly your own: they will no longer be concordant with those of your mount. The horse becomes something foreign, unpredictable. And riding becomes like a wrestling bout: it is all grappling, struggling, jerking this way and that . . .'

Ballas clambered into the saddle.

Crask looked at him. 'Still, it is a fine thing we have brisker transport. I shall be glad to rest my legs. And, in two days, we ought to be in Granthaven. Then – then we will bid each other farewell, yes? Heresh and I will travel to our safe place. And you – you will go wherever it is you are going.'

Ballas stared heavily at him.

'That is the plan, hm?' Crask licked his lips. 'We fulfil our half of the bargain – and you fulfil yours.'

For a long moment, Ballas was silent. 'You're foul company, Crask,' he said eventually. 'Whenever you speak, it is all prattle – you annoy me, like a squeaky wheel on a cart. When you're beyond earshot, I shall be happy. But as irritating as you are, your daughter –' he turned his gaze to Heresh '– is worse. When she is gone, I'll not weep.' He looked back to the eel-catcher. 'Our paths will split apart – I'll make sure of it. I won't spend a heartbeat more with you than I need.'

'So,' said Crask, 'there will be no sorrow in our parting?'

'No sorrow,' echoed Ballas. He stared at Crask – then shifted his gaze to Heresh. The woman was stony-faced, as if she detected something offensive in his words. Or something disturbing.

Ballas smiled. 'No sorrow,' he repeated.

Chapter 12

. . . and into their number came
The fifth pilgrim, from beyond the water,
And they accepted him, despite his strangeness,
For he claimed kinship with them,
And a common purpose . . .

After two days of silent, uneventful riding, they arrived at Granthaven – a large city of wooden buildings and muddied thoroughfares: a place almost, but not quite, as poverty-stricken as Keltherimyn.

As they rode into the town, Heresh began to dismount.

'No,' said Ballas, firmly.

'What?' replied the red-haired woman, blinking.

'Stay in the saddle.'

'I am sick of being on horseback,' protested Heresh. 'If I want to walk, I'll—'

'Get back in the bloody saddle,' growled Ballas.

Heresh paused.

'*Get in the saddle*,' said Ballas, sharply.

'Do as he says,' put in Lugen Crask, glancing uneasily at the big man. 'This is his adventure as much as our own. Let us be cooperative, yes?'

Heresh did as her father told her. Yet she started to say, 'I do not see why—'

'Two reasons,' snapped Ballas. 'Firstly, *I*'ve got to stay on horseback. What sort of man do you reckon the Wardens are looking for? The Church'll have described not only my face, but my build. I'm not a small man. If I'm on a horse, though, it isn't so obvious. So I ride. And if you dismount –' he glowered at Heresh '– and your father does the same, attention will be drawn to *me*.'

'And the second reason?' asked Heresh.

'Who notices a man on horseback?' replied Ballas. 'Who looks at a rider's face? No one. Walk past, and you see his horse – nothing else: only his horse. If anyone looks at you, it's only a glance.'

They rode slowly through Granthaven. The streets were not particularly crowded. Yet Ballas felt conspicuous, even on horseback, despite what he'd just told Heresh and Crask. It was true that most riders received a mere glance from any passer-by. But a glance – one from a sharp-eyed or suspicious-natured man – could be enough. He found it tempting to look at every passing face, to see if anyone was watching him with unusual intentness. Yet eye contact – however fleeting or casual-seeming – could easily make someone memorable to another person. Scowling, Ballas kept his gaze fixed on his mare's neck. When he looked up, it was merely to ensure that there was no danger present: no Wardens or clergymen.

He glanced sidelong at Crask.

'Where does this quill-master live?' he said, quietly.

'Assuming he lives at all,' began Crask, 'for, as I said, many years have passed—'

'*Where?*'

'His home lay upon Granthaven's eastern edge,' sighed Crask. 'It was a comfortable – even luxurious – place. It had underfloor heating, a bathing pool, a private stable . . . and windows. They, more than anything, are its most noticeable feature. Most buildings in Granthaven have shutters. But Jonas Elsefar preferred glass panes. For most people, they are objects of vanity, a type of architectural boastfulness. For few can afford them. They glitter most often in church buildings, and the homes of wealthy merchants. But among the common folk, they are rarities.' He raised a finger. Still, for Elsefar they were almost a necessity. They say he preferred to work in natural light. He found candlelight intolerable. For it is impure light – light without force or clarity. It placed great strain upon his eyes.'

It took half an hour to cross Granthaven and reach its eastern edge. The houses were constructed mainly of wood, yet there were also a few grey-bricked edifices. A couple were fitted with windows – yet only one was connected to a stable. Dismounting, Ballas, Crask and Heresh approached the front door.

Ballas looked heavily at Crask.

'No foolishness,' he said simply.

Crask blinked, puzzled.

'Say nothing that will bring us trouble,' growled Ballas. 'Don't mention our scrap in the marshes. Don't tell the quill-master we are on the run. Don't say that we have killed Wardens – for men don't often find such news reassuring. Better if he thinks you are an old ally, asking a favour. And no more.'

'And you? What will he think *you* are?'

'It doesn't matter,' said Ballas, shrugging, 'as long as he does what we ask.' He rapped thrice upon the door. After a short pause, it swung open.

A middle-aged woman stood on the threshold. She had blonde hair, tied sharply back in an austere, shrewish manner. Yet her face was daubed with make-up: her lips were painted soft red, and rouge placed a sunset tincture on her cheeks. On her fingers, two golden rings shone; the stones were large, and looked ungainly upon the thin bands. She looked first at Ballas, then at Crask and Heresh.

'Yes?' she asked, simply. Her voice was thickly accented, yet the *ss*-sound at the single word's end hissed clear – as if self-consciously spoken.

Ballas suddenly understood. The woman's severe hairstyle yet almost whorish make-up; her peasantish accent and expensive but vulgar rings . . . These contradictions suggested that she had not been born into wealth, but had acquired it. The habits of her past mingled with the affectations of her present.

Who was she? wondered Ballas. The quill-master's wife?

He hoped not. Such women were often harridans. They controlled their husbands like hunt masters controlling unruly hounds: with shouts, threats, thrashings. She might make matters difficult. She might not allow the quill-master to help them.

She gazed down her nose at her visitors.

'Well?' she prompted.

'We are seeking Jonas Elsefar,' said Crask, bowing slightly.

'Jonas Elsefar?' The woman frowned. 'That name is unknown to me. For certain, he does not reside here. You have the wrong house.'

The door began to close.

Ballas grabbed the door's edge, stopping it. The woman blinked.

'We've come a long way,' he said darkly. 'Don't be rude to us.'

'I told you, this man . . . this Elsefar – he doesn't live here.'

Ballas lifted his chin. 'But he lived here once?'

'I—' began the woman.

'*He lived here once?*'

The woman nodded, curtly. 'He was a vile man. A *cripple*. In a former life, he had surely been a sinner. For those who demonstrate ill virtue in one life return as hobbled, shambling creatures in the next. Yet – yet he had incredible arrogance. His legs were ruined, he could not easily climb a flight of steps – yet he loved himself as much as the healthiest and most virtuous of men. He was like a rat that imagines itself a lion. A vulture that thinks itself an eagle.' She shook her head. 'I do not like to speak of him. It is thought bad luck to talk of cripples. Speak of them, and you add their infirmities to your own. That is what the wise folk say.'

'Where does he live?' asked Ballas.

The woman smiled – a thin, malignant smirk. 'At the copying house, on Brewhouse Street. A horrid place for a horrid man.'

After receiving directions they rode to Brewhouse Street. The copying house was a long single-floored building, situated halfway along the street. It had a faintly churchlike appearance, partly because of its black brickwork, partly because of the arched windows set into it. A tiled roof tilted upwards, the dark slates glittering with frost. Over the door hung a sign: a quill poised over a parchment.

The window glass was scrubbed spotlessly clean. Through it, Ballas saw row upon row of wooden desks. Behind them sat a legion of scribes.

'What tack ought we take?' said Lugen Crask, wonderingly.

'Tack?' grunted Ballas.

'Do you wish to merely walk in there? Or will your . . . your campaign of discretion persist?' Crask gazed into the copying house. 'The men in there look bored. If so much as an ant entered the room, they would notice it – and notice, too, every detail: the width of its mandibles, the degree of shine upon its skin . . . They would commit you to memory in a trice.'

Crask spoke correctly. Ballas thought for a few moments.

'Go inside,' he said, 'and bring the quill-master out here. Give him some story that won't raise suspicions.'

'Such as?'

'Use your wits,' snapped Ballas.

Crask disappeared into the copying house. From a safe distance, Ballas watched through the window. As Crask stepped inside, every scribe looked up. He said something, then crossed the floor, vanishing from Ballas's view.

'Your father had better make no mistakes,' grunted Ballas, glancing at Heresh. 'For his sake – and your own.'

The red-haired woman shook her head. 'You disgust me,' she whispered.

'Three nights ago, you tried to kill me. I find *that* disgusting. Luckily, you are flat-footed – your footfall woke me up.' He paused, glancing sideling at her. 'That, and your fragrance. You hadn't washed for days, yet still you were sweet-smelling. Some women – the best sort – seem to sweat perfume.' He looked back through the window. 'Tell me: do you reckon it's disgusting that *I* didn't kill *you*?'

Heresh was silent for a few heartbeats. 'I do not believe you did me a kindness,' she eventually said, quietly. 'If you spared me, it was for your own reasons. Yes – now I understand. If you *had* killed me, my father would have refused to help you. While I am alive, you have something with which to threaten my father. The thought of my death frightens him. He will do anything to ensure I do not perish.' She laughed, sourly. 'You are the foulest breed of man. You cannot inspire loyalty, so you depend upon threats.'

'Loyalty's a flimsy thing,' grunted Ballas. 'Fear, though, is far tougher.'

'And you will make Jonas Elsefar fear you?'

'If needs be,' said Ballas, nodding.

'And if he has no children you can threaten?'

Ballas didn't reply. Not immediately. Through the window, he saw Crask returning to the door. Behind him was a squat, white-haired man, with a broad face locked in a scowl. He moved with great awkwardness, supporting himself upon a pair of wooden crutches. His legs were only half-capable of taking his weight. He advanced laboriously, swinging his legs forward, rocking himself upon them – then swinging them forward once more. There was an ungainly agility to this procedure, as if he had performed it all his life. His legs were tied at the ankles, so that they could provide a single pillar of support.

Ballas watched him approach the door.

'Children? Loved ones?' he said, shaking his head. 'Nah. I'd need only to tip woodworm upon his crutches. Or kick him into a pool of water.'

The door opened.

Crask emerged. Moments later, the quill-master followed.

Jonas Elsefar's eyes were green-hazel, and burned with a steady distaste – as if everything appalled him. His mouth was thin-lipped, but wide; silver stubble glittered on a solid jaw. His shirtsleeves were rolled to the elbow, exposing forearms latticed with veins: the consequences, thought Ballas, of using the crutches. Dark ink blotched his fingers.

His gaze darted from Heresh to Ballas. He paused, eyeing the big man closely. Then he coughed.

'This man –' he tilted his head to Crask '– says you have a job for me. Something you'd rather not make official. Something you'd sooner keep from my masters – and have me do on my own.' He rolled his shoulders, as if relieving sore muscles. He glanced at his crutches. Then he sniffed. 'I am the best copyist in Druine. The fastest, the most precise. From dawn till dusk, I labour in there –' he jabbed a thumb towards the copying house '– making copies of all manner of documents. Scholarly treatises, legal texts, prayer sheets and architectural plans – I can reproduce exactly anything you'd care to put on a parchment. I can even create forgeries that seem of equal – even *greater* – authenticity than the originals.' He looked at Ballas. 'As such, I do not sell my talents cheaply. As such –' he paused '– I do not sell them at all. My employers insist I work only for them. You must approach them, if you wish to use my talents.'

The quill-master spoke rapidly. When he finished, he spat on to the ground.

Ballas watched him closely. 'You said you copy prayer sheets—'

'Yes,' interrupted the quill-master, 'and many pieces of a religious nature. Hymnals, the works of theologians, collections of psalms—'

'You labour for the Church?' said Ballas.

Elsefar looked at him. 'The Church? No. They send various pieces to my employers, to be copied – as do many people. My dealings with the Church are those of a whore with her bedfellow: I perform a service, they pay me, and beyond that there is nothing.'

'Does it trouble you,' said Ballas, 'that you act as a whore for the Church – when they once would've killed you?'

Elsefar frowned. 'What are you speaking of?'

Ballas looked to Crask. 'Doesn't he know of your association?'

'I thought it wisest to keep it quiet,' said Crask. 'In the copying house, every ear was pricked . . .'

'You copied forbidden texts,' said Ballas, gazing intently at Elsefar. 'And this man smuggled them.'

'We never met,' Crask said to Elsefar. 'But that was the usual arrangement, was it not? It was safer for all, if we knew nothing of each other.'

The quill-master looked closely at Crask. 'Did you know Cappel Beck?'

'The name is not familiar,' said Crask. 'I worked most frequently with Aldras Cagrille.'

'Cagrille, Cagrille,' murmured Elsefar – then nodded. 'I remember Cagrille. He was captured, was he not?'

'Captured and hanged.'

'But you were not?'

Crask exhaled. 'Through good fortune, rather than fair planning. When the Church apprehended me, I possessed only false texts; they imprisoned me for twenty years. But beyond that: nothing.' He glanced uneasily at Ballas. The big man said nothing.

'You were lucky,' muttered Elsefar, shifting slightly. 'Many men went to the gallows. Or a cage elemental. A few found themselves upon the Penance Oak.'

'They were dark times . . .'

'But it was a darkness we chose for ourselves.' A strange smile flickered on Elsefar's lips. 'And now, you are here to ask a favour, yes?' He looked Crask up and down. 'What do you want from me?'

Lugen Crask glanced at Ballas.

'We can't talk of it here,' said the big man. 'We have to go somewhere quiet.'

'Very well.' With his dragging, forward-swinging steps, Elsefar led them along a narrow street to a windowless wooden building. Inside, upon a bare floor, two dozen beds were set out. The blankets were spun from coarse wool. Odours of decay hung in the air – of damp fabric, rotting; and of wet wood, crumbling to splinters.

Crask took them to a bed in the far corner.

'This,' he said, gesturing along the room, 'is my home. Once I lived in a fine place, on the town's rim. There I was warm and comfortable, and was left mercifully alone. Here, however, I dwell alongside my fellow copyists. It is not a pleasant existence. A man such as me –' he glanced at his legs '– craves solitude. For, in company, one is forced to taste mockery – to hear, again and again, the same jests, the same insults.' Grunting, he sat down on the bed. 'I shall not pretend I am contented.' He propped his crutches against the bed. 'Now: we have silence. So tell me your business. Do you have something you want copying? Something ornate, something delicate? Something requiring a fine touch?'

'Once,' said Ballas, 'you copied maps. That's true, yes?'

Elsefar nodded. 'Maps of every nature. Maps charting smugglers' routes, and watercourses, the paths of ancient armies, the ways trodden by the Four . . . Druine's geography has disparate significances for many men. They seek different things from the Church's land.'

'And the land that isn't the Church's?'

Elsefar blinked. 'All land is the Church's,' he said.

'Belthirran isn't,' replied Ballas.

The quill-master smiled. 'That is true . . . if you consider Belthirran a land at all. For all we know, it might not exist. It could be merely an idea, a dream, a phantom thought . . .'

'There are maps showing a way over the Garsbracks to Belthirran,' said Ballas.

'Such maps once existed.' Elsefar nodded. 'I copied many of them – and each was different to the other. If each was to be trusted, there had to be a million safe tracks over the mountains. And Belthirran would have been overrun by travellers.'

'I am seeking such a map.'

'For what purpose?'

'That's my business,' said Ballas sourly. 'Were there some maps you thought more trustworthy than others?'

Elsefar shrugged and said nothing.

'I have to find the one that you reckon is best,' Ballas persisted.

'None survive,' said the quill-master. 'When the Church grew aware of the trade in forbidden texts, we – that is, everyone with a hand in the business – thought it wise to destroy all the evidence. I can recall making a bonfire of my own parchments. There were many pieces that greatly pleased me – pieces in which my skills were strongly evident, pieces that would have bolstered my reputation . . . The flames, smoke and dark ash upset me. It was one thing to *sell* such documents; but to obliterate them?' He shook his head. 'Of course, the Pilgrim Church confiscated some documents, from other smugglers and quill-masters. Perhaps they still exist. Perhaps, in holy fervour, the Church incinerated them. It is impossible to tell.'

Crask looked at Ballas. 'I told you it was so,' he said, folding his arms. 'Our journey has been wasted.'

'Many journeys end in failure,' commented Elsefar. 'Be they journeys of the body, or of the soul . . .'

'I have to find a way over the mountains,' said Ballas suddenly. '*I have to find Belthirran.*'

A silence descended. Then Lugen Crask began to laugh.

'I ought to have guessed. Yet . . . yet it is such an absurd idea, I had no inkling . . . You wish to escape the Church by hiding in Belthirran – in a land that might not exist. That might, as Elsefar says, be mere rumour.'

Ballas ignored the former smuggler. 'If I'm to stand a chance, I've got to find a map, and it must be the one most worthy of trust.'

Jonas Elsefar grew very still. 'Like your friend,' he said, flicking a gesture at Crask, 'I think you are mad.'

'Help me,' said Ballas, 'and you'll be rewarded. Get me a map—'

'As I said, there *are* no maps. But perhaps—' Elsefar paused. 'Perhaps you will not need one.' His gaze grew contemplative. He looked past Ballas, as if some thought hung visibly in the air. 'Maybe I can help you . . . for a price.' His gaze drifted to Ballas. He looked the big man over from head to toe. 'You are not wealthy,' he observed.

'If you need money,' growled Ballas, 'I'll find some.'

Elsefar shook his head. 'I was about to say that you are fortunate, for your poverty does not concern me. I have an errand for you.' Taking his crutches, he struggled to his feet. 'On Blackberry Row, there is a tavern: the Scarlet Ghost. Behind it, you will find a park – just a patch of grass, a pond, some trees . . . Go there at eveningfall. We shall see how we may benefit one another.'

Using Crask's money, Ballas rented a lodging room in the Scarlet Ghost and stabled the horses. Inside, with Crask and his daughter, he waited for darkness to settle. Despite the tedium, no one spoke.

Ballas knew why.

For days, a question had preoccupied Heresh. Now it preoccupied her father, too. Ballas saw it in the old man's glances – his eye-flashes of fleeting scrutiny; and, when he believed Ballas was not looking, in his protracted stares, as if every aspect of Ballas's appearance, from his face to his clothing, might yield some insight into his true character.

Lugen Crask knew Ballas was a killer. But now he wanted to know . . . *needed* to know the extent of his ruthlessness.

Only after their meeting with Elsefar had this curiosity truly emerged. Ballas knew the exact moment. Crask had been mocking him for seeking Belthirran. Mid-sentence, his voice had wavered, his laughter thinned – *that* had been when Crask had realised the danger he was in. For he had understood, suddenly, that he knew Ballas's plans and that, with such knowledge, he posed a threat to Ballas. For if Crask were to inform the Wardens – or if the Wardens were to extract the secret from him – Ballas's chances of success would be jeopardised.

In the lodging room, Crask's silence was fraught, nervy – the silence of a man whose life depends upon a dice-roll.

Ballas wondered idly what he *would* do with Crask, and his daughter, when their usefulness was finished. He had scarcely thought about the matter.

He shrugged inwardly. Either way, it was of no odds.

Evening seeped through Granthaven's streets.

Ballas left the tavern and strode into the park. It was a clear night. Moonlight silvered a long thorn-hedge, a few leafless larches and a pond, its surface ice-plated. At the park's edge, though, darkness gathered. It was most dense between two large, squarish buildings: a block of hard blackness, into which the moonlight sank and vanished, like a piece of bright jewellery tossed into a fathomless sea.

A hunted man, Ballas mistrusted darkness. It unsettled most men, one way or another. But if they merely *feared* it concealed some mysterious threat, Ballas had to assume that it really did. When a slow dragging noise, punctuated by a *clack* after dull *clack* of one hard object upon another, drifted from the darkness, Ballas did not act as most men would have: he did not ponder the noise's source and wait for it to reveal itself. He slowly drew his dagger and approached it.

As he drew close, Jonas Elsefar appeared. On his crutches, he hauled himself into the park. On his forehead, sweat glimmered – each bead a blob of molten silver. Muttering, he sagged back against a larch, exhausted.

Ballas grew still. Tilting his head, he listened; but he heard no noise except Elsefar's breathing.

'I haven't been followed,' gasped the quill-master.

'You are certain?'

'Of course.' Muttering, he lifted the flap of a hip bag. Then he took out a whisky flagon. 'Every winter,' he said, 'the cold seems sharper. Every winter, I feel that I am nothing but ice. It is one of the perils of age. Most men fear infirmity; but I am already infirm. To occupy my mind – my ageing brain – I must find a different complaint. So it is the weather. In the winter, it is the cold; in summer, the heat.' He took a deep sip. An expression of relief crossed his face. 'I would offer you a mouthful,' he said, recorking the flagon, 'but you must keep a clear head, if you are to fulfil your part of the bargain.'

'Yes, the bargain,' muttered Ballas. 'What'd you have me do, Elsefar – and what do I get in return?'

'I cannot offer you a map of the mountains,' began Elsefar, slipping the flagon back into the hip bag. 'But I can give you the name of a man who has crossed them. A man who claims that, if the elements had not conspired against him, he could have reached Belthirran.'

Ballas stared heavily at him. 'A guide?'

'No,' said Crask. 'Like myself, he is old – his exploring days will be over. But he understands the mountains. I have copied many accounts of the journey to Belthirran. Most, I mistrusted. They had the false lustre of fiction. And their authors were not men of integrity. They sought fame. They sought money. They were liars, intending to profit from the trade in forbidden texts. But this man? He did not want fame. In fact, he avoided it, as if it were something noxious. He wrote his account anonymously, and scarcely a soul knew it was his work. And he did not want money, for he was already rich.'

'Who is he? A merchant? A Servant of the Church?'

Elsefar smiled. 'Later,' he said, raising a finger. 'Once your work is done.'

'And what *is* this work, Elsefar?'

'Work that a man such as you –' a gesture took in Ballas's form '– will be very familiar with.'

Ballas frowned.

'*Killing*,' whispered Elsefar.

Ballas blinked, surprised. He hadn't thought about what Elsefar would demand in exchange for his help. But even if he *had* given it thought, *much* thought, he wouldn't have expected what the quill-master had just said.

'You reckon I am a killer?' He gazed firmly at the quill-master. 'That I go easily to blood?'

Elsefar nodded. 'You have a murderer's sheen,' he said. 'Killing does not particularly please you. You do not think it a sport. But when needs must, you do not hesitate. In your eyes there is a clarity, like that of a bird of prey. Something watchful. Something unflinching. I confess that it disturbs me. For I am weak, and in matters violent, the thoroughfare runs only one way.' He shrugged. 'Your colour is red, my friend. Not sunset red, or the red of a rose. But the red of the wilderness. And,' his voice took on a casual tone, 'there is this to consider.' He drew out a furled parchment. 'Read it,' he said, proffering it.

Ballas took the scroll. Unrolling it, he peered at the quill-script: the letters swirled neatly, and on the top four rows they were larger than elsewhere, the ink more thickly daubed.

Decree of Righteous Annihilation:
Issued by the Pilgrim Church's Most Devout Servants
On the fourteenth day of the twelfth month
In the year five hundred and twelve, after the Melding.

Ballas breathed out.

In his chest, his heart thudded – it banged upon his ribs like a fist. Licking his lips, he glanced at Elsefar.

'Read it,' repeated the quill-master. 'I assure you, it is genuine.'

By Order of the Blessed Masters, the decree continued, *the man named as Anhaga Ballas, who has caused the highest offence to the Four, the Pilgrim Church and Druine is, by whatever means, to have taken from him his life, which, like that of any mortal, was once divine, but has now become a thing abhorrent.*

Unto every citizen, regardless of rank, wealth, age or sex, falls the duty, in accord with the Four's will, of killing Anhaga Ballas. To this end, no method is prohibited – for the action is holy. To this end, no contrivance of circumstance, or duplicity, or manner commonly thought blasphemous, is prohibited – for the action is holy.

Anhaga Ballas is in height six feet and eight inches, his hair is black, like raven feathers; his eyes are of a green-brown hue, and he is of a heavy build. His features are broken, the nose naught but disfigured gristle, his face scarred upon the cheeks; and, upon his forehead, is a wound, shaped like a week-old moon, and this shall become a scar. His voice is deep, and when he talks his accent is that of the southern region of Hearthfall.

Upon the provision of proof of his death, a reward will be administered to those who, by that deed alone, will have cleared from their souls the marks of all previous sins.

By Order of the Blessed Masters.

'The Blessed Masters,' said Elsefar softly, 'are seldom guilty of understatement. But here they excel themselves. They are desperate to see you dead, Anhaga Ballas. Decrees of Annihilation are seldom issued. They are dangerous – all across Druine, men who bear the mildest resemblance to yourself will be in jeopardy. Dozens may die, so that your death might come about.'

'Where did you get this?' Ballas felt his sweat dampening the scroll.

'Where but the copying house? It arrived yesterday morning from Soriterath. We have been instructed to quill two thousand copies, and spread them throughout this part of Druine. They are to be be mounted upon every church gate and cathedral doorpost. And, so that sinners may join the hunt and absolve themselves, they will be nailed to the walls of every alehouse and every brothel bedchamber. Soon, every class of man, and woman, will be watchful. And they won't grow lax or forgetful: the Blessed Masters have seen to that. You will notice that your crime has not been specified. This will provoke curiosity. What has he done, to deserve a Decree of Annihilation? Your ill deeds will become rumour. Every mind that thinks rarely of anything but gambling and ale will suddenly turn philosophical: *what* crime could be so bad? Eventually, the nervous will start to fear you. The brave will wish to prove their strength by killing you. Soon, superstitious gossip will spring up: Anhaga Ballas will become more than a man – he will be demon-possessed, an emissary sent by dark spirits, he will be Gatarix reborn . . . Your death will be desired with greater and greater strength. And, in time, your death will come. No man can elude a whole nation's wrath. Not for ever.'

Elsefar took the scroll from Ballas. Yet the big man could still feel the parchment against his skin.

The park seemed utterly silent. Ballas gazed at the shadows. They no longer struck him as sinister. He wished only to embrace them. To stride into them and be consumed by whatever hazards they concealed. He hungered for oblivion . . .

Yet the sensation passed.

He grunted. 'Have you copied the Decree?'

'Not yet,' said Elsefar. 'Fulfil your half of the bargain, and I will not do so. Naturally, we are not the only copying house in Druine that has been assigned this job. Sooner or later, everyone *will* know of you. But perhaps a little time can be bought. Do as I ask and the Brewhouse Street copying house will not be transcribing the Decree.'

For a short time, Ballas was silent.

'You spoke of killing,' he said eventually.

From his hip bag, Elsefar pulled out a square of parchment. Upon it, penned in dark ink, were three faces, each exquisitely drawn: the quill-work was so vivid that the faces seemed on the verge of moving – the lips twitching with speech, the eyes blinking. Underneath each face was a list of places: a mix of taverns, brothels, gambling dens and houses.

'These are the men I want you to kill,' said Elsefar.

'Who are they?'

'My employers.'

Ballas glanced up.

Elsefar nodded. 'I know what you are thinking. A man in my circumstances ought to be grateful for whatever work he finds. After all, what use is a cripple?' He clenched his jaw. 'Do not presume these men purchase my services out of charity. They employ me because I am the best there is. The fastest, the cleanest of hand . . . Yes: the best, if not the most modest. In a single day, I do the work of forty men – but for a single man's wage. And that is the problem.' He glanced at Ballas. 'I am not permitted to leave their employ. I wear no shackles, yet I am still a slave. My employers supply my lodgings – my damp, stinking, flea-infested room. For this, I pay rent – a rent that scarcely leaves me enough money from my wages to buy food. If I could, I would seek cheaper lodgings, away from the copying house. But there are none cheaper than those provided by my employers. So I am trapped. My rent is paid not in advance but in arrears: thus I am always *owing* money . . . If I were to leave the copying house, I would be in debt and then – my employers are ruthless. Damn it!' Elsefar smacked his crutch-ferrule upon the grass. 'Why do vulgar men dress up their brutality, their primitive schemes, in such elaborate garb? Does it make them feel intelligent?' He looked evenly at Ballas. 'They want me to stay at the copying house. They know that only the threat of death will keep me there. So that threat is made. They disguise it as some convoluted system of rents and wages . . . Yet if I go, they will kill me. It is that simple. Now, Anhaga Ballas: will you kill them – and release me?'

Ballas thought for a moment. 'How do I know you are not lying about the explorer? About the man who says he has crossed the mountains?'

This amused Elsefar. 'I am hiring you to commit murder,' he said. 'In itself, that is a crime. I could hang for it. What is it they say about shared guilt encouraging trust and honour?' His expression darkened. 'If you wished, you could betray me. You could inform the Wardens – which is not likely, I admit. But if you were captured who is to know what you would say in the moments before your death?'

The last sentence rang in Ballas's ears. He knew what Elsefar was driving at. He was Ballas's best chance – his *only* chance – of finding someone who could lead him to Belthirran. What choice did Ballas have but to trust him?

'If you are lying,' said the big man, 'I will find you, and kill you.'

'I know, I know,' said Elsefar. 'And because of that alone, you know I will not betray you.' Struggling closer, the quill-master prodded the list of locations on the parchment. 'These are the favourite haunts of my employers. The chances are that you will find them there.' He looked up at Ballas. 'I presume we have made a deal?'

'Yes.'

'Be true to your colour, Anhaga Ballas.'

The first two killings were not difficult.

From the parchment, Ballas chose as his first target a square-jawed, heavy-browed man named Brander Shan. Shan was a gambler. His haunts, identified by Elsefar, were those where a man could test his luck, and his powers of judgement. A warehouse where bare-knuckle bouts were fought. A long oval mud-track where dogs raced in torchlight. And a few outwardly ordinary houses inside which dice-games were played.

As Ballas trod from place to place, seeking his quarry, he wondered whether Shan was having a good night. Was he thriving? Was Mistress Fortune treating him kindly? Or was he cursing his ill luck? Would he consider his death in keeping with the evening's flow – a mere tightening of his general gloom?

Ballas found Shan in the Grinning Wolf – a loud, smoke-clogged tavern, with a circle chalked on the floorboards.

Shan sat near the circle's edge, drinking. He was bigger than Ballas had expected. And Elsefar's sketch hadn't captured the cold, dull cruelty of his eyes. Shark's eyes, thought Ballas. The eyes of a creature that follows its compulsions – its hungers and thirsts – yet never experiences pleasure. Only satisfaction.

Ballas couldn't hope to kill him in the common room. It was too crowded and, once the deed was done, he'd have no chance of escaping.

So he walked behind the tavern and, clambering over a high wooden fence, stood in the shadows of the pissing yard – and waited.

Drinker after drinker came out of the rear door to relieve themselves upon the muddy ground. With every fresh footstep, Ballas touched the knife tucked behind his belt. He felt his throat grow dry, his heart thud. It had been a long time since he had killed in cold blood. A long time since he had premeditated another's death. It did not thrill him. It gave him no sense of power. It was a means to an end, nothing more. He thought only about the reason why he had to kill. What the killing would bring him. He thought of the explorer Elsefar had mentioned. But mostly he thought of Belthirran.

Ballas was recalling his dream of the Land Beyond the Mountains . . . was seeing again the fields and cattle and distant buildings . . . when Shan appeared.

Ballas sank back into the shadows.

A second man followed Shan. They stood side by side, pissing on to the frozen mud. They talked of insignificant things – women, ale, a cock-fight they had just seen. The second man finished pissing but did not return to the tavern. He lingered near Shan and continued talking. Ballas cursed, silently. Then shouting sounded from the tavern.

'They've started,' said the man, moving to the door. 'I don't want to miss a second of it.' He glanced at Shan. 'Which bird did you bet on?'

'The darkest one,' replied Shan, slurring slightly.

'Bastard,' muttered the man. 'I wagered on the other. Which means, in short, that I have lost. This is your night, Brander. All the luck is yours. How much have you won already?'

'I haven't been counting.'

'Pah! Usually it's the losers who don't keep track . . .'

'A man cannot stay lucky for ever,' remarked Shan.

The other man went into the tavern.

Shan fumbled his childmaker back into his breeches. As he turned, Ballas strode forward – and slammed the dagger into Shan's lower back. The man gasped, his body tensing. Looping a forearm around his throat, Ballas jerked him backwards and snapped his neck. Shan's corpse slith-ered to the ground. Stooping, Ballas wrenched out the knife. Then he climbed over the fence, into the street.

As he walked away, he heard laughter from the pissing yard.

'Hey, Brander,' came a man's voice. 'Feeling worse for wear, eh? Come on, get up! You've won again! It was a short enough bout. The dark bird was savage. I've never seen anything like it.' There was a pause. Then: 'Shan? Sweet grief! The Wardens – summon the Wardens!'

Ballas picked up his pace.

Ballas found the second man at the first place he looked: the copying house. The man was seated behind a desk in a small office, adjoining the room where, during daylight hours, the scribes worked. Now, except for the second target – named Caggerick Blunt – the copying house was empty.

He was thin, bald-headed. Sagging folds hung under his eyes, as if he hadn't slept for months. Judging by his list of haunts, he did nothing but work: if he hadn't been in the copying house, he would have been in any one of a number of warehouses, or at a second office, further across the city.

As Ballas stepped through the door, Blunt looked up.

'Yes?'

'Egren Callen?' asked Ballas, on purpose giving the name not of the man seated in front of him but of the man he intended to kill after him.

'Who are you?' Blunt squinted.

'A messenger from Soriterath. Are you Egren Callen?'

'No.'

Ballas muttered, as if this displeased him. 'Where can I find him? I have something for him.'

'Tonight, I believe he is at his home, on Harvest Street.'

'Where is that?'

Speaking briskly, Blunt gave Ballas directions. Yet gradually, his voice slowed. Uncertainty flickered in his eyes. He peered intently at Ballas's face . . . at his forehead. His uncertainty changed to recognition.

Raising his fingers, Ballas touched the crescent-shaped scar.

'Yes,' he said, softly.

Springing forward, he drove a right hook hard into Blunt's cheek. The man's eyes rolled back and then he clattered to the floor. Moving around the desk, Ballas kneeled by the unconscious form. Drawing his knife, he cut Blunt's throat. Blood sprayed from an artery, speckling Ballas's tunic front.

Grunting, Ballas rose. He wiped his dagger blade clean on his leggings. Then he left the copying house.

That had been twenty minutes ago. Now Ballas walked quickly over the paving slabs of Harvest Street. Ahead stood a three-floored building, crafted from dark brick. Though not vast enough to be considered a mansion, it *did* exude wealth. It was surrounded by an eight-foot wall of weather-scrubbed stone. Beyond that, a few poplars speared towards the night sky. The poplars and the wall had been described by Blunt. Ballas halted. He had reached Egren Callen's home.

A set of gates were set into the wall, forty paces away. Two men were on sentry-go. In informal garb, they were not Papal Wardens – yet they *were* armed, each bearing a knife and a short sword. Part of a private guard, Ballas realised. Muttering, he backed into the shadows of a shop doorway.

The final killing would not be as easy as the first two.

If he approached the guards, he would be seen, and he doubted that could overpower them both – not if each carried a sword. And if he *did* succeed, the noises of combat would alert the other guards who were undoubtedly patrolling the grounds around Callen's home. Ballas tapped his fingertips lightly with his knife, thinking.

Then he released a deep breath.

The only way into the grounds was over the wall. Tucking his knife into his belt, Ballas left the doorway and ran noiselessly across the street.

Despite the grandeur of Callen's home, the wall was crudely constructed: a sharp-edged mass of interlocking stone lumps like the drystone walls found in some of Druine's rural regions. That was good, Ballas thought. At least there would be hand holds.

The big man spat on his hands. Then he jumped and grabbed the wall's upper edge. Grunting, he began hauling himself up. But his own weight surprised him. He felt like he had an ox's bulk. His muscles strained, and grew hot. He felt his face flaring red as blood gathered under his skin. Swearing softly, he hung motionless for a few heartbeats. Then he let go, dropping back to the ground.

He glanced towards the gates. The guards were talking among themselves. They hadn't heard his descent. Or the rubbing of his clothes against the stones.

Ballas looked up at the wall.

'Come on,' he urged himself in a half-whisper. 'Don't be so bloody weak.'

He jumped up again. This time, using his upward momentum, he dragged himself on to the top of the wall. Through the poplars, he glimpsed half a dozen figures, moving slowly through a large, well-kept garden. He could see scabbards at their hips. And knife sheaths strapped to their belts.

He swung down from the wall and hid behind a poplar bole.

Ballas felt a dull pain in his hands. His palms were bleeding, cut open by the stones. He wiped them on the back of his leggings. Then he wondered how he was going to leave the grounds. Over the wall again? Or through the gate – for, after the killing, he'd have no real reason to be discreet?

It did not matter – not yet.

Keeping close to the wall, and the poplars' shadows, Ballas crept swiftly around the grounds, keeping his gaze on Callen's home. The building was in darkness, every window a patch of black. Cursing, Ballas wondered if Blunt had been mistaken. Perhaps Callen was *not* at home that night?

Then, to the rear of the building, he saw a lit third-floor window. The window was hinged fractionally open and the curtains hung slightly apart. Crouching behind a holly bush, Ballas listened. At first he heard only his own breathing. And noises of the night: a cart rattling along a distant road, a breeze stirring the poplar branches. Then he made out another sound, coming from the window. Though faint, it was clear – and unmistakable.

A woman's groans. They sounded over and over, rhythmically and with increasing speed. They did not spring from suffering, merely from a type of near-painful pleasure.

The woman was rutting.

In the darkness, Ballas felt his loins stir. His tunic was blood-splashed and he had killed two men that evening. Soon he was to take the life of a third. Yet arousal touched him. He felt his throat go dry.

Maybe, when all the killing is done, I'll find a woman for myself, he thought. It's been a black evening, and I deserve a little light . . . the light that glints in a whore's eyes. He wondered, suddenly, if there would be whores in Belthirran. And taverns. And ale and wine and whisky.

Then he thought of the Pilgrim Church: of the Wardens he had killed, and those he had not encountered but who would be hunting him; of the Lectivin Nu'hkterin, and of the death of Gerack upon the Penance Oak.

Ballas felt suddenly uneasy. Frightened, even. It lasted only an instant. Yet it was enough to assure him that it didn't matter if there were whores in Belthirran. Or drinking houses. Only that he could find the Land beyond the Mountains.

He blinked.

Never before had he suspected that a desire to avoid pain could be more powerful than the desire to attain pleasure.

He spat on to the grass. Then he looked up at the window. The woman's copulation sounds continued.

Rising, Ballas completed his circuit of the building, trying to find a back door that might not be guarded. There was none. Swearing, he moved close to the building, and stole towards the front door.

There was a single guard – a tall man of middle years. His face had the stark slenderness of an axe blade. His eyes were tiny, and glittered sharply as he surveyed the grounds. He looked attentive, vigilant. He chewed slowly upon something. Tobacco, perhaps. Or a knot of flex-weed. One hand rested on his sword hilt.

Ballas watched him carefully.

He could easily surprise the guard. If he moved fast enough, he could plunge his knife into the man's throat. Then he would be able to enter Callen's home. But, of course, the killing would draw the other guards' attention. They would attack. He would have no choice except to fight.

Ballas drew a breath. He carried only knives. He'd have little chance against six or seven swordsmen. It would be necessary to steal the slain guard's sword. Then, because he couldn't fight all the guards at once, he'd have to vanish into the darkness and pick them off one at a time.

A difficult task. Yet he had no choice.

Standing upright, he started to draw his knife. Then he paused.

The thin-faced guard was calling to a companion. 'Ghallarin,' he said, his voice loud in the quiet air. 'You got any more tobacco?'

'What?' replied a guard, a hundred yards away.

'Tobacco – you got any more?'

'Yeah.'

'Lend me some, will you?'

'I've already given you a gobful.'

'I've used it . . .'

'Bloody hell – things don't last long with you, do they? It's the same when you're drinking. One instant the tankard is full, the next it's all gone. Tell me, do you ever *taste* it? I don't think so. You might as well be supping salt water . . .'

'Just bring me some more tobacco,' said the thin-faced guard, irritated.

The other guard sighed, audibly. 'Come and get it yourself,' he said. 'I'm not your bloody servant.'

It was if some god of killing had blessed Ballas. As if it had, in return for the blood he'd shed, made things easy for him. The guard moved away from the door and strode towards his friend. Seizing his chance, Ballas emerged from the shadows and opened the door. The hinges were well oiled, and silent. As he crossed the threshold, into a pitch-dark ante-room, he glanced back. The thin-faced guard was still walking towards his colleague. The other guards continued their patrols. They hadn't seen Ballas. They did not even suspect anyone was there.

Ballas closed the door.

A few threads of moonlight had pierced the darkness. Now they were extinguished. There was nothing except blackness. Groping, Ballas found a second door. He grasped the ring-handle and twisted. The handle turned a fraction – then jammed.

'Locked,' muttered Ballas.

Kneeling, he took a lock-pick from his pocket – just an elaborately toothed-and-indented bone splinter. He worked upon the lock for a few seconds. Inside, something shifted – then clicked. Ballas twisted the handle once more. The door creaked open.

Ballas stepped into a long corridor. Moonlight poured through a row of arched windows. A carpet covered the floor. Upon the walls hung paintings, their images indistinct in the weak light.

Ballas unsheathed his knife. Then he followed the corridor to a large, echoing room. At the far end, a stone stairwell rose into the gloom. Ballas climbed it to the second floor. Here he found himself in another corridor. He followed it, then ascended a second, narrower staircase, emerging on to the third floor.

Ahead, a door stood slightly ajar. A strip of hazy firelight spilled out. Ballas smelled smouldering herbs: the sort from the Distant East that, when burned, give off a fragrance reputed to inflame passions. Silently, Ballas approached the door. He cocked his head, listening. No sound came from inside the chamber. No feminine groans of delight. No masculine grunts of lust.

Drawing a breath, Ballas swung open the door.

In an instant he took in the bedchamber. Deep red rugs covered the floor. Candles flickered within niches. In the opposite wall, there was a window: heavy scarlet curtains hung half open.

And there was a bed: a four-poster, veiled in a red gauzelike fabric. Upon it sat a young woman. She had a pleasant, farm-girl type of face: plump, large-eyed and full-lipped. A gentle blush coloured her cheeks. Her dark hair tumbled on to her chest; a few strands were sweat-stuck to the side of her face. She was staring at her fingernails, and humming. When Ballas entered, she did not look up.

'You were quick,' she said. 'By the Four's mercy, I am hungry. What have you brought?'

Saying nothing, Ballas closed the door.

'Spiced apples,' said the woman, brightly. 'I crave spiced apples. Have you got any? And cheese – that pale, crumbling cheese from the south. What is it called? Oh, I cannot remember. My brain is all a-fuddle. Lovemaking gives me an appetite, and steals my wits. No matter. Whatever you have brought will be enough.' She turned her face to Ballas. Then she froze. Very slowly, her large eyes blinked. She tilted her head. She seemed like a fawn transfixed by torchlight.

'Who . . . who are you?'

Ballas strode towards the bed. The girl recoiled, scrambling over the mattress towards the far side of the room.

'*Who are you?*' she repeated. Then panic seized her: Ballas saw it flare in her eyes – a hot, wild light. Springing forward, he grabbed her forearm and dragged her off the bed. He clamped his hand over her mouth. He felt her lips – soft, warm – against his palm.

'Make a noise, and I'll cut you open,' he said, lifting the knife to her throat. 'Understand?'

The woman struggled.

'*Understand?*'

The woman stopped squirming and nodded. She wore a nightgown of white linen: a surprisingly heavy, inelegant piece of clothing.

'Where is Egren Callen? Answer no louder than a whisper.' Ballas moved his hand an half-inch from her mouth.

'He has gone to the privy,' she said. 'Then he is to bring me food.'

Ballas took her to the corner by the door. 'Do nothing foolish,' he said, 'and you'll live. All right?'

The woman nodded.

'Tell me,' said Ballas, 'who are you? Callen's wife? His mistress? Or a whore?'

'A whore.'

Good, thought Ballas.

No whore valued a client's life over her own – no matter how well he paid her or how gently he treated her. The woman wouldn't interfere. She'd simply let Ballas do what needed to be done.

Muffled footsteps came from the corridor. The woman's breathing faltered. With his free hand, the one not gripping his knife, Ballas lightly took hold of her upper arm. Something bumped dully against the door.

Ballas waited for the door to open.

And waited.

A voice from the other side said, 'Elspeth, I told you to leave the door open! My hands are full; I can't reach the handle. Stir yourself, and help me.'

Ballas swept the woman towards the bed. She stumbled, sprawling upon the mattress. Spinning round, Ballas seized the ring-handle and wrenched open the door.

Egren Callen stood on the threshold. In his arms he held a silver serving tray, laden with bread, cheese and two mugs of steaming liquid. He was a youngish man, with neatly cropped black hair. His eyebrows were very dark, and thick stubble covered his jaw. He wore a silken dressing gown and a pair of leather boots: an absurd combination, intended merely for the walk to the privy and the larder.

His gaze met Ballas's.

For a moment nothing happened.

Then Ballas punched Callen in the face, hard. The young man staggered backwards into the corridor. The blow had been powerful; blood spurted from Callen's nose. Yet he did not fall. Charging at Ballas, he cracked the serving tray edge-on into the big man's forehead. Sparks flared in Ballas's vision. Grunting, he stumbled back a step.

Then wet darkness swept over his eyes.

Swearing, he dragged his hand across his face. His palm came away soaked in blood. The blow had split open his forehead. For a moment he could see. Then blood poured into his eyes again.

Sleeving it away, he saw Callen sprinting towards his clothes, heaped at the far side of the bed. Swearing, Ballas ran at him – just as Callen, snatching at his tangled breeches, unsheathed a dragger from the belt. Ballas swung an uppercut that slammed shut Callen's jaw. The young man toppled backwards against the wall, upending a bedside table. A bowl of burning herbs tipped on to the floor. His knife held low, Ballas advanced.

Callen scrambled to his feet. With his free hand, Ballas wiped blood from his brow – again and again.

'A problem, stranger?' gritted Callen, grinning balefully.

Ballas said nothing. A blood-trickle crept into his eye. For an instant he was half blinded. Callen leaped at him. His knife blade jabbed towards Ballas's stomach – but the big man knocked his hand away. Jumping forward, he drove his dagger down at Callen's collarbone. The young man dived sideways. Overbalancing, Ballas tripped headlong. Blood poured into his eyes once more. Wiping it away, he spun and hurled the knife where he thought . . . where he *knew* Callen would be.

In the firelight, the knife flashed. Ballas's aim was true: the weapon headed straight for the young man. Yet Callen had seized the whore and jerked her in front of himself.

Time stood still. The dagger hung suspended, as if gripped by some invisible hand. There was a cold gleam on Callen's eyes. And in the whore's eyes Ballas could see . . . was *certain* he could see the dagger's reflection: a tiny splinter of light, glowing in each dark iris.

The dagger spun, slamming into the whore's breastbone. She teetered back against Callen and looked down numbly at her nightdress. Blood blotched the linen. She gasped, faintly. Then she collapsed, face down on the mattress.

Turning, Callen ran for the door.

Leaping over the bed, Ballas intercepted him. Dropping his knife, the big man punched Callen in the face, again and again. Each blow shook the young man's body. Each punch landed with such force that Callen seemed incapable of resisting. He simply *allowed* Ballas to strike him. Like a man adrift on a storm-struck ocean submits to the raging waters.

When Ballas stopped, the young man's face was a face no more – just a glistening blood-mask. With each breath, a bubble of blood swelled and popped on his lips.

'Who . . . are you?' he rasped.

Ballas did not reply. With studied deliberation, he stooped to retrieve his knife. When he looked up Callen was stumbling towards the window.

Ballas frowned, curious.

The young man swung open the window. Then he clambered out on to a ledge. Very carefully, he edged out of view.

Ballas walked to the window.

The ledge was wide – so wide that even a punch-drunk man could walk along it.

Pressed flat to the wall, Callen tried to shout. 'Guards – help me!' His voice was an inaudible croak. 'Guards . . .'

Ballas watched him coolly.

Callen returned his gaze. 'I have money . . . if you are a robber, I can give you much, and I will say nothing to the Wardens. I swear it! I will—'

Ballas hurled his knife. Once more, his aim was true. And this time, there was nothing to stop it striking home.

The blade sank into Callen's thigh. The young man gave a startled cry. Then he reflexively lifted his foot, taking weight off the damaged limb.

In that instant, his balance left him.

His arms flailing, blood drizzling from his mouth as he screamed, he fell backwards . . . fifty feet on to a patch of stone tiles. He struck the ground with a sound that was half thud, half crunch. A lone guard heard it.

'Sweet grief! Oh, sweet grief! Callen – he has fallen!'

He looked up at the window. Ballas stared down at him.

'There is someone there! In Callen's room!'

Other guards ran over. They gazed up at Ballas.

Ballas stared down calmly at them. To escape, he would have to fight his way through the guards. Men who were husbands and fathers, brothers and sons . . . whose death would spread grief among the innocent. Among those who were to suffer merely because they loved them.

Ballas grunted. It would not be a problem. Not for him.

Later, much later, after Ballas had left Callen's home and no longer felt in his fist the heft of a sword stolen from a guard . . . no longer felt in his shoulders echoes of the jarring crunch of steel striking bone . . . he returned to the Scarlet Ghost.

Darkness cloaked the tavern. Ballas tried the front door; it was bolted shut. Silently, he stood underneath the window of his lodging room. Stooping, he picked up a few small stones and tossed them at the shutters. They rattled against the wood. Retrieving several more stones, he repeated the action.

The shutters opened.

Lugen Crask peered out. 'Who is there?' he hissed – as if he were a strong, brave man who would retaliate against any threat, any unwanted guest.

'Go downstairs,' said Ballas, 'and open the front door.' To his own ears, his voice sounded odd – flatter than usual. And thick with fatigue.

He walked to the front door. After a short wait, he heard bolts slide. The door opened. Lugen Crask stood on the threshold. In his left hand he held a candle.

'Be quick,' he whispered. 'We mustn't wake the landlord. It would be a terrible thing, to be reported to the Wardens for such a petty thing as . . . oh, I do not know: but this feels like trespass. A man ought not to move furtively through another's home.' He glanced back, through the dark common room. 'Hurry,' he added.

Slowly, Ballas stepped through. He walked heavy-footedly behind the serving bar, and took a whisky flagon from a shelf.

'What are you doing?' Crask sounded frightened. 'That . . . that is theft. We must be careful – isn't that what you insisted? All that business about staying on horseback?'

Ignoring him, Ballas went up the steps to his lodging room. Crask followed close behind. Once they were inside, Crask shut the door and lit a tallow lamp. Orange-yellow light filled the room. Upon the bed, sleeping atop the blankets, lay Crask's daughter. The sudden light woke her. She opened her eyes – and stared at Ballas, her expression unreadable.

Ballas glanced at Crask. He too was staring – but his feelings were apparent. His mouth gaped, his eyes were wide.

'What . . . what has happened? Where have you been? What have you done? Oh, sweet grief: tell me you haven't fought with more Wardens?'

Ballas caught his reflection in a small wall-mirror. Blood-splashes speckled his tunic and leggings. More damp reddish-brown flecks covered his face. Dried blood covered his hands; it looked like he was wearing gloves of Caginnian silk.

He uncorked the flagon and sat on the floor. He took a deep mouthful. The hot liquid swirled down his throat. It burned softly as it went, and Ballas sagged back against the wall.

Crask and Heresh gazed at him as if he had undergone some shocking transformation – as if he had turned from a merely terrible creature into something truly appalling.

Ballas closed his eyes. Even the darkness seemed red.

Chapter 13

And they travelled towards Scarrendestin,
A mountain of holiness
And great power . . .

Ballas awoke.

The taste of whisky hung thickly in his mouth. Beneath it, a different taste – something metallic, coppery.

Blood, he realised.

Grimacing, he opened his eyes. His chin resting on his chest, he saw first the blood upon his tunic front. Then that which coated his hands.

Grunting, he looked up.

Lugen Crask and his daughter were seated on the bed. They stared at him. Ballas wondered if they had been watching him all night. Shifting slightly, he felt his muscles ache: his shoulders, back, chest, legs . . . it seemed that no part of him had escaped the after-effects of strenuous exertion. He flexed his fingers: they were stiff, and the joints burned: the previous night, he had spent much time gripping a sword hilt. An unaccustomed activity – one that he hadn't indulged in for many years until recently.

He drew a breath. How many men had he killed? He could not remember. He hadn't kept track. He was a killer – not an accountant.

He looked at Crask. Then at Heresh. Both were pale, tired-looking. Behind them, light edged the window shutters.

'What hour is it?' asked Ballas, pushing himself upright. His voice was a whisky-scoured rasp. He looked at the flagon, gripped loosely in his left hand. Some liquid remained; he drank it in a single swallow. His throat was numb, and he hardly felt the whisky trickling into his stomach.

'Halfway between dawn and noon,' replied Lugen Crask. Licking his lips, it seemed he wished to say more. Yet he held his silence.

'I need fresh clothes. Bring me some.'

'What . . . ?' said Crask numbly.

'I can't wear these,' snapped Ballas, smacking a hand against his bloodied tunic. 'They'd draw attention, don't you think? You've got money. Buy me new clothes.'

'You . . . you cannot treat us like this,' said Crask softly.

Ballas stared heavily at him.

'You have already taken advantage of us. You have threatened us into doing your bidding. But now you have gone too far.' He glanced nervously at his daughter. 'Last night – what did you do? We – we cannot, *will* not help you, until we know. Up till now, your violence has been . . .'

'The word you are looking for,' said Ballas, 'is *useful*. I've kept you alive. If you want to live a little longer, you'll do what I say.'

'Whose blood marks you?' asked Crask, as if Ballas had not spoken.

'That is not your business.'

'*Whose blood?*'

'No one you'd know – or care about.'

'That is not an answer . . .'

'It's the only one you'll get.' Ballas slammed the whisky flagon on to the floor. 'Now: get me new clothes. All right?'

Sighing, Crask took out his purse and tipped a few coins into his daughter's palm. 'Do as he tells you,' he said, quietly. 'And be careful, yes?'

Rising, Heresh left the room. Crask watched her go. Then he looked evenly at Ballas. 'We shall not serve you for ever,' he said.

Saying nothing, Ballas got to his feet. He moved to a small table on which rested a water bowl. He rinsed his face, then rubbed away the dried blood-flecks.

'You will serve me,' he said eventually, 'as long as I say. Don't forget that the Wardens are still hunting you. Your daughter, like myself, is a killer.'

'We have brought you to Jonas Elsefar,' said Crask. 'We have fulfilled our promise. Does that mean nothing to you?'

Ballas gazed at himself in the mirror. A few blood-spots stained his stubble. He wiped them away. 'I don't know if Elsefar will be of use. Last night, *I* did *his* bidding . . .'

'What?' Crask frowned.

'You didn't expect him to help me for nothing?'

'Oh, so you performed some . . . some morbid errand, yes? To earn his loyalty . . . no: not loyalty – for no sane man could feel such a thing towards you . . . To earn his *compliance*, you . . . you did what, exactly?'

Ballas did not reply.

Lugen Crask picked at his beard. 'You *murdered* – that is it, isn't it? Oh, I don't expect you to answer. You prefer silence. As if a man who doesn't admit his crimes is not guilty.' He folded his arms. Something – fear, perhaps – had made him defiant. 'The Church is seeking you; and you do not want to die. That I can well understand. But it is said that a man's decency and courage are measured not by those things he does in life but by those things he *refuses* to do in order to *preserve* his life.' He looked Ballas up and down. 'You, though, are capable of any foulness, aren't you? Tell me, what is your trade?'

'I have no trade. I'm a vagrant – that is all.'

'And before that? No – do not tell me. Allow me to guess. It was something despicable, yes? What were you: a whoremaster? A thief? Hm? They are solitary professions. I cannot imagine you working alongside others. But maybe you did. Have you worked the seas, as an exporter of whores? And importer of forbidden herbs? Perhaps that is too great an effort. Maybe you were part of a raiding team. Yes, you have the look of a brigand—'

Ballas smacked an open hand against Crask's head – a powerful blow that sent Crask hurtling across the room. He struck the wall, then slid to the floor. Ballas stepped closer. The former smuggler curled into a ball.

'Do not hurt me! Please – I am sorry . . .'

Grasping his shirt collar, Ballas dragged him to his feet.

'Do not goad me!' snapped Ballas, wrapping a hand around Crask's throat. He slammed him against the wall. Crask groaned. Already, he was weeping. 'It ain't me who is a betrayer. It ain't me who broke trust to save his own skin.' He tightened his grip. 'Did you feel guilty, when you told the Church about your accomplices? When you gave their names, so yours might avoid being etched on a gravestone?' Turning, he hurled Crask across the room. The former smuggler crashed into the table. 'What'd you *refuse* to do, to save your neck? What'd sicken you so much you'd sooner die?'

Crask lay upon the floor, sobbing. 'I am not a brave man . . .'

'That's for sure,' spat Ballas. 'And you aren't honourable, either. I tell you now, Crask, fear is no excuse – for *anything*.'

'I am not a brave man,' Crask repeated – and the words fell easily but earnestly from his lips. Ballas sensed that, in the past, he had uttered them often. To himself, of course – for they weren't words to be spoken aloud. But in solitary moments, when Crask felt ashamed of his betrayals, they were there to lessen his guilt – to make the betrayals somehow ordinary. Someone had once told Ballas that if a man believed it was his nature to be fearful, he would also believe that anything that dispelled his fears was justified – as it was justified for a hungry man to kill for food. Crask wanted his betrayals to appear *inevitable*. He had betrayed his fellows, and it was beyond his abilities to do otherwise. Thus he couldn't be blamed. His base actions were merely misfortunes.

Ballas felt himself hating Crask. 'A man makes up his own mind whether to be brave,' he said. 'He reckons up whether it's worth it or not. You didn't think it was. That troubles you. If it didn't, you wouldn't be bleating that you aren't brave . . . that, in truth, you're a coward by birth, not by intent.' He drew a deep breath. 'Your daughter has a stronger heart than you. Do you know that she tried to kill me?'

Crask shook his head.

'I was impressed.'

'By someone who would murder you?'

'There was never a chance she'd succeed. I'm a light sleeper, and she's as heavy-footed as a sow. She tried and failed. In such circumstances, I can be forgiving.'

'And because you admired her spirit, you let her live?'

'Her spirit? No. Her *usefulness*. She doesn't fight well – but she doesn't shy away, either. Sometimes such fighters grow lucky. They kill through vigour, not skill. Your daughter may be one of them. And that makes me laugh.'

'Laugh?' asked Crask, puzzled.

'Aye.' Ballas nodded. 'I find it odd that a coward has sired such a woman.'

Crask gestured empty-handedly. 'I taught her to have the virtues I lack. They are present in herself, though she cannot see that they are absent in me. And she must never know. If she does . . . As you said once before, she would be broken-hearted.'

'And you fear that?' asked Ballas.

'Yes.'

'More than any other kind of suffering?'

'Of course.' In Crask's voice there was conviction: he had stated a bald, simple fact.

'Then there is hope.'

'Hope?'

'That you'll act bravely, one day.'

Footsteps sounded on the stairs.

Getting to his feet, Crask hurriedly wiped the tears from his cheeks. 'This talk of bravery,' he said, 'is but sanctimonious drivel.'

The door opened. Heresh returned, bearing fresh clothing: a pair of leggings and a tunic, spun from the coarsest wool Ballas had ever felt, and a cape of a fabric so thin that it would scarcely keep out the cold. Ballas suspected that the woman had deliberately sought the least comfortable attire she could.

Ballas took off his bloodied clothes and got changed. When he had finished, he said, 'Gather your belongings. We are leaving.'

'Where are we to go?' asked Heresh, folding her arms.

'It is better, daughter,' said Crask, putting a hand upon her forearm, 'not to ask questions. He is not a man who enjoys speaking.' Disdain crept into Crask's voice. 'He is a man of deeds, not words. You must have learned *that* by now.'

'Father, are you all right?' She peered closely at Crask. 'Your face is red, and your eyes—'

'I took a tumble,' he said, shaking his head. 'That is all.'

Heresh stared coldly at Ballas. The big man tied his cape and raised his hood. Then he led them out of the tavern, to the park. The day was clear, the sky a sharp winter-blue. The sun burned without real warmth. They were the only souls there. Grunting, Ballas sat down on a long stone bench. And waited for Jonas Elsefar to appear.

Long minutes passed. Across the city, a church bell tolled noon. Muttering, Ballas interlocked his fingers. He continued to wait. And wait . . .

Sighing, Crask kneeled by a patch of frost-shrivelled blooms. 'Golden jagwort,' he said, prodding one with a fingertip, 'Sleeping Morahnim, Galgrante, Coris, Blue-tear . . . Bah! These are all squalid plants . . . all disgusting, and common.'

'What are we waiting for?' asked Heresh, suddenly.

'Jonas Elsefar and I made a bargain,' said Ballas. 'I have done his bidding. Now he is to do mine.'

'Perhaps. Perhaps not. He is not here, is he? What hour did he promise to arrive?'

'Noon,' grunted Ballas.

'Sweet grief! The middle hour has long passed. It seems Elsefar has deceived you.'

'Be silent.' Ballas scowled.

'The cripple is not here. I'd wager everything I have that he will not appear.'

'I said *shut up*!'

'Do as he bids, daughter,' said Crask, hurrying over.

Ballas got to his feet. He paced around the park, feeling his anger grow, harden. *Had* the cripple betrayed him? He hadn't seemed like a deceiver. He was arrogant, self-centred – but a liar? A man without honour?

Ballas looked at the sun. It had edged well past its zenith.

Turning, Ballas said, 'Come with me.'

Following a jumble of alleyways and backstreets, they walked towards Brewhouse Street. Ballas was determined to find Elsefar. There was a chance that, even though he would no longer be working in the copying house – the previous night's murders had freed him from such obligations – he might still be dwelling at his old lodgings, those that were provided by his employers.

Moving along an alleyway, Ballas slowed down. Brewhouse Street lay directly ahead. A couple of Wardens patrolled back and forth. By now, Caggerick Blunt's corpse would have been found. Now that it was the scene of a crime, the copying house would be under guard. That was to be expected. Yet something surprised Ballas. A heavy woodsmoke odour hung in the air. And, faintly, the smell of roasted pork.

Frowning, he peered along Brewhouse Street.

'Sweet grief,' he murmured.

Elsefar's lodgings – the long, single-floored wooden building – had burned to the ground. Nothing remained except a jumble of charred timbers. Wall planks lay toppled flat; tumbled roof beams tilted upwards from grey-black ash. Squinting, Ballas could make out corpses – blackened figures burned fleshless and locked in their death throes.

He stepped back.

'Go to the Wardens,' said Ballas, turning to Heresh, 'and find out what happened.'

'Like myself, my daughter is being hunted,' said Crask urgently. 'And you would send her towards the hounds themselves?'

'Keep your hood drawn up,' advised Ballas. 'They won't recognise you.'

Her hood raised, Heresh approached a lone Warden. He stood near the lodging hall, gazing at the corpses.

'Did many perish?' asked Heresh, moving alongside him.

Blinking, he glanced at her. 'About two dozen,' he said. He was a youngish man, and unusually slender for a Warden. He exhaled, breath-vapour mingling with a few strands of smoke. 'A bad thing,' he said, shaking his head.

'It seems somehow worse,' said Heresh, 'when men die through accident, not intent. It is so . . . so absurd.'

'These men –' he gestured at the corpses '– were not killed by a mishap. They were murdered. A few escaped the fire. Some are in a terrible state; I doubt they'll see the next dawn. But others are more or less unhurt. And they tell us that the blaze was started on purpose. They know who is to blame, too.'

Heresh's gaze flickered to the alleyway. She glanced fleetingly at Ballas. In her eyes' depths he saw suspicion, mistrust – and a type of uncertain dread, as if she suspected him of starting the fire.

'Who bears the guilt for this deed?' she asked.

'A man who, they say, is as twisted in his mind as he is in his body. A copyist and cripple by the name of Jonas Elsefar. His legs are withered, and he moves around on a pair of crutches. As he moves, the ferrules knock against the ground – they make a sound, they say, like the snapping of a crab's pincers. And this sound was heard last night, moments before the fire started. The survivors have no doubt: the blame is Elsefar's. When they tried to escape, they found the door was locked. Which is strange, for only during daylight hours, when the lodging hall is empty, is the lock set. They blame Elsefar for that, too.'

'He sounds like a wicked man . . .'

'His crime may run even deeper.'

'Oh?'

'Last night, the three men who employed him were murdered. Naturally, the cripple could not be responsible. But it isn't beyond him to hire an assassin. And we have a suspicion who that might be, as well.' The Warden handed Heresh a square of parchment. She read it, then glanced up. Ballas thought a little blood had drained from her face.

'A Decree of Annihilation,' she said.

'He was seen, last night, near a tavern where one of the men was murdered. And, at another victim's home, half a dozen guards were slaughtered – a feat of incredible violence: violence which is but an echo of his earlier deeds.' The Warden hesitated. 'He has killed many Wardens. Whether he is skilful or simply mad, I do not know – but he is dangerous. Do not fear, though,' he added. 'Neither he, nor Elsefar, will escape us. Within days, we will have them.'

'You sound certain.'

'The city gates are closed,' replied the Warden. 'They shall not open until we have him. Except, of course, to allow more of our number to pass through.'

'Fresh Wardens are coming?'

'Hundreds. We shall swarm through this city like fire ants, and we shan't rest until we have apprehended the killer.' He smiled, his eyes glinting mischievously. 'To be truthful, all this excites me. How often are Decrees issued? The last was forty years ago. Is this not a thing to tell one's grandchildren?'

A second Warden appeared, bearing a small mallet. Together, they nailed the Decree to a pole of blackened wood.

Heresh returned to the alley.

'Did you hear?' she asked, softly.

'Yes, every word,' said Ballas. 'And it changes nothing.'

'What . . . ?!'

'We must still find Jonas Elsefar,' said the big man. 'He must keep his half of our bargain.'

'And then?' demanded Crask. 'The gates are barred! We cannot leave!'

'We shall think of something,' said Ballas, shrugging.

For two days, they sought Elsefar. They scoured places where a man such as he – physically frail, and perhaps frightened for his life – might go to ground. Almshouses, dossing halls, taverns that Wardens seldom entered . . . They visited, it seemed, every such place in the city. Wary of being spotted, Ballas sent Heresh into these establishments, whilst he remained outside with her father. Lugen Crask feared for his daughter's safety. He feared for his own, too. He no longer confessed such things to Ballas. Perhaps he knew the big man would be unsympathetic. Yet his unease was evident. When Heresh entered Elsefar's possible bolt-holes. Crask sweated heavily, wringing his hands. Blood drained from his chill-pinkened skin. He looked like a plague victim.

Still Elsefar eluded them.

More Wardens began to arrive at Granthaven. At first their increasing numbers were scarcely noticeable. Ballas glimpsed the occasional extra black tunic, stitched with a blue Scarrendestin symbol. But none of them proved troublesome. It was, if not easy, far from difficult to avoid capture.

Gradually, though, this changed.

After a few more days, the streets were thronging with Wardens. At night, sheltering in a derelict warehouse, Ballas fancied he could hear the city gates creaking open and the noise of firm-soled leather boots stamping through the streets. Like the Warden at the burned-out lodging hall had promised, they surged like ants into the city. Soon, it seemed that every glance revealed a Warden.

One evening, as Heresh slept, Crask broke his silence. He confessed his fear in bitter tones.

'We shall not find Elsefar,' he said. 'In the fairest circumstances, it would be absurd to carry on looking for him. Granthaven is large, and we are few: how are three of us to root him out? But now, with Wardens everywhere . . . What chance do we have? None.'

He stared expectantly at Ballas.

'We carry on searching,' said the big man.

The next day, they did as Ballas promised. Once more, likely hiding places were visited. Once more, Elsefar could not be found.

The warehouse was no longer a safe refuge. It lay upon a street that, though small, was now patrolled frequently by Wardens. Ballas, with Crask and his daughter, moved southwards, to a jumble of half-derelict houses. No one lived there – except for a few stray dogs. The roofs were ripped away, and the stones were damp: yet a frugal shelter could be found.

During the night, they decided to take turns at keeping watch.

When Ballas roused himself to take over from Crask, he found the eel-hunter in a state of near-panic.

'I cannot live in this fashion,' he said. 'I am not built for such a test of nerves.'

'You used to be a smuggler.'

'What of it?'

'Didn't you ever feel on edge?'

Crask gazed angrily at him – as if he'd missed some fundamental point. 'There is a universe of difference,' he said, 'between bearing a few parchments across Druine's remotest territory, seeing scarcely a soul for days and . . . and this *blood sport*. What are we but deer entrapped in some private forest? We can run here and there – to a degree. We can hide here and there – to a degree. But we can never *escape*. We can't even relax. And it is *your* doing, Anhaga Ballas. If you hadn't gone to my marshes . . . if Culgrogan hadn't told you about me . . . Damn it all! If he were here, and alive, I'd slit his throat!'

'Tomorrow,' said Ballas quietly, 'we'll change our plans. We will look for ways out of Granthaven.'

'The city is sealed.' Crask laughed hollowly. 'There is no way out. Only Wardens are permitted to enter.' He looked sharply at Ballas. 'You are not intending to act like a fox pursued by hounds . . . You do not imagine you can run *through* the pack – simply cut among them, believing they will not spot you? I warn you: a Warden's eyes are sharper than a hound's. And they can scent—'

'Stop rambling,' grunted Ballas.

'I am tired,' said Crask – yet it was more accusation than apology. Getting to his feet, he said, 'Besides – it is a fair point, is it not? How are we to leave, hm?'

'The gates can't stay shut for ever,' said Ballas.

Granthaven imported most of its food. With the gates shut, none would be entering the city. Before long, the stores would be empty: all the grain, vegetables and meats would be gone. Though a large city, Granthaven had little farming land. Ballas had overheard talk that already the cattle were being slaughtered and the winter wheat harvested. Once people got hungry the Wardens would have no choice but to open the gates.

Ballas was mistaken.

For eight days, the gates remained shut.

Even living with little human contact, other than that of Crask and his daughter, Ballas became aware of increasing hunger in Granthaven.

He overheard talk of domestic privation – of empty larders and sparse rations. Upon the air hung smells of poverty cooking: bone-broth, vegetable soup, roasted cow- and pig-fat – these odours supplanted the usual ones of gravy-rich beef and crackling-covered pork shanks. Eventually, every man turned scavenger. In Granthaven, as in all of Druine, it was forbidden for ordinary citizens to bear arms. Yet men started to fashion crude bows and arrows and hunt stray dogs. Finding it impossible to steal food, since there was no food left, Ballas took up this practice: the dogs, undernourished, yielded tough, unappetising meat.

Occasionally, Ballas overheard conversations that betrayed the citizens' feelings. Two men, on a dog hunt, walked past the slum in which Ballas was hiding.

'I pay my taxes – but for what? To live on dog meat? Curse everything! Look at us! We work hard, and give a fifth of our earnings to the Pilgrim Church. How do they repay us? By shutting the city gates. By starving us.' He looked unhappily at his bow and arrow. 'I don't want my children eating cur-flesh. Is it holy, to keep our bellies empty? They starve us, just as much as potato blight and cropfall do – and why? So they might capture a single man. We go hungry, so a sinner may taste justice.'

'Don't blame the Church,' said the second man. 'Blame the sinner. *He* is cause of our suffering. I don't know what his crime is. But, clearly, it is serious: why else would the Decree have been issued?'

'Whatever he has done,' retorted the first, 'it hasn't harmed *me*. Or my family. It is the Church that makes us suffer, do you hear? The Church.'

Gradually, the city's discontent turned to violence. There were riots. The shops of those who normally supplied food – the fishmongers, greengrocers and butchers – were looted. When there was nothing to steal, they were set alight, as if flames could vanquish hunger. Wardens, though plentiful, at first had trouble controlling the citizens. Order was restored – by violence. A few deaths . . . a few sword slashes and dagger thrusts and loosed crossbow bolts had a powerful effect. The citizens were angry. But none of them wanted to become martyrs.

Some, though, died at their fellows' hands.

Ballas heard a group of women gossiping.

'They have got him!' said one, excited. 'The man in the Decree – he has been caught!'

'Thank the Four,' replied another. 'What are the Wardens going to do with him?'

'The Wardens? Oh, they had no hand in this. A group of weavers tracked him, and found him, and slaughtered him. He's strung up, down on Blackstone Lane . . .'

Curious, Ballas went to Blackstone Lane. The corpse dangled upside down from a signpost, its arms and legs bound, its clothing blood-drenched. It did not resemble Ballas. Though broad-chested, it was two hand-spans too short and the eyes were the wrong colour: a glacial blue shone from the bloodshot whites. But, supposed Ballas, the body more or less matched the Decree's description. As if to prove this, a copy of the Decree was nailed to the corpse's chest.

Eventually, the citizens wondered if the sinner would ever be caught.

'Perhaps he is dead. They say he has accomplices – an old man and a young woman . . . Perhaps they have all perished, from hunger or the cold.'

'Or they may have taken their own lives,' speculated another. 'I couldn't live, knowing the Wardens were hunting me. In the Church's hands, their deaths would be terrible. It would be far easier to drink a gentle poison, or to open the veins of one's wrists.'

Ballas, Crask and Heresh changed their hiding place every day. The city had become oppressive, claustrophobic. Crask's notion of themselves as deer in an enclosed forest seemed accurate. The hunters would soon come, Ballas knew. They could not be avoided for ever.

On the twelfth day, Ballas left their current hiding place – an abandoned woodstore – carrying his bow and arrow, seeking a stray dog to kill. He walked furtively through Granthaven's streets, avoiding other people, knowing that if he was merely glimpsed the alarm would be raised. He disliked acting with such discretion. He disliked listening for footsteps other than his own, or clattering hooves, or the creaking-open of window shutters . . . disliked anything that might indicate the presence of someone else – someone who could prove a threat. He disliked retreating into alleyways at the slightest suggestion of danger. He disliked, more than anything, his growing sense of claustrophobia. He had felt it on the moors. And now he felt it in Granthaven: the sensation of being entombed. The sky stretched upwards to infinity, there was plenty of air to breathe . . . yet it seemed he was buried alive.

He had no choice but to grow used to it. To accept it as the nature of things – at least for now.

At least until he reached Belthirran.

Ballas heard claws rattling on frozen mud. Nocking an arrow to his bowstring, he stepped back into a doorway. A black and white dog trotted past. Its fur was filthy. Ribs showed through its skin. Yet its eyes were bright. It looked healthy, more or less. An habitual scavenger, it was in a better state than many of Granthaven's human occupants. The present conditions of want, of hunger, were familiar to it.

Following the alley, the dog paused. For a few moments it sniffed the ground. Then it turned and doubled back.

Cutsing softly, Ballas stepped from the doorway. Raising the bow, he took aim – then froze.

From somewhere, there came shouting.

'By order of the Pilgrim Church,' began a man's voice, 'open your doors and step outside! Stand straight, and keep your faces uncovered.'

Ballas crept to the alley's entrance. In the road beyond, near a row of wooden houses, a group of Wardens had assembled. Some were genuine Wardens – those whose full-time job it was to serve the Church. Others were ordinary citizens, temporarily granted the status of 'Under-Warden': they possessed powers of arrest and lawful killing. But they did not wear uniforms. For badges of office they had, pieces of stiffened blue cloth, cut into Scarrendestin triangles and suspended from thongs around their necks. The true Wardens were relaxed, authoritative. The Under-Wardens seemed tense – and it was a tension they obviously savoured. In every man's eyes, excitement glinted. They were part of a great, dangerous adventure. They bore weapons – and could use them with impunity, if the need arose.

'Outside!' shouted a black-bearded Warden. 'Every citizen must vacate his home, and step into the street. No man, woman or child must remain indoors.'

A door opened. A thin, raggedly dressed woman appeared.

'What is going on?' she asked, her voice a rasp – she was a whisky-drinker, Ballas suspected.

'Are you alone in this building?' asked the black-bearded Warden.

'Yes – except for my children who were, until moments ago, sleeping . . .'

'Bring them outside. We must search your home—'

'For the magicker?'

'The magicker?' echoed the Warden, puzzled.

'From the Decree.' The woman lifted her chin. 'That's what he is, right? That's what everyone reckons. Why else would the Masters want him so much? Why else would we be made prisoners in our own city, except to help you lot catch such a man?'

The Warden's composure returned. 'Bring out your children,' he repeated. 'Obstruct us, and you will be arrested – understand?'

'He isn't in my home. Do you think I'd let someone like that near my offspring?'

'We are to search every building in Soriterath. Now, do as I tell you – or it'll be the cage elemental for you.'

Further along the road, more Wardens poured from an alleyway. Swearing, Ballas ran back to the woodstore.

Inside, upon the stone floor, a fire had been lit. Heresh sat nearby, a filleting knife in her hand. Lugen Crask was putting together an iron spit, stolen from a tavern's kitchen. As Ballas entered, the eel-catcher looked up.

'The hunt was not fruitful?' he said, disappointed.

'We have to leave. There is trouble.'

'What kind of trouble?'

'A new hunt's begun. The Wardens are moving through the city, peering under every bloody stone . . . Get up!'

As one, Crask and Heresh rose.

Crask said, 'Ought we to be alarmed? There aren't enough Wardens to search the city from top to bottom – are there?'

'Every damned citizen has been made an Under-Warden. Or so it seems.' Ballas strode out of the woodstore. He still held the bow and arrow – a flimsy weapon, crafted from an ash branch and catgut. Cursing, he tossed it to the ground.

'What are we to do?' asked Crask, wringing his hands.

'The Wardens are coming from the north,' said Ballas, 'so we move south.'

'And then, once we reach the city wall?' Crask's eyebrows shot up. He flattened a palm against his forehead. 'That is their plan, is it not? To – to drive us to the south, to herd us like sheep . . . Eventually, they will find us. We will be trapped at the city wall, with nowhere to run. Then the Wardens will just roll over us . . . Yet you would send us south? You would play into their hands?'

'What else can we do?' Ballas turned on the eel-catcher. 'If we go north, we die. If we head east or west, they will be on us in moments.' He spat on the ground. 'If we go south, we stay alive – for a while, at least. It will give us time to think. To plan.'

'To plan,' echoed Crask, murmuring. 'We have no options. What is there to plan *for*?'

Ballas ignored him. 'We need horses,' he said.

They walked briskly through Granthaven. As they went, Ballas sensed the Wardens, half a mile to the north. He thought of their single-minded purpose – and realised that, in all probability, they would succeed in their aim and kill him. There could be no escape from Granthaven. Not with the city gates barred.

Ballas couldn't be certain, but he suspected he was soon to die. He didn't feel afraid. Or angry.

Merely surprised – surprised that he should die on such an ordinary day. The sky was its usual winter blue, the sun a fierce frozen gold. At dawn, the magpies had cackled with their normal coarseness. Everything behaved as it always did. The sky, the sun, the magpies – they hadn't altered. The world was blind to Ballas's circumstances. Or uncaring. Either way, his death would be inconsequential. Like any man, he would decay into bones, rotting flesh, tendons . . . Or maybe his corpse would be burned. If so, the fire would devour him as it would any lump of meat. Then again, maybe he would be fed to dogs. They would eat him like they would any piece of carrion.

For a few seconds Ballas felt utterly alone. Then he grunted. The magpies understood perfectly what Ballas now understood: his death did *not* matter.

Yet . . . yet he still wanted to find Belthirran.

The Land Beyond the Mountains sang to him. He craved Belthirran *more* than life itself. To escape the Church would be a fine thing – not because it would keep him from death. But because it would mean that he had found Belthirran.

That was the true incentive to live on. To survive.

Such thinking made no sense. Why crave a place of refuge more than his own life?

Ballas snorted, then shook his head. This was a poor hour for deep thinking. Such things he should leave to philosophers.

The three fugitives stole the first horse, a chestnut gelding, from a tethering post outside a tavern. The second and third, black mares both, they snatched from a stable adjoining a private residence. They cantered south, putting distance between themselves and the Wardens.

The light began to fade. Into the perfect blue, clouds drifted. Bruise-black, water-bloated, they crawled through the sky like warships through the sea. As they arrived, the sun departed, vanishing behind the horizon. Evening crept in.

They halted upon a circular patch of open ground. Dismounting, Ballas noticed a faint burbling noise. Handing the reins to Heresh, he said, 'Wait here.'

He walked along an alley, on to a stream bank. Beyond the stream, a hundred yards away, the city wall thrust skywards: black-bricked, forty feet high, unscaleable. Iron spikes crested its upper edge. If the Wardens had any sense, they would have set clusters of broken glass there too. No Wardens patrolled the wall. Not on this side. More likely, they would be on the moorland side, waiting for Ballas to clamber over the top and swing down on a rope, or to risk an uncontrolled fall, hoping the tussocked ground would treat him gently.

Ballas's gaze followed the stream. It flowed through the wall by way of a sluice. For a moment, Ballas wondered if he could crawl through, out on to the moors. Then he saw the black bars of a lowered portcullis.

For a time, he watched the stream. Rain started to fall. Heavily. The stream's surface jumped with every droplet.

Licking his lips, Ballas returned to the open ground.

'Do you have any ideas?' asked Crask. Despite his dislike of the cold, despite his cross-moorland grumblings of two weeks ago, Crask hadn't raised his hood. Raindrops crawled down his forehead. Similarly, Heresh's hood was lowered. Strands of hair, come loose from her ponytail, plastered her skin. Her dark eyes were intent. Yet they betrayed fear. She did not want to die.

It wasn't any dream of Belthirran that provoked her desire to live. But something else. She liked life, Ballas realised.

Or, at any rate, preferred it to death . . . whatever death held, whether it was the Eltheryn Forest followed by the paradise as promised by the Four, or the pitiless oblivion predicted by renegade philosophers.

'Wait here,' said Ballas. He walked away from the open ground and followed an alley to a tavern. He stepped inside. The common room was empty, but for the tavern-master. The tavern-master, a broad man of middle years, grew tense. His gaze flickered to the wall.

Ballas looked in the same direction.

A Decree of Annihilation, nailed to the brickwork.

Striding over, Ballas tore down the parchment. He tossed it into the fire. Then he approached the bar.

'A flagon of whisky,' he said.

The tavern-master took a flagon from a shelf and handed it to Ballas. Silently, the big man left the tavern, returning to the open ground.

Climbing up on his horse, he took a deep swig from the flagon. Then he offered the vessel to Crask.

'This won't solve anything,' said Crask. Yet he accepted the flagon and gulped a mouthful. 'Sweet grief,' he murmured, shuddering. He gazed intently at the bottle. Then he held it out to Heresh. 'Daughter,' he said, 'if I have been a poor father – if ever I have failed you – if I kept you too long in the marshes, when other circumstances would have pleased you more . . . forgive me. All I have done, I have done out of love.'

'Be quiet,' said Ballas softly. 'Say nothing that'll embarrass you later on.'

'There will be a "later on"?'

'Do as I say, and you will live,' replied Ballas.

'You cannot promise such things.' Crask's voice was flat – except for a faint shaking when he shivered from the cold. 'You cannot say that we shall—' He glanced at Ballas, then fell silent.

Ballas stared fiercely at him.

Crask smiled, edgily. It was hardly a true smile, just a forced quirking of the lips. He was frightened. Yet he understood that he could not show it. Glancing at Heresh, he said laughingly, 'If he says we shall live, live we shall. If anyone in Druine is well qualified in avoiding death, it is this man. We have seen it before, haven't we, my girl?' He looked hopefully, earnestly, at Heresh. 'His virtues are not ours. Indeed, we might think them vices . . . But they serve a purpose. They will help us.'

Heresh drank from the flagon. Then she passed it to Ballas. The big man took a long swallow, downing a third of the whisky.

'The Wardens will come out of that alley,' he said, gesturing to the opening from which they had emerged minutes ago. 'There'll be a few on horseback. But most will be on foot.' He held out the whisky to Crask. 'Drink.'

Crask took the whisky.

'We must ride through them,' said Ballas flatly.

'You jest,' said Crask, the flagon an inch from his lips.

'We ride through them,' said Ballas, 'as if they were nothing but barley stalks. Darkness is falling. If we get beyond the Wardens, the night will hide us.'

'I can smell burning.' It was Heresh who had spoken. She was holding the flagon, handed to her by her father.

'And I can hear screams,' said Lugen Crask, tilting his head.

Half a mile away, orange fire-glow rose into the gloom.

'There were houses back there.' Crask frowned. 'I remember them clearly – a row of shanty buildings. Nothing more than huts. The Wardens are burning them down!'

'And those who dwell within,' said Heresh. 'Those screams are for more than the loss of some dwellings – they're cries of agony . . .'

'The Wardens cannot do this!'

'Their bloodlust has risen.' Ballas stared at the alleyway. 'That'll help us.'

Heresh drank from the flagon. 'How?' she asked coolly.

'Their discipline's gone. Perhaps the Wardens might've behaved themselves. But the Under-Wardens?' He shook his head. 'They've got no training. And no sense of duty. Each man wants to kill. They'll come thundering out, as wildly as marsh eels – and we'll cut through them.'

'You are an optimist.' Crask smiled – and Ballas sensed his response was genuine.

'The whisky is good, yes?' murmured the big man.

Crask nodded.

Ballas took the flagon from Heresh. He drained it, drinking down the last fiery drop. Hoofbeats sounded in the alleyway. And the clatter of boots.

'Through them,' repeated Ballas, 'and into the night.'

In the alleyway a horse appeared – a black gelding, with a white star on its forehead. Ballas hurled the flagon, which struck the animal on its star. Whinnying, the horse reared up, dislodging its rider. Then it bolted back along the alley.

Shouts erupted.

'*Now!*' roared Ballas.

They surged forward into the alley, Ballas at the front, Crask and Heresh close behind. A dozen men, Wardens and Under-Wardens, stood ahead of them – then they cried out as Ballas's mount ploughed through them. Hooves cracked bone and split flesh. Keeping his head down, Ballas hurtled onward.

Suddenly his mount panicked. Rearing, it tumbled Ballas from the saddle. As he struck the ground, a set of hooves flashed over him, pounding his body as they went. Cursing, he dragged himself to his feet. He glimpsed Crask riding away. Then two Wardens sprang at Ballas. He rammed a fist into the first man's mouth, bursting his lips and splintering his front teeth. The second Warden drew his knife, but Ballas kicked him in the crotch, then toppled him with a skull-splitting head-butt.

A rider passed Ballas. Turning, the big man glimpsed a Scarrendestin triangle on a tunic front. And a sword, arcing towards him. He leaped backwards. The sword point etched a track across his upper chest. Ballas stumbled. The rider turned, and rode at him once more. He slashed out with his sword again but this time Ballas ducked under the blade. Grasping the man's wrist, Ballas yanked him from his saddle. As he fell, Ballas stamped down hard on his neck, snapping it. Snatching up the slain rider's sword, he whirled round.

A Warden and Under-Warden were almost upon him. As the Warden drew his sword, Ballas swung his own blade clean through the man's forearm – a savage, bone-cleaving hack. The Warden's lopped-off hand fell and lay on the ground like a pallid crab. Screaming, the Warden pitched to his knees. Ballas kicked him hard in the face, tumbling him backwards. The Under-Warden faltered. Swinging the sword horizontally, Ballas sliced into his neck so that his half-severed head flopped sideways as blood fountained up.

From somewhere, Heresh cried, 'Watch out behind!'

Pivoting, Ballas raised his sword to block a Warden's down-swinging cut. Tilting the blade, he deflected the blow. Then he slammed a left jab into the man's nose. As the man stumbled, Ballas drove the sword through his neck.

Another cry rose: '*No!*'

Amid the noises of death – amid the stuttering rasps and gurgles and croaks of the maimed – the whinnying of horses . . . this sound stopped Ballas in his tracks.

From the corner of his eye he glimpsed Crask. The eel-catcher was staring along the alley. Ballas followed his gaze.

Heresh lay on the ground. Three Under-Wardens were kicking her. Blood covered her face and drenched her tunic.

Ballas hurled his sword at the first Under-Warden. Spinning as it flew through the air, the blade sank into his lower back. The two remaining Under-Wardens turned. Ballas threw himself at the first one, knocking him off his feet. Falling, he cracked his skull on the alley wall. The second, a large man, hurled a punch into Ballas's face. Ballas staggered. The man unsheathed a dagger, and struck at his foe. Blocking the blow, Ballas grabbed the man's tunic and they fell grappling to the ground. Kneeling upon his chest, Ballas punched the man twice in the face – then faltered.

He felt as if someone had thumped him in the stomach. A thudding pain filled his guts.

Ballas groaned.

Then he punched the Under-Warden over and over, in the face and throat and body, until he felt the man's ribcage contract and heard the whistling rasp of his final breath.

Ballas got to his feet. Shakily.

He looked along the alley. No Wardens or Under-Wardens remained standing. Some had fled. Most had died.

'My daughter!' said Crask, dismounting.

He ran to Heresh. The young woman was covered in blood. As Crask approached, she pushed herself upright.

'Oh, sweet grief – I am so sorry!' said Crask, gripping her shoulders.

'It is blood, and nothing more,' said Heresh. She touched her nose, which had been broken. And her lips, which had been split open. 'I am a little dazed. But that is all.'

'We must retrieve the horses,' said Crask, 'and ride far away from here.' He looked at Ballas.

The big man felt strange. He felt *weak*. It wasn't a pleasant weakness, like that of drunkenness. A darkness hovered behind it. Numbly, Ballas dipped a finger in the blood pouring from the sword wound high on his chest.

'Do not worry,' said Crask. 'We will find you a physician! Such an injury, for a man like you – why, it is nothing! A gnat bite!'

Without speaking, Ballas reached lower. His fingertips touched something smooth. A knife hilt, sticking out from his stomach.

Ballas's legs buckled.

Crask ran over.

'Do not die!' he said. 'Do you hear me? My daughter and I . . . we *need* you. Be strong, do you hear? We will find you a physician. We will . . .'

Crask's voice trailed off. Ballas understood why. In the distance there was shouting. More Wardens were coming. The men who'd escaped from the alley had summoned help.

'Get up,' breathed Crask, seizing Ballas's tunic front. 'Damn everything, but *get up!*' He tugged vainly at Ballas's tunic.

Ballas felt his senses grow dull. Every noise grew muffled, every image drifted in a blur across his eyes. Seizing Crask's wrists, he broke the eel-catcher's grip.

'Bring me a sword,' he said, his voice scarcely audible.

Turning, Crask sprinted to a fallen Warden. Bracing a foot against the dead man's shoulder blades, he wrenched out the sword stuck in his lower back.

Returning, he handed it to Ballas. The big man seized it. Yet there was something wrong with his sense of touch: he couldn't feel the hilt. He held it tightly, yet the leather-wrapped grip yielded no sensations.

Cursing, Ballas tried to stand. As he rose, his legs buckled – his muscles had little strength. He sagged against the wall. Then he slid to the ground.

Cartwheels rattled close by. Then a voice rang out, harsh-edged and clear.

'Get on,' it said.

Laboriously, Ballas turned his head. On the open ground stood a cart. On its driving bench sat an old man, bald-headed, hunched like a vulture.

'Get on,' he repeated, 'or you will be killed. And that would displease Elsefar.'

'Elsefar?' mumbled Ballas.

'Let us think later,' said Crask, placing an arm under Ballas's shoulder, 'and act now.' He glanced along the alley. 'Come on. Try to stand. Make an effort.'

With Crask's help, Ballas got to his feet. Leaning heavily on the eel-catcher, he staggered towards the cart.

As they approached, Crask said, 'He is hurt.'

'We will deal with such things later,' said the cart's driver calmly.

Ballas heaved himself up on to the cart-back and sprawled limply on the boards. Dimly, he felt a lurch as Crask climbed up alongside him. Then the cart tilted again, and Ballas caught Heresh's scent.

The cart's driver said something – but Ballas couldn't tell what: he was growing deaf.

A rustling darkness swept over him. He smelled damp leather – a tarpaulin, he realised.

He fell into swirling blackness.

Chapter 14

. . . As they journeyed, the Pilgrims began
To mistrust the pale stranger,
Whose name was Asvirius, espying within him
A dark fire . . .
. . . Of the sick, he healed none.
Nor granted voice to the mute,
Strength to the frail . . .

Something drew Ballas out of the black well of unconsciousness. Grunting, he opened his eyes. He found himself lying on blankets, in a cold, black-bricked room. The walls were bare. A few niches held candles, flickering fitfully. One contained a skull. A jagged patch of darkness marked its pate; the bone had been smashed through. Empty eye sockets gazed blackly at Ballas.

'The martyred Cadaris Brante,' came a voice.

From a doorway stepped the man Ballas had seen on the cart. In the poor light, the bald, hunched figure seemed more gaunt than he had before. Age creases seamed his face. His eyes glittered as he touched the skull with a fingertip.

'Cadaris the Sufferer, Cadaris the Forest Walker. Soon he will be beatified. Sainthood awaits him. As soon as the Masters give the word, this relic – and, trust me, it is truly Cadaris's skull: it is not some false, soon-to-be-disproven antiquity, such as a sandal strap belonging to the Four, or a shard of Scarrendestin diamond – this relic will be taken to the Esklarion Sacros and blessed, then granted a permanent place in Soriterath's cathedral. I do not covet Cadaris's skull. But, I confess, I shall be sad to be without it. I sense that it contains a little of Cadaris's spirit. It provides good company. Do you know the tale of Cadaris? He was a brave and holy man. He dwelled, as a hermit, in Wildthorn Forest. He lived upon the fruits of the earth. He ate berries, roots, nuts. And he dwelled placidly among animals that are more often enemies to man: wolves, boars, serpents.

'One day, a group of bandits came into the forest. During the evening, they decided to amuse themselves by digging out a badger and presenting it to their dog – a small, fierce creature, well acquainted with badger-baiting. Naturally, it fell upon the animal.

'From a different part of the forest, Cadaris heard the badger's yelps of pain. And the bandits' laughter.

'Following the sounds, he found the bandits. Without hesitation, he swept up the badger, releasing it into the undergrowth. The bandits were furious. They avenged themselves upon Cadaris. They beat him, and mutilated him. They burned out his eyes, they broke his arms and legs.

'Then they sliced open his stomach. They tipped an ants' nest into the wound, then closed it up again. The ants ate away at him from the inside. His agonies were indescribable.

'Of course, Cadaris perished. And did so to save an animal. An unusual exchange, do you not think: a human's life for a beast's? But the Four preached that all lives are equal. If an animal's life is to be taken, it must be done with respect and solemnity. A hunter must pray for his quarry at the moment of slaughter. No animal must be slain just for pleasure.

'These are considered the most trivial of the Four's principles. Yet Cadaris obeyed them most earnestly. His piety was rare – and unconditional. I admire him, more than any other martyr. His presence comforts me.'

Turning, he opened his raincape. Underneath it he wore dark blue robes. Around his neck, a Scarrendestin pendant glinted.

Ballas started to rise.

'Be still,' said the man, placing a hand on his shoulder, 'or your stitches will tear.'

'You are a priest,' growled Ballas.

'How else do you think I got you safely through the Wardens? How else do you think I prevented them from searching my cart? Yes, I am a priest – and one of no small standing.' He gestured around the room. 'This is the crypt antechamber, beneath Granthaven Cathedral. And I am Father Rendeage.' He draped his cape on a low table. From a cloth bag, he extracted jars of ointment and a bandage roll. 'You have no cause to trust me. You are subject to a Decree of Annihilation, and I am of the Pilgrim Church. I ought to crave your death and wish you a thousand sufferings.' He paused, looking directly at Ballas. 'But it is not so.'

'Why not?' groaned Ballas, sitting upright.

'Because I am a holy man.'

'Yes, and I'm a sinner, a fugitive . . .'

'I am a *holy* man,' snapped Rendeage, emphasising the word. 'A holy man before I am a priest, before I am a Servant of the Church. I obey the Four's will – not the Blessed Masters'. Where one concurs with the other, that is fine – and it makes life less troublesome. But where there is disparity . . . I bow my head to the divine, not to the earthly.' He gestured upwards, not to the ceiling but beyond it: to the cathedral overhead. 'The Four said, "*Lock not the doors of your church, for no man is a trespasser in the house of the Four. The man virtuous and the man ill-tainted shall lodge side by side, without judgement, and from all hazards be protected. Only the Four, within the Eltheryn Forest, shall measure a man's goodness and his wickedness.*"' He drew a breath. 'You are safe here. But I do not know for how long. It is but a matter of time before the churches are searched. The Masters are reluctant: for such an action suggests that there is disunity within the Church. But it will happen, sooner or later.'

Ballas gazed at Rendeage's robes, and his pendant. 'You brought me here – you healed me, yes?' He touched the bandages, wrapped around his waist where the dagger had struck.

'Yes.'

'What'll happen, if you're found out?'

'I shall be tried,' said Rendeage. 'Then I shall be executed.'

Ballas grunted. 'You are taking a chance, holy man.'

'I am risking my life,' agreed Rendeage. 'But in return, I shall save my soul.' He sighed. 'Now, do you hunger? And thirst?'

Ballas nodded. The priest left the chamber, returning a short time later with a wine flagon and a piece of beef. Ballas bit into the beef. Then he uncorked the wine flagon. Taking a swallow, he found the taste familiar – yet he couldn't quite recall from where.

'I must leave you,' said Father Rendeage. 'But we will speak later. There are things you and I must discuss.' He hesitated, staring closely at Ballas. 'You are a free man. I cannot force you to remain here. But I can tell you that there is no safer place in Granthaven. Step outside, and you will become Wardens' prey. Stay, and – for now – you will be protected. Your friends have acted wisely. They have not set foot outside the cathedral. They are in the next chamber, if you wish to speak with them.'

With a nod, Rendeage left the room. Ballas chewed on the beef and drank from the wine flagon. His stomach hurt: he could feel the tug of the stitches every time he moved. He glanced at the martyr's skull, pale within the niche. Then, getting up, he went through the doorway.

In the next chamber, he found skulls – dozens of them, resting on shelves fashioned within the brickwork. The effect was momentarily disturbing. Every shadowed eye socket seemed trained upon him. He felt as if he had stepped into a large crowd – as if these assembled bone relics were a living audience, attentive and expectant.

A couple of tallow lamps were burning.

Lugen Crask and his daughter were seated upon a rug. Crask appeared unharmed. But bruises darkened Heresh's face. An eye was swollen half-shut. Her lips were split. The crippled quill-master, Jonas Elsefar, sat upon a chair in the corner. His crutches were propped against the wall. He looked at Ballas closely, his expression unreadable.

Lugen Crask got to his feet. 'Father Rendeage insisted on you sleeping in the other chamber. He thought it unhealthy for a man to regain his health in a place such as this . . . that is, in an ossuary. Certainly, it would be a shocking thing to wake up to, don't you think? Akin to waking into a nightmare . . . to waking into some pit of hell.' He smiled, nervously. 'I told him you weren't of a queasy temperament. I said a few bones would not perturb you. But he insisted. Instead, this has become *our* lodgings. A touch macabre, perhaps. Too much like something from a grisly fairy tale . . . Yet we are secure here.'

Ballas drank from the flagon.

'The priest says you are fortunate to be alive,' continued Crask, into the silence. 'The blade pierced your gut, true – but every major innard remained unscathed. He says your recovery will be total. There will be no hint of injury, except for the scar. But what man frets over such a thing? In a woman's eyes, scars are marks of virtue, are they not?'

Ignoring Crask, Ballas walked over to the quill-master, Elsefar.

'We struck a bargain,' he said, gazing down at the cripple. 'I've done what you asked. Your employers are dead.'

'I know, I know,' nodded Elsefar, looking up. 'I admit that I am impressed. I saw Caggerick Blunt, upon the floor of his office. A deeply pleasing sight. It moved me.'

Ballas couldn't tell if Elsefar was speaking sarcastically.

Lugen Crask said, 'And did it please you to see those boys burn – the ones in the lodging hall?'

'We have spoken of this before,' said Elsefar impatiently. 'You have slept for two days, Ballas. And for those two days this fellow has been a one-man plague of sanctimony. Yes, I set light to the lodging hall. Yes, many perished. But Crask cannot understand that those whom I hurt deserved to suffer. Those "boys" mocked me. Every day, year after year, they took amusement in ridiculing something beyond my control. I cannot walk. I cannot run. No woman will even glance at me – except in revulsion. And they found it amusing. If you could hear the jibes, and feel them strike home . . . each as sharp, as piercing as the dagger that entered Ballas's stomach—'

'You burned them alive!' snapped Crask.

'And their mockery burned *me*!' Elsefar's voice rose, angrily. 'Have you no inkling of *my* suffering? To be cursed in this fashion?' He struck his useless legs. 'To arrive into this world, unable to jump and run . . . unable to walk the hills. To swim in rivers. My birth was cursed, through no fault of my own. Yet I suffer for it.' He sat in agitated silence. Then he calmed himself. Drawing a breath, he said, 'Our circumstances have changed.'

He met Ballas's gaze.

'I cannot honour our old agreement. Not unless it is reshaped into a form that suits me better. That suits us *all* better.'

'I warned you,' said Ballas, 'that if you broke your promise, I'd kill you.'

'Kill me,' said Elsefar, 'and you murder your sole chance of escape.' His gaze flickered from person to person. 'Accept my new conditions, and we live. Refuse, and we perish.' He shifted slightly. 'I do not ask much. Merely that, after we escape, you transport me to Bluewater Wilds, fifty miles from here. It will involve a small detour, on your way to the mountain-guide. But not by far.'

'Why do you want to go to Bluewater?'

'I have . . . I *had* a home there. I lived at the Wilds during the years I copied forbidden texts. It is in the middle of nowhere. No paths lead to it, there are no villages close by – it is safe. I used to live off the land. I will do so again. And I will also be alone. A pleasing thing, I think. I am a solitary creature. Humankind sickens me more and more each day. A hermit's existence will bring me the greatest happiness. I will live like Cadaris, though I shan't sacrifice myself for *anything*.' He coughed. 'I ask only that we escape together, and you take me to the Wilds.'

'He is no position to make bargains.' Crask moved alongside Ballas. 'He wants to live as much as we do.'

'Untrue,' retorted Elsefar. 'Look at me. Do you suppose my life is joyful? And that my future, even if I reach the Wilds, will be a wellspring of delight?'

'You'll be taken to the Wilds,' said Ballas. 'Now, how do we get out of Granthaven?'

Elsefar pointed down. 'The sewers.'

'There aren't any.' Ballas frowned. 'On the streets, there are no gutters—'

'They are no longer used,' replied the quill-master. 'They were built three centuries ago and depended on the River Blackrush to sluice through them, carrying the filth away to a water-drop on the moors. But the Blackrush dried up. Now it is no more than a stream, just a trickle flowing near the city's edge. The sewers were closed, the gutters paved over. This was a hundred and fifty, maybe two hundred years back. Nowadays, most people have no knowledge of the tunnels under the city. I suspect that even the Pilgrim Church has forgotten.'

'But *you* know of them,' muttered Ballas.

'Once, years ago, I was asked to make a copy of the map, to be stored in the Archive Hall on Bracken Street. The sewer network is as complex as any labyrinth. If you wish to find your way out, you will need the map. Of course, retrieving it from the Hall might prove troublesome.' He smiled. 'But you, Ballas, have performed tasks far more difficult.'

Feeling tired, his knife wound throbbing, Ballas returned to the other chamber. Settling down on the blankets, he glanced at Cadaris's skull. Would it matter to Cadaris if he was made a saint? Or if, left unbeatified, he – his skull, that was – lodged for eternity in a niche, beneath a cathedral?

Footsteps sounded.

'May we talk?' asked Lugen Crask, appearing on the threshold.

'The priest, Rendeage – what sort of man is he?' asked Ballas, ignoring the eel-catcher's question.

'A devout one,' replied Crask.

'Untrue.'

'Oh?'

Ballas lifted the wine flagon. 'Holy wine.'

'Are you certain?'

'I have drunk it before,' said Ballas, recalling the wine he had stolen from Father Brethrien, many weeks ago. 'I recognise the flavour. It can be drunk only as part of a church service. By doing this –' he took a swallow '– I am committing blasphemy. More than that, it's sinful to drink wine at all. The Four preached against it.'

'You are mistaken. It was not the Four who prohibited wine but the Church. And that is what makes Rendeage unusual. He is a churchman in title – but not spirit. He follows the Four. Not the Pilgrim Church.'

'He said as much,' said Ballas. 'But I don't know whether to believe him.'

'If the wine isn't proof enough,' said Crask, 'remember that he brought you safe through the Wardens.'

'You reckon we can trust him?'

'Elsefar does,' said Crask, 'and I doubt the cripple enters lightly into such arrangements.' He nodded, a touch curtly, as if talk of the quill-master left a bad taste in his mouth. 'Once the Wardens started hunting him, he sought refuge with Rendeage. And he asked the priest to help us.' He drew a breath. 'Rendeage is a strange man. But perhaps that is because he *is* truly holy. And such holiness is a rarity.'

A thunder of footfalls came from overhead.

'The worship hall lies directly above,' Crask explained. 'Twenty feet up there –' he pointed to the ceiling '– are a hundred people – ordinary people, loyal to the Church – who would tear each of us apart.' He grew quiet. Father Rendeage's voice sounded. The floorboards muffled the words. But the steady, drawn-out rhythms of sermon oratory were clear.

'I am weary,' said Ballas. 'I'm going to sleep.'

The hint was clear – yet Crask lingered, suddenly uneasy.

'What?' asked Ballas.

'I wish to offer you thanks.'

Ballas frowned.

'You saved my life. But more than that, you saved my daughter's. I . . . the debt I owe is so great, it cannot be repaid. I am grateful.'

The big man gazed levelly at Crask. 'I saved your daughter because she, and you, are useful to me.'

Crask watched him uncertainly. The eel-catcher's gaze seemed to probe the big man. As if seeking some clue that Ballas was lying. As if hunting a sliver of honour.

The eel-catcher's shoulders sagged. Turning, he left the chamber.

Ballas slept. When he woke, he found that the knife wound had bled slightly – yet the stitches had held firm. Grunting, he got to his feet. A little wine remained in the flagon. He drank it, then went into the next chamber.

Crask, Heresh and Elsefar were present. So was Rendeage.

'The sleeper awakes,' the priest remarked. 'I trust you slept comfortably? It is said that in crypts man finds his deepest repose. The dead exert a calming influence. Their stillness is contagious.'

'What hour is it?' asked Ballas.

'The evening has deepened,' replied the priest. 'We are but hours from midnight. Soon I will be abed. I called merely to see if you require anything.'

Ballas raised the flagon. 'Wine. That's all.'

Nodding, Rendeage left the room, going up a flight of steps.

'If every priest was as free with his alcohol,' said Crask, watching him go, 'Druine would bristle with the pious – and the drunk.'

'Prepare yourself,' said Ballas, turning to Heresh. The red-haired woman was sitting cross-legged on the floor. A brazier was burning and in the warmth she had stripped down to breeches and shirt. 'We're going to the Archive Hall.'

As Heresh stood, Lugen Crask did the same.

Ballas shook his head.

'What?' queried the eel-catcher.

'We're going alone, your daughter and me.'

Crask blinked. His expression was unreadable. Ballas knew exactly what he was thinking. He was recalling Ballas's words, days earlier, praising the vigour with which Heresh had fought – her courage, her decisiveness: two virtues that Crask knew he lacked.

'She will be in danger,' he said eventually. 'I cannot be parted from her.'

'Father,' said Heresh, casually taking her cape from a wall-hook, 'Ballas knows more of such matters than you and I. If he says it shall be just him and me, then so be it. I am certain his reasons are sound.' She turned to Ballas, expectantly. For a moment, Ballas wondered if she recognised the true reason – if she saw in her father that which he saw in himself.

'If there are two of us,' said Ballas, 'we can move with greater stealth. And she's lighter-footed than you, Crask. She has the benefits of youth.'

Sweat glistened on Crask's forehead. 'It does not please me,' he said. 'It doesn't please me at all—'

'Don't argue,' said Ballas.

'Swear you will look after her.'

Saying nothing, Ballas returned to the other chamber. As he pulled on his tunic, covering the bloodstained bandages around his gut, Father Rendeage returned with a wine flagon.

'You are leaving,' he observed.

'We shall be back.'

'It is not my business,' began Rendeage, 'but where are you going?'

'I can't remain here for ever. There are things I've got to do, if I'm going to leave Granthaven with my skin whole.'

'That much is obvious. I never expected your tenancy here to be eternal . . . But I ask again: *where* are you going? The streets are dangerous. There are Wardens on every thoroughfare and corner. They are as plentiful as maggots on rotten pork.'

'You liken the Church's lawkeepers to maggots?' asked Ballas, surprised.

'Forgive me. I have insulted maggots. They batten upon the dead; but they do not kill.' The priest adjusted his robes. 'Yesterday, many innocents perished. Sweeping through the city, the Wardens lost control. Fires were started, those men who obstructed the Wardens – accidentally, without ill purpose – were cut down. It was as if every Warden had been driven mad by the pleasures of the hunt.'

'I'd expect that from the Under-Wardens,' said Ballas, sweeping up his cape. 'But the proper Wardens? They are well trained . . .'

'They are but men.' Rendeage shrugged, sadly. 'And men of a rough nature. Their inclinations, in life, are not upwards but downwards. When the Under-Wardens began misbehaving, the Wardens quickly followed. It was a chaotic time. And for the crimes, no one will be punished. Neither Warden nor Under-Warden.'

Ballas took the wine flagon from the priest. Uncorking it, he took a long swallow.

'The Pilgrim Church hungers for you,' said Rendeage carefully. 'Why?'

'That is my business.'

'If you fear it will appal me so greatly that I shall hand you over to the Wardens,' murmured Rendeage, 'you are mistaken. I have granted you sanctuary – and I have done so unconditionally.'

Ballas ignored him.

'Your crime – is it tied up, somehow, with Belthirran?' persisted Rendeage.

Ballas looked up sharply.

'Do not be alarmed,' replied the priest. 'Elsefar told me of your intent. And I admit that it makes sense.'

'You know of Belthirran?'

The priest shook his head. 'No more than any other man. Just rumours, hints – you know there is no proof that Belthirran exists?'

'Yet you say I'm being sensible in seeking it . . .'

'You cannot remain in Druine,' said Rendeage. 'Nor can you flee to the Distant East: every port and harbour is being watched. So what remains for you but Belthirran? You are acting logically. I cannot argue with that.' Pressing his hands together, he touched his fingertips to his lips. 'Once more: why are the Church pursuing you?'

'Because of my crime,' said Ballas, annoyed by the priest's questions. 'I've sinned, they want to punish me – it's obvious.'

'You have not sinned.' Slowly, Rendeage shook his head. 'Or rather, if you *have* sinned, it is of no odds – the Church aren't after you because of that.'

'What are talking about?'

'A Decree of Annihilation has been declared. The purpose of such an act,' said Rendeage, almost whispering, 'is not to punish a wrongdoer – it is to prevent more harm. The Decree says you must be killed. By whatever measures, you must be ripped out of existence, so that you will not be able to trouble Druine – *at some future time*. If the Masters wished to punish you, they would insist on your capture. Then you would be handed over to them, so that they might exact retributive suffering. They would not leave it to the common folk.'

Rendeage squinted.

'The Decree demands *annihilation* – not apprehension,' he continued. 'That distinction is crucial. They see you as harmful, Ballas. You are a threat; you must be obliterated. *That* is why the Decree was issued. For some reason, they fear you.'

For a long time, Ballas was silent. He hadn't thought much about the Decree. The different implications of death and of capture hadn't occurred to him. Yet he remained puzzled.

'I am no threat to the Church,' he said, frowning. 'I care nothing for it! Yet . . . yet perhaps . . .'

'Yes?'

Ballas stared flatly at Rendeage. 'My crime was a dark one. I attacked a Blessed Master. I reckon I might've killed him.'

Rendeage did not seem shocked – only interested. Tilting his head forward, he said, 'There have been rumours. A Master named Muirthan has not been seen for some time. Normally, he would preside over the great ceremonies: of all the Masters, he is the finest orator. Yet at the Earth Blessing, at Soriterath Cathedral, he was not present. Nor did he attend the Winter Prayers.'

'The Masters tried to put me on the Penance Oak,' continued Ballas. 'To escape, I had to kill – so kill I did. I saw a man perish on the Oak. It is a vile death, the worst I've ever seen. Maybe the Masters reckoned it angered me . . . turned me into a rebel. Maybe they expect me to start an uprising. Like Cal'Briden did.'

'It is possible,' said Rendeage. 'But the Masters are not, I think, so nervous. They do not think that they can be brought down. They consider true rebellion to be unlikely. Which it is, of course.'

'But I know other things . . . about the Oak.'

'Speak on.'

Ballas briefly recounted the events of the night he was almost nailed to the Oak. He spoke of the Lectivin, of the magick it used – and of his cell-mate Gerack's suffering.

Rendeage closed his eyes, slowly. He seemed genuinely pained. When he opened them they were moist.

Ballas frowned, puzzled.

'It is nothing,' said Rendeage, waving a hand. He swallowed, and when he spoke his voice was strained. 'True: you *do* know things . . . things that might threaten the Church. After all, we have spent six hundred years vilifying Lectivins . . . saying they were evil incarnate. Yet if it were shown that the Church employed one . . . And magic: how fiercely it is forbidden! Forbidden to all, it seems, but the Masters.' He lifted a knuckle to his lips.

'Such things would turn many against the Masters. So it would seem they have good cause to silence you. Except . . .'

Ballas tilted his head questioningly.

'. . . They know you'd never be believed. Say what you have seen, and you would be declared mad and locked up. Only your fellow lunatics would believe you.' He exhaled. 'There must be something more. Why were you arrested in the first place? Why did the Masters wish to place you on the Oak?'

'I killed a Servant of the Church,' said Ballas – and, briefly, felt again his knife sinking into Carrande Black's stomach. 'He tried to murder me.'

'Why?'

'I had a trinket he wanted . . . an iron disc, set with precious stones.' For the first time in a while, Ballas thought of the disc. He saw the rubies, the gemstone, the drifting sparks. And he saw – inexplicably – a flash of blue-silver light. It shot dazzlingly across his vision. He had no idea what it was. Where it had come from. It was a memory, he supposed. Yet it surprised him, in a way that memories seldom did. Grunting, he rubbed his eyes.

Heresh appeared. She was dressed now in a woollen jumper and black cape.

As Ballas moved to the door, Rendeage said, 'I will think upon this matter, while you are away.'

Ballas and Heresh climbed the crypt steps, emerging through a door into the worship hall. They left the cathedral, stepping cautiously out on to the streets.

A few Wardens strolled past. Ballas drew Heresh back into the doorway. He watched the men disappear along the street. Further off, a second patrol stood on a street corner, chatting.

'Father Rendeage says that more Wardens arrive every day,' said Heresh. 'Despite their failed search – or because of it – their numbers are being increased.'

'That's good news,' murmured Ballas, his voice heavy.

Heresh looked at him, puzzled; moonlight was reflected in her eyes.

'There'll be fewer Wardens out *there*.' Pointing, Ballas indicated the land far beyond the city gates. 'So when we leave, we may be left alone for a while.'

'For a pragmatist,' commented Heresh, 'you're capable of great self-delusion.' She looked intently at the big man. 'We won't have a second's peace. Not until we are dead.'

Ballas glanced along the alley. 'Come on,' he said, stepping out.

They moved through the darkened streets. A cold moon shone overhead:

a curved splinter of ice-white light. They kept close to the fronts of buildings where shadows pooled. They kept their footsteps as near-silent as they could on the frosted thoroughfare mud. Their progress was slow. It was as Rendeage had claimed: the city teemed with Wardens, and Ballas became aware that they might be concealed off the streets as well. Crossbow-armed Wardens might be perched upon rooftops – *would* be perched there, if they had any sense. Others might be watching from windows. Or alleyways. In the narrow streets over which buildings loomed Ballas felt dangerously exposed.

He looked at Heresh.

Her hood was pulled up. In the moonlight, her face was pale, her eyes anxious. Yet she kept pace with Ballas. One hand hovered near a dagger, hidden under her cape. She was ready to fight. Perhaps such a prospect did not please her. But she understood that blood was the price of survival. It wasn't something she'd learned slowly, over time. But something she had realised, in a heartbeat, in the marshes, when the Warden Jasper Grethinne had planned to murder them.

You are truly not your father's daughter, thought Ballas. Once, Crask must have possessed a little daring, or recklessness – such qualities would have been needed when he was smuggling forbidden texts. Yet they no longer existed. Perhaps, when the Wardens had caught him and had threatened him with execution, they had been driven out of him. Sensing the closeness of his own death, a man often discovered what he truly was. Crask had found that he lacked bravery. And he had accepted it. Instead of perishing, he had struck a deal with the Church.

What would you have done, in your father's shoes? wondered Ballas, glancing at Heresh. Would you have acted as he did? Or would you have gone to your grave?

Briefly, Ballas wondered what he himself would have done. It was one thing to fight when there was no hope of survival. But when there *was* hope of a escape, of a reprieve . . . Such hope, however slim, could burn away a man's loyalty to his fellows. Friendships, promises – they swirled up in smoke.

'We are here. It's as Elsefar described,' said Heresh.

They halted. The Archive Hall was a large, dark-bricked building. Unlit arched windows overlooked the street. A short flight of steps led to an oaken door. Ballas grasped the ring-handle.

'Locked,' he grunted, twisting.

'Should we break it down?'

'Hold this,' Ballas said, handing Heresh a small lantern in which the shutters were closed, allowing no light to escape.

He took a lock-pick from his pocket – the same carved splinter he'd used to break into Egren Callen's home. Kneeling, he worked at the lock. Moments passed. Then a weight dropped inside the lock.

The door opened.

'You were a thief, hm? That was your trade, wasn't it?' Heresh looked intently at Ballas.

'Among other things,' grunted the big man.

They stepped inside. As Ballas closed the door, a slithering rattle sounded – then a dull snap. The lock was a sophisticated model. When the door had shut, the lock had reset itself.

Ballas stepped forward. His boot soles rasped on a wooden floor. Rustling echoes swirled into the dark space. They indicated a deep, hollow vastness. The scent of parchments – musty, grave-deathly – hung in the air.

'Open the lantern.' He spoke softly. Yet his voice sounded sonorous.

The lantern shutter slid aside. A tiny flame flickered, giving out a haze of pale light, and the Hall became dimly visible. Though still shadowed, three floors could be seen, each linked to the other by a single staircase. On every floor there was nothing except shelves, crammed with texts. There were leather-bound books, the gilt letters of their spines glinting in the lamplight; scrolls, neatly heaped; and folded parchments, tucked tightly against one another.

Heresh sighed. 'Elsefar did not mention that the place was so big. We don't have a hope of finding the map. I don't even know where to start looking.'

Sniffing the air, Ballas raised a finger to his lips. He detected a thin but dense odour, drifting from the dark. He sniffed again. The smell persisted.

'What are you doing?' whispered Heresh.

'There's someone here. Someone who knows we're here too – and who doesn't want to be found.' He looked at her. 'I can smell smoke from a candle that's just been snuffed out.'

They walked briskly, following the smell. They reached a closed wooden door. Kneeling, Ballas sniffed the door-bottom, where it failed to meet the floor properly. The extinguished-candle odour was strong. Rising, he drew his knife. Then he pushed open the door.

The lantern-light illuminated a small, bare-walled room. Upon a table stood a flameless candle, dark smoke rising from its wick. A pallet-bed rested against the far wall. A young man was kneeling on it. He wore a woollen jerkin over a long white nightshirt. His face was thin and tapered crookedly, as if an unseen hand were pushing his jaw slightly to one side. His brown eyes flared in terror at the sudden light. Scrambling backwards, he cowered in a corner, seemingly trying to squeeze himself into the bricks themselves. In his right hand he held a book. In his left, a long knife – a type used for cutting parchment.

Springing forward, Ballas swatted the knife from the young man's hand. The blade flew glinting across the room. Snatching his wrist, Ballas hauled him to his feet.

'Please! Don't hurt me!' cried the young man.

He must have been at least eighteen years old, yet he had the gawkiness of an adolescent. His limbs were spindly. Ballas could feel his wrist bones against his own palm.

'Who are you?' hissed the big man.

'Please, be merciful!'

'Answer me, damn it! Or I swear I'll rip your bloody guts out!'

The young man's knees buckled. Sliding to the floor, he curled into a ball. 'You are the sinner,' he said. 'Oh, sweet grief! I knew I shouldn't have stayed here! I knew I should have gone home!'

Ballas reached out to grasp his nightshirt collar. But Heresh placed a hand on his wrist. Ballas glanced her. She shook her head, then kneeled beside the young man.

'You will not be harmed,' she said, 'if you do as we say. Do you understand?'

The young man nodded.

'Now, tell us who you are.'

'The archivist's apprentice,' he said, wretchedly.

'You know your way around this place?' growled Ballas. His tone was hard, forceful – the apprentice's whole body flinched.

'Do you?' asked Heresh, more gently.

'I've been here two years,' replied the apprentice, 'and my knowledge of the Hall is as good – almost – as my master's.'

'Then you can be of use,' said Ballas. 'On your feet.'

The apprentice got up. And shivered. His gaze flitted anxiously from Ballas to Heresh, then back again. 'You are the sinner,' he said once more, 'from the Decree . . .'

'Yeah,' agreed Ballas. 'And you were going to kill me?' He gestured at the parchment knife.

The apprentice shook his head. 'I – I wished only to save myself.'

'Then we're not too different, you and me,' said Ballas. 'To save your own life, you're willing to kill. And so am I. The woman spoke the truth. Help us, and you'll leave here unharmed. Understand?'

'I don't want to die.'

'Then be sensible,' replied Ballas. 'In here, somewhere, there's a map of the sewers under Granthaven.'

'Sewers? There are no—'

'Don't argue!' snapped Ballas. 'You must find it – and quickly. All right?'

The apprentice breathed out shakily. 'I didn't want to sleep here. But my master made me. He said someone must remain with the books, so that none are stolen.' He shook his head, angrily. 'My master is a fool. What use am I against someone like you? Or against anyone, for that matter. For all his learning, he can be damnably stupid!'

The apprentice took a lantern from the table. Ballas ushered him into the Hall.

'A map of the sewers,' murmured the young man. 'If it truly exists, it will be up on the third floor. We keep all the architectural documents up there.'

They climbed the stairways to the third floor. Countless parchments were stored around the room's edge, squeezed into twenty-foot-tall cases. The middle of each floor was empty air, a central well around which ran galleries overlooking the lower floors. Approaching the oak balustrade, Ballas looked down. He could see little except darkness, yet he felt a mild touch of vertigo. He was, he estimated, eighty feet above the ground. He sensed the black emptiness below, and saw in his mind's eye the hard floorboards at the bottom. He stared, and the momentary unease passed. Grunting dismissively, he turned to the apprentice.

'Well?' he said.

'This way,' said the young man, leading them further along.

They halted. The apprentice peered at markings etched into a case. Then he nodded. 'It is in here somewhere,' he said, gesturing at the ranked parchments.

'Find it,' said Ballas.

'It may take some time,' muttered the apprentice, frowning. He glanced unhappily at Ballas. 'My master's traits ill suit him to his trade. He is an archivist – yet he is also slothful, and disinclined to place things in order. When I said it is in here *some*where, I was not talking idly. This section is a jumble. I do not—'

'*Find it.*' The big man's voice roared like thunder. The apprentice recoiled, growing calm again only when Heresh placed a hand on his shoulder. He looked uneasily at her.

'The sinner,' she said, eyeing Ballas, 'has a few virtues – but patience is not one of them. Work quickly, and you will please him. As soon as the map is found, all will be well.'

The apprentice got a wheeled ladder from further along the gallery and rolled it to the shelves. Climbing to the top, he took a parchment from the upper shelf, looked at it, shook his head, then replaced the document. He repeated this action for the next two parchments. Heresh had spoken correctly. Patience was not a virtue that Ballas possessed. The big man's skin bristled, his guts knotted in frustration. The apprentice's movements were delicate, over-careful – prissy, even.

'Get down,' said Ballas.

The apprentice stared from the top of the ladder.

'Must I say everything twice?' shouted Ballas.

The apprentice scrambled to the floor. Gripping the sides of the ladder, Ballas clambered to the upper shelf – then swept down its contents. A pile of parchments tumbled flapping around the apprentice. Ballas stepped down to the shelf below and did the same again – and again and again, until he leaped from the ladder and cleared the bottommost shelves.

The apprentice stared wide-eyed, as if Ballas had committed sacrilege.

'Find the bloody map,' said Ballas. 'When you've looked over a parchment, throw it aside.'

Kneeling, the apprentice did as he was told. He worked quickly now. Parchments were unfolded, scrolls unfurled; he swept his gaze over each and, finding them unsatisfactory, tossed them into a heap to one side. The young man's eyes glinted. He seemed happy, as if taking a perverse joy from the procedure. Ballas wondered if, accustomed to order, he was enjoying the creation of chaos. Perhaps his future, as an archivist, would consist of nothing but the careful treatment of texts – and, right now, he was savouring his sole period of recklessness. Ballas sniffed. Often, educated men loved most the practices of the ignorant.

Heresh touched his shoulder, then led the big man away from the apprentice.

'What are you going to do with him?' she asked, at a whisper. The apprentice continued scanning the parchments. 'He will deduce, sooner or later, that we plan to use the map to escape from the city. Sweet grief – he has probably already done so. And for us, that is dark news. If he tells the Wardens—'

'He won't,' said Ballas.

Heresh looked at him uncertainly.

'I'll tie the boy up,' explained Ballas, 'and leave him in his room. His master won't be back before dawn. By then, we'll be well away. As soon as he's found the map, we'll go back to the cathedral. We'll get your father and Elsefar, and leave this piss-awful city.'

Heresh looked calmly at Ballas. 'It would be more efficient to kill him. His silence would be assured.' In her voice, there was a type of dark suggestiveness.

'You want him to die?'

She shook her head. '*I* don't. But *you* do,' she replied. 'It is in your nature to be ruthless.'

'Ruthless? Maybe. But I'm not . . .' he groped for the proper word '. . . *indiscriminate*. When the need arises, I kill. But otherwise?' He shook his head.

Heresh's stare did not falter. 'Perhaps you'd be doing the boy a favour.'

Ballas frowned.

'Think what you have done to him. You have forced him to do your bidding – to aid a sinner, to help the subject of a Decree of Annihilation escape capture.'

'*Forced* him.' Ballas nodded. 'He isn't helping us because he wants to. But because he has to.'

'I doubt the Wardens will be sympathetic to that argument. It is his duty to try to kill you – isn't that what the Decree says? *Unto every citizen, regardless of rank, wealth, age or sex, falls the duty, in accord with the Four's will, of killing Anhaga Ballas.* He has hardly tried, has he? He sat on his pallet-bed, cringing in fear. Nothing else. In itself, that makes him a criminal.' Heresh drew a breath. 'He is not strong. Look at him: he was probably the runt of his parents' litter. But such types are often sharp-minded. Many people apply to become archivist's apprentices. Only a few are accepted. He isn't a halfwit, Ballas. Perhaps he has already worked out that if he doesn't try to kill you he will be arrested.'

Ballas shook his head. 'He's too frightened to think clearly. He can't see past the present moment.' He shrugged. 'And if the Church decides to punish him – so what? I can't be blamed for their cruelty.'

They returned to the apprentice. The young man continued sifting through the texts, inspecting each of them. Eventually, he reached the final one. He unfolded it, and peered closely at it. His strangely contented expression faded. He looked anxiously at Ballas.

'What?' said the big man.

The apprentice did not speak – he merely turned his face to Heresh.

'The map is not there?' asked the red-haired woman.

The apprentice shook his head. 'I am sorry . . .'

'Pilgrims' blood,' murmured Ballas. 'Are you certain? Did you check every parchment? You'd better not have made any errors, boy—'

'I did my best. And the sewer-map is not here.' He wrung his hands – a mannerism belonging to someone far older. 'I never make mistakes. That is why my master employs me. He says I am as keen-eyed as—'

'Pissing hell!' snapped Ballas. Once more, he felt suddenly claustrophobic. The city of Granthaven seemed no larger than a prison cell. The sky, the air, the mud of the roadways – all seemed to conspire to imprison him. He swung his boot through the parchments, scattering several over the balustrade. They drifted soundlessly into darkness before pattering on to the floor below.

'Do not kill me,' said the apprentice. 'Please – I have helped you as far as I can! I . . .' His voice trailed off. A frown touched his brow. His gaze drifted to the next case of parchments. 'Perhaps . . . perhaps there has been overspill.'

'Overspill?' said Ballas.

Rising, the apprentice wheeled the ladder to the case. Monkey-nimble, he clambered up. He took down the first parchment, glanced at it, then replaced it. He did the same for the second. Ballas felt his anger rising—

—Then the apprentice said, 'I've got it!'

Ballas looked up, surprised.

'I've found it!' said the apprentice, waving a folded rectangle of parchment.

At that instant a dull boom rolled through the Archive Hall. Startled, the apprentice swayed upon the ladder, grasping a rung to steady himself. Heresh looked to Ballas, her eyes wide. A second boom rang out. Ballas moved to the balustrade and peered down.

Through the windows he made out a group of figures. Squinting, Ballas estimated there were eight or nine of them – perhaps more. Several torches blazed, the fire glimmering upon the glass.

There was a third thud. The door shook on its hinges.

'Open up!' someone shouted. 'Or I swear we'll smash our way in!' The voice was that of a man in his late teens: it had a jarring unevenness, as if it was yet to find its proper timbre.

Ballas turned to the apprentice. 'Give me the map.'

His face pale, the apprentice tossed Ballas the document. 'Who is out there? What are they doing?'

'We must have been seen,' said Ballas, tucking the map behind his belt. 'Is there a back way out?'

'The hall can be entered, or left, only by the front doors.' The apprentice clambered shakily from the ladder. 'There is no other way—'

Another boom sounded. Then a rattling crash, as the lock burst and the door slammed open. A dozen men poured on to the ground floor. Three held torches. The flames sent shadows sprawling across the walls. The figures moved to the centre of the floor where they stood motionless, scanning the Hall for any other living souls.

'We know you are here, sinner!' shouted a figure. 'We can bloody sense you, you evil bastard! We are here to do the Church's bidding. We will fulfil the Decree of Annihilation. The only question is, do we kill you quickly – or slowly? Show yourself, and we shall be merciful. But hide, and we'll take our time when we butcher you. We'll rip out your guts and garland you with them. We'll slice out your heart and thrust it down your throat.'

Ballas drew back from the balustrade. 'Stay silent,' he whispered to the apprentice.

'Are we to fight them?' asked Heresh, her voice steady.

Ballas did not reply. It was impossible to know what to do. Creeping back to the balustrade, he stared down at them. In the torchlight he discerned the faces of young men – each one scarcely out of adolescence. He recalled a group of youths outside a tavern, getting soused on ha'penny jugs of cider. He thought that he and Heresh had passed unnoticed. Clearly, he had been mistaken.

He drew a breath.

This was to be the young men's finest hour, Ballas realised. They would kill the sinner – and for ever after they'd talk of their courage. They would use Ballas's death to lure women into their beds. They would boast loudly of it in taverns, earning the admiration of their fellows. And, once they settled and had children, they would present themselves to their young as near-legendary figures: as noble, and courageous as anyone from the old myths.

Ballas sensed their excitement. And knew that it crackled perilously close to fear.

'Let us see how brave they are,' he murmured, drawing his knife.

Moving to the balustrade, he hurled the weapon downwards. It vanished into darkness, reappearing an instant later as a firelight-struck flash of gold. The blade spun before sinking into a torch-wielder's throat. The youth pitched backwards, flinging the torch in the air. It struck the ground, burning happily on the wooden floor. Another youth snatched it up, stamping out the flames as he did so.

Several others stared at the corpse.

'Malcrin?' One figure kneeled, touching his fingertips to the knife hilt protruding from his friend's throat. 'Sweet grief – he is dead!' He looked up at the balustrade. But Ballas had already stepped back. 'Look – look what he has done!' the figure persisted. 'He has used magic, surely! No man's aim is so true—'

'He was lucky,' said a second figure. 'Even sinners enjoy occasional good fortune.'

Something moved in the corner of Ballas's eye. The apprentice was running away, his nightshirt flapping around his ankles. He sprinted to the staircase, then hurried down to the figures.

'I am a friend!' he shouted, as he drew close. 'A friend to you, and no ally to the sinner! I promise you: I crave his death as fiercely as you do! Were I strong enough, I'd have gralloched him myself!'

He half-stumbled to the figures.

'I am the archivist's apprentice,' he explained, moving into the torches' glow. 'He made me do his bidding!'

'He is up there, yes?' asked a figure.

'Him – and a woman, who acts as if she is . . . a sweet, harmless thing. But how can she be, when she keeps such vile company?'

'And there are no others?'

'None. And I promise you, neither of them is a demon. Or a magicker. If they were, they wouldn't have needed my help. They are but ordinary people – that is all. You need not fear them.'

Huddling together, the young men plotted their next move. Suddenly, the apprentice spun on his heel and raced out of the Archive Hall. One of them tried to grasp his nightshirt collar. But the apprentice was too fast. Ballas watched him vanish out of the door, into the street.

'Bastard!' said one of the youths loudly. 'Now we must act with haste. Otherwise . . .' His voice softened to an inaudible whisper.

'Otherwise what?' finished Heresh, looking to Ballas.

'Otherwise,' said the big man, 'there'll be Wardens here, and those young men'll be robbed of their glory.'

'Then we too must act with haste,' said Heresh. 'But I don't see—'

'Wait.'

Ballas thought a moment. Then he strode to the balustrade.

'You're seeking me, right?' he shouted. His voice shook the walls, and threatened to blast the windows from their frames. As one, every figure jumped. 'If you want to take my life, come to me. We'll see how well you do.' Ballas gestured to Heresh. She moved to stand beside him. 'We're waiting for you. We aren't going anywhere. After all, where can we go? It's up to you.'

'What in the Four's name are you playing at?' hissed Heresh, seizing Ballas's forearm.

'I'm letting them know where we are,' said Ballas. 'And I'm offering us up as bait. Now,' his voice dropped, 'we must see how smart they are. If they split up, with one group going that way –' he gestured around the far side of the gallery '– and the other going this way –' he gestured in the opposite direction '– they can trap us. We won't be able to run. And perhaps we'll prove easier to kill.'

'And if they aren't smart?' queried Heresh. 'If they come as a single group?'

Ballas did not reply.

The figures climbed the first staircase. Then the second. At the top of the third, they paused: a knot of dark, shadow-garbed shapes, half-haloed in torchlight. Then they broke apart, forming two groups. One group moved off to the gallery's far side. The other headed towards Ballas and Heresh.

Ballas grasped the woman's upper arm. 'Stay with me,' he said.

'Where are we going?'

'Just do as I say.'

The nearest group moved cautiously forward.

'Come on, sinner,' said the youth at the front. Of his features, Ballas discerned only shadows: eye sockets, darkly pooled, and a pockmark-stippled jaw. 'Don't bring us up here and then run away. Our offer still stands. Show yourself, and we'll slaughter you quickly. Play cat and mouse, and your sufferings will seem endless. Be grateful we're offering you a choice.'

Ballas glanced towards the other group. They were moving steadily along the far side of the gallery. Soon, they would turn left, go along another side, then turn left again, emerging behind Ballas.

The big man continued edging backward. Then he halted.

The pockmarked youth grinned. 'Now I see you,' he said, squinting. He tilted his head, curious. 'So: *you* are the sinner, eh? The man hunted by every Warden in Druine.'

Ballas glanced back. The other group came into view. Ballas moved his mouth close to Heresh's ear. He caught a faint tang of female sweat. 'Go to the top of the staircase,' he said, very softly. 'I will clear us a path.' He looked at the youths. 'It'll be harder than hacking through a nettle patch. But whatever happens, get yourself to the staircase.'

Drawing her knife, Heresh nodded.

The pockmarked youth sneered. 'Oh, you've a taste for a fight, have you?'

Saying nothing, Ballas raced towards the group. While he was still several yards away, he flung himself down on to the floor and *rolled*, crashing through their legs. A few fell; leaping to his feet, Ballas punched a torch-bearer in the stomach, hard. Wheezing, the young man slumped against the balustrade. The torch slipped from his fingers. Ballas caught it before it hit the floor. Spinning, he smashed the torch into the face of the nearest youth. A flurry of sparks shot up. The pockmarked fellow ran at Ballas. The big man brought the torch down on top of his head. The youth's hair caught alight, blazing like a beacon. He screamed – until Ballas rammed the torch into his face . . . Then he made choking, gurgling noises.

Ballas glanced up.

Heresh had reached the stairway. Head-butting another youth out of the way, Ballas ran along the gallery, reaching her in seconds.

'Go down!' he snapped. 'And be quick!'

The other youths were running over. Moving quickly, Ballas grasped a tall case of parchments. Growling, he brought it crashing down upon the stair-top. Parchments slithered over the floorboards. Stooping, Ballas thrust the torch into them. Bone dry, they burst into flame. The youths ran towards Ballas. Gradually, their pace slowed.

They halted, uncertain.

Their gazes flitted from Ballas to the fire. Then to Ballas again.

Ballas raised the torch. He did not speak. He did not have to. The youths understood the situation. Soon, the parchment-case at the stair-top would be burning so fiercely that they would not be able to pass. They would be trapped on the third floor – the highest gallery in the Archive Hall. To leap over the balustrade would mean a quick death – not escape. If they wished to leave alive, they would have to get past Ballas.

And Ballas, his upraised torch flickering, would not permit it.

Ballas inhaled the smoke from the fire. The smell evoked something. It was faintly familiar. He frowned, trying to remember – and thought once more of the museum in Soriterath where everything had begun . . . thought of the parchment-filled room in which the curator had concealed the iron disc . . . thought of the small fire that he had accidentally started but neglected to douse . . .

The flames on the stair-top were taking hold now. Ballas jumped through them. A few sparks flared in his leggings and tunic. He patted them out.

A couple of youths approached the fire, seeking to imitate Ballas.

Standing on the stairs, Ballas raised the torch. The youths hesitated. Then the flames surged higher, and they vanished from sight.

Ballas walked briskly down the stairs.

At the bottom stood Heresh, pale and shocked. Ballas untucked the map from his belt.

'We have what we came for,' he said. 'Now we must go.'

Already, flames were creeping along the third floor. The youths backed away into darkness . . . darkness that would soon flare bright with the advancing flames.

Ballas knew what would follow. Some youths would burn. Others would clamber over the balustrades and jump.

All would perish. It was merely a question of which death each young man preferred.

He took Heresh's wrist. 'The apprentice will be summoning help,' he reminded her. 'We don't have much time.'

Turning, they left the Archive Hall.

At a half-run, Heresh and Ballas returned to the cathedral. They passed through the worship hall and went down into the crypt. As they entered, Lugen Crask got to his feet.

'What has happened?' he asked, alarmed. He gestured at Ballas's blood-speckled tunic. 'Trouble?'

'Yes,' replied the big man. 'We have to go.'

'My daughter, are you—' began Crask, turning to Heresh.

'I am unhurt,' said the red-haired woman. 'But Ballas is correct. We must go – and go now. Our plan has been discovered.'

Crask swore.

The cripple Elsefar said, 'Give me the map. Within the city, there'll be an entry point to the sewers. We must locate it before we leave.'

Ballas handed over the map. The quill-master unfolded it on the table. He ran his fingertips over it. 'Ah, yes – this is my work,' he said, nodding dreamily. 'Surprising how strongly one's handiwork can bring back the past to one. I executed this one summer morning. And now, I can almost feel that season's heat.' Blinking, he leaned close to the map.

Father Rendeage emerged from the other chamber.

'Ballas,' he said, 'we must speak – privately.'

The holy man's breath smelled of wine. Yet there was nothing drunken about his manner. His eyes burned with a nervous intensity.

'I am leaving,' said the big man. 'I have no time for talk.'

'It is important,' said the priest. Stepping close, he said quietly, 'I know why the Church are hunting you. Or at least, I *think* I do. It would serve you well to know.'

Ballas glanced at the others. Then he followed the priest into the adjoining chamber.

From its niche, the skull of the martyr Cadaris watched them. Father Rendeage dragged a hand over his bare scalp. For a moment he seemed unable to find the right words.

'Come on, priest,' said Ballas. '*Speak*.'

'I have been consulting this,' he said, patting a thick leather-bound book upon the table. 'It is a directory of magical objects that I, as a priest, must be especially aware of. Inside, there are items from many cultures, some eastern, some western; some extinct, some extant.' He paused. 'You spoke of an iron disc.'

'Yes.'

'Describe it.'

Ballas shrugged. 'It was about so big.' He made a circle with his thumbs and forefingers. 'There were four rubies around its edge. And a blue gemstone in the centre. It was the gemstone that caught my eye. It looked valuable.'

Rendeage made a strange, quiet sound. 'The rubies were not rubies. And the gemstone . . .' He paced back and forth. 'What do you know of magick? Of *Lectivin* magick?'

'Apart from what I saw at the Oak, nothing.'

'The Lectivins were a magical species. They had grasped the forbidden arts far more than we had. So much so that they devised ways of communicating with the dead. During the Red War, this gave them an immense advantage over us. A soldier slaughtered in Mecanarde could tell his colleagues, situated miles away, how the battle was faring in the north. Reinforcements could be summoned; tactical advice supplied. Often, to transmit such information, Lectivin soldiers would kill themselves. Then their cohorts could speak with them. We lumbered on with foot messengers and carrier pigeons. The Lectivins sent information almost instantly right across Druine.'

'For all the good it did them,' muttered Ballas. 'We slaughtered them. We smashed them into nothingness.'

'We outnumbered them,' Rendeage replied. 'We reproduced with greater ease and frequency than they did. Thus they couldn't compete with our numbers.' The priest tugged at the cuffs of his robe. 'We defeated the Lectivins because we cannot resist temptation. Because we submit to the faintest tug of lust.'

'A pleasing thought.'

'Not for the Pilgrim Church. But that is by the by.' Rendeage waved a dismissive hand. 'The Lectivins spoke to their dead through a device known as the *sivis*. There is no precise translation. The most satisfying equivalent is "monument". In our culture, a monument is any testimony to the dead. Usually, the term means something large, grand: a statue or edifice. For the Lectivins, the scale was unimportant. They were magical creatures. Familiar with the world of souls, and the edges of the Eltheryn Forest, they did not construct monuments of remembrance. The Lectivins did not remember their dead. They *spoke* to them.

'The Lectivins created many *sivis*, and they were used not merely during the War, but in periods of peace as well. They enabled the Lectivins to seek advice from their ancestors. From long-dead rulers, philosophers, engineers. Even magickers. Any Lectivin at all from the past.

'And maybe that is why the Pilgrim Church wants you dead. Maybe they believe you have used a *sivis*, and learned something terrible, something dangerous from it.'

'Horseshit,' murmured Ballas. 'I'm not a magicker. I wouldn't know how to work this . . . Monument.'

'It would not be difficult,' said Rendeage. 'You would only need to expose the middle gemstone to moonlight. No magical talent of your own would be needed. The stones you thought were rubies are, in fact, *skiverns*: energy stones. They contain the necessary magick. With their help, the moonlight would take shape, and become . . .'

For the second time that day, Ballas glimpsed blue-silver light. This time it *was* a memory. He was certain of it. Concentrating, he tried to recall further details. He groped beyond the blue-silver. Yet grasped nothing.

Rendeage stared intently at Ballas. 'You look as if you were remembering something.'

'I reckon I was,' said Ballas. 'But it's gone now.'

'That is to be expected. A man who uses a Monument sees into the Eltheryn Forest. It is a world of the dead, of spirits. Our memories can recall only things of the corporeal world. We have not been created for retaining glimpses of the afterlife.'

'Then what use was the Monument to the Lectivin generals? If they could remember piss-all, what was the point?'

Rendeage sighed. 'The directory –' he touched the book '– does not say. And I am no expert upon matters magical. But, as I say, it seems the Monument lies behind the Decree. The Church fears you, Ballas.'

'It's got no reason to. I'm no threat. I want to leave Druine – not destroy it.'

The priest seemed uneasy. 'I admit I am troubled. I do not know how the Monument acts upon a man. How its purpose is served. Maybe the Church knows more than I do. And that is why you trouble them.'

Lugen Crask appeared in the doorway.

'We are ready!' he said, his face flushed. He lingered a moment, then vanished into the other chamber.

Rendeage trembled. 'I fear I have made an awful mistake. I ought never have granted you sanctuary.'

Ballas wondered if the priest realised he was speaking aloud. Nonetheless he said, 'You'd better pray I get to Belthirran. Once I'm there, I won't trouble the Church.'

Ballas moved to the door.

'Wait. I have a question.'

Ballas felt an urgent impulse to leave. With every passing second, more Wardens would be assembling in the streets above. The apprentice would have told them of Ballas's need for the sewer map. Already, they would be seeking a map of their own – trying to learn where the fugitives would enter the sewer. And from where they would leave it.

Yet he paused. There was desperation in Rendeage's voice.

'You said the Penance Oak provided a vile death. Was . . . was it truly so bad? Did the prisoner suffer as fiercely as you described?'

Ballas did not speak. He simply nodded.

Rendeage gave a quiet groan. 'Go,' he said, softly.

In the next chamber, Ballas found Crask helping Elsefar up the steps. The climb was a struggle for the cripple. Striding over, Ballas knocked away the quill-master's crutches. Then he slung him over his shoulder like a sack of potatoes.

Elsefar did not protest.

They hurried up the steps and through the worship hall. Slipping out of the front doors, Ballas whispered, 'Where've we got to go?'

'On Clarion Street there is a brothel,' said Elsefar. 'Keep going north-east, and I shall guide you when we are close.'

Ballas heard footsteps and shouting. Turning, he saw a mob gathering outside the cathedral. Someone struck the door with a dagger hilt.

'Open up, Rendeage! We know of your guest . . . The sinner is with you, isn't he? We demand entry!'

The dagger-gripping man turned the ring-handle. To his surprise, the door opened. The mob poured through.

Ballas realised he had been wrong. The apprentice hadn't gone to the Wardens. He had clearly told the first person he'd met – an Under-Warden, perhaps. Or an ordinary citizen. Within minutes, a crowd had assembled.

'They will kill him,' said Heresh tonelessly. 'They will find we are not there, and they will tear him apart like wolves.'

They moved northwards, towards Clarion Street.

Someone knocked violently on the cathedral door. In the crypt Father Rendeage started, surprised. Listening, he heard shouting – the bricks and wood of the building muffled the words, but he detected anger.

'They are here,' he said flatly, his voice echoing. He hadn't really expected to get away with it. He knew that someone, somehow, would discover he had sheltered the sinner. That he had prolonged the city's agonies by hiding him away, while the gates remained sealed and people starved.

He gazed at Cadaris's skull.

'Tell me, am I to become a martyr? I have obeyed the Four's teachings.

I have helped the needy. I have honoured my oaths . . . Yet, in doing so, have I not jeopardised the Pilgrim Church? Have I not saved the life of a man who – perhaps – threatens it?' He lowered his voice. 'Is it not absurd that the Four's virtues, when applied in real life, might destroy the Church?'

He didn't know what danger Ballas posed. But he knew, now, that he ought to have left the big man to die.

He touched Cadaris's skull, tracing his fingertips over the impact hole. 'I have gone too far . . .'

Rendeage closed his eyes.

He had behaved recklessly. Moreover, he'd been self-indulgent. He had *enjoyed* harbouring the sinner.

It was a type of adolescent stubbornness. A callow disrespect for a powerful, centuries-old institution: the Pilgrim Church. He had saved Ballas as a gesture of defiance. A tiny vengeful act that had filled him with a vulgar sort of happiness – as if he'd shouted an obscenity at the Blessed Masters. He loved the Four, not the Pilgrim Church.

It hadn't always been so. Rendeage had taken up the priesthood late in life. A quarter of a century ago, in his fifty-fifth year, he had enrolled at the Seminary at Braensigate and, three years later, had come out garbed in the blue robes, and Scarrendestin pendant, of a clergyman.

For the first five years of his service, he had made no distinction between the Church and the Four. He had believed that the Church's laws and procedures were the Four's will perfectly enshrined. He had believed the Four themselves could have formulated the rules governing Druine.

He had performed his duties immaculately, unquestioningly, and with pride and satisfaction. He had tended the sick. He had administered Final Blessings. Weddings, Coming-of-Age Ceremonies . . . Everything the Church demanded, he did. He was a flawless example of the priesthood.

When he found that a girl, only fifteen years old, was practising magick . . . when he heard of this young healer, using her talents to remedy agues, blood-taints, disease . . . he didn't hesitate to apprehend her and turn her over to the Wardens. Her fate was to be an unpleasant one: she would be transported to Soriterath, and there placed upon the Penance Oak. This didn't perturb Rendeage. She had behaved contrary to Church law. She had to be punished. Even when her mother begged him to spare her, and shrieked and wept and clawed her face when he refused, Rendeage remained unmoved. He had sent many to the Oak. The girl was to be treated no differently.

Several weeks later Rendeage travelled to Soriterath. He was to visit the Eskalrion Sacros, in order to receive a fresh clerical posting: the Blessed

Masters had determined his talents were best used not in the small church where he was presently preaching but in a cathedral – the cathedral at Granthaven.

To reach the Sacros, Rendeage crossed Papal Square on foot. For the first time in his life he saw the Penance Oak. At first, in the light of a winter noon, it seemed unexceptional: it might have been any oak, uprooted from any forest and replanted in Druine's holiest city. As he drew closer, though, this changed. The branch-borne heads became visible – the heads of those guilty of holy crimes. Blasphemers, apostates, heretics . . . and magickers.

It surprised Rendeage to see the girl healer there. He hadn't imagined that, after so long, only now would she have been placed upon the Oak – he had supposed that justice, when dealing with such criminals, would be administered swiftly.

Yet there it was: the head of the same blue-eyed, blonde-haired girl whom he'd delivered to the Wardens.

It hadn't been long upon the Oak. The flesh had scarcely started to rot. Of course, in the weeks before her execution, the girl healer had been incarcerated. That, it seemed, had taken its toll on her. Her skin was thinner, a little of the healthy, farm-girl plumpness of her face had vanished. Lesions marked her cheeks. Her hair was greasy and, even now, lice flourished among the strands.

Rendeage stared at her. At her eyes, her skin – at the nail in her forehead and the bloodied stump of her neck.

There was a peculiar beauty to it all. It exuded *rightness*. It was entirely proper that the Oak should exist. That sinners should be lodged there. That their lifeless eyes should stare at the Sacros, the heart of the Pilgrim Church. It even seemed right that magpies should peck out those eyes and crows feast upon the unliving flesh.

Rendeage saw the girl healer – and felt satisfaction. He had played his role to perfection. He had acted as the Church demanded. He had been a priest without flaw . . .

Suddenly, he felt weak. The ground seemed to tilt, the sky lowered, the day's light became first punishingly bright, then oppressively dark. Shivering, rubbing his eyes, he realised that the outer world hadn't altered. No earthquake had shaken Papal Square. The light had stayed constant. Rather, something inside himself had changed. He had been struck by a revelation, and it nauseated him.

Staring at the Oak, he found that he couldn't look upon the girl healer as someone who had suffered. She seemed merely a trophy, like the stuffed animal heads that might decorate a huntsman's walls. He viewed her as proof of a job well done. As a testament to his devotion to his priestly duties. She might as well have been a message of praise from the Blessed Masters. Or the promotion, from church-priest to cathedral-master, that he was in Soriterath to receive.

And that, surely, was a violation of the Four's teachings. The Four preached sympathy and empathy – because these were the seedbeds from which compassion grew.

Yet Rendeage felt nothing for the girl healer. She was young and, despite her sins, innocent: but her death satisfied him.

Rendeage accepted the Master's offer, moving to Granthaven Cathedral. But thoughts of the girl healer persisted. Gradually, Rendeage began to pity her. And he felt ashamed – ashamed at the ruthless fashion in which he'd delivered her to the Wardens. Ashamed at his failure to consider, even briefly, her plight, her suffering. He realised he had been *too* devoted to the Church. So much so that he had forsaken the Four.

It occurred to him that the Pilgrim Church itself, with its cruel practices – not merely the Penance Oak but the cages elemental, gallows, public stonings and many, many other things – had forsaken the Four.

He refused to abandon the Church. Instead, he vowed to be a *holy* priest. A priest obedient to the Four. Not to the earthly institution existing in its name.

And from this, a type of rebelliousness grew. It pleased him when the Church's demands conflicted with the Four's and he chose the latter. It made him feel virtuous. It made him feel holy.

Now, though, he wondered if this had been wise. For it had compelled him to rescue Ballas. And if Ballas were to destroy the Pilgrim Church – Rendeage didn't know how that could be done, or if Ballas was really capable of it – but if he destroyed the Church, what would become of the Four's teachings?

For all its flaws, the Church kept the Four's flame burning. Without it, the Four would be forgotten, their principles vanishing under a thick layer of dust.

'What if I have committed the greatest of evils?' Rendeage grew cold. 'What if I have ripped the keystone from the Church, and the whole structure will soon crumble?'

Footsteps sounded overhead. There were people in the worship hall.

Rendeage looked into the eye sockets of Cadaris's skull. For an instant, they did not seem empty. He thought he glimpsed living eyes within: opal green, exuding utter calm. Then the hollow blackness returned.

'Guide me, Cadaris,' he whispered.

Father Rendeage climbed the steps to the worship hall. A group of twenty or thirty men stood in the aisle. Several carried torches, their light filling the hall.

The men were talking. When Rendeage appeared, they fell silent. They seemed to hesitate – and Rendeage realised that, though they were probably going to kill him, they had felt a reflexive pang of reverence. He was still a priest. He still wore his blue robes and Scarrendestin pendant.

'Where is the sinner, priest?' asked a man at the front of the group. He was tall, swarthy, and rot-toothed. 'Show him to us.'

'He is not here,' said Rendeage.

'He's been seen,' replied the rot-toothed man. 'One of us saw him come here just a brief time ago . . .'

'If you had been vigilant,' said Rendeage, 'you would also have seen him leave. Search my cathedral if you wish. You will not find him.'

The man clenched his jaw. 'You harboured a sinner, priest.'

'It was my duty, as a man of the Four—'

'It was your duty to *kill* him. Didn't you read the Decree of Annihilation?' The man tensed aggressively. 'Where has he gone? Will he return?'

'He will not return,' said Rendeage, 'and do not I know where he is.'

The rot-toothed man moved toward Rendeage. The rest of the group followed, slowly. 'You lie, priest.'

'I speak only the truth.'

'*You lie!*' Leaping forward, he struck Rendeage backhandedly across the face. The priest staggered, then clambered on to the dais behind the altar.

'You are in a house of the Four,' he said. 'There must be no violence. Think of your souls! Do you wish to face damnation . . . do you wish to wander eternally the Barren Lands beyond the Eltheryn Forest? For your own sake, leave me be!'

'It's *your* soul that's in danger,' retorted the rot-toothed man. 'You're the one who protected the sinner. We –' he glanced back at the group '– are doing the Four's work. We're going to track him down and slaughter him.'

'That will not make you good men,' said Rendeage. Yet he didn't hear his own words. He wasn't even certain what they meant. He was aware only of the crowd steadily drawing closer. And of a strange calm that had settled upon him. It was resignation, he supposed. It soothed him.

He backed away. The crowd neared the dais.

Three Wardens stood at the far end of the hall. Rendeage hadn't previously noticed them. He wondered if they had gathered these men together. For certain, they were doing nothing to stop them. They watched, impassively.

Rendeage frowned.

A fourth figure stood beside the Wardens. It wore a brown woollen robe, the hood drawn up. It was short of stature, its head rising level with the Wardens' chests.

Squinting, Rendeage tried to see under the hood. He couldn't make out the figure's face. Only a patch of skin was visible. It was pale, almost bloodless: as white as altar marble. It was stretched tightly over bone.

Rendeage wondered who he was. Clearly, he was ill: his pallor suggested poor blood. Or maybe a canker. But why – why would the Wardens bring him here, to witness a priest's death? What purpose would it serve?

Rendeage's speculation ended abruptly.

The crowd clambered on to the dais. The rot-toothed man strode over. Kneeling, Rendeage murmured a prayer. He felt the heat of bodies close by. Then something smashed into his face, toppling him.

'Guide me, Cadaris,' he repeated.

Chapter 15

He had powers of a magical nature,
As did every Pilgrim – yet his were drawn
From the dark well of himself, not the benediction
Of the creator-god . . .

They moved through Granthaven – Ballas, carrying Elsefar over his shoulder, Lugen Crask, and his daughter, Heresh, who carried the crippled quill-master's crutches. They ducked from darkness to shadow, shadow to darkness, avoiding the Papal Wardens. They stole along like foxes, Ballas thought, darting from grove to undergrowth to rock outcrop, constantly seeking places to hide. It took no effort to carry Elsefar. Though scarcely thin, the cripple weighed little: he seemed barely heavier than an effigy crafted from straw.

They walked on, following a narrow road.

Ballas sensed the presence of the Wardens a heartbeat before they appeared. Still carrying Elsefar over his shoulder, he shrank into a doorway. With no time to hide, Crask and Heresh remained in the road.

'What is happening?' whispered Elsefar, unable to see the Wardens.

'Shut up,' murmured Ballas. Kneeling, he slid Elsefar from his shoulders and set him on the ground. The quill-master scowled at this rough treatment. Yet he stayed silent.

There were two Wardens.

'Who are you?' said the first, approaching Crask. 'What's your business, out at this late hour?'

'We are citizens of Granthaven,' said the eel-catcher, spreading his hands wide. 'And we are . . . we're following a rumour.'

'Speak plainly,' ordered the Warden. 'What do you mean: "following a rumour"?'

'A rumour of blood, of death,' said Crask, haltingly. 'And . . . and loyalty to the Pilgrim Church. Divine work is being done, and we wish to witness it. Wish, even, to take part – if we are capable, and it is not too late.' He glanced towards the doorway. He looked desperate. Crask was not a natural liar, Ballas realised. 'The sinner has been caught,' concluded Crask. 'We've heard he's at the cathedral. We want to observe his death.'

The Warden raised his eyebrows. 'This is the truth?'

Crask nodded vigorously.

The Warden turned to his companion, fingering his sword hilt. 'I was starting to wonder if he'd ever be captured. I too would like to watch him die.' He looked at Crask. 'How long have you lived in Granthaven? Your accent isn't from these parts. Nor do your footsteps suggest you're familiar with this city.'

'What do you mean?'

'You're going the wrong way for the cathedral. You ought to be heading in *that* direction.' He pointed back along the road.

'You jest,' said Crask, feigning amazement.

'You're about a mile from the cathedral.'

Crask pulled a disappointed face. 'My sour luck continues. Never, *ever* am I treated kindly by fortune! This is typical. I miss out on . . . on watching history being made – and why? Because my sense of direction is poor.'

'Hurry,' said the Warden, 'and perhaps you'll see the aftermath. With the sinner gone, there will be celebrations. Yourself and your . . . ?' He looked questioningly at Heresh.

'Daughter,' said Crask

'. . . Will have a fine time.' The Warden peered intently at Heresh. 'What are these?' he asked suddenly, prodding Elsefar's crutches, which Heresh held in her hands. Reaching out, he took the crutches from her. He gazed at them, frowning. Then he looked at Heresh once more. Moving close, he gazed at her hair – hair that, even in the torchlit half-dark, was visibly red-hued. 'I know about you. And you,' he added, looking at Crask. 'Your descriptions are nailed to every Warden-house wall. You travel with the sinner. You are in league with him – as is the scribe from the copying house –' he lifted the crutches '– who owns these.' He grasped Heresh's forearm. 'You have made a grave error, woman.'

Heresh glanced at the doorway, where Ballas was unsheathing a knife. 'I suspect the error is yours,' she said.

Striding from the doorway, Ballas slammed the knife into the Warden's chest. The man gasped, blood spraying from his mouth. As he slithered to the ground, Ballas drew the Warden's sword. The second Warden unsheathed his own weapon. Running at Ballas, he swung the blade in a fierce down-stroke. If it had hit home, it would have hacked open Ballas's skull-top. Lifting his sword, Ballas deflected the blow, and forced the Warden's sword tip to the ground. He planted his boot upon it. The Warden jerked at the weapon. His sword remained trapped under Ballas's foot.

The big man punched the Warden in the face. The Warden stumbled backwards. Ballas swung his sword horizontally and the blade cut deep into the man's neck. The Warden fell, lifeless.

Ballas tossed aside the sword. Returning to the doorway, he lifted Elsefar over his shoulder.

'You impress me,' said the quill-master. 'For a man of your size, you are surprisingly light-footed. You could be a dancer if you weren't so ugly.'

'Where is the brothel?' asked Ballas, stepping around the dead Wardens.

Elsefar guided them hurriedly through the city. Again and again, they were forced into the shadows as patrols passed. After the exhilaration of combat had ebbed – after his hands had ceased trembling, and the dull satisfaction of having preserved his own life had faded – Ballas found he was angry. Not at the Pilgrim Church. Or the Blessed Masters. But at those who served them. Which, in light of the Decree, was everyone in Druine. There was hardly a soul who didn't want him dead. Who wouldn't murder him while he slept. Who wasn't watchful for the moment when they could become Druine's hero, by destroying the sinner. Across the land, there would be groups of men similar to the youths in the Archive Hall. And because they were his enemies, Ballas despised them. Their desires were perfectly natural, of course: what red-blooded man would shun fame and all its trappings? What man would baulk at the hunt, when the quarry was so highly prized?

And perhaps . . . perhaps some actually believed the promise of the Decree that the sinner's killer would be absolved of all their sins, and would be assured of a place in the Eltheryn Forest.

Even so, Ballas felt nothing but rage towards them. So they wished to save their souls – to Ballas's mind, that didn't matter. It enraged him that they should seek salvation at his expense.

After a while, they arrived at the brothel. It was an ugly, two-floored structure, built from ochre-tinted stone. Curtains masked the upper window, but on every sill a red lantern blazed. Over the doorway hung a sign: the customary daub of a candle burning with a scarlet flame. Yet there was something slightly different about this design. Something that Ballas thought was unusual. Thick strands of smoke twisted from the candle flame. Brothel signs rarely bore such details. Ballas glanced briefly at it, yet gave it no further thought.

He set Elsefar on his feet and Heresh handed the quill-master his crutches. 'The entrance to the sewers,' said Elsefar, 'must, of course, be found by going *downwards*. Into a cellar, perhaps.'

'It may prove awkward.' Crask fidgeted. 'What if it is a . . . a bed-chamber, hm? Things might become, ah, indelicate. No man enjoys being interrupted.'

Ballas glanced at the eel-catcher. Then he stepped inside the brothel.

He found himself in a long uncarpeted hallway. There were doors on either side, all of them shut. Sounds of copulation floated out: men grunting like animals, whores moaning as if their lovers were genuinely gifted. At the far end of the hall, a flight of stone steps led down underneath the floor.

Ballas walked quietly down the steps, Heresh and Crask close behind him. Elsefar struggled along a few paces further back.

The steps halted at a door. Ballas pressed his ear to the wood. From within, there came no noises of fornication. Only silence.

Yet the room was occupied, Ballas knew. A lantern-smoke scent drifted out.

Ballas pushed open the door.

The room beyond was medium-sized, the floor covered with crimson rugs. Red, green and yellow paint-swirls decorated the walls – a garish tangle of loops, whorls and wild curves. The same random designs marked the ceiling. Half a dozen men sat or slouched upon the floor. Ballas reached reflexively for his dagger. Then he paused. The men hadn't seen him. Their eyes were blank. Whatever they saw . . . whatever images fed their minds, they did not originate in the physical world. One gazed at a rug. It was a plain red rug, yet he stared intently at it – as if it were a thing of infinite complexity, as if it were a doorway to a scene of wonder. He smiled dreamily, rocking from side to side.

Another man peered at a magpie feather. Tilting it, he watched metallic reds, blues and greens gleam and intermix on its surface. Like the first man, he seemed pleased.

Ballas looked around the room.

Everyone seemed locked in a vague rapture. One man gazed at the ceiling, another at a a wooden board painted with a bright jumble of diamond shapes. Still another gazed at his own palm, fascinated.

In the centre of the floor stood a wooden box. Inside bristled a tangle of brownish weed.

'Visionary's root,' murmured Crask, behind Ballas.

Heresh stepped through. 'I have heard of this,' she said. 'It is outlawed, isn't it? The Pilgrim Church thinks it unholy. It can earn you a place upon the Oak. They say it conjures hallucinations—'

'It conjures *truths*,' came a voice. An old man blinked, as if waking. He rubbed his eyelids with his fingertips. He was bald, except for two strips of shoulder-length hair growing from above his ears. He sported a long salt-white moustache. He had a small, round face, a-scrawl with creases. His teeth were brown-yellow. He looked immeasurably aged – yet, even though he was seated cross-legged, he looked comfortable enough. 'It brings wisdom, insight . . . In ancient days, to acquire such knowledge – that is, knowledge of the infinite, knowledge denied our ordinary powers of apprehension – one had to put out one's eyes. Now, though, we have adopted Eastern practices.' He gestured at the box. 'One need not mutilate oneself to grow wise. That is progress, is it not? One must look beyond one's own shores, if one is to move onward. Otherwise, all is stagnation.'

He interlaced his fingers.

'We are all seeking knowledge here. Our practices may be mistaken for decadence –' he indicated the man gaping at the magpie feather '– and futility, but it is knowledge that moves us . . . that summons our ecstasy.

'A mouthful of visionary's root – I despise that term; I prefer the Eastern name, *gakria* – a mouthful can make perceptible, in an instant, more than a lifetime of study can reveal.' Stooping, he took a pinch of root from the box. 'The brothel-keeper brings this to us. It is some of the most potent I have ever taken. This much –' he held it up '– is enough to reveal the universe's deepest secrets. I can hear the music of the spheres, and the celestial breathing of the Four. Remarkable.' He lifted the visionary's root to his lips. Then hesitated. 'Sometimes, when I chew upon *gakria*, I see the Eastern hand that harvested it. I see the hand's owner, and then that owner's thoughts blend with my own. He has no secrets from me. His lusts and longings, delights and tragedies, are exposed: they glint as brightly as diamonds upon black stone. And, when the *gakria* is swallowed, one exists beyond time. Once, I entered this room in summer, and left in autumn – yet it seemed only heartbeats had passed. There is no finer thing, no finer thing: and that, I trust, is why you are here? To acquire an education?'

Ignoring him, Ballas grasped a rug and hurled it aside. The man who had been staring at it, who had seen infinity within its fibres, started. He was young, and faintly foppish. He turned his dark eyes accusingly to Ballas. 'I was using that! It was a marvellous . . . I was . . . seeing . . .' He drifted away. His gaze sank to his boots. They transfixed him. His happy, abstracted expression returned.

'What are you doing?' asked the old man. 'No: wait – I recognise you!' He raised his hands. 'By all that is good, I am here with most famous man in Druine! Or the most notorious – but then, what is the difference between fame and notoriety . . . except approval?'

Ballas glared balefully at him.

'Oh, do not be angry! I am pleased you are here. The Pilgrim Church is not *my* church. My religion is *gakria*. It is a far better faith, for it requires no faith at all. Everything is proven. One need not speculate, need not imagine. And besides –' he smiled a smile of absolute innocence '– one can learn much more from the wicked than from the good. Why? Because truly wicked men are rare. One seldom has the privilege of encountering them. They say the rebel leader Cal'Briden was wicked: and now they say that you are wicked too. What was your crime?'

Without answering, Ballas drew his dagger and jammed it between two floorboards. Working it back and forth, he prised a board up far enough to slip his fingers underneath and tore the floorboard out. Blackness lay below. He ripped up the neighbouring floorboard.

'Clearly, your crime wasn't verbosity,' muttered the old man. 'And, to be honest, it hardly matters. For a crime is but the symptom, or manifestation, of the stuff of true interest: the mind, the life, of the criminal.' He put the visionary's root in his mouth. Then he chewed slowly, luxuriantly.

Ballas pulled up floorboard after floorboard, until he had made a large gap. He took a lantern from a niche and lowered it into the dark underboards space. Five feet below lay a rock floor. In the centre rested a jagged-edged stone, the size of a cauldron.

Gripping the floorboard edges, Ballas lowered himself through. Setting the lantern on the ground, he gripped the stone. Grunting, he heaved it aside, exposing a wide hole, through which he pushed the lantern. The flickering light shone out along a tunnel, cut through dark rock. Rising, Ballas hauled himself back up through the gap in the floorboards.

'I've found them.' Pointing to Elsefar, he added, 'You first.'

The quill-master passed his crutches to Heresh. Gripping Elsefar's tunic collar, Ballas lowered the cripple through the gap. Clambering back down, the big man took hold of Elsefar again, this time manoeuvring him into the stone tunnel. Elsefar, his legs near-useless, sagged against the tunnel wall.

He recoiled, crying out. 'There is something in here! Something that moves . . .' He dropped to the ground. 'Sweet grief . . .'

'What is it?' asked Ballas.

'I do not know,' replied the quill-master. 'On the wall . . . there is something on the wall. It is . . . *writhing*.'

Gripping the lantern, Ballas squeezed through the opening and on into the tunnel. Lantern light shone out. Ballas froze, perturbed. The walls *rippled*. The darkness seemed to swell and recede. He moved the lantern closer.

Countless lizards clung to the wall. Pale-fleshed, sleek-bodied, their eyes white globes, they froze in the sudden light. They plastered not only the wall but the sewer ceiling. Their spraddle-fingered hands gripped the stone.

Elsefar sighed. 'Reptiles,' he said simply. 'Damned reptiles . . . Never have I seen the purpose of such things They are revolting.'

Heresh passed Elsefar's crutches down through the opening. Ballas gave them to the quill-master, then climbed back into the room above.

'Go down,' he said, passing the lantern to Heresh. The red-haired woman disappeared through the gap in the floorboards.

Crask leaned close to the old visionary's-root-loving man. The old man spoke softly to the eel-catcher. Scowling, Ballas said, 'Crask, over here. We have to go.'

The old man talked for a few seconds. Then Crask moved away. The eel-catcher disappeared through the floorboard-gap.

Ballas felt the old man's gaze upon him. Brown-tinged saliva trickled from the corners of his mouth. He chewed slowly on the visionary's root. His eyes – tiny, almond-shaped – stared fixedly at Ballas. They had a trance-like glaze. But also an alertness, a vigilance. It seemed that while the old man stared at Ballas, he also stared *beyond* him: he was seeing both Ballas and something else.

Scowling, the big man turned away. He slipped through the gap in the floorboards, then squeezed through the opening into the sewer tunnel.

Ballas took the map from Elsefar. He peered at it in the lantern light. It was neatly drawn, in bold black ink. It showed the city's outline and, within it, the sewer system. Ballas grunted. Despite Elsefar's immaculate quill-work, the map wasn't easy to read. The sewer system was fantastically complex: a near-indecipherable jumble of tunnels.

In his mind's eye, Ballas worked out a route through the sewers. Glancing at the scale, he calculated that they had to walk roughly five miles. He didn't think their progress would be brisk. The sewer ceiling was so low that he had to stoop. It would be impossible to carry Elsefar, so the quill-master would have to move himself along. Eventually, they would emerge on a tract of moorland, half a mile beyond Granthaven. And then . . . Ballas hadn't looked that far ahead. For the time being, he had to concentrate solely on escaping from the city.

They made their way through the sewers. Elsefar moved with surprising speed. Noises reverberated through the tunnel. Every sound – every footfall, cough or crack of Elsefar's crutch on the stones – echoed, once, twice, thrice. Lizards twitched on the walls and ceiling. There were also spiders, nestling in the split bricks. Bred in a lightless world, they were as pale as the lizards. Crask appeared intrigued.

'This sewer,' he said, 'is a world within itself. And these lizards and spiders depend upon one another for survival – even though each is the other's predator. The lizards are of the *crenkali* breed. They dine upon insects and arachnids. The spiders are *movvali* – or something similar. They are parasites; they feast on the lizards' blood. And they also use the lizards as, ah, *hatcheries*. They inject the lizards with their eggs – which, as spiders' bodies are warm, soon hatch. The infant spiders, trapped within the lizard, have to eat their way out. In doing so, they obtain much-needed nourishment. For the lizards, it is an agonising death. But for the spiders, a healthy start to life.' He scratched his jaw. 'Eventually, one species will gain the upper hand. The lizards will eat all the spiders. Or the spiders will kill so many lizards that there won't be enough of them left for the spiders to lay their eggs in. The surviving species will leave the sewer. They will live elsewhere. But eventually they'll come back, for their prey will also have returned. And, once more, their grisly partnership will continue. This cycle will recur over and over, for ever. There will be warfare, then peace; warfare, then peace.' He shook his head, wonderingly. 'Such things amaze me. Tell me, Ballas: do such things not interest you?'

Ballas shrugged. 'Should they?'

'You are from Hearthfall,' said the eel-catcher. 'I recognise your accent. It is farming country, is it not? They call it the Agrarians' Province. I understand it is a place of remarkable beauty. And peace.'

'I grew up on a farm,' Ballas agreed. 'But animals don't interest me.'

'No?'

'I lived among them,' said Ballas. 'They didn't seem strange. Or exciting. Just ordinary.'

'Ah, that is where you and I differ,' said Crask. 'I was raised in a city. There were few animals. There were birds, of course: crows, magpies, pigeons. And the occasional tatty, threadbare fox. But nothing of genuine interest. So the natural world was foreign to me. It seemed exotic, thrilling. Even the marshes, with its eel populace, never ceased to delight me.' He looked to Ballas. 'Why did you leave Hearthfall? I cannot understand why a man would quit such a place. Did you offend someone, hm? Sleep with another man's wife? Brawl with the shire-reeve?' He laughed at the archaism: there hadn't been shire-reeves since the Pilgrim Church had gained control of Druine.

Ballas did not laugh. A memory swam into his consciousness. He saw his home: a white-walled farmhouse, set amid fields of cattle. It was a hot day: sunlight winked through the smooth straw-thatch. The grass glinted, each stalk glass-bright. The front door stood open, revealing a patch of cool interior shade. A wolfhound snoozed by the doorstep, its fur a steely grey-blue. Ballas could taste something . . . could taste steak, covered in rich gravy. He had just eaten his midday meal. Now it was time to bring home the supper. In his right hand he held a fishing rod. Over his shoulder he wore a leather bag, crammed with lures and spare line. He shouted a farewell to his mother, who was inside the cottage. Turning, he walked through the village, and climbed the steep slope to Knucker Pond, where Druine's finest trout flickered from bank-shadow to surface and down again . . .

In the sewer, Ballas halted. He felt sick. Panic flooded up from his guts, locking his limbs, making his skull feel unbearably light. Sweat broke out on his brow. Suddenly weak, he leaned against the wall.

Crask frowned. 'Something troubles you?'

Ballas did not reply. He could hardly speak. His heart hammered, his breathing came in stuttering gasps.

'You . . . you are not ill? The blood has gone from your face. Oh, sweet grief: this is a poor moment—'

'Shut up,' said Ballas heavily. 'Shut up, about lizards and spiders and . . . I don't want to listen to your talk. You chatter like a bloody housemaid.'

'I was merely breaking the silence,' said the eel-catcher, stunned.

'I'd rather have silence than your pissing chat.' Ballas wiped a hand across his mouth. He forced from his mind the images of his home. Pushing himself away from the wall, he continued walking.

For a long time, they pressed on. Ballas looked carefully at the map, over and over. One sewer passage was indistinguishable from another. If they were to become lost, there would be little hope of regaining their bearings. It was as if the architects, whilst designing the sewer, had wished instead to fashion a labyrinth.

They walked on in silence. Ballas's anger at Crask's questions and the memories they had provoked had brought a dark mood down on the group. No one spoke, for no one dared: Ballas's sudden anger had shocked them. This surprised him. A short time ago, they had watched him slay two Papal Wardens. They would've noticed how little he cared for their suffering. Yet this did not startle them. Ballas glanced at Crask and Heresh.

They have grown used to me, he thought. And perhaps they have grown used to their circumstances. He thought back to the evening on the river bank when Heresh had told him he disgusted her. How quickly that has changed, woman. How rapidly you have come to understand that this is not a world for the soft-hearted.

As they proceeded, their footsteps were the only sounds – those, and the *crack-crack* of Elsefar's crutches.

Until Ballas detected a different noise. Something distant, something scarcely audible.

'Wait.' He halted the group.

'What is it?' asked Elsefar. The quill-master was sweating with exertion: he had found the walking difficult.

'Be quiet,' murmured Ballas. Tilting his head, he listened to the sewers. For the first time, he noticed a faint movement of air – a breeze rustling through an opening far away. Concentrating hard, he heard something else.

Footfalls.

Their muted echoes drifted through the sewer tunnel. They came from further back along the way the group had come. They were being followed, Ballas realised. By four, maybe five men, moving at a slow jog.

Ballas turned to the group. But, listening, they too had heard the echoes.

'Wardens, surely,' said Crask, licking his lips.

Ballas nodded.

'What ought we do?' asked the eel-catcher.

'We can't outrun them,' said Ballas.

'No?' asked Crask. 'It seems only one of us is too weak . . .' He looked at Elsefar.

The quill-master nodded. 'I ought to ask you to go on without me and save your own skins. That'd be noble, wouldn't it? The stuff of poems and songs. But Ballas will not permit it. Why? Because he is kind-spirited? Because he and I are friends?' He shook his head. 'He needs me. He needs to know what *I* know. I still haven't revealed the name of the mountain-guide – the man who can take him to Belthirran.'

'Such information will be useless if you are dead, Ballas,' said Crask. There'll be other people who know of this guide. Other people who know of other guides, some more reliable, perhaps . . .'

'We won't leave Elsefar,' said Ballas flatly.

'Ballas—' began Crask.

'We will *not* leave him,' repeated the big man, irritated. 'There is no need to.'

'What are you suggesting?' asked Crask. 'We are miles from the way out of these damnable sewers. *Miles*. What should we . . .' Sighing, the eel-catcher closed his eyes. 'We are to fight, yes?'

Ballas nodded.

'Forgive me,' said Crask, 'but you test yourself too often. There'll come a time, soon enough, when your luck runs out. You'll grow tired, or careless, and—'

Ignoring him, Ballas unfolded the map. He scrutinised it for a few moments. Then he started off along the passage. 'There is a good place further on,' he said.

He led them to a point where the passage divided, one branch heading to their left, the other to their right. Ballas inspected both branches, finding the one to the right slightly wider. 'I'll stay here,' he said. 'The rest of you, get into the other passage. When the Wardens get here –' he indicated the fork '– they'll pause, wondering which way we have gone. While they are doing that, we strike – understand?'

Crask nodded. The eel-catcher's skin grew pale. He unsheathed a small knife and passed it nervously from hand to hand. His daughter remained completely calm. Reaching behind her head, she unfastened her loose ponytail. Red hair spilled to her shoulders. She tied it into a fresh, tighter ponytail. Then she disappeared into the passageway. Crask followed her, then Elsefar.

Ballas went into the right-hand passage. He closed the lantern shutters, reducing the light to a frail gleam. He sat on the brick floor. Drawing his knife, he rubbed the blade with his sleeve, polishing away dried blood. His reflection became visible. He gazed at it, seeing how tired he looked. Pouches of loose skin hung under his eyes and, despite the food provided by Father Rendeage, he was still underfed from the time when, with the city gates locked, no food had been arriving in Granthaven. He touched the scar on his forehead. The bruising had subsided. Now the flesh had healed. The crescent-scar was fully formed. Ballas turned the knife, watching his reflection appear, then disappear. He felt tired, but it wasn't simply the fatigue of physical effort. Everything sickened him. The Church, the Wardens, the Under-Wardens and every civilian who pursued him. Crask annoyed him; he was a man full of fear, and that irritated him. The eel-catcher tried to control his unease, true. But even this angered Ballas: it merely reminded him that the fear existed. And that, in a man, repelled him.

The eel-catcher's daughter was a different matter – slightly. She was more decisive, more strong-willed. Yet her inexperience tested Ballas's patience. She had vigour, but lacked cunning. A part of him acknowledged this was unfair. Living out in the marshes, with no threat greater than the eel-infested waters, how could she possibly have acquired a decent grasp of combat? Nonetheless, she made Ballas bristle with impatience.

And Elsefar – Ballas was unsure what to make of the quill-master. Certainly, he was cunning and self-serving. That was to be expected. But it presented problems. What was to ensure that, once Ballas had taken him to his 'safe place', he would reveal the mountain-guide's name and location? He would reveal *a* name, for sure. But there'd be nothing to guarantee it was genuine. Ballas might find himself seeking a man who did not exist. And, if he returned to Elsefar's safe place, intending to exact revenge – Elsefar would not be there. The safe place might simply be a ruse.

A flake of blood clung to the knife blade. Ballas picked it free, then tossed it to the floor. A lizard scampered out of the shadows. It sniffed the flake. Then, deciding it preferred living blood, the reptile climbed the wall to a cluster of spiders. It thrust its maw among them, and chewed. Some spiders scattered. Others vanished down the lizard's gullet.

'The lives of lizards and spiders,' came a voice, 'are almost as barbarous as our own.'

Lugen Crask appeared.

'How many Wardens are chasing us? Could you tell?'

'Half a dozen, more or less.'

'Do you suppose they have got a map from somewhere? Or are they merely following us, and trusting in luck?'

'Just following us,' grunted Ballas. 'They won't have had time to find a map. Not many people know about these sewers. Perhaps the Wardens don't even realise how much of a maze they are, and didn't reckon on needing a map.'

'Six men,' said Crask, quietly. 'Do you think we can beat them?

'We've faced worse odds.'

Crask shivered. 'I'd give anything for a mouthful of whisky.' He rubbed his arms. 'It'd make me feel braver.' He hesitated – then released a slow breath. 'Ballas, speak frankly. What are you?'

Ballas frowned. 'A stupid question. I'm a man, being hunted by the Church . . .'

'There is more to you than that. I have been watching you. You are a thief and a killer – in both activities you are accomplished – and *relaxed*, even. And *that* is what puzzles me. You have a talent, Ballas. A grim and bloody one, perhaps. But your abilities outstrip those of many men. You kill quickly, cleanly. And you *think*. For any situation, you can come up with a plan. It may be messy and dangerous – but it seems always to be the *best* plan. And there is—'

'What I am,' said Ballas, 'is my own business.' He wondered why Crask should be so suddenly curious. Did he believe that they wouldn't escape the Wardens, and wanted to satisfy his curiosity before he died?

Unprompted, Crask explained.

'The old man, in the visionary's-root den, said he had a vision. When he chewed the weed and gazed upon you, I mean.'

'So?'

'He said that, in its form, it was a typical vision. He saw three chalices, each filled with a different substance. The chalices denote the past, present and future conditions of one's soul. In the first chalice – your soul's past – there was wheat. That meant that, to begin with, your soul was contented. You were happy.'

'Horseshit,' muttered Ballas.

'The second chalice – your soul's present health – was filled with blood.'

Ballas laughed loudly, coarsely. 'That means violence, or something, I suppose.'

'It means . . .' Crask groped for the proper word '. . . turmoil. And, yes – violence.'

'It seems that those who take root,' muttered Ballas, 'become predictable.'

'The blood was that of a lioness,' continued Crask, unperturbed. 'For, in the background, such a beast lay dead. Its throat had been slit. This indicates that there was, ah, something *noble* about your violence. But also something tragic. You see, the lioness's stomach was swollen – she was gravid.'

Ballas muttered something to himself.

'The third chalice,' began Crask.

'Yes?' interrupted Ballas, bored and irritated. 'What was it this time? More blood? Or bloody goat's piss?'

'The third chalice,' breathed Crask, 'was empty.'

Ballas glanced up at Crask.

'The old man could not understand it. Your soul existed in the past, and – obviously – exists in the present. Yet it is not there in the future. Which makes no sense. Because souls endure. They do not pass away, they do not vanish. They endure after death. They leave this world and go to the Eltheryn Forest. They *remain*, Ballas. They are not scrubbed out of being.'

'Pah! You reckon it's smart to trust an old idiot who's been eating visionary's root? You reckon such men are wise?'

'It is said that visionary's root *does* provide insight. That is why the Church outlawed it.'

'The Church outlawed it,' said Ballas, thinking back to the barge-master, 'because it created visions that people were half-witted enough to believe in.'

Crask shook his head. 'I – I can't help thinking there is something in it. Such practices, if they fail to bear fruit, do not endure—'

'People enjoy visionary's root,' said Ballas. 'They like it because it makes them feel wise. But they aren't wise. Pilgrims' blood! At least we drunks are honest: we know it does nothing except make us happy. We don't dress it up as something deep.'

'In the Distant East, the caliphs employ *gakria*-eaters as advisers . . .'

'In the Distant East,' said Ballas, 'widows are burned alongside their husbands' corpses. And they eat dogs – because they *want* to, not because they have to.' He snorted. 'Don't look to the East, Crask. It is a place of dust and stupidity.'

Crask grew very still. 'You are telling me that all I have spoken is false?'

'Yes.'

'And that in your past you did not act nobly?'

Ballas nodded.

Crask smiled. 'There is something I did not tell you. In the old man's vision, the lioness whose blood fed the second chalice was blind.'

'What of it?'

'It suggests a particular type of ignorance. The lioness did not know what it truly was. It did not know it was noble. Nor do you understand what you are.'

Ballas stared evenly at Crask. 'Horseshit,' he said.

'When we last escaped the Wardens, you saved my daughter's life. And I think I saw something there . . . a glimmer of something that once was in you, but now—'

Footfalls echoed along the sewer tunnel. Crask started, surprised.

'Concentrate on the Wardens who are coming,' said Ballas, rising. 'Not on those we've already avoided.'

Crask left Ballas, returning to the left-hand passage. Ballas shuttered the lantern completely, and the sewer tunnel sank into darkness.

In the dark he saw the three chalices. And the blinded lioness.

'You are an idiot, Crask,' he muttered.

Footsteps hammered along the sewer tunnel. Lantern light pierced the gloom. Shadows sprawled over the walls. Rising, Ballas gripped his knife hilt tightly. A faint melancholia lay upon him. It was a product, he presumed, of his tiredness. As his anger had been. Often, when he was weary, dark moods preyed upon him.

He thought fleetingly of Belthirran. And his unhappiness lessened, then vanished. It would be worth staying alive if he could reach the Land Beyond the Mountains. All the sick feelings that pressed upon him – his bitterness and anger – would fade away.

Watching the tunnel, he licked his lips.

The lantern light brightened. The footsteps drummed louder. A group of Wardens ran out of the dark. Five of them, Ballas counted. In the gloom, their features were indistinct – a massing of shadows. The Scarrendestin triangles stitched on to their tunic fronts were visible. So too were their swords and knives.

Approaching the forking passages, they halted.

'Which way, do you think?' asked a Warden.

A second Warden sniffed the air – and Ballas sprang at him, driving his knife blade into his stomach. Spinning, Ballas drove his fist into the face of the Warden who'd spoken, felling him. A third Warden drew his sword, but Heresh hurtled out from the other passageway, ramming her knife into his side. It was a clumsy, poorly aimed strike. The blade didn't sink even hilt-deep. Yet the blow startled the Warden. Crying out, he instinctively reached to cover the wound. Crask sprinted out and kicked him hard in the guts. The Warden sank to his knees, the sword slithering from his fingers. Crask retrieved the weapon, and hacked awkwardly at his back. It was a powerful blow, but because of Crask's clumsiness the blade scarcely pierced the Warden's flesh. Snatching the sword from Crask, Ballas delivered a neck-splitting chop. The man slumped, dead.

'Look out!' shouted Heresh.

Whirling, Ballas raised his sword, blocking another Warden's down-stroke. Blades clashed, flinging off sparks. Deflecting the Warden's blade, Ballas stepped forward, smashing his forehead into the Warden's nose. He collapsed, dazed.

One Warden remained standing. He glanced fearfully at Ballas. Then, turning, he sprinted away along the tunnel.

Drawing back his arm, Ballas hurled the sword at the Warden as if he was throwing a spear. The blade sank into the fleeing man's lower back. Crying out, he fell face down.

Ballas gestured at the other Wardens who were sprawled on the ground. 'Make sure they're dead – those two I only knocked out need killing, for a start,' he told Crask, then walked over to the sword-struck Warden.

Wrenching out the sword, he rolled the Warden on to his back. Ballas noticed something unusual about the man's tunic. Though fashioned from the usual blue cloth to indicate service to the Church, the Scarrendestin triangle bore bright red edges. Ballas realised he'd seen this design before. Seen it without realising it: on the tunics of the Wardens supervising the putting of heads on the Oak.

They must be Wardens of the highest rank, thought Ballas. Wardens that the Masters trust absolutely.

Ballas sat on the Warden's chest. 'How many more of you are in the sewers?'

'None,' replied the Warden, his voice rasping.

Ballas looked at the sword – then threw it aside. A more precise tool was needed. He pulled out a thin-bladed knife. 'I'll ask you again,' he said, touching its tip to the Warden's eyeball. 'How many Wardens are on their way?'

'None,' repeated the Warden. 'But you'll die anyway. You are still being followed.'

This puzzled Ballas. Had Under-Wardens entered the sewers? Or citizens of Granthaven?

'Who are you talking about?' demanded the big man.

'I cannot tell you.'

'No?' Ballas tapped the blade's tip against his eye. The Warden blinked, wildly. Then he tried to turn his face away. Grasping his jaw, Ballas forced him to stare upwards. He pressed knifepoint to eye socket. 'Who?' he asked, simply.

'I have sworn an oath,' said the Warden. 'I shall not break it. I *cannot* break it.'

'Cannot?' Ballas shook his head. 'I could make a saint curse the Four. I could turn a nun into a whore in a heartbeat. Don't reckon your oath counts for anything.'

'I didn't speak loosely,' said the Warden. 'I *cannot* tell you. For my oath is binding in a way you can't imagine.'

'We shall see,' said Ballas. Delicately, he scraped the knife tip over the man's eyelid. It broke only the thinnest layer of skin. No blood emerged. Only tears as the Warden's eyes watered furiously beneath their not-so-protective membranes. 'Who is following us? Tell me, and I'll spare you.'

'What good will that do me? If I fail to kill you, I will forfeit my own life. My failure will not be tolerated.'

'Then I'll grant you an easy death. I'll open an artery, and you'll feel like you're falling asleep.'

'There'll be no escape in death. Not for me. I'll still be punished.'

'This is your last chance,' said Ballas, flatly.

'Nothing has changed,' replied the Warden. 'I cannot tell you.'

Ballas sank the blade into his eye socket. The Warden's body jerked rigid. He cried out – a long keening noise, half-shriek, half-sob.

'Tell me,' said Ballas, gently.

'I can't! Be merciful – please!'

Ballas moved the knife to the other eye. He lightly touched the blade to it.

'Oh, by the Four's goodness: don't do this to me!!'

Ballas sank the knife tip a quarter of an inch into the eyeball. The Warden screamed – and, as if he hadn't willed it, he said, 'It is Nu'—'

He fell silent abruptly. Then he arched his back, dislodging Ballas from his chest. The big man sprawled on the ground. The Warden's body went into a frantic spasm. He clawed at the brick floor. His jaw hinged madly, teeth clashing. His less-damaged eye quivered feverishly in its socket. The tendons on his neck ridged out.

For a moment Ballas believed it was a ruse. A false fit, intended to give the Warden a few seconds in which he could formulate a plan.

Then Ballas saw the flames.

A tongue of blue fire sprang from the Warden's chest. Others erupted from his stomach. And then from his eyes – each a stabbing cone of flesh-blackening light. Steam swirled from his body and the Warden hissed like a grasshopper tossed on to a red-hot grill. His tunic shrivelled. His hair sizzled to nothing. Soon the flames covered him. Yet still he writhed: a dark outline of a man, enfolded in dazzling, consuming blueness.

Eventually he grew still. The flames died down. A few lingered, but now these were ordinary flames – yellow-orange, swaying softly.

Suddenly Ballas understood. He knew what was pursuing them.

'Come on,' he said, snatching up the lantern.

The others stared at the Warden.

'How – how did that happen?' Crask gaped. 'Surely, there was magick in it—'

Ballas listened for footsteps. He couldn't hear any. That was good. At least their pursuer was some distance away.

For the time being.

'We have to get out of here,' said Ballas. 'We are being followed. And I don't reckon we can outfight it.'

'*It?*' Crask frowned.

Saying nothing, Ballas snatched up a sword. It would be of little use, he knew. But its presence comforted him.

He moved to go deeper into the sewers. Jonas Elsefar grabbed his arm. He drew Ballas down, and whispered in his ear, 'I don't know what is coming after us. But remember, Ballas: it is in your interest to make sure that I live. If I die, you'll never find Belthirran.'

Ballas glanced at the quill-master. Then he strode away.

They continued through the sewer tunnels. For the sake of speed, Ballas carried Jonas Elsefar. The low ceiling prevented him from slinging the crippled man over his shoulder, as he had in the streets of Granthaven. Instead, he bore the quill-master across his chest, as if he were a sleepy infant. Though Elsefar wasn't heavy, it was awkward for Ballas, stooping to keep his head clear of the ceiling, to proceed like this. Yet it was faster than allowing Elsefar to propel himself onward.

Crask watched Ballas. The big man felt the eel-catcher's gaze upon him. He was frightened, Ballas knew. And his fear was not focused upon

Wardens but on the nameless threat that pursued them through the sewers. The menace that had caused the Warden to burst into flames and that Ballas had not yet named.

They hurried on. It was Crask who first detected an unfamiliar noise.

'I hear something,' he said, halting.

Ballas paused. He felt Elsefar's body against his chest: a sharp-edged jumble of bones. The quill-master breathed heavily.

Crask looked back down the tunnel. 'Listen,' he said. 'It is faint – but there is definitely something there.'

Ballas did as he was asked. In the far distance, he heard a dull rasping sound – as of leather rubbing against stone. It grew slightly louder. As it did so, it took on a different quality: though still rasping, it seemed also to *chatter* – as if an infinity of tiny sibilant voices were speaking over one another.

Crask looked wide-eyed at Ballas. 'Is this it? The . . . the thing that chases us? That will destroy us?'

'I don't know,' Ballas replied honestly.

Suddenly, at the end of the passage, the darkness of the wall and ceiling *twitched*. Then it thickened, growing almost solid. Spreading over the brick-work, it raced towards Ballas and the others. The rasping chatter grew in volume. Yet it was still far from loud. The air moved, slightly.

Crask raised the lantern. Its yellow glow swept over the ceiling. And was reflected back by innumerable white eyes. Lizards' eyes.

Clinging to the walls, lizards coated the dark bricks: a dense blanket of pale shapes, so tightly clustered and moving so purposefully that they seemed a single organism. With frantic urgency, they raced along the sewer. Jostled by their kindred, a few lost their grips, falling to the floor before scrambling back on to their feet and vanishing along the tunnel. The rest surged onward, scrambling over one another. Their bodies brushed against each other, producing the rasping sound.

Crask lowered the lantern. 'I do not understand,' he murmured. 'What are they doing?' He looked at Ballas, his eyes alight with sudden defiance. 'What is hunting us? For certain, it is not men who frightened the lizards: they did not run from us, or from the Wardens. So what is it, hm? What thing, capable of conjuring flames from a man's body—'

'A Lectivin,' said Ballas, sharply. Turning, he carried on walking briskly. He was afraid, he realised. He doubted that, even if he tried, he could force himself to stand still. Like the lizards, he was compelled irresistibly onwards.

Crask scampered alongside him. 'You are jesting, surely? Lectivins no longer exist. They were slaughtered during the Red War! And those that survived, those that remained upon the island Lectivae, were obliterated!'

'One remains,' said Ballas. 'The Church has preserved him.'

Ballas had little choice, but to recount – in the briefest terms – the events of the night he had almost been placed upon the Penance Oak. He spoke of Gerack's agonies and his own escape.

For a long time no one spoke. Then Elsefar laughed – a high, wheezing sound. 'It seems you are worrying needlessly, Ballas. You have filled us with false fear. You have thwarted the Lectivin once already. Surely you would be able to do it again.'

'The priest, Rendeage, reckons not. The Lectivin was part-way through a magical ritual. It was distracted and I managed to surprise it. Now, though, he'll be alert.'

'This Lectivin – what caste was he?'

'Rendeage says he was a hunter.'

'The most bestial breed of Lectivin,' said Crask, thoughtfully. 'Elsefar, you – *we* – have cause for worry. Sweet grief! Historians say that, during the Red War, a single Lectivin hunter could kill fifty human fighters. *Fifty*,' he repeated. 'And how many of us are there? Four – one of whom can't stand up without help!'

They redoubled their speed, half-jogging through the sewers.

'That Warden – he intended to kill us,' continued Crask. 'Yet I can't help but pity him. The oath he swore . . . the oath of secrecy . . . Such things were common among Lectivins. As soon as they could speak, they were forced to swear allegiance to Lectivae. If ever they nursed thoughts of betrayal – if they ever even *doubted* their country's greatness – they were obliterated by fire. It seems such oaths can bind men as well as Lectivins.'

They carried on for a short time. Then Ballas halted, abruptly. Something was wrong. The passage diverged into three separate passages. Ballas had half-memorised the route through the sewers – yet this branching was unfamiliar. Turning to Heresh, who held the map, Ballas clicked his fingers. The red-haired woman unfolded the map.

Ballas peered at it. He was certain that he had taken no wrong turns. On the map, he retraced their steps and found that the tunnels corresponded with those down which they had travelled. They had followed the map exactly. Yet now the map did not match the actual layout. The passage should have continued straight onward, finally swerving left before splitting in two. Instead, they were confronted by three possible routes.

Ballas swore. 'The map is wrong,' he said. 'The bloody map is *wrong*!'

'Let me see,' said the quill-master.

'If you have copied it badly, Elsefar, I'll rip you apart!'

'I do not make errors,' retorted the quill-master. 'And never have done. Now give it to me!'

Heresh handed the map to Elsefar. The quill-master looked it over, then tapped a line of quillscript in the top right-hand corner. 'This explains it,' he said quietly. 'This is not a map at all. Rather, it is a *design*.'

'What's the difference?' snapped Ballas.

'Oh, come,' said Elsefar tightly. 'Think for a moment. A map describes what *is*. A design, what *might be*, if the plans are brought to fruition. Now, this document is labelled "Version the Second". So there might be other versions: a third, a fourth, a fifth . . . as many as it took the architect to settle on the final sewer layout. Clearly, he rejected this version. The central area of the sewers satisfied him, true enough. But its outer reaches, where we are now?' He shook his head. 'The design has taken us this far. But it'll lead us no further.'

'Damn it all!' shouted Crask. 'You have doomed the lot of us, Elsefar! You should've known the map was only half-useful! And when Ballas gave the bloody thing to you . . . Sweet grief: you should have noticed there was something wrong! You should have seen—'

'It would be wise,' interrupted Elsefar, 'to keep your voice low. Better if we don't make it too easy for the Lectivin to find us.'

'If I were to shout, if I were to beckon it towards us, it would make no difference. Hunter-caste Lectivins are practically blind. They follow scents – and soul-glow.'

'Soul-glow . . . ?' The quill-master frowned.

Crask nodded, angrily. 'When a Lectivin imbibes visionary's root, it is capable of sensing the light of a man's soul. To him, it shines as strongly as torchlight.'

'It is foul luck,' remarked the quill-master, 'that he will have followed us through a *gakria* den. It seems that, in escaping the Wardens, we have helped their most dangerous weapon.'

'The Lectivin would've already had visionary's root,' said Ballas. 'The Church gives it to him, I reckon. He was eating it at the Penance Oak. None of this is important. Not now.' He looked around. 'We have to find a way out.'

They stood silently. In this featureless underground maze, where no sun shone nor moon glowed, it would be treacherously easy for them to lose their sense of direction. Ballas tried to think. Near the sewer exit, he'd perhaps see a little light from the sky. Maybe outdoor noises – bird-song, wind blowing across grass – would drift through the passage. But that was a long way off, Ballas thought. They might still be miles from the way out.

He clenched his jaw. 'We'll have to take a chance,' he said. 'We'll have to make a guess at the right way, and hope we're lucky.'

He looked at the three passages. Each seemed no more promising than the others. Shrugging, he stepped into the left-hand passage.

'Wait!' said Crask, urgently.

Ballas halted.

Crask pointed to the central passage. 'This will lead us out of the sewers.'

'Have *you* been eating *gakria*?' asked Elsefar sardonically. 'Are you being guided by a vision?'

'A vision? No. Merely a lizard swarm.' He gestured at the ceiling. Lizards surged into the passageway. 'Their senses are extraordinarily acute. They will be able to *smell* the outside world. And it is to the outside world that they are fleeing.'

Ballas raised his eyebrows. 'So, Crask, you *do* have a use, after all.'

They hurried along the middle corridor. Elsefar gradually became a burden in Ballas's arms. Ballas's muscles were tiring, and the quill-master seemed to grow heavier and heavier, as if he were turning to lead. Sweat prickled Ballas's forehead. He breathed in thick, sullen gasps. A peculiar tension seized Elsefar's body. The quill-master knew he was an encumbrance. Perhaps he was afraid that Ballas might drop him. More likely, he feared he would be abandoned – tossed away, like cargo from a sinking ship.

'Remember that you need me,' he told Ballas quietly. 'Remember that in me all hope is invested. Without me, you shall never set foot in Belthirran.'

After a time, a sliver of light pierced the dark. They halted. Ahead, a heap of rubble blocked the passage. Overhead the ceiling sagged: at some earlier time, it had half collapsed. Light slid through a small gap in the tumbled brickwork. Pale lizards squeezed through the opening. Breathing deeply, Ballas smelled wet grass. Sodden soil. The sharp tang of frost.

He set Elsefar down on the floor.

He started clearing away the rubble. He seized brick after moss-tufted brick, tossing it back along the corridor. A dull thunder of echoes rang out. For a moment Crask and Heresh didn't move.

'Help me!' shouted Ballas.

As if a spell had been broken, father and daughter joined Ballas in his labours. They worked quickly, vigorously. The brick's sharp edges cut their hands, yet they toiled on. As they did, the lizards continued disappearing towards the sunlight. They brushed Ballas's skin. They clambered over the big man's hands. Those that dropped from the ceiling and found themselves upon the floor clambered over him. Their tiny feet clawed the back of his neck. Padded over his head. He ignored them.

The gap widened. Light poured into the passage. Eventually, there was space enough for Ballas to squeeze through.

He found himself on a circular patch of brickwork. Ahead, the sewer had completely collapsed. The floor lay buried under a weight of moorland earth. The downfallen ground had ripped itself in half, exposing a buried wall of slick limestone, twenty feet high. There were few visible handholds – only the occasional fissure and crease in the stone. Around its upper edge, grass stalks swayed. Beyond them, a grey sky was visible. Drizzle drifted down, prickling Ballas's face.

The big man blinked.

Heresh pulled herself through the gap. Crask followed. Working hand over hand, Elsefar dragged himself through.

The quill-master gazed at the rock face. 'What are you going to do, Ballas?'

The big man shrugged. 'The way ahead is blocked. Perhaps that's no bad thing. The ceiling's fallen, true – but by doing so it's given us a chance of an earlier escape from this place.'

'How do we get out?' demanded Elsefar, agitatedly.

'How do you reckon?' replied Ballas.

'Do you expect me to climb? Look at me: do I strike you as someone who can do such things?'

'In truth,' said Crask, 'I do not believe *I* will manage it. I am not an agile man. My hands aren't strong and I've no head for heights.'

Ballas turned to Heresh. She simply shook her head.

Ballas swore. Then Elsefar, seated on the rubble, said, 'It is getting closer.'

Ballas turned to him.

The quill-master had grown pale. 'I can hear it.'

Ballas moved his ear to the gap. There were footfalls – a succession of soft *dab-dab-dabs*, each one hardly heavy enough to strike an echo but moving briskly, as if their owner were moving as quickly as a cat. Even as Ballas listened, he heard them grow louder. The Lectivin was approaching at great speed.

The others looked at Ballas.

'We cannot fight it,' said Crask. 'We all know that – and you've admitted as much yourself. We've come all this way, only to be trapped.' He glanced at his daughter. Grimacing, he tried to put a little resolve into his voice. 'There has to be *something* we can do. We mustn't just accept our fate. It would be . . . foolish.'

Stooping, Ballas removed his boots. Then his socks. The wet stone chilled his bare feet.

'You have thought of something?' asked Crask, unable to keep a note of desperation out of his voice.

Nodding, Ballas approached the wall. Reaching up, he found a finger-hold. He dragged himself upward, then gripped a thin ledge with his toes. Grunting, he reached higher – then fell, his skin sliding on the slippery limestone.

He landed heavily.

He glanced at the others. They stared at him, uncomprehending.

Ballas began climbing once more. This time, he gripped the rocks with a type of delicate firmness. He made himself aware of every fractional loss of grip. Every small slip of his fingertips and toes. He noticed each alteration in the limestone's texture – its patches of roughness and the rarer areas of glassy smoothness. He climbed slowly, determinedly.

Halfway to the top he heard Elsefar swear.

'The bastard! He is abandoning us! Ballas: you reeking whoreson!' The quill-master's voice rose to a shriek. 'Have you forgotten what I said? *You need my help!*'

'He needs to live,' Crask corrected him flatly. 'What use are you to a dead man?'

Ballas reached the top. He dragged himself over the edge, sprawling out on the grass. The moors stretched out around him. After the sewers, the open expanse dizzied him briefly. He got to his feet.

Ballas heard Elsefar screaming from the sewers. 'I don't want to die! You pissing betrayer, Ballas! You stinking wretch!'

Ballas swept his gaze across the moors. Ahead, there grew a small copse of rowan trees. Further off, a cluster of Skelfenian pine. One of the trees was lightning-blasted. The bolt had split the trunk, and the greater part of the tree had fallen, remaining attached to the bisected trunk by a flap of rotting wood.

Ballas looked down into the sewer. Elsefar had dragged himself away from the gap. Now he was cowering at the opposite side. Crask and Heresh stood beside him. The eel-catcher gripped the sword that Ballas had taken from the Warden. Both he and his daughter stared at the gap, frightened, expectant.

'Throw me the sword!' shouted Ballas.

Crask looked up.

'Throw me the bloody sword!' repeated Ballas.

'Don't be a fool!' said Elsefar. 'Don't give *him* our only weapon – our only defence!'

After a pause, Crask hurled the sword upward. It was a weak throw, and badly aimed: the blade clattered against the rock wall, then dropped back down. It missed hitting Elsefar by an inch. The quill-master swore violently. Snatching up the weapon, Heresh tried to fling it to Ballas. Her aim was good, the force of her throw sufficient: Ballas grasped it adroitly by the blade, his fingers clear of its edge, and then strode to the fallen pine.

With several fierce downstrokes, Ballas hacked the bulk of the tree body from the lower trunk. Then he grasped the upper branches. Turning, he dragged the pine towards the sewer-hole. The tree was extremely heavy. The blood gathered in Ballas's face; he felt it pulsing under his skin. Pain lanced through his shoulders. And through his fingers where they curled tightly around the branches. He felt as if he were dragging the corpses of a hundred men. Growling, swearing, he hauled the tree over frost-silked grass. Eventually he reached the edge of the sewer hole.

He peered down.

He half expected to find the others dead – or at least to find the Lectivin amongst them.

But they were alone.

'Turn your faces to the wall!' he shouted.

'It is getting close!' shouted Crask. His voice wavered. 'It is loud now – it cannot be too far away!'

'Do as I say, and perhaps you'll survive,' called Ballas impatiently. 'Now: turn your faces to the bloody wall!'

They did as they were told. Crouching low, almost to his knees, Ballas braced his shoulder against the tree trunk's shattered stub. Grunting, he pushed – hard. His unshod feet slipped on the grass. Cursing, he scrambled back up and tried again. He dug his toes into the frozen earth Flesh tore. Through his numb skin, he felt the wet warmth of blood. The pine inched slowly forward. The branches inched over the edge of the drop. Then, as if some brake had been released, the tree's weight shifted over the empty air. The tree trunk rose, and the pine crashed downwards into the sewer hole.

Ballas looked down. It seemed that fortune had favoured the others. The tree had not struck them.

'You'll have to climb,' shouted Ballas. 'Do you hear? Once you get to the trunk, I'll help you. Understand?'

They nodded.

'Elsefar, you go first.' The quill-master opened his mouth to protest. 'You won't need to use your legs,' shouted Ballas, 'only your arms. You must have *some* bloody strength in them!'

Muttering sourly, the quill-master seized a few branches. Laboriously, he began heaving himself up. Ballas turned and jogged back to the pines. Using the sword, he chopped through a lower branch. When he returned to the sewer hole, Elsefar had almost reached the trunk – from which no branches grew.

'There's nothing to grip!' he yelled.

'Take this,' shouted Ballas. He slithered the branch over the edge. It lay within easy reach of Elsefar. But the quill-master seemed frightened to let go of the trunk. Scowling, Ballas said, 'Grab hold of it, you idiot! Or I'll knock you off with it!'

Grimacing, Elsefar seized the branch. Stepping back, Ballas hauled him out of the sewer hole. First, the quill-master's head appeared above the rim. Then, reaching out, he grasped a grass clump and dragged himself on to the flat ground. He lay upon his back, gazing at the sky. His chest rose and fell. 'That was awful,' he said. 'I've never suffered such a torture. Not for a long time, anyway.'

'You're alive,' Ballas said. 'Be grateful.'

'What do we do now?' asked Elsefar, sitting up. His wiped his palms on his breeches, an oddly lethargic gesture. 'Which way do we go? I can see no Wardens – that is something. But they will come here soon enough. We don't have much time to waste.'

Grabbing his tunic collar, Ballas dragged the quill-master away from the sewer hole.

'What—?!' complained Elsefar angrily.

Saying nothing, Ballas took the branch. He lowered it into the sewer hole. Already Heresh had climbed as far as the smooth pine trunk. Without hesitation, she grabbed hold of the branch.

Elsefar sneered. 'Do not be an idiot, Ballas. You need my help – not theirs. Leave them for the Lectivin. They are nothing to you.'

Ballas ignored him. He pulled Heresh from the hole. She clambered out on to the moorland. She was sweating, yet her skin was pale. She looked anxiously at Ballas.

'Be quick,' she said. '*Please*.'

Ballas moved to the edge. Crask was climbing up the fallen pine. He climbed as if it were the most unnatural act imaginable, clutching awkwardly at the branches. He wore an expression of deep concentration. Suddenly, he looked up.

'It is here,' he said. 'I can hear its footfalls. Not their echoes but the footfalls themselves. Sweet grief, it is here!'

'Get a grip!' snapped Ballas. 'Keep climbing!'

Crask did as he was told. As he neared the smooth trunk, a branch broke under his foot. He found himself hanging, his legs scrabbling at empty air. Then he located fresh footholds. He climbed up to the trunk. Ballas lowered the pine branch. Crask grasped it. Ballas started drawing him up.

Heresh cried out, pointing.

Through the gap clambered the Lectivin, Nu'hkterin. It was dressed identically to how it had been on the evening, many weeks ago, when it had tried to put Ballas upon the Oak. It wore a coarse brown robe, with the hood drawn back. Its pale skull-top glistened as drizzle fell on it. It looked upward. In the dawn light, its stark-boned heavy-browed head seemed dazzlingly pale – as if its skin had been polished bright. Its scarlet-irised eyes flared with some emotion. Anger, perhaps. Or blood-hunger. Its lips peeled back, exposing sharp-tipped teeth . . . teeth brown-tinged with visionary's root. It fingered the curved knife hanging from its belt.

It looked at Crask. Then at Heresh.

Then its gaze fixed upon Ballas. Its expression altered. The fire ebbed from its eyes. Its lips slackened, slipping over its teeth. The Lectivin, though of the hunter caste, – though more animal than thinking creature – grew thoughtful.

Ballas met its gaze.

The Lectivin's eyes narrowed. Its brief reverie lifted. Snarling, it sprang on to the pine. It climbed quickly, its movements spider-like. Its short-fingered hands grabbed branch after branch. Within seconds it was halfway up.

Jumping, it reached for Crask's legs. Somehow, Crask saw the move. Crying out, he swung his legs upward. The Lectivin's sharp-nailed hands grasped at air. The creature dropped a short distance, then grasped a branch.

Swearing, Ballas hauled Crask out on to the moor. The eel-catcher scrambled from the sewer-hole, then sprinted away.

The Lectivin had reached the tree trunk. The slick wood scarcely hindered it. Jabbing its fingernails, each as tough and sharp as a beast's talon, into the hask, it continued climbing. Ballas knew it'd be on the moorland within seconds. And then? Then it would kill them all.

Ballas thought quickly. He gripped the end of the tree trunk. Growling, he lifted it high enough to get a shoulder under it. The Lectivin froze. Swearing, Ballas gave the pine a fierce push. It swung backward. For a moment it stood perfectly vertical: a bizarre parody of a tree, with its root end upward and branch end down. Then something – whether momentum or the Lectivin's weight – dragged it over. It crashed backwards into the sewer hole. The Lectivin, realising that it was about to be crushed, scampered nimbly around the trunk. The tree thundered to the floor. The Lectivin sprang clear, landing upon its feet.

Then it started climbing the limestone wall. Or tried to. Its fingernails prevented it from getting a grip: they skittered wildly on the slick stone. They were too smooth, too inflexible. The Lectivin abandoned its efforts.

Hissing, it gazed upwards. Its eyes flashed with rage. Then it vanished through the gap, back into the sewers.

'Are we safe?' asked Crask, approaching cautiously.

'It has gone,' Ballas confirmed.

Crask was trembling. When he spoke, the words came quickly – yet he seemed to be trying to slow them down. 'Historians say that there were no animals on Lectivae. None on the ground nor in the sky.' Suddenly he laughed. 'We did it,' he said, peering into the sewer hole. 'We escaped . . .' Grinning, he clapped Ballas on the arm. 'You are a piece of work, my friend. Truly – a marvel.'

'We'd better move on,' said Ballas, scanning the moorland.

They started out over the frost-clasped grass. Then they halted as Elsefar cried, 'Wait – what of me?'

Ballas turned. The quill-master was seated upright on the ground.

'Where are my crutches?' he demanded.

'I did not bring them,' said Crask, shrugging.

'Nor I,' replied Heresh.

Ballas stared into the sewer hole. Elsefar's crutches lay at the bottom, half hidden by the fallen pine. Ballas's boots were beside them. Scowling, the big man became aware of the frozen grass under his feet. At the moment, he could feel nothing. Soon, though, cold would seep through. His bones would ache. More seriously, if his feet were cut, he might take a blood-taint.

Muttering, he strode to the pines. Using his sword, he hacked off two longish branches. Then he proffered them to Elsefar.

'They're not perfect,' said Ballas, 'but they'll have to do.'

'Not perfect?' The quill-master scowled. 'The top parts must be padded! Otherwise they'll skewer my underarms.'

Ballas thought for a moment. Then he dug up two thick tussocks.

Grimacing, Elsefar stuck them on the crutch-tops. Ballas hauled the quill-master upright. Elsefar tried out the crutches, jamming the tussock-padded ends under his arms and taking a few leg-swinging steps. 'No good,' he said. 'No good at all. The right is too long.'

'I'm no craftsman,' said Ballas. 'And you're ill placed to moan.'

He glanced at his feet. The cold was making itself felt. Lugen Crask also looked at Ballas's feet.

'Sweet grief,' he said. 'Bear's paws! Shall we be moving on, though?' The eel-catcher grinned. A happy light danced in his eyes. Ballas understood why. Crask had been seconds from death. The Lectivin had almost grabbed him, yet he had emerged unscathed. The near miss exhilarated him. He felt *alive*. He had gazed into the black pit of death – he had, deep inside, believed he was about to perish – yet he had escaped death. For a short while, the world would acquire new properties for him. Everything would gain clarity – and it would intoxicate him. The frost would appear whiter, sharper, cleaner. The grass, greener. The tiniest familiar things – the clothes he wore, the lines upon his own hands – would provoke mild raptures.

Ballas felt none of this. Only a dull need to find Belthirran.

They walked northwards over the moorland. They were exhausted, and their pace was slow. Crask's smile did not waver. His daughter was seized by a similar breathless happiness. They chatted to one another, sharing their wonderment. Ballas was uninterested in their words. Their companionship. But he knew they'd be joking about their adventure. They'd be mocking Nu'hkterin whilst praising the lizards. They'd look upon the sewers are something terrible yet adorable: a place of awful foreignness, yet home to a memory they'd prize for ever.

After a short time, Crask halted. 'Forgive me,' he said, 'but the excitement is all too much. I have to, ah . . . you understand?' He gestured at a cluster of limestone blocks.

Ballas nodded.

Crask disappeared behind the blocks. The group continued walking, slowly. Ballas pondered idly what their next move should be. Feeling frost-sharpened grass underfoot, he realised that the most urgent thing would be to obtain a pair of boots. But how? He shrugged inwardly. The same way that he had, for so long, got what he needed. He would steal them. If they encountered anyone upon the moors – a merchant, perhaps, or a huntsman – they would attack him, and take anything of use. Then they would kill him. For he, like anyone who laid eyes on them, would be able to tell the Wardens of their whereabouts and the direction in which they were travelling. How would the others take to this? wondered Ballas. Elsefar wouldn't bat an eyelid. The quill-master seemed unconcerned about human life. After all, he had instructed Ballas to murder his employers. And by his own hand he had burned alive dozens of scribes.

But Heresh and Crask?

They had grown accustomed to killing, in order to preserve their own lives. But murdering for a set of boots?

Two black shapes flapped past Ballas's face. Startled, he stepped back, raising his sword. A pair of black crows alighted on a limestone block. Then they flapped down to the grass beyond.

Looking towards the horizon, Ballas resumed his train of thought.

It didn't matter whether Crask and his daughter approved of his actions. But perhaps, for harmony's sake, it would be better to gain his boots without bloodshed. If they found a town, they might also find a cobbler's shop, which they could steal from. And they would—

A cry split the air.

Ballas whirled. The cry sounded again, from behind the blocks. Ballas sprinted around them. And froze.

A brown-moustached Warden appeared to be hugging Crask. He held the eel-catcher tightly against his body. Crask's eyes were rounded, his mouth agape. Suddenly he fell away from the Warden. Blood soaked his lower tunic. A dagger hilt protruded from his stomach. Gasping, he dropped to the ground.

Ballas wondered briefly where the Warden had come from. Had he been hiding behind the rocks all along? No – Crask would have cried out far sooner.

On the ground, the second crow watched Ballas. Around its body a blue light glowed. The creature grew larger and, as it did so, its beak shrank back into its skull, its eyes narrowing. Its puffed-out chest grew more shallow. Its wings broadened. Its feathers faded, to be replaced by a black tunic – blazoned with a Scarrendestin triangle.

A second Warden gazed at Ballas. His eyes were dull, as if he had suffered unimaginable pain. Yet a vigilant gleam lurked in them.

Ballas blinked – then swung his sword horizontally into the first Warden's face. The blow half-cleaved his skull. The Warden fell, his blood gushing. The second Warden drew his sword and lunged at Ballas. Ballas deflected the blow, the clash of steel ringing out across the moors. Ballas stepped back, observing the Warden. He was almost as tall as Ballas. And leaner. He moved with a near-feline grace. Springing at Ballas, he hacked with his sword at Ballas's ribs. Ballas raised his own sword – but only just in time. The blades met, and the jolt nearly wrenched Ballas's sword from his hand. Gasping, Ballas retreated a few steps. The Warden attacked again, lifting his sword high, then slashing it downward at Ballas's shoulder. Ballas danced aside. The blade whispered down his tunic sleeve. Cursing, Ballas hazarded an ungainly cross-strike at the Warden. The Warden parried it with ease. Ballas trotted back yet more steps.

'Did the Lectivin send you?' he asked. 'Are you his creation?'

The Warden didn't reply.

'His magick made you, yes? Of course it did. What else could've done it?'

'There are many more like me,' said the Warden.

'Like you? You mean, those that've sworn oaths to the Lectivin?'

'He trusts us,' said the Warden, 'for he knows we cannot disobey. He has ordered me to kill you. So I shall do so.'

Leaping forward, he snaked out his sword at Ballas's neck. The big man stumbled back. His heel struck a stone concealed by the grass. For a second he stayed upright but unbalanced. Then he fell on to his back.

The Warden swept his sword down, slashing at Ballas's chest. Rolling aside, Ballas heard the blade crunch into frozen soil. He scrambled to his feet, just as the Warden launched another strike. Ballas blocked it clumsily. He had scant time to brace himself, to clench the muscles in his wrist. The blades impacted, and Ballas's sword spun from his grasp.

The Warden smiled. He walked closer to Ballas, moving at a relaxed pace. There was no need to hurry now. His prey was unarmed. And exhausted. He took a step closer. Then he swung his blade across Ballas's stomach, intending to slice it open. Ballas arched himself forward, drawing in his gut. The blade's tip brushed his tunic. Growling, the big man hurled himself at the Warden. As he did so, he grasped the Warden's arm, pinning it across his chest. Both men fell, Ballas landing on top of the Warden. Straddling his ribcage, Ballas planted his left knee on the Warden's free arm, holding it to the ground. With his free hand, he grasped the other man's sword-bearing arm above the elbow. He braced it against his chest, and bent it slowly back against the joint. The Warden howled. Gristle grated, tendons popped. There was a slow tearing sound, as the muscle fibres pulled apart. Ballas released the arm only when it was utterly ruined. It flopped upon the grass, hinged back against the elbow.

Rising, Ballas retrieved the sword. He planted his foot upon the Warden's chest. He contemplated sinking the blade through his throat. Then he decided against it.

He stabbed it through the Warden's scream-widened mouth. The blade's tip pierced the back of his throat, skewering him to the ground.

Ballas stepped back, heart pounding.

Then he remembered Crask.

The eel-catcher sat on the grass, propped half upright against a limestone block. His daughter was beside him, her arm around his shoulders. She looked frantically to Ballas.

'You must do something,' she said.

Ballas kneeled in front of the eel-catcher. He peered at the knife wound. The blade was lodged hilt-deep. He looked at Crask's face. Blood greased his lips. He gazed unfocusedly at the horizon. His breathing was a wet rasp. He blinked, then vomited a gobbet of blood.

'Don't die,' whispered Heresh. 'You cannot die – not now; not after everything.' She turned to Ballas. 'There must be something you can do. Something *we* can do. A physician – we must find a physician. Please – you must . . .'

Crask's gaze drifted from the horizon to the ground. Then he turned his face to his daughter, slowly, as if the movement cost him much strength.

Their gazes met.

'Father?' said Heresh, uncertainly.

Crask opened his mouth – then something in his gaze altered. The life-light faded. In its stead appeared the reflection of the grey gleam of dawn. He sagged forward, then sank sideways, sliding away from his daughter.

In a vague fashion, Ballas supposed that he owed his life to Crask. If the man hadn't realised they ought to follow the lizards they might still be wandering the sewers. The eel-catcher had annoyed Ballas, true. Yet Ballas had never wanted his death.

Heresh hugged her father's corpse. She buried her face in the crook of his neck. Ballas stood fifty yards away – yet he could see her shoulders shaking as she wept. He sensed the immensity of her grief. She was suffering an immeasurable agony – an agony so profound she'd never imagined it could exist. Some emotions were so fierce, Ballas knew, it seemed incredible that they did not physically tear apart the sufferer.

Jonas Elsefar approached.

'I hate to speak of practical matters,' he said, 'but we must keep moving.'

The quill-master squirmed on his newly made crutches.

'The Wardens'll care nothing for her unhappiness. They will still be hunting us. So too will the Lectivin. It is folly to delay another instant. The sooner we get to my home – my new, safe home – the better.'

Ballas did not reply.

Elsefar jabbed a crutch tip into the ground. 'Have you lost your wits? What are you waiting for? The girl's grief to run its course? I warn you, a woman's misery *never* blows itself out. Stay here for a million days and nights, and still she'd weep. What is she to you, Ballas? What was her father? Nothing. A means to end, that is all. Her purpose is served. Have you forgotten that? Now she is nothing but a hindrance. If she wishes to stay with her father,' he sniffed, '*let her*.'

Ballas disliked the quill-master.

'She is nothing to you,' Elsefar repeated. 'The only thing that matters is that you get to Belthirran.'

Ballas hesitated. Elsefar spoke sense.

'Leave her,' the quill-master said. 'We're wasting time. Can't you hear sand slipping through the hourglass? Think upon this: to reach Belthirran, you'll have to cross the mountains. In fair weather, it is thought an impossible task. But in midwinter frost and snow?' He shook his head.

Ballas turned to Heresh. To his surprise, he found she was on her feet.

'We cannot leave him here,' she said. 'Not where wolves and buzzards can get at him. We must bury him.'

'We've no time,' said Elsefar impatiently.

'And we've no tools,' said Ballas. 'We can't dig a grave with our bare hands.'

'We cannot abandon him. We must do something . . .' Heresh lowered her gaze. She drew in a sharp breath. 'It is your fault, you bastard! This is all your doing!' She slapped Ballas across the face – a sharp blow, which the big man made no attempt to avoid. 'If you hadn't come to the marshes – if you hadn't dragged us into all this – my father would still be alive!' She pounded her fists against Ballas's chest. Ballas could have easily grabbed her wrists and stopped her. Yet he let her continue.

Eventually she grew still.

'There *is* something we can do for your father,' Ballas said quietly.

'What would you care?' hissed Heresh, glowering.

'I *don't* care,' replied Ballas. 'I'm only saying that there's a way of keeping your father's . . . your father safe. It'll only take a few moments. Take it or leave it, woman.'

Ballas told her of his intentions. She consented. Slinging Crask's body – limp, blood-wet – over his shoulder, he walked a hundred yards to a heap of grey boulders. Ballas was not an educated man. But he had been told that once volcanoes had studded the land. They had spat forth lava that hardened into boulders such as these. Each was a rough, elongated sphere, no larger than a child's torso. Each was porous, and weighed no more than a sack of grain.

Ballas set down Crask's body. Then he hefted aside a boulder, exposing a dark space beneath. He moved more boulders, until he had exposed a wide opening. He granted Heresh a moment to look upon her father a final time. Then he lowered Crask feet first into the blackness. He felt Crask's boots make contact with stone. Gripping his collar, Ballas allowed the body's knees to buckle, until they rested on the stone. Then Ballas gently released him. Crask pitched softly forward, his back bent and head lowered. As if, in death, he were praying.

Ballas replaced the boulders, sealing Crask underneath.

Heresh wished to speak with her father. Leaving her alone, Ballas walked to Elsefar. The quill-master wore an impatient expression. Ballas detected his unspoken thought: We should abandon her. Time is slipping away. With every passing moment, the odds of you reaching Belthirran grow longer . . .

Belthirran – the word flashed in Ballas's skull, and he felt a dry, hard thirst for the place, and an overwhelming urge to go now, without delay . . .

'We are leaving,' he told Heresh, striding over to her.

She had been talking to her father . . . had been whispering into the heaped boulders. She started.

'I need a short while longer,' she said, a touch of resentment in her tone.

'Stay if you want. But I'm going.' It was true that he no longer needed Heresh. Her purpose, and Crask's, had been to take him to Elsefar. That had been accomplished weeks ago. Once the city had been sealed, Ballas had remained with them, suspecting that they might prove useful. Which Crask certainly had: he had enabled Ballas to escape the sewers.

But Heresh? What use was she? What use was she *now*?

'Remain here as long as you like,' said Ballas. 'We've nothing to do with each other any more.'

Heresh turned to look at him. 'What?'

'We are done with each other, you and me. You're free to do as you wish.'

She looked suddenly frightened. 'You cannot go without me,' she said, rising. 'You cannot leave me alone. Not now. I'll walk with you. For a while, at least.' She glanced abjectly at the boulders. 'My father spoke of a place where I may be safe. My uncle's home. In a few days, I'll find my way there. But not yet. I can help you, Ballas. There are things I can do which you cannot. You are distinctive-looking. Every man who sets eyes on you will know you're the fugitive. But me? I am unknown – for the time being. There are many red-haired women. But few men of your size . . . and none that bear such a scar upon their foreheads. I can bring you ale from taverns. If you need anything from a market place . . . if you need fresh weapons, or horses . . . *anything* . . . I will be able to buy them without being recognised. And I can fight, can't I? Not well. But not badly, either. I know how to hunt, too. And light fires. I can make your journey less arduous.'

Her eyes glittered, desperately.

She fears solitude, Ballas realised. She had been uprooted from her home. Her father had died. She was utterly alone. Everything would appear cold, uncaring towards her. The pale sky cared nothing for her. The winds blew and the rains fell unfeelingly. Druine, the whole *world*, was suddenly peopled by strangers.

Ballas understood these sensations.

He understood why Heresh wanted to remain in his presence. He was the only familiar thing that had, so far, endured. Their time together had been brief. He had led her into deep unhappiness. Yet he was all that she had – a flame that burned her, but at the same time provided the only light within the greater dark.

Heresh hated him, he was sure. But, for the time being, she needed him.

Ballas shrugged. 'Do what you will.'

He and Elsefar set out across the moors. Heresh followed, ten paces behind.

Chapter 16

. . . and he kept secret the full strength
Of his magic, and the pilgrims grew wary,
For his secrecy was profound, and he craved
Power upon power . . .

They moved across the moors.

Things were different now, Ballas knew. He had not expected the Lectivin to pursue them – for it to be sent out by the Church like some hunt-hound. Nu'hkterin was the Church's deepest secret. A secret that, if revealed, could threaten the entire institution. Yet the Blessed Masters were willing, now, to take that chance. To let Nu'hkterin move among Druine's citizens. To have entered the sewers, it would have had to pass through the visionary's-root den in the brothel. Would the root-eaters have thought it a mere hallucination? Or maybe they hadn't had time to think anything at all: surely the Lectivin would have been instructed to destroy all witnesses.

It was a measure of the Church's keenness to capture Ballas that they should employ the Lectivin so openly. Ballas recalled Father Rendeage's words: *A Decree of Annihilation has been issued. The purpose of such a thing is not to punish a wrongdoer – it is to prevent more harm.* But what *sort* of harm? Of such things Ballas had no understanding – nor did he care to acquire any. He had to reach Belthirran. *That* was all that mattered. He cared not whether the Church collapsed or thrived. He simply wanted to cross the Garsbracks, and find the Land Beyond the Mountains.

The Lectivin troubled Ballas. He did not know what it was capable of. It could cause a man to burst into flames. Or adopt a crow's form. It could follow a man, as Crask had claimed, by his soul-glow . . .

What else could it do? What other talents did it have?

There were crows on the moors. The birds gathered in dark clusters. Whenever Ballas saw them, he grew uneasy. What if they were Wardens?

When he approached some, they flapped away, apparently alarmed. They did much the same when he hurled stones at them. Perhaps, if they'd been Wardens, they would have acted differently. Maybe they would have transfigured into men, and attacked. But Ballas did not know. When the group crested low hills, then sank into the dips on the far side, it did not seem that the crows followed. They did not soar overhead, or skim discreetly over the land, hundreds of yards away. They seemed uninterested in the travellers.

Nonetheless, they disturbed Ballas. They were a problem that he did not want to have to deal with.

As night fell, the group found itself several hundred yards from a village that was perched on a rise near a stream. Drizzle was no longer falling but a nocturnal cold had seized the land. It was tempting to seek lodgings. But the risk was too great.

They struck a sparse camp amid willows growing near the stream. They spent an icy night huddled together. Heresh did not speak. Preoccupied, she wept softly. Elsefar complained about the cold, for a time. Then he grew resigned to his discomfort. Muttering, he sank into a restless half-sleep.

Ballas slept easily. When he woke, the sky was still dark – yet a blueness glowed on the horizon. Dawn was breaking. Leaving the others at the willows, he walked into the village. The streets were silent, empty. From a stable, he stole a steel-grey mare and hitched it to a cart standing outside a butcher's shop. When footsteps sounded, he hid in a doorway. A young man came along the road, whistling cheerfully as if he were a substitute for those song birds that had fled the winter. He was almost as tall as Ballas – but very thin. He walked in long ungainly strides, and squinted short-sightedly.

As he passed the doorway, Ballas punched him on the side of his head. His whistling ended in a dull *toot*. He fell unconscious to the mud. Ballas dragged him into the stable, stole his boots – which, despite being too narrow, fitted him comfortably enough – and tied him up with a set of reins.

Ballas rode the cart back to the willows.

'That should speed things up,' said Elsefar, pleased.

Following Elsefar's directions, they rode in a north-westerly direction. They maintained a fast pace, the cart jouncing over the tussock-studded ground. As evening approached, they arrived near a range of high, forested hills. The day had been cloudless. Now the setting sun glinted on every twig-tip. The forest was broad, and deep. Ballas estimated that it covered fifteen, maybe twenty square miles. It was a place of silence. Of seclusion. It did not surprise him when Elsefar said, 'We are here.'

They halted.

The quill-master pointed one of his crudely fashioned crutches at the forest. 'This place was my refuge when the Church was herding up those who traded in forbidden texts. And it shall be my refuge once more.' Manoeuvring himself carefully, he swung down from the cart. He sniffed the air, inhaling forest scents. 'For a man with my disability –' he tapped his legs with a crutch '– this is not easy terrain. To move from spot to spot is hard work. But survival? That is another matter. If one plans ahead, one can live in something approaching ease. The forest is full of good things. There is food of some sort everywhere, if you care to look. And have the patience, and skill, to lay traps. I lived here for ten years. A long time. Come. I'll take you to my home.'

'Wait,' said Ballas. He walked to the cart. Heresh clambered from the cart-back. She looked exhausted. Her eyes were red-rimmed, the whites bloodshot from constant weeping. She gazed at the forest. She seemed to see the trees, yet not absorb their presence. She knew they were there. But they meant nothing to her.

Ballas unhitched the cart. Then he removed the harness from the horse. Slapping its rump, he startled the creature into a cross-moorland canter. Lifting the shafts, he rolled the cart to the edge of a deep, fast-flowing river. He gave it a single push and it splashed into the water. It sank, then resurfaced, showing only a wheel, a shaft and its side. The heavy current pulled it away.

'Such caution,' said Elsefar, at the forest's edge, 'is not needed. No one ever comes here. They never walk past the forest, or set foot inside it. The nearest village is thirty miles away. It has a forest of its own, which the villagers use when they wish to hunt or gather timber. There are no roads close to here. This forest is halfway to nowhere. Its seclusion is almost absolute. That is why it is so safe. That is why I chose it.'

They walked through the forest. There were no paths, but the trees – a mix of oak and sycamore – were widely spaced. Occasionally, their paths were blocked by thorn bushes: huge, densely coiled barbed stalks, impossible to pass through without injury. But this was not a problem. They merely retraced their steps and took a slightly different route.

It had been a long time since Ballas had been in a forest. He had forgotten how soothing such places were. The scent of wet, living wood; the perversely wholesome tang of rotting vegetation; the subtle, sap-thick frequence of mosses . . . It all calmed him. The trees had a gently mesmerising effect. They lulled him into a happy trance. Unthinkingly, he stepped over protruding roots, walked around deep puddles. For the first time in weeks, he felt vaguely restful.

They walked for an hour. Increasingly excited, Elsefar no longer moaned, or sniped, or sported a disdainful expression.

'We are almost there,' he said, looking around. 'I recognise these trees. These grasses. And . . . yes: look!' He pointed to a patch of ground. Peering through the fading light, Ballas saw a snare tied from catgut. The catching loop lay slackly around a rabbit's leg-bone. Around this, other bones were scattered.

'You shouldn't leave snares set, if you aren't going to take your quarry,' said Ballas. 'You're a poor huntsman, Elsefar.'

'I survived,' said the quill-master. 'I see nothing *poor* in that. And besides, it was ten years ago. These are ancient bones.' He drew another deep breath. 'A full decade . . . The beauty of forests,' he said, 'is that everything changes – yet stays the same. Things renew themselves. New mosses and moulds sprout up. Yet the forest remains as it always was. I had forgotten how much I liked it here.'

'Why did you leave? Was the Church getting close?'

'Of course not,' said Elsefar. 'They would never suspect that anyone lived here. If you are wise, Ballas, you'll give up your ridiculous search for Belthirran.' A sneering note entered his voice. 'Instead, you'll find yourself a deep forest and settle down.' He grew quiet. 'I left because the solitude did not suit me. But now, I return to it gladly. I can see more clearly its virtues. There is no one here to taunt me. No sick, half-witted souls like the scribes at the copying house.' He wiped a hand across his mouth. 'Like those I had to avenge myself upon.'

He continued walking, agitated again.

They emerged on to a patch of open land. The river, into which Ballas had tipped the cart, snaked across the forest floor. A wooden board crossed from bank to bank at the watercourse's narrowest point. On the opposite side, ten yards back from the river, there was a cave. The entrance was hung with goatskins.

'I am home,' said Elsefar, simply. His agitation vanished. He crossed the bridge, and touched the skins. 'A little rotten,' he said, thoughtfully, 'but that is to be expected. No matter. They can easily be replaced.' A barrier of rope-tied branches stood propped alongside the cave entrance. Elsefar struck it with his crude crutch. 'Still sturdy. I crafted this myself, of course,' he said, glancing back at Ballas. 'There are boar in the forest. Sometimes, they'd wander in while I was sleeping. So I fashioned this: a door of sorts.' He grinned, exposing tiny yellow-edged teeth. Then he ducked through the skins. Ballas followed, then Heresh.

The cave was dark. Elsefar rattled about in a far corner. A flint struck against steel. A spark flared, and a lantern was lit.

'The oil is still good,' said Elsefar, peering at the lantern. 'A fine omen, don't you think?'

The cave was practically unfurnished. Rotting blankets were bundled against a wall. A jumble of objects was clustered in the corner. Cups, bowls, spoons, all carved from wood. A dozen pouches, stuffed with herbs. A thicket of quills and a mound of decomposing parchment. In the centre of the floor there was a circle of stones and inside it was a heap of dark wood-ash. A spit was erected over the fire. There was also some unused firewood, and a bowl of moss kindling.

'Build us a blaze, Ballas,' said the quill-master.

Ballas complied, first igniting the kindling from the lantern flame, then heaping the firewood. The wood was slightly damp – yet it soon caught alight.

Elsefar was delighted. 'Everything is more or less as I left it. A little sodden, perhaps – a little, ah, degraded with time. But so what? Nothing lasts, yes? Nothing remains eternally perfect.'

He shook out a clay cooking pot. A few spider corpses floated out. Elsefar wiped out the pot with his hand. 'I do not know about you,' he said, glancing at Ballas, 'but I am hungry. We have travelled far, over awkward ground. And I wish to eat before I sleep. Fill this with water, will you? Then I'll heat it up, and if you get what is needed from the forest, I'll make us a broth.'

Ballas filled the pot from the river. Crask told him which roots and berries to gather from the forest, and whereabouts they grew. Ballas stepped into the darkness. Crossing the river, he dug up a clutch of *skanndag*-root, delving it from the leaf-mould-nourished earth. From a spiky *grende* bush he collected several pouchfuls of berries. He picked mushrooms sprouting from an oak's roots, and gathered numerous other ingredients.

Then he returned to the cave. Heresh was sitting against a wall, staring at the fire. Elsefar peered into the pot. 'Your timing is good,' he told Ballas. 'The water will soon boil. Did you find all I asked for?'

'Yes,' replied Ballas. 'You're making Wayfarer's Broth.'

'You're familiar with it?'

'I've had it before,' nodded Ballas.

'When times are lean, and hunger bites,' said Elsefar, taking the roots, berries and mushrooms from Ballas, 'one can depend upon Wayfarer's Broth.' He looked around for a moment. Then he grimaced. 'I can't find my knife. Might I borrow yours?'

Ballas cleansed the blood-caked blade in the river, then gave it to Elsefar. The quill-master cut away the tough rind of a *skanndag* root. Ballas left him to prepare the meal. The quill-master worked quickly; soon, he tipped the ingredients into the boiling water. After a while, the broth was ready: an odour, something like a forest in summer's heat, filled the cave.

Elsefar spooned the broth into two bowls. Partway through the third, he paused. 'You'd better pull the door across,' he said. 'The boars might be drawn by the scent.'

Rising, Ballas sealed the cave mouth with the makeshift door. When he returned, Elsefar offered him a bowl. Grunting, Ballas accepted it. Elsefar held another bowl out to Heresh.

She shook her head.

'You must eat,' said Elsefar.

'I'm not hungry.'

'Have you forgotten the Church is pursuing you? Have you forgotten you must keep your strength up?'

'He is right,' said Ballas, spooning broth into his mouth. It had a peculiar taste – a mix of sweet juice and old wood. Yet it was palatable enough. 'We'll leave at first light. I don't want you slowing me down. Understand?'

Reluctantly, Heresh took the bowl. She ate slowly, steadily – as if the broth were a medicine to be consumed, not a meal to be enjoyed.

Ballas soon emptied his bowl.

'I am tired,' he said, blinking.

Elsefar watched him from the fire's edge. 'Then sleep.'

Something nudged Ballas's shoulder. Heresh leaned against him. He pushed her away. Her eyes flickered, as if she were struggling to keep them open. The bowl slipped from her fingers, spilling leftover broth on to the floor. She rocked drowsily from side to side. Then she sagged against Ballas. Her breathing was deep, and even: as if she were sunk in a fathomless sleep.

Exhaustion swept over Ballas. It was an unnaturally intense and sudden fatigue.

He looked at Elsefar.

'You have poisoned me,' he said.

'I do not believe that this safe house –' Elsefar gestured at the cave '– is safe at all. Not with the Lectivin prowling Druine. Not with those terrible crow-Wardens.' He shook his head. 'If the Church's forces catch up with me, what hope will I have? I am hiding from them – they will resent that. I have been your accomplice – that will earn me a place upon the Oak. But if *I* approach *them*, bearing a gift of immeasurable value? If I present them the head of the sinner? And the flame-haired lady who travels with him? They will realise that I am not the Church's enemy. They will understand that I have been just a puppet, worked this way and that by yourself. I burned the copying house down – but so what? *You* made me do it. Just as you made me leave Granthaven.' He held out his hands, palms upward. 'They will forgive me, Ballas.'

'They'll forgive *nothing*,' growled Ballas. 'Because they don't have to. They'll kill you, Elsefar. It'll be a bad death . . .' Ballas grimaced. His vision swam. The fire blurred, its light surging and ebbing in intensity.

Elsefar seemed amused. 'Do not fight it, Ballas. Lugen Crask – poor, dead Lugen Crask, butchered while he was having a piss: an ignominious demise, yes? A man should perish while holding his sword, not his cock . . . Crask said you have been poisoned before. He claims your constitution is extraordinarily strong. Alas, it shall not be strong enough. I have given you *somnaris*. In small doses, it aids sleep. In large amounts, it kills. And you, Ballas, have eaten a *huge* amount.' He knocked the bowl with his crutch's tip. 'You mistrust me. Yet still, you look away while I am serving you your food. You should have been attentive. The girl, though, has had but a sleeper's dose.'

Ballas frowned, puzzled – if Elsefar was to kill them both, why preserve Heresh's life, albeit temporarily?

Elsefar caught his confused look.

'Oh, come now, Ballas – my legs are ruined, not my childmaker! She is a fine piece of work, the eel-catcher's daughter. I have never rutted with a red-haired girl before. It must be rather like sticking a poker in a fire. Visually, I mean . . .' He grinned. 'Submit, Ballas,' he whispered. '*Submit*.'

'Not . . . yet,' slurred Ballas, forcing himself to his feet.

Elsefar blinked.

The room spun. Ballas swayed, then sagged against the wall. Elsefar got himself upright. Edging sideways, he kept the fire between himself and Ballas.

Ballas glanced at him. Then he stumbled towards the wooden chopping board, where Elsefar had cut the vegetables. Grasping the knife, he turned to Elsefar.

'Do nothing foolish,' said the quill-master. 'You are too slow to kill even me.' He moved further around the fire. 'Look at yourself. You can scarcely move.'

Ballas stared hard at Elsefar. He knew that if he threw himself *through* the fire, he'd have a chance of plunging the knife into the quill-master's guts.

He took a step – then halted. A thought swirled up from somewhere.

Ballas faltered.

'I . . . do not . . . *want* to kill you,' he said, his voice sluggish. He could hardly keep his eyes open. 'You know the explorer . . . who will take me to Belthirran.'

'You never tire of that idiot dream, do you?' said Elsefar. 'Your only journey, my friend, will be to the Eltheryn Forest – or to Hell, perhaps.'

Leaning against the cave wall, Ballas moved slowly around the fire. Elsefar kept his distance. Suddenly, Ballas stood up straight – and crashed himself through the makeshift door-cover, into the dark night outside.

He fell heavily; above him, stars swirled – and continued swirling, even after he had temporarily stopped moving. Groaning, he stirred himself and crawled towards the river.

Dragging footsteps sounded behind him.

'Do you intend to *crawl* to Belthirran?' asked Elsefar, laughing. 'A feat in itself, I admit – and ambitious, since you still don't know the way.'

Reaching out, Ballas tossed the knife towards the river. It fell inches short, and lay glinting on the dark mud. The dragging footsteps sounded again, moving quickly now. Grunting, Ballas clawed his way to the knife – just as Elsefar's crutches appeared in his vision, on the river bank.

'Crafty,' said Elsefar, stooping to pick up the blade. 'But also very, very stupid. You are dying; I have no need to dispatch you. Heresh is the only one I need kill by physical deed. True, I intend to use the knife. But I could equally well use a shard of stone – to open an artery, say. Perhaps I could beat her to death. Or burn her. It wouldn't matter if she were unrecognisable: I'm sure the Masters would take my word for it, when I declared she was your companion—'

Rolling on to his back, Ballas grabbed one of Elsefar's crutches and yanked it away. The quill-master stumbled, then started to fall. As he dropped, Ballas swung the crutch into his face. It connected squarely with his teeth.

Struggling on to all fours, Ballas crawled to Elsefar. Slowly, deliberately, he threw the first crutch into the river. Then the second. They floated briskly away on the moonlit water.

Ballas picked up the knife. He held it in front of Elsefar's eyes – then hurled it into the water. It sank with a muted splash.

'What have you done?' asked Elsefar, his eyes wide.

Ballas did not reply. Darkness flooded over him. He collapsed face down, and sank into sleep.

Ballas woke.

During his slumber, he had not moved. He still sprawled on the river bank. The water swirled palely in dawn-light. Out of the corner of his eye, Ballas saw frost covering his sleeve: a film of sharp crackling whiteness. Closer to his face was a puddle of vomit, also frost-capped.

Groaning, he pushed himself up on to his knees. The skin around his neck ached. A dull pain throbbed in his throat. He was cold – it seemed as though his bones, if struck hard, would shatter like ice.

He struggled on to his feet. He stumbled, the ground seeming to lurch beneath him. Then he regained his balance. He felt sick – but it was a sickness no worse than that of a hangover. His eyes burned, the roof of his mouth was raw with vomiting. He staggered numbly into the cave.

Heresh lay upon her side, sleeping. Her shoulders lifted and fell with every deep breath. She appeared unmolested: her clothing hadn't been tampered with. That was good, thought Ballas. Elsefar's fortunes suddenly growing sour, he had lost his ardour. With his knife and crutches gone, survival had become his priority – not copulation.

It didn't take Ballas long to find Elsefar. On his hands, the quill-master had hauled himself about half a mile through the forest. Dragging behind him, his legs had crushed an easily visible track through the undergrowth. Ballas found him curled up at the base of a thorn bush, sleeping. He had clearly chosen the wrong track and had found his path blocked. Whereas it seemed he had previously managed to crawl through such vegetation – his tunic was ripped, his hands gashed and bloodied – he had found this final obstruction too much. Exhausted, he had given up hope.

Grabbing his collar, Ballas yanked him upright.

Elsefar woke. Crying out, he swung his hands feebly at the big man – each blow half slap, half punch. Grunting, Ballas released him. Elsefar dropped to the ground, then pitched face first into the thorn bush. Saying nothing, Ballas dragged him out. The quill-master groaned, writhing like a hooked fish. Again, Ballas pulled him upright. Lacerations on his forehead and cheeks were bleeding. A stray thorn had pierced his lower lip, hanging there like a piece of primitive jewellery.

Ballas slung him over his shoulder. Then he carried him back to the cave.

Heresh was kneeling on the river bank, retching into the water. 'What has happened?' she asked, looking up.

'He poisoned us.'

Ballas sat Elsefar against an oak tree. The quill-master shivered – from cold, and from fear. 'You need me,' he said, staring evenly at Ballas. 'Without me, there'll be no Belthirran. It is true – you *know* it is. You said as much last n—'

'Shut up.' Ballas struck Elsefar sharply across the face with the hard palm of his hand. The sound of skin upon skin rang cleanly, crisply, into the air.

'If you kill me, you'll—' began Elsefar.

This time Ballas punched him: a skull-jolting blow to the cheekbone.

'Another sound,' said Ballas, 'and I'll do worse than kill you. Sit still, be quiet – and I might let you live.'

Ballas removed his belt. Kneeling, he looped it around Elsefar's stomach and the tree trunk, so that the quill-master was bound to the oak. Ballas tightened the belt as far as it would go. Then he buckled it up.

Elsefar struggled briefly against his bonds. 'What are you going to do with me?'

'What is the explorer's name? Where can I find him?'

'Release me, and I'll tell you – but no sooner.'

'You will tell me *now*,' said Ballas, 'or I'll leave you here for the boars to eat.'

Elsefar grimaced. 'How do I know you won't do that anyway? You aren't a man to be trusted. And . . . and you have a grievance with me.'

'In many ways,' said Ballas easily, 'you and I are moulded from the same clay. There are things you want – and to get them, you'll do the foulest things. You'll lie, cheat, steal – and kill.' He shrugged. 'That is the world's way, though. And it is my way. But sometimes . . . sometimes people like you and me must help one another. You can give me what I need to survive. And I can do the same for you.'

Elsefar chewed his lip. 'You promise you will untie me?'

'My promises are worthless,' said Ballas. 'But you know that if you don't tell me what I need to know, you'll stay here *for certain*. Within days, you'll be dead. You'll freeze and die of thirst. Or, as I say, the boars will get you.'

'It seems I have no choice,' said Elsefar sourly.

'All men have a choice,' replied Ballas. 'In your case, you choose between a chance of life and the certainty of death.'

Elsefar exhaled. 'Go to Greenleaf Village. It's about two hundred miles due east from here—'

'I know where it is,' Ballas said, nodding curtly.

'Seek out a man named Seppemus Scallen. He is the one you require.'

'What is his profession?'

'The last I heard he was a farmer.' Elsefar shrugged, as far as he could with his arms bound. 'Tell him that I sent you, and he might help you. Bribe him, and you will have greater success.'

'Seppemus Scallen, of Greenleaf Village,' murmured Ballas.

'Yes,' confirmed Elsefar.

Ballas stood up. 'Keep an eye on him,' he told Heresh. 'There's something I must do.'

'Wait!' snapped Elsefar. 'You promised to set me free.'

'And I will do, soon enough,' said Ballas.

Returning to the cave, Ballas gathered the bags he had used the previous night when collecting roots and berries from the forest. Then he stepped back outside.

He crossed the river and, for a short while, did at dawn exactly what he'd done at nightfall: he harvested those things that could be mixed into a broth. Except that now he dug up far larger quantities. When the bags were full, he returned to the cave and emptied them upon the floor. Then he returned outdoors and did the same again. Heresh and Elsefar watched him. Both seemed puzzled. But whereas Heresh's confusion was a numb, passionless thing, Elsefar appeared deeply agitated. In a whisper he demanded, 'What are you doing? What game is this?' over and over.

Ballas ignored him. After a while, a good store of food was heaped on the cave floor. Ballas then peeled moss from a few tree trunks, and collected several armfuls of dead branches. These too he put in the cave.

He unfastened Elsefar from the oak trunk. Then he dragged the quill-master into the cave. Heresh followed, curious.

Ballas gestured at the roots, berries and mushrooms. 'It'll take me about a fortnight to get to Greenleaf Village,' he told Elsefar. 'You've got about three or four weeks' worth of food there, and enough firewood to cook it. When I find Seppemus Scallen, and he proves to be what you claim, I'll send Heresh back with more food – and other things you'll need to survive: knives, a new set of crutches . . . Without those, you are useless. You can't look after yourself, Elsefar. You'll have to depend on the food I've brought. You won't exactly be enjoying a banquet each evening. But you won't starve, either. Unless, of course, you've lied to me . . .'

Heresh stared at Ballas, her eyebrows raised. 'I don't want to come back—'

'Be quiet,' said Ballas sharply. 'You'll do as you're told.' He swung his gaze to Elsefar. 'If Seppemus Scallen isn't what you say, or if he doesn't exist at all . . . Heresh won't return. And you'll die.'

Taking hold of Heresh's arm, Ballas pulled her upright. 'This is a good time to go. You'd better pray you see this girl again,' he added, gesturing at Heresh. 'For what is she to you now – except life? So long, quill-master.'

Ballas led Heresh outside the cave. They walked several steps from the cave-mouth, then halted.

'What are you doing?' asked the red-haired woman.

Ballas raised a finger to his lips. 'Wait.'

From within the cave came sounds of sobbing. Then, suddenly, Elsefar cried: 'Come back! Please – come back! I have misled you! I was mistaken!'

Heresh started back to the cave. But Ballas stayed still.

Elsefar called out again. 'Please, for mercy's sake – *come back*!'

Only now did Ballas return to the cave. Elsefar's face was red and tears were pouring down his cheeks. 'I am sorry,' he said – then, from somewhere, he managed a nervous laugh. 'Forgive me,' he wheezed, 'but I got my names jumbled. I only just realised . . . it suddenly struck me . . .' He grimaced. 'You must find Athreos Laike. *He* is the explorer you seek.'

'Where does he live?' asked Ballas, kneeling.

'Dayshadow Town, at the base of the Garsbracks. He owns the quarry there. He is a man of some wealth, I understand.'

Ballas repeated the name to himself. Athreos Laike. Dayshadow Town.

'And who is Seppemus Scallen?' he asked.

'Oh – merely a quill-master I once knew,' said Elsefar diffidently. 'I am old. In my memory, one name dwells where another ought to be. Forgive me. Isn't it said that to err is human?'

Ballas shrugged. Then he swept up in his arms the food store from the cave floor. Striding outside, he dropped it in the river.

Elsefar didn't speak.

Ballas picked up the firewood and kindling and threw it in the water.

'W-what . . . ?' stammered Elsefar. 'I – I have told you who you must find!'

'*This* time you have,' said Ballas. 'But before, when you thought it was safe to lie . . .' He shook his head. 'Some men only turn honest when their life depends on it. You are such a man. Sometimes, so am I.'

Turning, Ballas ushered Heresh from the cave.

'Come back!' shrieked Elsefar. 'You cannot do this! I shall die! Sweet grief, *I shall die!*'

'After days of lies,' muttered Ballas, 'he speaks a truth.'

'You truly intend to leave him?'

Ballas nodded. 'The cold will destroy him. Or, as I said, the boars.'

They left the forest. As they stepped on to open moorland, Heresh touched Ballas's shoulder. She pointed to the distance. A group of grey-silver shapes were bounding towards the forest.

'Wolves,' said Heresh softly.

Elsefar's cries were dimly audible. He shrieked for help, for mercy . . . yet these cries, twisting hoarsely in the air, only summoned those things that would kill him. Soon, he would perish amid snarls and gleaming teeth.

The wolves vanished amid the trees. Turning, Ballas walked away.

They headed northwards through a fresh fall of drizzle. Ballas did not consider the seasons to be entities governed by a calendar's strictures: summer didn't truly arrive on Wisten's Day, nor winter on the day of

Winter Prayers. As a vagrant, he had learned that the seasons were inconstant, wilful. They came and went when they pleased. Their presence could be observed only by looking *outward*, at the world. Winter, for instance, existed as a particular type of coldness. Not the crisp cold of autumn, which spoke faintly of impending renewal. But an aggressive, bone-splitting cold that chimed icily with death. According to the Pilgrim Church's calendars, winter had gripped Druine for a month and a half. Yet only now was a true winter cold evident. Evident, too, were other markers of the Fierce Season. The fallen leaves were scarcely noticeable: they had traded their sharp browns for the sullen, stinking blacks of death. The frosts lay thicker – as thick, almost, as snow.

And this troubled Ballas.

If he was going to cross the Garsbrack Mountains, he would need to beat the snows. He accepted that snow lay upon the peaks, even during the swelter of summer. But if it clogged the lower slopes, it would be near-impossible to climb the mountains.

It might prove near-impossible even in the best of circumstances. But at least he would know the way. Surely the explorer Elsefar had spoken of would supply a map. Then the ascent wouldn't be a test of route-finding but of straightforward endurance. It would be a physical rather than an intellectual trial. And that suited Ballas. He was accustomed to physical pain and hardship.

On the first night since leaving Elsefar's home, Ballas and Heresh encamped in a gully a few hundred yards from a stream. They took turns at keeping watch. The next day, Ballas acted in a way that, since he had begun fleeing the Church's forces, had become familiar: he slipped into a nearby village, stole a couple of horses, then returned to Heresh.

They rode in silence. This too, Ballas noticed, was typical. Except when Crask had been present and his nervous blathering had relentlessly filled Ballas's ears, the big man seemed to render mute those around him. No one made small talk. Not the barge-master, many weeks ago; not Heresh, riding with him now. Ballas approved of this. He disliked chatter.

For two days they rode onwards. In the pre-dawn dark, Ballas performed another robbery at another village. This time he stole a couple of whisky flagons. The following evening, after striking camp against a wind-blocking upthrust of rock and dining upon the meat of a moorland sheep, Ballas offered the whisky to Heresh.

She shook her head.

'It will help you,' he said.

'Help me?'

Ballas stared intently at her. Since her father's death, she had cried incessantly – while riding, while setting up camp – while sleeping, even. Her noise irritated Ballas. He understood it – yet it grated upon his nerves to hear the deep misery of another person.

'It'll soothe you.'

'I don't want it.'

'Go on.' Ballas held out the flagon. 'Take it.'

'I said that I don't—'

'Out of respect for your father, yes? You reckon you ought to suffer as much as you can, to prove how much you loved him?'

Heresh appeared momentarily surprised. 'Yes. That is the reason.'

'It's horseshit,' said Ballas. 'You're suffering enough. Drink.'

'My father is dead. I shan't do anything that will make me forget . . . I shan't drink myself into oblivion.'

'Oblivion?' Ballas laughed, loudly. 'Sweet grief, woman – you aren't a drinker, are you? This –' he wagged the bottle '– doesn't bring *oblivion*. It brings a sort of darkness – a sort of *twilight*. You'll won't forget your father's dead. But you won't ache as much.' He sighed. 'Beside, it'll clear your head. It doesn't always bring fog, you know. Sometimes . . . sometimes, when drunk, you stop worrying at things. You stop stirring things up. The water's left alone long enough to go clear. Then you understand a little better.'

'Understand? What is there to *understand*?'

'Just drink,' ordered Ballas.

Heresh complied. She took a recklessly deep gulp of whisky. Then gasped, as if she had swallowed a burning coal.

In silence, they took turns drinking from the flagon. After a while, Heresh was drunk. Her eyelids were heavy, her voice slurred slightly. There were different depths of drunkenness, Ballas knew. Heresh had reached the point where she hadn't lost control of her tongue – but spoke honestly instead.

'On the morrow,' she said, 'I will leave you.'

Ballas drew a breath.

'I am sick of this. I am tired of being wet and cold and outside on moorland. I am tired of sleeping under the stars. And, more than anything, I am tired of being hunted . . . No: I am tired of *running away*. I want to go somewhere safe, where I can simply hide. My nerves can't take much more of this.' She looked at Ballas. 'I have an uncle. He will take me in – my father promised it.'

'You said you'd go with me to Dayshadow.'

'I have changed my mind,' said Heresh.

'You made a promise.'

'I swore no oath.'

'You didn't have to,' replied Ballas. 'You begged to come with me. I said you could because—'

'—I'd be of some use to you?' She closed her eyes. 'I shan't be treated as . . . as a tool. As something to be used. Not any more.'

'Then I'll kill you.'

Heresh looked directly at Ballas. 'After all we have suffered . . . After Granthaven, after the sewers . . . After I saved your life, more or less, in the marshes—'

'After all that, aye.' Ballas shifted, slightly. 'You know where I'm going. You know I have to get to Dayshadow. Leave tomorrow, and by nightfall the Wardens might have you, and – believe me – you aren't strong enough to keep a secret. They'll make you tell them where I am. What my plan is. And that isn't a chance I'll take.'

Heresh laughed, disbelievingly. 'So I must travel to Belthirran with you?'

'Come with me to Dayshadow,' said Ballas. 'We'll find Athreos Laike. Then, once I've started up the mountains, you can go wherever you like. The Wardens won't follow me then – no matter what you tell them. And if they do – so what? I'll have a head start. They won't be fast enough to catch me.'

Heresh drank from the flagon. 'For a man who is so practical,' she said, after a pause, 'you can also be incredibly . . . fanciful.' She handed the flagon to Ballas. 'You are level-headed in many ways. When something must be done, you charge in and do it. There is no hesitation. No procrastination. As soon as the thought appears, the deed follows.'

'It keeps me alive.'

'It may also kill you.' Leaning back, Heresh stared up at the stars. 'You are going to climb a mountain – the most treacherous in Druine. Why? To find a place that probably doesn't exist. Need I repeat what you have heard already? Belthirran is a myth, a rumour. Yet you look upon it as a certainty.'

'What choice do I have? If I stay in Druine I shall die, sooner or later. The ports are blocked: I wouldn't be able to find a ship to take me to the East. So where remains? Where does the Church hold no sway?'

'You don't seek Belthirran out of necessity. You *crave* it in its own right. Every time you utter its name, a light flares in your eyes. In the marshes, when my father drugged you, you spoke its name, over and over. You were in a deep sleep, yet your lips moved, and you uttered "Belthirran . . . Belthirran". You *hunger* for it – and no man hungers for a last resort. He goes there grudgingly, and without excitement.' She lifted her chin. 'What will you do if you cross the mountains and find Belthirran does not exist?'

'It *is* there,' said Ballas. 'There *is* such a place as Belthirran.'

'What if you are mistaken?'

'I'm not,' replied Ballas firmly.

Heresh stopped talking. They drank more whisky. Heresh passed the flagon back to Ballas, then fell asleep. Ballas raised the flagon to the sky. The moonlight silhouetted the liquid remaining inside the vessel: the flagon was half full. This pleased Ballas.

He thought about Heresh's words and for a heartbeat he felt himself doubting, too. What proof did he have that there truly was a Land Beyond the Mountains? And that it would provide sanctuary?

These thoughts flickered briefly – then died.

Belthirran existed.

He could *feel* it. It was there, within him, as a quickening of the blood, a nervous tightening in his guts.

He supposed Heresh had been right, when she said that it was no longer a last resort for him – but something he craved. He had *dreamed* of Belthirran – that was true. Some might argue that he had confused the dream-place with Belthirran; and, having done so, was chasing a figment of his own imagination.

This wasn't so.

Ballas knew the difference between dreams and reality. He knew how quickly a dream's potency dwindled. A dream might alter the dreamer's mood – might make him, once awake feel joyful or melancholic. But this passed after a short time. The dreamer's waking mood would find its proper balance: a balance determined by the real world.

For Ballas, Belthirran's influence had not diminished. It had grown. In a vague way, he realised that it didn't matter if he died – as long as he died in Belthirran. Belthirran was no longer a mere refuge. But, in some inexplicable way, a *home*.

A thought struck Ballas. It was perverse – yet weirdly coherent. Maybe – he could scarcely bring himself to think it – maybe becoming the Church's enemy . . . maybe killing Carrande Black, a Servant of the Church . . . had actually been the greatest stroke of good fortune. It had led to much suffering. But, ultimately, it might turn out to be the source of the greatest comfort.

Life is strange, Ballas thought – for the first time in his life.

Chapter 17

As they neared Scarrendestin, the true Pilgrims
Grew fearful, for Asvirius trod
With urgency and feverishness, as if
The mountain were a prize to be grasped . . .

For several days, they rode northwards. The weather worsened. The frosts grew thicker; hail fell, a white fury pounding the land. Ballas and Heresh kept away from the roads. At night, they encamped by whatever sparse shelter they could find. They ate whatever the moors yielded: sheep, goat, fox . . .

On the fourth morning, they crested a rise.

In the far distance, through drizzle, Ballas saw something he mistook at first for a low bank of cloud: a huge slab of greyness, blocking the horizon.

Then he understood.

'The Garsbracks,' he murmured. 'The mountains . . .'

All day, he and Heresh held their northwards course. The mountains seemed to grow no closer. They hunkered countless miles away – a dull, impenetrable, unshifting vastness. Their stone was dark, its grey so deep as to be almost black. Only their lower slopes were visible. The clouds hung low, revealing little except the foothills. Dayshadow Town appeared only during the afternoon's dying hour. Built from the mountains' stone, the buildings could scarcely be discerned. They seemed to merge with the rocky heights, appearing only briefly as the light shifted. From far away, Dayshadow seemed just an extension of the mountain – and not a place in its own right.

Drawing closer, the mountains' size became more apparent. The air grew still. The north wind, which had whipped up the rain and hail and had gusted incessantly into Ballas's face, died back, blocked by the Garsbracks. And this motionless air permitted a quietness unlike any Ballas had experienced. The grass stalks did not rustle. The trees did not creak. No wind moaned through the limestone outcrops. There was nothing to distract the ear from the sounds of living creatures. With astonishing clarity, Ballas's mount's hooves crunched upon the frost. Each hoof-fall seemed a soft explosion. A stonechat's *chh-chh* cries were sudden, and shockingly loud. The moorland sheeps' bleats, always dull and flat, gained an unexpected full-bloodedness – for the first time, they sounded as if they came from some wholly living, wholly sentient creature.

The effect disturbed Ballas.

On any Church-approved maps, the Garsbracks were the northernmost edge of the world. Beyond them, nothing existed.

For an instant, Ballas felt this was true. The Garsbracks stood at the end of the world. As if the forces of creation had planted them there in order to say, *There is no more.*

'You are mad,' said Heresh, softly.

Ballas looked at her.

'Do you truly believe you can climb those mountains – and go beyond them?'

Ballas drew in his breath. Then nodded.

'Such an ambition would be understandable,' said Heresh, 'if you were drunk. But you are clear-headed now, aren't you? Yet still it persists.' She shook her head. 'You will die.'

Ballas shrugged.

'You will die,' Heresh repeated, 'for nothing greater than an illusion.'

As night fell, they entered Dayshadow.

They rode through the quiet streets, passing between the grey stone buildings. They needed to find out exactly where Athreos Laike lived. They followed a back alley towards a row of taverns. Ballas hung back in a side street while Heresh approached a man who had just stumbled drunkenly from a drinking house. He wore loose work clothes: a pair of leggings and a shirt, both stitched from a thick fabric. A thin layer of dust clung to these garments. He looked like he was in his fourth decade, no more. Yet he stooped as he walked, as if troubled by his back.

Heresh rode closer. 'Excuse me,' she said.

The man did not seem to hear.

'*Excuse me,*' repeated the red-haired woman.

He looked up, blinking. 'You speaking to me?' he asked.

Heresh nodded.

'I'm too tired to rut,' he said, shaking his head. 'I've been working all day, and I want to use my bed for sleeping – nothing else.' He gestured at the tavern from which he had emerged. 'There are others in there, though, a little stronger than me. Perhaps you'll have more luck with them.'

'What are you speaking of?' asked Heresh.

'You are a whore, yes?'

'Since when did whores ply their trade from horseback?'

The man laughed – then shrugged. 'You are right. I am sorry. But, as I said, I am tired – and as you can probably tell, I am also soused. It isn't my fault, though. The blame belongs to my profession. I start labouring at dawn; when dusk comes, and I down tools, I need ale to soothe my sore muscles. Alas, it soothes my mind too . . . soothes away every clear thought.'

'What is your trade?'

'I am a quarryman,' replied the drunk, 'like almost every man in Dayshadow.'

'Do you know Athreos Laike?'

'He pays my wages. Damn everything, he practically owns the Garsbracks – as far as any man does. He has the quarrying rights for this part of the range.'

'Does he live close by?'

'Walk towards the mountains,' said the quarryman, gesturing vaguely, 'and you will find his home near the foothills. You can scarcely miss it: it is the largest building in Dayshadow. A mansion, more or less.' He squinted curiously at Heresh. 'One of Druine's wealthiest men, it is said. One of the most tight-fisted, too. For all his gold, he lives frugally. It's reckoned there's no luxury in his big house. And he eats the same rations as you or I. The same oatcakes, the same vegetables – he could afford the finest. With his wealth, he could eat Glenshire beef for breakfast, flavoured with spices from the East. But he refuses. He eats like a bloody pauper. If you ask me,' he drew back his shoulders, 'it's obscene. To have so much money, and not spend it – it's like an eagle choosing to walk instead of soar.'

The quarryman staggered away.

Ballas and Heresh rode through the city, heading towards the northern edge. As they left the town proper, they came upon a large three-floored building built from Garsbrack stone. It was enclosed by a perimeter of railings. There was a garden – one that hadn't been tended for a long time. The lawn was a shaggy, weed-tangled wilderness. A lavender shrub bushed out luxuriantly, grown well beyond any useful size. The flower beds sported only winter-shrivelled thistles and nettles. Three or four armed men patrolled the garden. Squinting, Ballas saw they were neither Wardens nor Under-Wardens.

The big man hung back, in the shadows of the road.

Heresh glanced at him. Then she approached a set of gates.

'I wish to speak with Athreos Laike,' she said, dismounting.

One of the men strode over. 'The hour is late,' he said. 'Can't you come back tomorrow?'

'It is a matter of urgency.'

The man rubbed his jaw. 'Truly? He doesn't like having his rest interrupted . . .'

'Tell him that Jonas Elsefar has sent me.'

The man looked Heresh up and down. Then he disappeared into the house. A short while later he returned, walking beside a middle-aged man dressed entirely in black. He had a thin face, with small deep-set eyes. He was short and puny-looking: he had the spindly limbs and round shoulders of a petty bureaucrat.

'Are you Athreos Laike?' asked Heresh. There was a note of incredulity in her voice.

'I am his servant.' His voice too was thin. There was something limp about his entire form. As if some unseen force had sucked all energy, all passion from him. 'What is your business with my master?'

'We wish to talk with him,' said Heresh. 'We come upon Jonas Elsefar's recommendation.'

The servant frowned. 'That name isn't familiar to me.'

'It will be familiar to your master.'

'My master prefers solitude to company,' said the servant. 'Why do you come?'

Heresh licked her lips. 'It is a private matter.'

'There are many who would see my master on *private matters*. Then, once granted an audience, they bore him with trivia and complaints. Again – why must you see Athreos Laike?'

'Can you not take my word that . . . that . . .' Heresh faltered. She was not an accomplished liar, Ballas realised. She had flashes of guile, true. But a genuine liar could utter lies as easily as truths.

Suddenly Ballas sensed that lies would not be needed.

He heeled his mount forward a few steps. Emerging from the shadows, he said, 'It concerns Belthirran.'

The servant looked up. He started, surprised by the big man's presence. 'Who are you?'

'I travel with the woman,' said Ballas, keeping his hood drawn up. 'We must see Laike together.'

'You wish to *ridicule* him, do you?' asked the servant. 'He shall not be made sport of – I won't permit it.'

'I don't understand,' said Ballas, frowning.

'Oh, come now,' said the servant, folding his arms. 'Is it not the way of men to mock those of achievement? Those who have accomplished something of such magnitude that it can scarcely be believed? My master has climbed the Garsbracks. If he wished, he could have gone on to Belthirran. An incredible endeavour. A *unique* endeavour. Yet it amuses people. It coaxes laughter from the small-minded . . . from the weak, the inept, the unexceptional. Why? Envy, I suspect. And that urge, which often accompanies such green anger: the urge to destroy all that is great. To tear it down. To obliterate it. Or – if such things prove impossible – to deny its greatness. My master is a remarkable man. Yet people seek to reduce him by mockery. They wish to convince others that he is a nothingness. Moreover, they wish to convince *themselves*. For in their envy, they feel shame, too. Shame that *they* are not great. That they lack his abilities, his resolve. *He* is as eternal as the mountains. *They* are as temporary as rain.'

'I've travelled a long way,' muttered Ballas, 'and I don't intend to mock your master. If anything, I'm here to praise him.'

'Praise him?'

'And ask for his help.'

'Help in doing what?'

Ballas paused. 'I want to do as your master did. I want to find Belthirran.'

The servant laughed. '*You*?'

Ballas nodded.

'I do not wish to be cruel, but look at yourself. You are hardly a healthy specimen, are you? One must be in the very best physical condition to—'

Swinging down from his horse, Ballas moved close to the servant. He drew back his hood, exposing the horseshoe-shaped scar on his forehead.

The servant blanched. 'You . . .'

'Yes, me.' Ballas nodded.

The servant seemed unable to breathe. 'You are the . . .'

'For many weeks,' whispered Ballas, 'I've been hunted by the Church. They haven't caught me yet. That proves I'm determined, doesn't it? That, like your master, I have *resolve*.' He drew his hood back up. 'And trust me, little man: I've resolved to see Athreos Laike. I don't believe he'll refuse me.'

'Wait here,' said the servant, going back into the house.

Ballas looked beyond the house, to the Garsbracks. In the nocturnal gloom, the mountains were indistinct. They existed as a mere thickening of the darkness. For a moment, Ballas felt that they were, in some inexplicable way, the *origins* of the night's dark – that the darkness poured from them, and seeped across Druine: that, at every day's end, they birthed night.

The servant returned. He unlocked the gates, and gestured for Ballas to step through.

'My master has consented to see you,' he said, his voice quiet. He gestured to one of the armed men. The man strode over. 'Take care of their mounts,' instructed the servant. 'Ensure that they are stabled, watered and fed.'

Nodding, the man led the horses across the garden.

'You must demand nothing of my master,' said the servant, walking slowly towards the house. Ballas followed, Heresh at his side. 'In permitting you to meet him, he is being gracious. Remember that he is a man of wealth, power and achievement. He does not tolerate fools. That said, he seldom tolerates *visitors*, of any type. I suspect you intrigue him. After all –' he looked at Ballas '– you are now one of Druine's most famous men. Whatever fate you meet, you will be remembered. As a villain, of course. Like Scarlet Enfrique, the Convent Rapist. Or Madren Halter – the Cutpurse of the Northern Roads. Perhaps you will exist, in Druine's memory, for as long as Galdrin Sentricke . . .'

He led them up a flight of steps and into the house. They entered a large, echoing hallway. The servant lifted a lantern from a wall-hook. Then he took Ballas along a series of corridors.

The drunken quarryman had not exaggerated. Athreos Laike did not live in luxury. The floors were carpeted, the walls had hangings – yet both were plain, bearing not even the simplest designs, and were woven from inexpensive coarse wool. Their purpose was merely to conserve heat. Of which there was little, Ballas noticed. No woodsmoke-smell could be detected in the corridors – nothing to suggest that elsewhere in the building fires blazed. The house was dark, too. No candles burned in the wall niches. The servant's lantern provided the only light.

He took Ballas through a bare-walled room. An opened door led out on to a veranda. Upon the tiled expanse stood a figure in a pale robe. Its back was to Ballas. It seemed to be gazing at the mountains, several hundred yards away.

It was of slender build; white hair fell to its shoulders.

'Master,' said the servant, 'your guest is here.'

'Good.' A hoarse, grating voice – yet strangely rich. 'But he is not alone?'

'There is a woman with him.'

'Send her away. She does not interest me.' The figure shifted, slightly. 'She may wait in the banqueting hall. See that she is provided for.'

'As you wish, master.' The servant touched Heresh's forearm. 'Follow me, please.'

The red-haired woman looked at Ballas. The big man nodded.

Heresh allowed herself to be led away.

Ballas stared at Athreos Laike. The explorer's robe was stitched from linen. It could have provided little warmth. Yet Laike seemed untroubled by the cold night air.

'So,' he said, still gazing at the mountains. 'Jonas Elsefar sent you.'

'He said you'd help me find Belthirran.'

'Is he in good health?'

Ballas paused. 'He is well enough.' He thought it wise not to mention the way he had abandoned the quill-master. And the wolves he'd seen racing into the forest.

'A pity,' murmured Laike. 'I met him only once, when I delivered to him the account of my journey up the mountains. He was extremely talented: he made many copies, some quite elaborate, of my work. He also ensured that they would be distributed across Druine. He had contacts, you see . . . But he was also sour-hearted. He believed his affliction justified his wickedness. I trust he still bemoans his infirmity?'

'He does.'

'He believes fate has cursed him.'

'I reckon it can't be pleasant to be crippled.'

'It was his own doing,' said Laike, shrugging. 'Did he not tell you *how* he came to be crippled?'

'He was born that way.'

'That is his tale, yes,' said Laike. 'Perhaps now, after years of self-pity, he has even started believing it. But it is a lie, Ballas. And the truth is far less wholesome. To keep the story short: he strangled a whore, in a brothel at Tarminster. She was no ordinary whore, but one imported from the Distant East. Such girls are rare, and highly prized. The whore Elsefar killed was new to her trade. She hadn't acquired the false manners a whore requires. When Elsefar dropped his leggings, she laughed. In his rage, he murdered her. Of course, the whoremaster couldn't let this pass. He had invested heavily in the girl. To punish Elsefar, he thrust a blazing scalpel into his thigh muscles, just above the knee. This, I understand, was an apt retribution: in Eastern traditions, one who destroys another's possession – particularly his cattle – is injured in this way. Why, I do not know: the East is a mystery to me.' He laid his hands flat upon the balustrade at the veranda's edge. 'In his self-pity, Elsefar has forgotten he engineered his own ill fortune. A terrible man. The worst I have met.'

'I thought you and he were friends,' said Ballas.

'Associates, and that a long time ago – nothing more.'

'Then I'll tell you the truth: Elsefar's dead.'

'By your hand?'

'More or less.'

Footsteps sounded. The servant returned, bearing a wine flagon and two goblets. He filled the first goblet and carried it to Laike. The explorer accepted it wordlessly. The servant prepared Ballas a goblet. The big man took it, with a nod of acknowledgement. The servant left the room.

'Masharrian red,' said Laike, perching the goblet on the balustrade. 'One of the most expensive wines in Druine. This particular flagon is forty years old. It is worth more than most people's homes. I hope you enjoy it.'

Ballas sipped the wine. To him, it tasted no different from Keltuskan red. He dimly acknowledged that years of whisky-drinking had shrivelled his taste buds.

'I have simple tastes,' said Laike. 'I dislike ostentation. Yet sometimes one ought to be lavish, in order to mark a special occasion. It is not every day that I have such a visitor as yourself. A man of repute. Of notoriety. Tell me –' he lifted the goblet to his lips '– why do you seek Belthirran?'

'If I stay in Druine, I'll be killed.'

'True,' said Laike, nodding his agreement.

'And I can't sail to the East. The harbours are sealed off.'

'That is also true.'

'What choice do I have?'

'A man always has a choice,' said Laike. 'You could retreat to the more remote areas of Druine.'

'Someone would find me, sooner or later.' In his mind's eye, Ballas saw the Lectivin hunter, Nu'hkterin. And the shapeshifting crow-Wardens. 'The Church has means you can't even guess at.'

'Do you fear the Church?'

'I've no desire to die.'

'That is not what I asked,' replied Laike sharply. 'Do you *fear* them?'

The Wardens and Under-Wardens didn't frighten Ballas. But the Penance Oak, the slow death upon the branches . . .

'Yes,' he replied softly.

'Fear will drive a man to great lengths. If he is in a burning building, he will hurl himself from the highest window, knowing very well that the fall will kill him. To escape a fierce enemy upon a ship, he will leap over the side, into the sea – knowing very well that the waves will drown him. But these are spur-of-the-moment reactions. They spring from a terrible, terrified reflex. But your decision to find Belthirran – though possibly as suicidal as the reactions of those others – is one that you have had time to contemplate. Yet still you persist. Belthirran offers you more than a sanctuary, yes?'

'Yes.'

'A chance to, ah, be born again?'

Ballas shrugged. 'Put it how you will,' he muttered.

Laike sipped at his wine. 'How do you know Belthirran really exists?'

The question, coming from Laike, struck Ballas as odd. 'I can *feel* it,' said the big man awkwardly. 'And besides – *you*'ve been there, haven't you?'

Laike didn't reply. Not for many moments. He ran a fingertip around his goblet's rim. 'Beirun,' he said, loudly.

The servant appeared. 'Master?'

'In the lumber room there is a casket of unpolished teak. Bring it to me.'

The servant disappeared. He was gone for some time, during which Laike stared silently at the mountains. The explorer turned his head slightly, exposing part of his profile. Through the gloom, Ballas discerned a strong aquiline nose and a sleek jaw.

'Have you ever set foot on the Garsbracks?' Laike asked, turning his face away once more.

'Never.'

'There is music up on the mountains,' said Laike. 'In the streams, in the underground springs. In the winds blowing around the rocks. In the shaking rowan branches and the slow, steady crumbling of the soil. I suppose that I love the mountains. Certainly, I hold them in higher regard than any man – or woman – I have met. Yet . . . yet I am destroying them. My quarries are eating into the lower slopes. Once, this did not trouble me. I believed that a quarry team of gods, labouring for eternity, could not diminish the mountains. But now I am not so sure. Man is the most destructive creature. We are ambitious and persistent. If we wished, we could set the skies aflame . . . we could dry out the oceans, and hunt to extinction every creature on the face of the world.' He sighed. 'But if I were not quarrying the Garsbracks, someone else would be. The stone is the finest in existence. And the most profitable.'

Laike fell silent. He didn't speak again until Beirun returned.

'I have it, master,' said the servant, holding the casket.

'Open it.'

Beirun did so.

'Hand the contents to our guest.'

Beirun took out a piece of bone – a cow's shoulder blade, Ballas thought. Beirun passed it to the big man. A map was etched into the surface. At the lowermost edge, the Garsbracks were represented by overlapping triangles. Above it was the outline of a land mass. Frowning, Ballas presumed he had the object the wrong way up. He turned it so that the Garsbracks lay to the north. And to the south, Druine.

He drew in a breath sharply.

The outline did not match that of Druine. Druine was large, sprawling; this other land mass was a ragged triangle, about a twentieth of Druine's size.

Ballas looked up.

'You are surprised?' asked Laike, tilting his head. 'I heard you gasp.'

'What is—' began Ballas.

'Beirun, leave us,' said Laike. 'Tend to the needs of our guest's companion.'

'As you wish.' Beirun departed.

'What is this?' said Ballas.

Laike held up a silencing hand. He appeared to be listening to something. The mountain's music? wondered Ballas.

The answer was less intriguing.

'Beirun has left us,' Laike said. 'He is beyond earshot now. That is good. I trust him with my life. He is devoted to me. I could not wish for a more loyal servant. But he is a simple creature. He is not . . . not designed for complexities. His world doesn't extend beyond the washing of clothes, the preparing of food . . . I have no wish to disturb his peace of mind.' Laike took another sip of wine. 'In your hands, Anhaga Ballas, you hold proof of Belthirran's existence. Proof that there is such a place. Proof that it is populated.'

Ballas gazed at the map.

'I found it close to the Garsbracks' highest point,' explained Laike. 'I confess it amused me, for it lay upon the *Druine* side of the mountain tops. I believed – and still believe – that it had been dropped by a denizen of Belthirran who'd been attempting the reverse of my own endeavour. Just as I sought Belthirran, they sought . . . whatever lay beyond their side of the mountains.'

'Unless,' said Ballas, 'it was made by someone from Druine. Someone who'd already been into Belthirran.'

'Unlikely,' said Laike. 'The map isn't a practical object. The coast is outlined – nothing else is represented. How can one navigate from something so vague? Rather, I'd say the map is a ceremonial object. Or a keepsake, to remind the intrepid Belthirran explorer of home. Such things are not unknown. Besides, in Druine maps are quilled on to parchment – not etched into bone.'

Ballas turned the map over in his hands. He felt exhilarated. Then doubt touched him. 'You say this is proof of Belthirran . . .'

'Yes.'

'But there must be more. You've seen Belthirran, haven't you?'

Laike was silent again. Then he shook his head.

'What . . . ?' gasped Ballas.

'I have not seen the Land Beyond the Mountains.'

'Elsefar said you wrote an account of—'

'The account was false,' said Laike. 'When I was young, I hungered for fame. Of all hungers, it is the most ignominious. The most degrading. For it forces a man to act immorally. To cheat. To lie about himself. To slander others . . . My account of the ascent was true – to a point. I went as far up as is possible. But I never *crossed* the mountains. It cannot be done, Ballas.'

A hollow feeling filled Ballas's gut. 'Why not?'

'Fifty feet from the summit,' explained Laike, 'there is a sheer rock wall. It is as smooth as glass. There are no handholds. Nor is there any way around it. I walked the entire length of the Garsbracks. The wall continues without interruption. One might as well be a spider trying to climb out of porcelain cup.'

Ballas felt irritated. 'You should've used a grappling hook.'

'I did,' said Laike easily. 'But the prongs wouldn't grip. I tried, over and over again. Each time, it slithered back down. Do not imagine it wasn't frustrating. To climb thousands of feet, and be thwarted by the final fifty.' A tightness entered his voice. 'I had already found the map. I knew Belthirran existed. I knew I was on the brink of a great discovery . . .' He looked up into the sky, his gaze distant, as if observing the stars. 'It was agony – the highest suffering. And I was a proud man. Arrogant, too. When I returned, it wasn't enough to say that I had gone as far as any man could. No: I had to have achieved the impossible. I had to have found Belthirran. So I lied.' He breathed out, sighing deeply. 'When I penned my false account, I thought it would be believed. After all, its description of the ascent was accurate, and persuasive. Only the later details were fictitious.' He shook his head. 'The reverse happened. My account of Belthirran was deemed untrue. And people thought, If that is a lie, the rest of his story must be untrue. No one believed I'd ever climbed beyond the foothills.' He sighed. 'It serves me right, I suppose.'

'Why didn't you show anyone *this*?' said Ballas, indicating the bone map.

'What?' murmured Laike, not turning.

'The map,' said Ballas. 'That's proof, isn't it?'

'It would be decried as fake. They'd say I had made it myself. Strange, isn't it, that a suspicious man can condemn the greatest wonders as false?

In such people, there is a poverty of spirit. It garbs itself as many things often thought virtuous: pragmatism, reason, diligence. Yet it is none of those. It is merely the voice of a decrepit soul. When I was younger . . . when I climbed, I was an extraordinary man. I say so not out of arrogance – no – but from honesty. I was not exceptionally strong. Nor exceptionally sharp-minded. Rather, my uniqueness lay in something usually considered a vice: I was reckless. To scale the Garsbracks, I took risks beyond imagination. Nothing perturbed me. The part of the mind that preaches caution – the part that, in most people, cries out strongly – was mute in me. The gullies, chasms, steep-sided rocks – none of those things unnerved me. Perhaps a man can only accommodate a limited number of urges. And my most powerful urge – for glory – drove out all others. I feared less than any other man. And *that* was why I reached – almost – the Garsbracks' summit.' He shifted, slightly. 'Tell me, Anhaga Ballas, does fear strike you easily?'

'No,' replied Ballas, truthfully.

'Does it strike you *at all*?'

'Sometimes.'

'That is natural,' replied Laike. 'But to have come so far, it is clear that fear never *debilitates* you. That is a good sign, I think. What is your profession?'

'I haven't got one.'

'No?'

'I've lived as a vagrant for . . . for a long time.'

'And before that?'

Ballas drew a breath. 'I was a soldier.' The words fell strangely from his lips. His voice sounded oddly distant to himself. As if *he* were not speaking, but someone else – someone he half-knew, but had not encountered in many years.

'Were you a *good* soldier?'

'I fought well enough,' shrugged the big man.

'Ah – so you saw action, then?'

Ballas licked his lips. 'Aye. Against Cal'Briden.'

This delighted Athreos Laike. He slapped his hand down upon the balustrade. 'Cal'Briden: the Rebel Merchant. The Blight-Upon-Druine. The man who, with his armies, sought to wrest control of Druine from the Pilgrim Church. In this, I scent an irony.'

'I didn't fight to help the Church,' grunted Ballas.

'No?'

'I fought because my wages depended on it.'

'You bore no personal grudge against Cal'Briden?'

'I disliked him.'

'Why?'

'He was of brigand stock,' replied Ballas uneasily. 'He was a raider. Such men are a pestilence.'

'When first Cal'Briden appeared,' said Laike, 'I was filled with optimism. Here was a man who would end the Church's rule. And after that, utopia would blossom. The Church's cruelties and injustices would be banished. In its stead, a new society would be installed. There would be peace, poverty would vanish . . . I was mistaken, of course. You are right, Ballas. Cal'Briden was a wicked man. He would have governed Druine badly. Worse, perhaps, than the Masters. Some say he enjoyed cruelty. For certain, he could scarcely control his soldiers. Or rather, he was undiscriminatingly permissive: he allowed them to commit all sorts of atrocities . . . I understand that his death was unpleasant. His throat was slit, as if he were a pig – in his own fortress, as well.'

'So they reckon. But I'm not here to speak of the past. My *future* concerns me – nothing else. Will you help me find Belthirran?'

'I have told you,' said Laike, 'that such a thing is impossible. Do you reckon I'm a liar?'

'Maybe you're mistaken. Or maybe you weren't reckless enough.'

Laike laughed softly. 'The present question is whether I am reckless enough *now*, is it not? Reckless enough to help you. After all, if I assist the sinner, I will make myself unpopular with the Church. Like you, I will face death.' He took a drink of wine. 'I must think upon this matter. If you wish, you may spend the night here. You will be fed. And Beirun will fill a bath for you. You desperately need a wash – you stink like a pig, my friend. If the Wardens wish to catch you, they need merely follow their noses.'

'Can I trust you?' asked Ballas flatly. 'What is to say you won't summon the Wardens?'

'If I wished to,' said Laike, 'they would be here by now.'

There was logic in the explorer's words.

'Enjoy a little ease,' said Laike. 'The past weeks must have been unpleasant for you. And, yes – you may take the wine. Finish it off. If you want more, ask Beirun and it will be brought.'

The servant took Ballas to a bathing chamber. A deep rectangular bath was set in the middle of the floor. It was full to the brim. Rose petals floated upon the surface, patches of pink amid the pale upswirls of steam.

'Athreos Laike accepts few guests,' explained the servant. 'But when he does, he treats them well.'

'Better,' said Ballas, 'than he does himself.'

'My master prefers a simple existence,' replied the servant. 'He rarely uses this chamber. When he does, the water is always cold spring-water, brought fresh from the mountains.'

'Your master is perverse,' grunted Ballas.

'He is *unusual*, I grant you.'

'To have such wealth—'

'And favour asceticism?' The servant smiled. 'Forgive me. But I have heard such arguments often before. You must understand: my master's life has been built largely upon self-discipline. He treats himself harshly. But it is a harshness that gratifies him. And it has good consequences. How old would you say he was?'

'Difficult to tell,' said Ballas. 'He didn't show me his face.' He paused, frowning. 'I'm being hunted by the Church. Everyone in Druine is entitled to kill me. Yet he didn't even turn and look at me. Wasn't he curious?'

The servant put a towel at the bath's edge. 'I am certain he has his reasons. My master never acts without purpose. As for his age: he is in his seventieth year. Yet he is as strong, as nimble, as an adolescent.'

'He isn't present,' said Ballas. 'You needn't flatter him.'

'Oh, but it is the truth. Perhaps you will find it hard to appreciate, but if you live cleanly, your body's natural decay will be greatly slowed.'

Pulling off his shirt, Ballas glanced at his ale gut. It drooped over his belt – though it wasn't as pronounced as it had been several months ago . . . before the Church began pursuing him. He tossed his shirt on to the bathside. Then he lowered his breeches. 'Bring me more wine,' he said, stepping out of the garment. He drained the flagon of Masharrian red. 'This one's dead.'

'As you wish,' said the servant, leaving the bathing-chamber.

Ballas lowered himself into the pool. He slid slowly, luxuriously, into the hot water. It was the most pleasant sensation he'd had for years. Closing his eyes, he felt steam ghosting against his face.

'Laike,' he murmured, 'you're an arse. What man would trade this for freezing spring-water?'

He ducked his head below the surface. Surfacing, he rubbed his face. Then he sagged back against the side of the bath.

After a while, the servant returned.

'Masharrian red,' he said, setting a flagon on the edge of the bath. 'You appeared to enjoy the last one.'

'It will do,' said Ballas, taking the vessel. He swigged a generous mouthful.

'My master says he will help you.'

Ballas looked up.

'He has agreed to assist you in finding Belthirran,' the servant elaborated. 'All will be explained tomorrow. In the meantime, relax. Once you have bathed, go to the banqueting hall. Food will be waiting.'

Ballas remained in the bath a long time. He tried to recall the last time he'd bathed in hot water. As a vagrant, he had washed – when he had washed at all – in rivers, streams, puddles. He was unaccustomed to such luxury. Such *comfort*. And it pleased him. Even the floating rose petals – though an effeminate, foppish touch – were gratifying in their way.

He left the bathing chamber only when the second flagon of Masharrian red was empty.

He found Heresh in the banqueting hall. She was seated alone at a long oaken table. Before her rested a plate of potatoes, venison and vegetables, soaked in rich gravy.

Warm, comfortable, Ballas grinned. 'This is the way to live, eh? Far better than hunkering out on the moors.' A place had been set for the big man. A platter of cold meats was laid out. He sat down. 'I doubt whether Belthirran could match this place.'

'The servant says you intrigue Laike. He thinks he sees a little of himself in you.'

'I doubt it,' said Ballas. 'He takes cold baths. He scarcely touches his wine. I dare say he eats little except vegetables. He's more like a priest I once knew . . .'

'There are more aspects to a man's character,' said Heresh, 'than his vices.'

'True. But none as dear to him.' He sprinkled salt upon the beef. The white crystals glittered.

Ballas ate contentedly.

'You seem in good spirits,' observed Heresh.

'I've a bellyful of wine,' he said, 'and I'm eating like a Master. Of course I'm happy.'

'I take it that Laike has agreed to help you?'

Ballas nodded.

Heresh tucked a stray lock of hair behind her ear. 'He believes Belthirran exists?'

'He *knows* it does.'

'And that you can find a way there?'

Ballas shook his head. 'He reckons it's beyond my grasp. Or anyone's.'

'Yet still he helps you?'

'Yes.'

'Absurd,' said the red-haired woman.

'And what are you going to do?'

'Laike is making arrangements for me to travel to my uncle's home,' said Heresh, quietly. 'He has assured me a safe journey.'

'He is a wealthy man,' said Ballas, taking a slice of beef. 'He'll be able to bribe you a passage across Druine.'

After several more flagons of wine, and much food – the servant brought a roasted pheasant and a selection of cheeses that Ballas ate greedily – Ballas allowed the servant to lead him to a frugal yet comfortable bedchamber. Between clean sheets, Ballas slept soundly. His slumber was deep, untroubled. When he woke, he felt utterly refreshed.

He went to the banqueting hall.

The servant brought him a large breakfast. With the unselfconscious urgency of a pig at a trough, Ballas gorged himself upon a countryman's breakfast: bacon, eggs, sausages, fried bread, mushrooms – all sprinkled with pepper and salt. He had not eaten such a breakfast in a long time. When he had cleared the plate, a second was brought, heaped high with the same food once more.

'My master believes you'll need to keep your strength up,' explained the servant Beirun, 'if you are to climb the Garsbracks.'

'Where is Laike?' asked Ballas, around a mouthful of egg – a trickle of yolk seeped on to his chin.

'He has matters to attend to. And he has elected to breakfast alone this morning . . .'

'On what? Nuts, berries – a field mouse's rations?'

'He is eating as you eat,' replied Beirun.

Ballas snorted. 'The scents of such grub –' Ballas waved an eating dagger over the plate '– must have overwhelmed him. Who can resist fried pig meat? Laike may be an ascetic. But he's still human.'

Ballas continued eating. He could see the Garsbracks through the window. In the dawn-fresh light, he could make out quarrymen toiling on the lower slopes. They were breaking the rocks with sledgehammers and chisels – laborious, back-breaking work. He thought of the Garsbracks' summit.

Of the rock face that, according to Laike, made it impossible to reach Belthirran.

The old man exaggerates, thought Ballas. He has already admitted he is prone to half-truths. And outright lies. Perhaps, up on the mountain, he was tired and disheartened – and the rock face only *seemed* unclimbable. Maybe he had lost his nerve . . .

The servant returned. After asking Ballas whether he had eaten his fill, he led him to a large room. On the floor lay a selection of mountain climbers' equipment. Ice axes, tough-soled leather boots, fur jackets and legging covers, rucksacks, ropes . . . The instruments of altitude survival. Athreos Laike kneeled among them, his back to Ballas. He folded blankets into a rucksack.

'He is here, master,' said the servant.

'I know, I know,' replied Laike softly. 'You are dismissed, Beirun.'

The servant left.

'I trust you enjoyed your breakfast?' asked the old explorer.

'I'm glutted,' replied Ballas. 'The best morning-meal I've had in years.'

'A mile to the east,' said Laike, 'there is a farm, where every creature thrives. They eat well, they forage, they breathe clean air. They grow strong; their taste is a thousand times finer than that of most animals that meet the table. Tell me: have you enjoyed the wine I served?'

'Of course.'

'And it rendered you drunk?'

'Drunk enough,' agreed Ballas.

'Good,' said Laike. 'It is essential that, before any long journey, a man must purge himself of his lusts. Come nightfall, we shall be deprived of all comfort. We might as well indulge ourselves while we can, yes?'

'We?' Ballas stared hard at Laike. The explorer fingered an ice pick: the point was savagely sharp.

'Yes,' said Laike, nodding, '*we*. I have decided to travel with you.'

It took Ballas a moment to absorb this. 'I didn't come here to find a travelling companion,' he said.

'I did not think so,' replied Laike. 'You wanted a map?'

'Yes.'

'Then you know nothing of the Garsbracks. The mountains cannot be transcribed on to parchment. Not with any precision. Why not just vaguely write, "Go up" – and leave the rest blank? That would be as useful as any elaborate chart. The route is treacherous. More than that, it is *intricate*. One might as well try to tabulate the hairs on a lion's back as attempt to record the way up the mountains.'

'What are you talking about?' Ballas said dismissively.

'All in good time,' said Laike. 'But do not be concerned. I will act as your guide.'

Ballas looked at Laike's white hair, the leanness of his body, and heard the hoarseness of his voice. 'You are too old to be climbing mountains,' the big man said bluntly.

'My faculties are undimmed.'

'Your servant said you think clean living will keep you young—'

Suddenly, Laike hurled the ice pick across the room. The movement was fluid, natural: the pick stabbed into a wall beam, and hung there, vibrating.

Ballas blinked.

'My faculties are undimmed,' Laike repeated. 'I am still strong. Still alert. I am a rich man – yet I have lived like one who, each day, must beat hunger.'

Then Laike did something odd. Something that, after the thrown ice pick, was unexpected. He reached for a blanket, rolled up on the floor. And missed the object, his fingertips pattering on the floorboards. He reached again. Again, he missed. Only on the third attempt did he succeed. He bundled the blanket into the rucksack. There was something self-conscious about his movements. Something simultaneously hurried yet deliberate.

Grasping his shoulder, Ballas twisted the explorer around. For the first time, Laike's face became visible. Once more Ballas saw the aquiline nose and sleek jaw. Now, though, he saw something else.

Athreos Laike's eyes twitched in their sockets. The blue-grey irises, the sight-absorbing pupils . . . They flickered this way and that, oblivious to the world of light.

Laike was blind.

The explorer sighed. 'My secret is out, yes?'

Ballas did not reply.

'Do not be perturbed,' said Laike. 'Look upon the ice-pick. Look where it has lodged.'

'You struck a beam. A fluke, rather than skill. Once I saw a crossbow bolt, loosed by accident, knock a starling from the air—'

'I will guide you,' interrupted Laike. 'I will take you up the Garsbracks.'

Ballas snorted – a cold, cruel laugh of derision. 'You cannot see,' he said. 'I dare say you couldn't guide your piss into a hole . . .'

'I love the mountains,' said Laike. 'I love them more than I love myself.'

'So what?'

'When I climbed the Garsbracks and reached the impassable point, I had no choice but to come back down. By then, winter had set in. Snow lay knee-deep – the purest snow I have ever seen. And in those heaped crystals lay my blindness.' Laike became very still. 'An icy winter sun shone. The snow reflected its light, dazzling me. I squinted, I stepped cautiously – yet I did not cover my eyes. Gradually, the light glared-out something within me . . . some subtle mechanism of my eye. I did not realise it was happening. I saw only a gathering darkness. I rested, expecting it to pass. But . . .

'It did not pass.

'I had been stricken with snow-blindness. My sight had been killed by second-hand light. I could see *nothing*. The brightest day was night. I was only halfway down the Garsbracks, and I was unable to see where my feet fell . . .'

'Yet you made your way down,' said Ballas, quietly.

Laike nodded. 'I made my way down,' he said, 'by the same means I will make my way back up. I have a strong memory. I can recall every crease, tuck and fissure in the mountains. Every false path, every dead trail. For thirty years, I have seen *nothing* – nothing except my final, near-fatal route up the mountains. It lingers here –' he tapped the side of his head '– as vividly now as when I first saw it. It is surprising what one can recall when a true effort is made. Upon the Garsbracks, my life depended upon it. I had to draw out in my mind every step I had taken. While climbing, I hadn't attempted to remember everything. Nonetheless, it had soaked in. That was fortunate. By thinking hard – by groping deep into my memory – I was able to retrace my steps.

'And I can do it now.

'Since the Garsbracks, I have lived in blackness. The only light comes from my imagination – and from my memory. Every day, I retrace my steps up the mountain. I have forgotten scarcely one thing. I still see it, Ballas: and it is *all* I see.'

Ballas stared incredulously at Laike. 'I won't be guided by a blind man . . . by a blind, *old* man.'

'My abilities are undiminished,' began Laike. 'I am still capable—'

'You are capable of *nothing* – except getting me lost.'

'That is not true!' snapped Laike, leaping to his feet. 'And you must stop speaking as if you have a choice. For who else will lead you up the Garsbracks? Do you suppose there are others like me, who have reached the summit? And do you imagine they would help *you*? Remember what you are, Anhaga Ballas. No one will assist you . . . no one except me.'

For this first time, Ballas grew curious. 'Yes,' he said, 'perhaps that is so. And it puzzles me . . .'

'Oh?'

'*Why* are you helping me?'

Laike opened his mouth – then shrugged. 'I shall not deceive you. I miss the mountains. For a long time, I've wished to climb once again . . . to struggle towards the top. But who would accompany me?'

'You are rich,' said Ballas. 'You could pay someone to go with you.'

Laike shook his head. 'No one is interested. I've asked a few climbers, but they always refuse. They believe the Garsbracks are too dangerous. And they don't wish to make things more difficult, by guiding a blind man – a blind, old man, as you say – up the slopes. I have offered great sums in exchange for help. But always I receive the same reply: *money is no use to a dead man*.' He interlaced his fingers. 'I would go alone, but the mountains have changed. Certain ledges will have crumbled. Some scree slopes will have slipped, leaving everything unfamiliar. To a man of sight, such things are but small hazards. But to me? For all their insignificance, they might still prove fatal.'

Ballas gazed at the ice pick, hanging from the wall beam. He touched fingertips to the cold metal. A thought struck him. What would Laike do, once they reached the summit? Once they came up against the impassable rock wall?

And, knowing such a barrier existed, why did he wish to climb at all?

Ballas shook these questions away. Such matters were irrelevant. He had found himself a guide – that was all that mattered.

Laike had spoken correctly. There was no one else who would lead him up the mountains. No one with the knowledge. Or the inclination.

Ballas licked his lips. It was farcical, he thought: a sightless man acting as a mountain guide. Still Ballas had no choice but to accept his offer.

'When do we leave?' he asked.

'Nightfall,' replied Laike. 'Better we go unseen, through darkness.' Grinning, the explorer slapped a palm down on the floor. 'At this hour, tomorrow we shall be up there.' He gestured through a window towards the mountains. 'Is it not the finest feeling? And is it not the greatest ritual –' he swept a hand out over the climbing equipment '– to gather what one needs for a long journey? Does it not inflame the blood? It has been many years since I last experienced such sensations. I had forgotten how sweet they are.'

The day passed slowly. Ballas sat in his sleeping room, drinking from a wine flagon and gazing at the mountains. He felt nervous, restless. An edgy desire to start climbing immediately gripped him. He feared that, at any moment, Wardens would raid Laike's home. Or Nu'hkterin would appear, the curve-bladed dagger in his hand.

Yet everything remained quiet.

Ballas's thoughts drifted. He contemplated the climb, sensing there would be hardships. But for many years, discomfort had been his constant companion. No matter how extreme the difficulties were, he would cope.

He thought of Belthirran, over and over again. The dream-fragment glowed in his mind: the lush fields, grazing cattle, distant cook-fire smoke . . . They beckoned him. The bone map Laike had found provided much encouragement. It signified a single thing: *Belthirran existed*. Ballas knew that if he grew doubtful, he would only need to think of the map.

As evening approached, the servant took Ballas to the banqueting hall. Laike and Heresh were present, seated at the long table. Food was served: a platter of cooked meats, sprinkled with herbs and glistening in gravy and grease. Ballas sat down and filled his goblet from a fresh wine flagon. He ate greedily, knowing he'd be deprived of such treats for a long time. Laike also seemed intent on consuming as much as possible – but if Ballas gorged himself in a bestial fashion, the explorer took his food methodically, passionlessly, as if it were a medicine. Heresh scarcely touched her food. She seemed preoccupied with the wine, drinking goblet after goblet. Ballas noticed that she smelled different. Her faint, feminine scent had taken on the tang of a tavern whore. She had been drinking throughout the day, Ballas realised. Now, wine-laced sweat seeped from her pores.

No one spoke.

The servant scuttled back and forth, bringing more food and drink. Eventually, when the meal was almost over, he lingered beside the table. There was something cautious, and expectant, about his manner. Like a dog expecting scraps.

Laike became still. Setting down his eating dagger, he turned his blind eyes towards the servant. 'Something troubles you, Beirun?'

The servant wrung his hands. 'I wish only to discuss practical matters.'

'Then do so.'

'Very well,' said the servant uncomfortably. 'I am merely wondering how long you will be absent.'

'However long it takes.'

Beirun grimaced. 'However long *what* takes? I see no purpose in going up the mountain. It is absurd. I truly cannot—'

'Do not concern yourself,' said Laike. 'Please: rest easy. You have served me for many years. You have come to understand my nature. Indeed, can you not predict my needs? Do you not sometimes execute an order before it is even given? You must know, therefore, that I never act rashly. Is that not true, Beirun?'

'It is, master,' conceded the servant. 'But you have never done anything like this before.'

'Are you concerned for my welfare?'

'No, master, for I know such a preoccupation would offend you.'

'Then . . . ?'

'I am worried for the quarry. What will become of it while you are away?'

Laike laughed. 'My agents will tend to it, of course.'

'And you trust them?'

'Naturally. I appointed them myself. I wouldn't surround myself with rogues. And I pay them enough to ensure their honesty.'

'Men are greedy,' murmured the servant. 'And what will become of here?' A gesture encompassed Laike's home. 'What should *I* do?'

'Perform your duties as normal,' said Laike blandly. 'Things will be a little easier for you. You will have no need to feed me, and—'

'What if you do not return?' interrupted Beirun. 'What . . . what if you suffer some mishap?'

'This talk is starting to bore me,' said Laike, irritated. 'I do not wish to approach the mountains with your questions ringing in my ears. I shan't let your fretfulness pollute everything.'

'Pollute, master?'

Laike slammed his hand flat on the table. 'I wish to enjoy the mountains. From start to finish, the experience must be *pure*. On the Garsbracks, the spring-water is unimaginably fresh. The air is so clean it *glitters*. The light is uncorrupted, it gleams like a spark in the creator-god's eye. The only thing that can befoul such a place is *Man*. Do you understand? So, I must leave all such thoughts behind. The quarry, my home, my commitments – the bleak trappings of my species . . . they must vanish from my mind. Otherwise, all will be tainted. Now: begone, Beirun. If you are needed, you will be summoned.'

The explorer turned the eating dagger over in his fingers – as if contemplating some violent action.

'Forgive me, master,' said the servant, leaving.

Laike tapped the knife-tip on the table.

The evening lengthened. Leaving Heresh in the hall, Ballas returned to his sleeping-room. Travelling clothes had been laid upon his pallet-bed. Removing his present garb – the sweat-fouled, blood-specked tunic and leggings – he dressed in his new attire. There was a silken vest, and underbreeches of the same material. These would retain his body heat while he climbed through the mountains' cold. Then there was a jumper and a pair of trousers, both of black wool. Ballas pulled them on. They fitted him perfectly. Next there was a pair of boots. They were large, heavy, fashioned from thick leather. These were slightly too tight. In time, though, they would stretch.

Ballas went looking for Athreos Laike. The old explorer was on the veranda, his posture identical to that during their first meeting. Ballas moved alongside him. It was a clear night: a half-moon shone, stars sparkled. Yet it seemed that the Garsbracks absorbed much of their light. Ballas remembered his earlier impression of the mountains. He had thought them the source of darkness. Now he realised this was untrue. They didn't birth darkness. They swallowed light. They drew the moon's quicksilver glow on to their slopes and, like rainwater, it trickled away into the gullies and fissures.

'Can you hear the silence?' asked Laike.

Ballas did not reply. It seemed an absurd question.

'All day,' continued the explorer, 'the quarrymen labour within the foothills. The sky shakes with their terrible, destructive noise: sledgehammers falling, chisels splitting rock . . .' He shook his head. 'I have lived badly. I have been destroying a beautiful thing. My crime is that of the rapist, the murderer . . .'

'Then why did you do it?'

Laike lowered his head. 'Why did I purchase the quarrying rights?'

'Yes.'

'I am blind – what trade can I hold?' He turned sharply to Ballas. 'I wish not to speak as Elsefar often spoke. I do not pity myself. I lost my sight through carelessness – and that is that.' He sighed. 'When I returned from the Garsbracks, I wished to stay close to the mountains. At the time, the quarrying rights were being sold off – not for the entire range, you understand. No. One could purchase only a small section of the lower slopes. With what money I had, I obtained an area about twenty paces square, a half-mile east from here. I was extremely fortunate: for within this area there was an underground stream, upon the bed of which nestled a cluster of small but exquisite diamonds. I sold them, and with the money bought more quarrying rights. Once you have money, it is easy to make more. My wealth grew. As did my stake in the mountains. Now, I own a five-mile stretch of the Garsbracks. It has made me very rich.' He shrugged. 'As I said, I am near to the mountains – which was what I wanted. And I have no need to live in an alms-house.

'That is why I break apart the Garsbracks. That is why I profane one of Druine's few wonders.'

Out of the darkness came a clattering of cartwheels. The noise was far off but clear. Laike jumped, startled. Then he tilted his head, listening.

'Find Heresh,' he said, 'and bring her here. Oh – and when you have done so, remain indoors. It is better if you are not seen.'

Ballas moved to the balustrade. A wooden cart rattled closer along a lane. Squinting, he made out a single figure on the driving bench.

'Who is it?' he asked.

'He will ensure Heresh arrives safely at her uncle's home. He is a good man – loyal, strong, sharp-witted. But he has his limits. If he were to discover that you and I were acquainted, and Heresh was your travelling companion . . . He would refuse to serve me. As would any man. Druine bristles with your enemies, Ballas. But soon such things will not matter.'

Ballas found Heresh in her sleeping-room. She was seated on her pallet-bed, drowsing.

'Wake up,' said Ballas, curtly.

She twitched, then opened her eyes. The whites were bloodshot, the irises unfocused. 'What do you want?'

'You are leaving.'

Getting to her feet, Heresh moved to a table in the corner. Upon it rested a bowl of water. She rinsed her face, then towelled it dry.

'So, we are to say farewell.' Her tone was bitter. 'Our parting shall not be tearful. You are a pestilence, Anhaga Ballas. You bring nothing but misery. Because of you, my father is dead. And I am condemned to a life of fear. Of watchfulness. Whenever I hear a football, I shall imagine it to be a Warden's. Whenever I see birds break clear of a forest-top, I will believe they've been frightened by the Lectivin. In every patch of darkness I'll sense a threat . . .' Grimacing, she tossed the towel on to the bed. 'You have saved my life, many times. And my father's. But only from dangers *you* have conjured. I cannot forgive you.'

'I don't *want* forgiveness,' said Ballas, darkly.

'No?'

'There's a cart waiting for you. Get on it and go – *that* is what I want. Then I can start up the Garsbracks.'

'You are vile,' said Heresh. She gazed intently at him. She no longer seemed unfocused. Sharp clarity lit her eyes. 'Let me ask you something. You still believe Belthirran exists, yes?'

'It exists,' nodded Ballas. 'Laike has shown me proof, so if you reckon—'

'And is it populated?'

'Yes.'

'If you get to Belthirran,' said Heresh, 'how do you know that the people will accept you? You'll be an outsider. A man from beyond the mountains.'

'They won't know where I'm from. I won't tell them.'

Heresh laughed – a harsh, shrill, harpyish sound. 'You idiot,' she said. 'Sweet grief – for the first time in days, something has amused me. What of your accent, Ballas? Do you suppose the Hearthfall burr is heard often in Belthirran?'

'Doesn't matter,' replied the big man. 'I'll pass myself off as a mute. Until I've learned a Belthirran accent. It won't be hard.'

She shook her head sardonically. 'You imagine Belthirran to be a marvellous place. Yet anywhere that welcomes *you* can't be a paradise. For you are a taint, an evil stain. You will not belong there. It will be their duty to keep you out. Any land that accepts you must, by definition, be awful. You belong in a midden, Ballas. You are a stinking wretch, suitable only for squalor, decay, bloodshed.'

'At least the Masters won't be able to find me.'

'Oh – the Masters are the only people you've offended? Is that what you are saying?'

Ballas didn't understand. 'You are drunk,' he said.

Heresh nodded sharply. 'What of it? A truth is true no matter who utters it. Wherever you go, there is upset. You anger people. You lie, steal, cheat. It is in your nature. You can't escape it. Leave Druine if you wish. But soon, you'll be hanted in Belthirran. Someone will seek to destroy you. You'll never find peace.'

Ballas's anger flared. 'What do you know of the world?'

Heresh flinched, surprised.

'What do you know, eh?' repeated Ballas. 'You've spent your life in a bloody marsh! What have you *seen*? What have you *done*? Piss-all, woman. Nothing except kill eels.'

Heresh drew a breath. 'I hate you, Anhaga Ballas. But I wish you luck.'

Her words surprised him. 'Bad luck, I suppose?'

'No. I hope that you find Belthirran. And that it does turn out to be a paradise. And the people count you as one of their own. And you live a long, happy life. And the Belthirran whores are the finest in the world. And the ale is cheap but pleasant upon the tongue.'

Ballas frowned. 'I don't understand.'

'I have learned that all life is a joke.' Heresh closed her eyes, as if the words pained her. 'You are a wicked man. Yet you thrive. Many have tried to kill you – yet you have escaped them all. My father, however, died. He was fair-hearted, . . . But he died. And it was a painful death. There is no logic to this. No sense. No reason. I can only assume everything is just a cosmic joke. And to be happy, you must choose whether to laugh or weep. The humour is in poor taste – but it is humour nonetheless.' Her eyes opened. 'I have chosen to laugh. Every savage irony, every harsh twist of fate, will fill me with mirth.'

There was a change in Heresh. Something deep, something brutal. The wine hadn't created it, thought Ballas. But it had given it strength.

'My father was a good man. He was not brave, I admit that much.

When he acted courageously, it was always a pretence . . .' She hesitated, gazing at Ballas. Some involuntary expression must have touched his face. Heresh smiled, knowingly. 'Yes, you are right, Ballas: my father did not merely lack bravery: he was a coward. When I was a young girl, I admired him, believing he had a lion's heart. But later, when I grew up, I began to understand that he had deceived me. This did not stop me loving him, though. Why should I turn away from him for lying, when the lies were born out of devotion? Even though we lived way out in the marshes of Keltherimyn, we were still treated badly by almost everyone who knew anything about us . . . about my father's old profession. He wanted me to believe he could protect me, no matter what happened. So he had to make believe he was strong and capable. But once I realised the truth about him, I found that *I* had to protect *him*. Not from other people, but from myself. Because if he knew I had seen through his ruse, he would have been heartbroken. It would have destroyed him.' She sighed, wearily. 'If you reach Belthirran, fate will have created another joke. The worst of us, finding the best of places. I shall laugh so fiercely that I'll spit blood. Good luck, Ballas. I hope you bring me such dark joys.'

Snatching up her cape, Heresh moved to leave.

Ballas caught her by the arm. 'I reckon I was wrong. There's a lot of your father about you.'

Heresh jerked her arm free. 'What are you talking about?'

'You're both cowards. But at least your father didn't choose it for himself.'

Heresh blinked, puzzled.

'Life isn't a joke. Your father was brave enough to treat it seriously. He was frightened, much of the time. But he made an effort. You, though? You're going to pretend nothing's important. Nothing matters. It isn't so – and you know it. But pretend that it is, and you have an excuse. An excuse for weakness. For turning away. Crask didn't ever do that.'

Heresh's expression tightened. 'You have no right to utter my father's name. How dare you speak of him, you bastard! He was a thousand times better a man than you!'

'Sure. But he's dead, and I'm not. Now laugh, will you – it's the kind of joke you reckon you like, isn't it?'

Heresh spat in Ballas's face. The warm liquid struck him on his cheek, then trickled down to his jaw. Slowly, he wiped it away.

'I hope you rot,' said Heresh, pushing past him to leave the room.

'One day I will,' said Ballas, half to himself. 'But not yet.'

* * *

For a short while, Ballas lingered in the sleeping-room, supping the dregs from a wine flagon left upon a table.

When he returned to the veranda, he saw a cart moving away along the lane.

'She has gone,' said Athreos Laike.

'Good,' grunted Ballas.

'I sense there is little love lost between you.'

'She's had her uses,' said Ballas. 'But, like those of any woman, they were few.'

Turning away from the balustrade, Laike said, 'Gather your things. The hour for leaving is upon us.'

In his sleeping-room, Ballas put on his rucksack. It was stitched from ox leather, waterproofed with animal fat. It was heavy, stuffed with provisions – a bland mix of dried meats and vegetables – and his fur clothing, which would be needed only on the upper slopes. On its outside, it was hung with various implements. An ice axe and a grappling hook each hung from a leather strap. There was a furled groundsheet, a raincape and a water canteen. Banded to the underside was a short bow; in a side pocket, two dozen arrows.

Ballas walked through the house. In the banqueting hall, he drank several goblets of water. He was thirsty – his throat felt like a parched river bed. He was nervous. A sensation that was largely unfamiliar. Yet, over recent days, it had struck him again and again. Licking his lips, he drained the final goblet and went out on to the veranda.

Athreos Laike was already there. He stood in his customary stance: hands flat on the balustrade, his face turned towards the Garsbracks. Upon his blind eyes, moonlight glistened: and, visible in each iris, the mountains hung reflected.

For a long time Laike didn't move. He appeared uneasy. Doubtful, even. Through his nostrils he inhaled breath after deep breath. As if savouring the corrupt odours of lowland humanity before rising into purer altitudes.

'Let us go,' he said abruptly. He clambered smoothly over the balustrade.

Ballas glanced back at the house. The windows were lighted, the veranda door stood open. It seemed almost as if Laike were abandoning his home.

Or maybe, he was leaving a place he considered – had considered for many years – a temporary lodging place.

Ballas looked further off. The lights of Dayshadow pierced the dark: frail glimmers, seeping from the town's houses, taverns, brothels. This, he realised, would be his final glimpse of Druine. Soon, he would be above cloud level. The lower world would vanish.

He stared hard at the lights.

He wouldn't be sorry to leave Druine. For a long time, it had seemed like a prison. Not merely since the Church had begun hunting him. No; Ballas had felt incarcerated long before that.

He knew no place other than Druine. Yet his departure would cause him no grief.

Then why this faint unease? Why did a tiny part of him wish to stay?

It didn't, Ballas decided.

Turning, he found himself confronted by the Garsbracks. Vast black slopes, surging into the night sky.

He feared them, he realised. They were unfamiliar, dangerous – and that was why he wished to remain in Druine.

He grunted dismissively. He would grow used to the mountains soon enough. Within a day and a night, they would cease to be strangers.

The doubts lingered for a fleeting heartbeat – then Ballas saw, once again, his dream of Belthirran: the placid sprawl of fields, the cattle and cook-fires and gently labouring figures.

His doubts evaporated.

Swinging over the balustrade, Ballas started walking.

Chapter 18

Upon Scarrendestin, the true Pilgrims
Sought to destroy Asvirius, for they recognised
His intent: he wished to steal their powers
As his own, and gain the powers of the mountain
And of the creator-god . . .
. . . And become a half-god,
Strong, unstoppable . . .

Over open grassland, they walked towards the mountains. Laike moved briskly but cautiously. In his right hand he held a staff, which he planted firmly into the ground with every step. With his left hand, he gripped Ballas's forearm. The big man guided him onward. Occasionally Laike's boots struck a rock. Each time he stumbled, but quickly resumed his determined pace.

They left the grassland and entered the quarry.

Offcut stone shards carpeted the ground. The mountain walls had subsided jaggedly, chiselled away by decades of labour. It seemed as if some elemental force had ripped away at the rocks. The terrain grew difficult for Laike. The scree shifted under them. Stone lumps littered the area. Again and again, Laike half-tripped. Once or twice, only his grip on Ballas's arm kept him from falling. Every time he lost his balance, he swore. His expression hardened to a mix of anger and shame. Under his breath he muttered, 'When this was mountain, not rubble, I could walk it with ease. *I* have done this . . . *I* have created this ruination.'

Ballas ignored him. He wanted to leave the quarry as quickly as he could. He fought an inexplicable urge to run into the foothills. To vanish amid the rock upthrusts, where no one could see him. Yet he resisted, patiently helping Laike take step after step.

Eventually, the quarry ended. A vertical rise confronted Ballas. It was twenty feet high, more or less. The stone was chisel-cropped, uneven: a jumble of gashes and juts.

'What do you see?' asked Laike.

Ballas told him.

'I shan't be able to climb it,' said Laike. 'Not without help. We have ropes, though. You know what you must do?'

'Yes,' said Ballas, unknotting a rope coil from the side of the rucksack.

'We have walked – what – five hundred paces?'

Ballas glanced back along the quarry. 'Something like that.'

'If memory serves – and I am certain it does – there will be a couple of rowans a little further on. They will make good tying posts.'

Ballas shrugged out of his rucksack. Slinging the rope over his shoulder, he started to climb. The chisel-shattered rock was full of easy hand- and toeholds. It took Ballas only fifty heartbeats to reach the top.

Hauling himself over, he looked for the rowans.

Laike had miscalculated. They grew fifty yards away – too far to act as tying posts. Ballas swore, loudly. His profanity rolled through the night air. From somewhere there came a skittering echo – as of one hard surface sliding over another. In the darkness around the rowans, something moved – a mere flash of dirty white. The moonlight glinted upon a pair of eyes. Ballas reached for his dagger, imagining that the Lectivin was there. But he glimpsed a pair of curved horns. And a tail.

A mountain goat stared at him.

Ballas swore again. Turning, the goat fled into the gloom.

Ballas tied the rope around a boulder, then tossed the free end down to Laike. Groping, the old man located it, then tied it around a shoulder strap of Ballas's rucksack, and a shoulder strap of his own. Ballas hauled the rucksacks up, then dumped them beside the boulder. He threw down the end once more. Looping it around his wrist, then tightly gripping it, Laike started to climb. Leaning back, allowing the rope to take his weight, he merely walked up the rock face. When he neared the top, Ballas grabbed his coat collar and heaved him over.

The explorer lay on his back, gasping. 'Hard work, for one of my years,' he said.

Ballas gazed at him.

'But do not be troubled. I get my breath back quickly.'

After a few moments, Laike got to his feet. Stooping, he followed the rope to the boulder around which it was tied. 'The rowans have gone?'

'They're over that way,' said Ballas, gesturing – even though Laike couldn't see his action.

'Too far away to be of use?'

'Yes.'

Frowning, Laike walked to the trees. For the first few steps, he remained cautious. Then he grew confident. He took long, easy strides, his staff clacking on the path. He was on familiar territory, Ballas realised. The quarry had disorientated him, for it had changed since he had last climbed the Garsbracks. But the rest of the mountain remained unaltered.

Laike halted near the rowans.

'I was not too far off,' he said, touching the branch tips.

Ballas carried over the rucksacks, and the two men pulled them back on. With his staff, Laike pointed to a block of stone lying close by. 'There is a fissure running down its upper face,' he said. 'It tracks down through the dead centre.'

Ballas looked. Laike spoke correctly: a soft-edged split creased the middle of the rock.

Laike's staff pinpointed a second piece of stone. 'Its surface is softly indented, so it resembles a bowl. And a groove passes over its lowermost edge, yes? It has been worn away by a trickle of spring-water, you see.'

Again, Laike was correct.

'Your memory isn't bad,' said Ballas quietly.

'My friend,' said Laike, 'it is *immaculate*. And for that you should be grateful.'

Laike set off walking. Now he moved as quickly as a sighted man upon flat ground. His staff clack-clacked, his boots scuffed lightly against the ground. They emerged on to a broad stone plateau. On the right, a roughly pyramidal rock stabbed at the sky; it was at least a hundred feet tall. On the left, the ground fell away, exposing a deep, rowan-cluttered gully. As he walked, Laike continued his game of landmark-naming. With a swipe of his staff, he identified a succession of idiosyncrasies in the landscape. A colony of rare red-leafed *firewort*; a cluster of gashes in the rock face; water-worn whorls on the ground; overhangs seventy feet above them, some rectangular, others elliptical . . .

Ballas grew irritated. He wondered why Laike continued pointing out aspects of their surroundings. And, having done so, demanded to know whether all was as he claimed. Was he showing off? Ballas wondered. It wasn't impossible. To be admired, Laike had falsified an account of Belthirran. Surely he would show off any genuine talent, any true achievement?

Perhaps there was another reason. Maybe, in remembering such tiny details, Laike was dragging up larger ones. He hadn't been on the mountains for over twenty years. Maybe he feared his memory wasn't as sharp as he supposed. Maybe this was a way of brushing the dust from it.

Ballas decided to tolerate Laike's game.

Gradually, the plateau narrowed. It became a ledge, three feet wide. A splashing sound drifted up from the gully. In the depths, Ballas could see a small waterfall. The tumbling water shone in the moonlight. At the waterfall's base, foam, glinting palely, frothed over black rocks. Ballas guessed that the gully was seventy feet deep.

'Beautiful, isn't it?' remarked Laike. The old man was facing away from Ballas. Yet somehow he must have sensed that the waterfall had caught the big man's eye.

Ballas shrugged. 'I've seen worse things.'

Laike pressed a hand against the rock wall. With his fingertips, he groped – and found a wrinkle in the rock. He seemed to caress it for a moment. Then he squirmed out of his rucksack.

'Do you need to rest?' asked Ballas, tightly. 'You promised you were in fine health—'

'Be silent.' Laike raised a finger to his lips.

Ballas stopped speaking.

The explorer became very still. Then, with alarming suddenness, he sprinted a dozen paces along the ledge and hurled himself out over the gully.

'Laike!' shouted Ballas, thrusting out a hand as if to catch the explorer.

Laike flew through the air above the gully. He wore an expression of serene concentration. Soaring through the darkness, he lost momentum and started to fall. A heartbeat later he was gone – consumed by the gully's darkness.

Ballas was too shocked to curse. A sick weightlessness filled his stomach – as if he too had fallen. He felt Belthirran retreating from him. His only hope of finding refuge, of reaching the Land Beyond the Mountains, had gone . . . had disappeared into blackness.

He stumbled forwards, staring into the gully.

'Laike! Where are you! Pilgrim's blood . . .'

'Do not be alarmed,' came a calm voice. 'All is well, all is well.'

Sinking to his knees, Ballas looked down.

The explorer stood on a second ledge, seven feet down the gully wall. 'Everything is as I remember,' he said, grinning. He rapped his staff upon the ledge. 'Come over, Ballas. Jump, as I did. But first, throw over the rucksacks. They will not aid your flight, my friend.'

'Are you mad?' snapped Ballas. 'You could've killed yourself!'

'Killed myself? I rather think I've saved my life. We must take this route, Ballas.'

'There's no safety in leaping over a bloody chasm!'

'There's no safety,' corrected Laike, 'in following that ledge any further.'

Ballas looked along the ledge. It seemed perfectly safe to him. It was wider than the one on which Laike stood. And it continued as far as the eye could see.

'You're mistaken,' said Ballas, hoarsely.

'You must trust me, Anhaga Ballas.' Laike spoke softly. 'Have I not climbed the Garsbracks before? Are you not the novice here?'

Scowling, Ballas flung the rucksacks down on to the ledge. Then he sprang into the gully, landing heavily upon the ledge. The ledge shook as his weight fell upon it.

'You are not a graceful soul,' said Laike, tilting his head.

'And you,' snapped Ballas, 'are a bloody fool! If you have to do anything dangerous, warn me first, yes? Stupid bastard.'

Laike smiled. 'Forgive me.' Stooping, he pulled on his rucksack. Then he walked away along the ledge.

Ballas followed. This ledge seemed infinitely more dangerous. Not only was it even narrower than the first, but by turns it rose steeply up, then sank sharply down. As if the gully-crossing leap had given him a taste for recklessness, Laike moved onwards at great speed. Ballas wondered if he was trying to prove a point. Laike considered the mountains his territory. He owned the foothills; and he felt spiritually conjoined with the higher slopes. Maybe he wished to demonstrate his closeness to the mountains by acting as if they could do him no harm. Maybe he wanted to impress upon Ballas that he, the explorer, was leading the expedition. And that Ballas was merely a passenger.

For a long time, they walked along the ledge. A thin sweat broke out on Ballas's skin. As they went higher, a breeze penetrated the rocks, fluting a single wavering note. Otherwise, there was silence.

Eventually Laike halted.

'Through here,' he said, gesturing to a v-shaped opening in the rock wall. They clambered through, arriving at a small cave.

'A good place to pitch camp, I think,' said Laike. 'We shall rest till dawn. Then we must press on, yes?'

From his rucksack, Ballas took some firewood and got a blaze going. Shadows sprawled over the cave walls. Laike settled contentedly in the cave mouth. Ballas crouched by the fire, warming his hands.

'We'll take turns at keeping watch,' he said.

'I doubt whether I would be much use.' Laike pointed to his sightless eyes.

'You aren't deaf,' said Ballas. 'It ought to be enough to listen. They reckon blind men have sharp hearing . . .'

'Do you think such vigilance is necessary?'

'I'm not going to take chances,' replied Ballas, prodding the fire.

'We won't have been followed.'

Ballas snorted. 'Have you forgotten how badly the Wardens want to catch me?'

'There's a difference between desire,' said Laike, 'and ability. Trust me: no one will find you here. Not tonight, at least. Rest easily. Sleep. Tomorrow there will be much walking to do.'

Moving deeper into the cave, Laike closed his eyes and fell asleep. For a while, Ballas gazed at the stars and moon. Then he too started to doze.

On the cusp of sleep, a noise startled him – hooves clattering, then the alarmed bleating of a goat. Ballas jerked wide awake. The goat bleated for a while longer. Then it quietened.

Under his breath, Ballas swore.

'That is why we are safe here,' said Laike.

The old explorer's eyes remained closed.

'What're you talking about?'

'The goat has made a terrible, fatal mistake,' said Laike. 'The same mistake that any Warden, if he were following us, would make. Tomorrow all will become clear.' Laike shifted slightly. Then he went back to sleep.

When Ballas woke, the following dawn, he felt as if he had not slept at all. His head throbbed, his throat was dry, his muscles ached. Groaning, he pushed himself up into a sitting position. Athreos Laike was already awake. Kneeling, the old explorer fed firewood into the fire. The flames leaped and twisted – yet the cave remained cold.

'Bad dreams?' asked Laike, his unseeing gaze locked on the fire.

'What?' muttered Ballas, taking a canteen of water from the depths of his rucksack.

'Your slumber was full of turmoil. You tossed and turned, like a man suffering a fit.'

Drinking from the canteen, Ballas recalled his dream. Or rather, a shard of it spun up from his memory. He had dreamed of the mountains. Of stones, boulders, rock faces. There was no drama he could remember. No imagined incident that might have provoked such contortions from his body. Just a jumble of images. Just fissures, cracks, seams in the rock. Perhaps he hadn't dreamed at all – merely remembered fragments of the climb so far.

No, he realised – he hadn't done so. For the rocks he had seen had been bathed in dark light: the light that spills from a cloud-jammed sky.

Rising, Ballas stepped outside the cave. The ground shone with frost. The stones were slippery underfoot. Walking carefully, he moved a few yards away, then urinated on to the ground. He watched the steaming yellow fluid melt the frost. Then he returned to the cave.

They ate a breakfast of porridge, cooked from the oat rations in their rucksacks. Shivering, Ballas kept close to the fire.

'The cold bites deeply when one is tired,' said Laike. 'It is important that you get a healthy night's sleep. Otherwise you will be making your journey a thousand times more arduous.' He patted the rucksack. 'I brought whisky. To stave off the cold, mainly – but if a few mouthfuls will help you drowse . . .'

Suddenly, a goat bleated – the same goat, Ballas presumed, that had startled him the previous night.

'Of course, of course,' murmured Laike. 'There is something you must see.'

They finished their breakfast. Packing the blankets, groundsheets and cooking implements into their rucksacks, they left the cave.

They clambered through the v-shaped opening on to the ledge.

'Tread carefully,' said Ballas. 'The ground is—'

'Frosted, yes – I know, my friend.' He touched Ballas's forearm. 'Winter is tightening its grip. Let us pray we reach the top before the snows blow in. If we don't, Ballas, you'll know how cold a man can truly get.'

They followed the ledge. Ballas was acutely conscious of the slippery ground. Every footfall, however solidly placed, slid a fraction of an inch. Leading the way, Laike moved slowly. He leaned slightly upon his staff. With his left hand, he gripped the rock wall.

Ballas gazed into the gully. He saw another, smaller waterfall. There was something awkward, something half-rigid about the movement of the water. It was on the cusp of turning to ice, Ballas realised. Already, a few icicles hung at the waterfall's edge. The rowans below sparkled: frost-sealed, their leaves glittered like polished blades.

Ballas decided to keep his eyes on the ledge.

After a few hundred yards, Laike called a halt. With his staff, he pointed across the gully to a flat patch of stone, squarish in shape, each side four paces long. Upon it stood the goat, lapping at spring-water trickling from a rock face.

'There. Do you see? That is the way the Garsbracks kill.'

Ballas scowled. 'The goat is alive. It doesn't seem unhappy – it's just standing there, drinking.'

'Drinking? Ah – then you are seeing, too, how the mountain can torture.' Laike lowered his staff. 'The goat is trapped. There is no escape from where it stands.'

Ballas looked intently. And realised that, contrary to first impressions, Laike was correct. The stone square led nowhere – it simply jutted over empty air. The goat had reached it by scrambling down a steep slope. This slope was smooth, and scarcely possible to climb back up. And if the goat did so, it would still be trapped: for at the top of the slope was a severe overhang, extending several feet. Its underside would act as a barrier to anyone – or anything – attempting to go beyond the slope. The goat couldn't possibly negotiate an escape route. Nor could a human, Ballas decided. Not even the tallest man would be able reach up and grasp the overhang edge and haul himself up.

Laike smiled. 'If one believed this arrangement had been *designed*,' said the explorer, 'we would call it ingenious, yes?'

Ballas nodded.

'The goat followed the ledge – the ledge *you* would have taken last night. The drop from the overhang does not appear too dangerous. And, viewed from above, the stone shelf on which the goat now stands seems to be the beginning of a fresh ledge, curving away around the rock face. It looks perfectly safe, Ballas. As safe as a deadfall to a fox.' He drew a breath. 'The goat is going to die. The torture comes from the spring-water. Deprived of water, it would survive only a few days. But now it will linger for weeks. Until it starves to death. A cruel touch, yes?'

Jumbled bones lay upon the stone. From the distance, Ballas couldn't tell whether they were animal or human.

'Who'd make a path leading to nowhere?' he said. 'It's bloody stupid . . .'

'Not all ledges are paths,' replied Laike mildy. 'Some serve such a purpose. Others do not. That one –' a staff-swipe toward the ledge '– was once a path, I think – but no longer. Many hundreds of years ago, long before Druine was founded – before history began, even – an earthquake shook the mountains. The paths were distorted, disfigured, torn apart. Many, as you said, lead to nowhere. They became traps. And the mountains, always treacherous, grew fatally dangerous. That is the thinking of some scholars. It is speculation, of course.

'But speculation that demands further speculations.

'For if there are paths, there are living creatures. But a path worn into stone doesn't always tell you what those creatures were. Certainly, they could be the work of goats' hooves. But maybe men once lived here.'

There was a strange catch in Laike's voice – as if he was contemplating some intoxicating mystery.

'Men lived on a mountain.' Ballas shrugged scornfully. 'That's hardly wondrous. Travel to the south, and you'll find many mountain tribes.'

'True.' Laike nodded. 'But what is to say that men *lived* upon this mountain? Maybe it was merely a crossing point . . . an obstacle to be negotiated, on the way to somewhere else?'

'Belthirran?' asked Ballas.

'"Belthirran" is the name we, as inhabitants of Druine, have given the

Land Beyond the Mountains. But yes – the place that occupies that area of the world. There is another theory – one I relied upon when composing my false account of Belthirran. Some believe that the land south of the mountains, and that to the north, communicated freely. They traded with one another, transporting goods over the Garsbracks. Perhaps they thought themselves one: a single country, divided by the mountains.

'When the earthquake struck, the lands were divided. Nothing could be done to rejoin them. What choice did the people have but to carry on as two nations, each isolated from the other? Thus Belthirran was born.'

Ballas felt light-headed. 'You reckon this is true?'

'It is unproven, but plausible. To my mind the bone map attests that there is *some* civilisation beyond the Garsbracks.'

Ballas experienced a surge of optimism. He felt as if he had already arrived at Belthirran: a kind of airy delight swept through him. Grinning, he said, 'We'd better be making tracks.'

'First,' said Laike, 'you must do me a favour. Grant the goat a quick death. They are pleasant creatures, and I hate to think of them suffering.'

Nodding, Ballas untied the short bow from his rucksack.

Their journey continued. At noon they paused, and Ballas ate a heel of coarse black bread. Then he drank from an outlet of spring-water. Laike had spoken truthfully: the water was almost indescribably pure – purer than the water of cities, of wells, of moorland streams.

After resting, the two men moved on.

The terrain – a mix of scree and loose rocks – caused Ballas discomfort. Within his knees, tiny agonies flared: a sharp, hot pain, as if a burning spike was stabbing within the joint, or pieces of the bone were grating against one another. His lower back ached. His leg muscles seemed infused with liquid fire. Occasionally, the ground levelled out and Ballas found himself on grass-covered ground that was soft, springy. This provided a little relief. Yet it was always a brief lull, a momentary escape. The rocks and scree returned, as did his discomfort.

At the middle of the afternoon, they stopped at a heap of boulders. It rose thirty feet, each stone lump crusted with frost-blackened moss.

'We must climb it,' said Laike. 'Are you well enough?'

'What?'

'Are you *capable*? You are struggling, my friend. If there were snow, your breathing would conjure an avalanche – for each exhalation is as loud as the snort of a rutting stallion . . .'

'I am fine,' Ballas said sourly.

'There is no shame in weariness,' said Laike. 'You are not a mountain man. You are strong, but that strength gives you no advantage here, because you are heavy. And you also lack stamina. You are accustomed to bursts of exertion – as when you are fighting. But the slog, the slow persistent toil of ascent? That is new to you.' His tone became lighter. 'Besides, you have hardly treated your body kindly over the years. The grain and the grape bring pleasure – but also infirmity.'

'I'm not infirm.'

'No, but your health is imperfect. Do you wish to rest?'

'No.'

'As I say, there is no shame—'

'We'll make the climb, then rest.'

'As you wish.'

Laike was the first to scale the boulders. Despite the frost and crumbling moss, he moved quickly and nimbly – as if there was something of the squirrel about him. Ballas wondered how detailed Laike's memories were. In his mind's eye, did he perceive every boulder, with perfect clarity? Or did instinct play a part, guiding his hands and feet to the safest stone every time?

Ballas followed, aware of his clumsiness. In his limbs, he felt every ounce of his body's weight. And every ounce of his rucksack. He clambered to the top, then sat down, groaning.

'Are you thirsty?' asked Laike, pointing at a spring close by.

'Nah.'

'I am,' said the old man, walking towards the trickling water.

Half numb with fatigue, Ballas gazed at the mountains. Many were so high that their summits were indiscernible; they vanished into the sky's stark blue. Waterfalls tumbled here and there: light-struck, a few flickered with rainbows. Ballas looked dully at the slopes, gullies and grass-patches – then he froze.

A figure was moving across a tract of scree, several hundred yards away. Ballas's vision was far from perfect, yet he knew instantly who it was.

Heresh.

Her red hair was a faint patch of colour against the grey stone. And Ballas also recognised the dark woollen travelling cape, given to her by Laike.

She should have been partway to her uncle's home by now. Not scrambling up the Garsbracks. Something must have happened. Something must have stopped her journey not too long after it had begun.

'Ballas – what troubles you?'

The big man blinked. 'Nothing,' he told Laike.

'Then what do you say?'

'Say?'

'Are you ready to move on?' The explorer rapped his staff on the ground. 'How often must I ask you, my friend? Three times I have—'

'I am ready.'

Rising, Ballas glanced towards Heresh . . . to the hardly discernible figure, alone up on the Garsbracks. Then he turned away.

They walked until evening approached and a thin darkness crept over the mountains. With the sun gone, the air grew still colder. A breeze blew – scarcely more than a soft rustling of air. Yet it was so icy that it seemed to peel the skin from Ballas's face.

They pitched camp between two large boulders, stretching a tarpaulin overhead to form a roof. Exhausted, Ballas did not bother lighting a fire. If Laike wanted a blaze, he could make it himself. Slouching against a boulder, drawing a blanket up to his chin, Ballas fell asleep instantly.

When he woke, it was dawn. Laike *had* built a fire, at the edge of the camp. It burned feebly – a few tiny flames, flickering upon a bed of ash. The explorer slept on the ground, his head upon his rucksack, his staff in his arms. He seemed peaceful, contented. As if mountain-sleep were something nourishing. Ballas had slept deeply. Yet he still felt tired. A dull weight hung behind his eyes. His body was stiff, as if it was acquiring the hard quality of the mountains' rock.

From a pouch, Ballas tipped a few beans into his palm. They were brown-black in colour, and round in shape. Laike had imported them from the Distant East. He claimed that they dispelled tiredness. That they could fill the weariest of men with vigour. Crunching them between his teeth, Ballas stepped out from the camp.

The day was cold, clear – much like the previous day. Ballas wandered a dozen yards away, unfastened his leggings and urinated.

A sudden noise disturbed him. It was not loud. Nor did it come from anywhere close by. It surprised him, for it was the sound of a human voice. Once more it rang out, drifting over the mountains. Ballas couldn't make out the words: the cry was muffled by distance and had lost its clarity to the confusion of echoes. Yet its tone remained expressive.

It was a cry for help. And it belonged to a woman.

From the camp, Ballas retrieved the bow and some arrows. The cry rang out again – thin, dull, tired: yet laden with pain and fear. The big man followed the sound, treading as lightly as he could over frost-coated grassland. After half a mile, he came upon a deep, broad gully.

Upon a ledge, thirty feet from the top, Heresh sat motionless, her head bowed. Her left arm was folded across her chest, as if shielding a wound. Blood soaked her travelling cape and caked her hands. Her hair had broken free of its ponytail, grease-dulled strands straggling over her face. She breathed heavily, her shoulders rising and falling.

Ballas ducked behind a rowan tree. He stared at the bow – at its polished wood and tautened string. Then at the arrows: copper-tipped, red-fletched.

He blinked. Then, nocking an arrow, he moved from behind the rowan and took aim. Heresh was an easy target – as easy as the goat had been the day before. He drew the bowstring tighter, felt it taut against his fingers.

Then a voice spoke. 'Trouble?'

Athreos Laike moved to stand beside the big man. 'I heard you leave the camp a short time ago,' he said. 'Then I heard someone calling for help. It is the girl, is it not? The woman who journeyed with you? I could recognise her voice.' He touched the bowstring with his fingertips. 'I noticed, too, that this weapon was missing. One need not be a genius to work out your intent. Where is she, Ballas? Upon a ledge?'

'Go back to the camp,' said Ballas.

'A ledge, yes? Of course – if she had fallen to the gully floor, she would not have survived.'

'It doesn't matter where she is. Go back, Laike. I'll sort this out.'

'If you kill her, I shall not guide you. Among mountain men, there is a code of honour. The injured, the despairing – they cannot be abandoned. I intend to be loyal to such principles. I have upheld them all my life. I shall not forsake them now.'

'Don't be an idiot,' said Ballas softly. 'What use would she be? Piss-all. She'd be nothing but a burden. She's injured. I reckon her ribs are broken. And beside that she's a bloody woman. She's got no place upon the mountains. She would slow us down. We've got to reach the top before the snows come in. We can't afford to be . . . be dragging a dead weight with us.'

'She is, as you say, injured. Yet she has made it this far up the mountains – and has done so *by herself*. Doesn't that suggest you are underestimating her? She couldn't have gone much further, of course. About a mile further on, the ground on that side of the gully falls away, and there is nothing except a quarter-mile drop to a rock bed.' Laike exhaled slowly. 'She is strong, Ballas. And resilient. The route she has taken is not easy . . .'

'She was probably hysterical. I reckon she didn't even know what she was doing—'

'Panic cannot endure for two days,' said Laike mildly. 'It burns itself out.'

Ballas shook his head. 'It's not important. Not important *at all*. Strength? Resilience? Horseshit to them both. She isn't coming with us. I'll grant her a quick death – a *clean* death. She won't know it is coming. She'll just wake up in the Eltheryn Forest – or in the sulphur pits of Hell. Either way—'

'I shall say it once more: take her life, and I will not guide you. Ballas, I will simply leave you here. Then you will die. And with you, your dreams of Belthirran shall also die. To die knowing one's ambitions are unfulfilled – that is a terrible thing. Perhaps the *worst* of all things.'

For a long time Ballas did not move. He held the bow poised, the arrow pointing at Heresh. Then, swearing, he hurled down the weapon.

Laike had brought a length of rope. Ballas secured one end to the rowan. The other he fastened around a piece of stone. Moving to the edge of the gully, he shouted, 'Woman! Wake up!'

Heresh raised her head. She stared uncomprehendingly at Ballas. Suddenly, she understood. Her eyes widened and she started to get to her feet.

'Please,' she began. 'Help—'

'Shut up! Catch this, all right?' Drawing back his arm, Ballas hurled the stone over the gully to the ledge. It struck the gully wall, several inches away from Heresh's head. Then it bounced, clattered off the ledge and vanished into the gully. The rope slithered tight; grasping it, Ballas drew the stone up again. 'This time,' he shouted, 'you'd better do as you are told. *Catch it*. Drop it, and that's it – we'll bloody well leave you there.' He threw the stone over. It cracked against the gully wall, above the ledge. Twisting, Heresh caught it – then staggered, grimacing. She curled her arm across her chest again.

'Yeah,' said Ballas, 'her ribs are broken. She's half crippled.' He looked at Laike. The explorer's expression was impassive.

Following Ballas's instructions, Heresh untied the stone, threw it away, then wove the rope into a makeshift harness, which she slipped over her upper body. Tightening it, drawing the rope against her chest, she winced. Ballas gripped his end of the rope, winding it around his fist. Stepping back from the gully edge, he shouted, 'Jump!'

Heresh stared up at him.

'Jump, damn it!'

Licking her lips, Heresh moved to the rim of the ledge. Then she halted. She peered into the gully, and froze.

'Pilgrims' blood,' muttered Ballas. Yanking the rope, he tugged Heresh off the ledge. Screaming, she tumbled into empty air. As she fell, the slack vanished from the rope. The harness squeezed her damaged ribcage. Her scream fractured into a rasping howl. She swung on the rope, smacking into the gully wall across from the ledge. Leaning backwards, heels jabbing into the earth, Ballas dragged her upward. Against his shoulder blades, his muscles locked solid. The rope pulled hard around his hands, constricting them painfully. Growling, he took step after strenuous step backwards until Heresh appeared over the gully's edge – first a dull glint of red hair, then a face clenched in pain. Striding over, Ballas grasped her arm, and manhandled her on to the grassland. She rolled on to her back, sobbing. Then she sat upright, leaning forward, both arms covering her chest. Her face was pale and tears streamed down her cheeks.

Ballas threw down the rope. 'There,' he said, turning to Laike. 'Now she's *your* bloody problem.'

A short while later, Ballas sat on a rock, drinking whisky, staring across the mountains. Before the journey could be resumed, Heresh's injuries had to be tended. Ballas left this task to Athreos Laike. And it seemed that Laike's ministrations were far from painless. From the camp, a hundred yards away, sounds of agony drifted: a mix of groans, yelps, gasps. The big man did not pity Heresh. He cursed her silently.

He cursed, too, Laike's code of honour. By insisting that Heresh was rescued, the explorer had jeopardised the ascent. As if it did not matter whether they reached the summit.

Which, of course, it did not – not to Athreos Laike. For he did not believe Belthirran could be found.

So why had he agreed to travel with him? Why, if he believed failure lay ahead?

Ballas hadn't asked himself this question before. Now, it preoccupied him. Sipping at the whisky, he suddenly understood. Laike didn't care about Belthirran. He simply enjoyed being up on the Garsbracks. For Ballas, the expedition was a serious matter. But for Laike, it was a mere holiday, a pastime, a pleasant recreation.

Angrily, Ballas hurled the whisky flagon at a heap of rocks. It shattered, shards flashing in the icy light.

'I hope you drank the last drop,' said Athreos Laike from behind Ballas. 'It is one of Druine's finest liquors. For half a century, it has been maturing. It would be villainous to waste it.' The explorer settled next to the big man. 'My servant, Beirun, betrayed me. He is a weak, timid man – and he loathes change. He believed that I would not be returning from these mountains. For twenty years he had served me – but now he believed that I was deserting him. He was vengeful, I think – and he exacted the vengeance of the weak: he turned the strong against me. He informed the Wardens of our alliance. Heresh had scarcely left Dayshadow when she was intercepted by the Church's men. She managed to escape, though. She ran through Briande Copse. And started to climb the mountains. She is a brave girl, resourceful. But you will understand that. You have known her far longer than I have.'

The explorer shifted to get more comfortable.

'When she fell on to the ledge, she broke her ribs – as you suspected. Her skin is cut, from the thorn bushes in the forest. And she is badly bruised. I am surprised that she is alive. She has endured much.' Laike hesitated. 'She says a Lectivin is seeking you?'

'Yes. One of the hunter caste.'

'He will fare well in these mountains. They are fast, and have much stamina. The mountain's convolutions will not trouble it, either. It will not find itself trapped upon a dead-end ledge, for it will be following your soul-glow – and that soul-glow, of course, will be giving away our route: the safe route. It is as if you have left behind a trail of footprints. We will have to be wary.'

'Wary,' murmured Ballas, sourly. 'If you wanted to be wary, you'd have let me do away with Heresh. She will be slowing us down. Perhaps the Lectivin will catch up with us before we find Belthirran.'

'So what?' said Laike, rising. 'By nature, you are a killer. If the Lectivin appears – kill it.'

For two days, they walked through the mountains, moving upwards into thinner air. Laike led the way, Heresh at his side. Despite her injuries, the young woman maintained a respectable pace. Despite her pain, she did not complain. She listened, as if genuinely curious, when Laike pointed out the Garsbrack's ingenious hazards: the dead ends, from which no way back was possible; the bewildering webwork of ledges and ridge walks; the gullies that, though easy enough to enter, permitted no escape. She enjoyed the explorer's talk; and the explorer enjoyed talking, sensing perhaps that she was more interested than Ballas had ever been. Walking behind them, Ballas was unsure whether Heresh truly cared. Or whether the old man's chatter was merely something to distract her from the pain and discomfort of her battered body.

On the first night, they made camp. They ate the food from Ballas and Laike's rucksacks, sharing it with Heresh. Ballas noticed that Heresh's gaze was as sharp, as reflexively watchful as it had always been. Yet something was absent. The gentle hardness of her strength of mind had faded: in its place there was timidity. An understanding that, despite having survived so many things in the lowlands, she was, here in the mountains, fragile. Ballas wondered if her broken ribs had humbled her. Or whether the mountains themselves – a place wholly alien to someone raised in the marshes – were to blame.

On the second evening, they struck camp against a tall boulder. The tarpaulin slanted from boulder face to earth, once more creating a roof. Laike had wandered off, to wash in a stream. No food remained in the rucksacks. Ballas had to find a goat to kill and, sitting in the camp, he restrung the bow and selected the arrows. Heresh had gathered firewood. She struck a flint and steel, aiming at a small pile of moss kindling. Sparks flared; yet the kindling did not take. She tried over and over to light the moss. At first, her failures amused Ballas. He enjoyed a type of dark gratification: she was useless, a hindrance, he had said so from the start, and now she was proving him correct: a task as simple as fire-lighting was beyond her.

Then he grew annoyed. Every *snick* of flint and steel, every impotent spark-flash, angered him.

He snatched the flint and steel from her. With a single strike, he lit the kindling. Smoke coiled up from the moss, which he picked up and placed in Heresh's hands.

'Blow on it,' he said. 'You can manage that, I suppose? You can bloody *breathe* without fouling things up?'

Silently, Heresh obeyed.

'Why are you here, eh?' asked Ballas.

Heresh did not speak.

Lashing out, Ballas struck the kindling from her grasp. 'Answer me.'

'I can't light a fire,' she said, retrieving the moss, 'if you hinder me like that.'

'Why are you on the bloody mountains?'

'I had no choice. Surely Laike has told you—'

'Yes,' interrupted Ballas. 'But there are other places you could have gone.'

'Really? Tell me where, Ballas. For I don't believe that there is anywhere safe in Druine.'

'That doesn't explain why you are here.'

'I am here because there is nowhere else.'

'You intend to live for ever on the mountains?'

Heresh looked up, puzzled.

'You're going to stay here until you die? You're going to settle down here? Maybe screw a billy goat, and raise a few kids?'

'You're obscene,' said Heresh, slipping the smouldering moss beneath a clump of twigs.

'Yeah, perhaps. But I don't pretend to be something I'm not. Nor do I lie about my ambitions. I'm seeking Belthirran. And I reckon you're doing the same now.'

Heresh became still.

'I was being hunted by the Church. Belthirran was my only hope of survival. Yet you mocked me. You thought me a fool. But now – now *you* are hunted, and desperate. So: what happens? You start hungering for Belthirran. Suddenly, it isn't the dream of an idiot. Nah. It's a truth. An aspiration. Something that *must* exist; something you *want* to exist.'

'Laike has spoken of the evidence. But this morning, he told me of the bone map . . .'

'You didn't know about it when you started, though,' countered Ballas. 'And has he told you of the rock wall? That cannot be climbed?'

'He has.'

'And it doesn't trouble you?'

'It troubles me,' said Heresh. 'But once we are there . . .'

'Yes?'

'We will find a way. Isn't that the way of things? There is a problem that seems insoluble. But once you are there . . . once it is in front of you . . . In the alley, in Granthaven, when the Wardens were approaching – there was no way out. Yet somehow, we found one—'

Ballas snorted. '*I* found one. You simply did as you were told. And that's the size of it, I reckon. You expect *me* to take you to Belthirran. Tell me this, then: why should I help you? You thought me a halfwit. You say I'm obscene. You spat in my face, at Laike's home. What do I owe you? Why should I help you?'

'Laike says that if you don't, he, in turn, will not help you. In fact, he will leave you here.' She looked up: a flicker of defiance had returned. 'Are such arrangements not familiar to you? Have you not forced people to do your bidding, upon threats of death?'

Muttering, Ballas left the camp.

Rain-fat clouds blotted the sky. A luminous darkness lay over the mountains – and an airlessness, as if every living thing was holding its breath. Ballas tramped two hundred yards over grassland, towards a grazing goat. Halting, he nocked an arrow and took aim.

His eyesight blurred, the goat flickering in front of him.

Swearing, Ballas lowered the bow. He was tired. So tired that his eyes couldn't focus clearly. He hadn't slept properly, not for a long time. Every night, he *did* fall asleep. Yet he never woke refreshed and renewed – only exhausted. The dreams of stone persisted. Their contents were a mystery. He couldn't recall anything about them – except that, in some way, they were about stone. He had expected that, after a few days on the mountains, they would have stopped. But it seemed he would have to endure them indefinitely. And the climb would pass in a haze of weariness.

Yet his desire to find Belthirran was undiminished. More than ever, it filled his thoughts, possessed him, forced his heart to beat, his muscles to keep working.

He aimed at the goat.

The first arrow pierced the animal's upper leg; the second, its throat. Using his dagger, Ballas cut out some slabs of meat and a few edible innards. Then he pitched the remains into a gully.

Thunder tolled, shaking the mountains. At first, the rain was almost too light to feel: it was detectable only by grass stalks trembling and stones darkening. Then it gained strength, crashing down as if the clouds were flinging fistful after fistful of iron nails. After a few moments the rain became hail. The grassland was bombarded with icy white pellets. They bit at Ballas's face and rattled upon his cape. As he jogged to the camp, lightning flashed.

Laike had returned. 'On the Garsbracks,' he said, over the noise of hail drumming on the tarpaulin, 'a storm is the herald of winter.'

There was more thunder, fresh lightning.

'The Fierce Season has found us,' said the explorer. 'Now our struggles begin.'

Chapter 19

And the Pilgrims cast out
Asvirius, but the Lectivin did not submit
Gently, and a battle struck the Mountain . . .
. . . The sky blackened, the waters rose,
Birds fell dead from the air . . .
. . . Not since Creation had such magick crackled
Through the world of substances . . .

'Pilgrims' blood,' said Ballas, as he woke.

His body shook. His eyes felt raw, as if they'd been scraped with sand. In his throat, bile swirled; he felt tired, sick, and half-frozen to death. Once more, he had dreamed of stone. Once more, the meaning of the dream eluded him. As always, though, waking was uncomfortable – and this morning, it was worse than before. He felt feverish, more or less.

An ague, he thought. I've got winter sickness – or something.

He rubbed his face. His hands were cold upon his cold skin. Cursing, he sat upright, and looked around the camp. Heresh was already awake, eating a piece of goat meat that had been cooked the night before. But Laike was nowhere to be seen.

'Where is the explorer?' said Ballas, thickly.

'You look ill.'

'Where's the bloody explorer!' snapped Ballas.

'Outside,' replied Heresh. 'Everything . . . everything has changed.'

'What do you mean?'

'Look for yourself.'

Rising, Ballas stepped outside. All night, after the hailstorm, rain had fallen. Now, every grass stalk and stone was sealed in ice. A hundred yards away, a waterfall was frozen solid, its foam white, its depths a glowing blue. A wind blew – it played over his skin like a razor blade fashioned from ice. In such sudden cold, Ballas groaned. Then he hugged himself.

'Beautiful, is it not?' said Laike, gesturing.

'I am bloody dying.'

'I remember when I saw these high slopes in winter. In my memory,

I see them now: there is nothing, in all Nature, to compare with it. Does it not move you, Ballas? Does it not make you grateful to be alive?'

'Alive? Are you stupid, Laike? This ice could kill us. The ledges are covered in it. Or don't you remember that part?'

'I remember,' said Laike mildly. 'And I have taken precautions.'

In the camp, Laike took two roughly oval-shaped metal frames from his rucksack. On the undersides, inch-long spikes protruded. On the upper sides were two sets of leather straps, each with a buckle stitched to it.

'Crampons,' said Laike, handing them to Ballas. 'They fasten over your boots. They'll help you grip the ice.'

Ballas strapped them on; Laike took out his own pair, and did the same.

'A fine invention,' said the explorer. 'Far better than merely driving nails through one's boot soles.' Laike lifted a knuckle to his mouth. 'Of course. Forgive me, Heresh: but I did not expect you to be joining us. I have only two pairs, and each is of a size too great for your feet. But all is not lost. Take a rope, and tie one end to yourself and the other to myself or Ballas. If you slip, you will not fall – at least, not too far.' He offered the woman a rope.

Heresh took it, then paused.

'Well,' said Laike, 'who is it to be: myself or Ballas?'

Heresh glanced at Ballas, then at Laike. 'You,' she told the explorer.

'Ballas is far stronger than me,' he said. 'Heavier, too. If you suffer a mishap, he is best equipped to save you.'

'I won't place my life in the hands of someone I mistrust. Not if I can help it.'

'Very well. There is also another matter,' continued Laike. 'That of your clothing. The mountains are far colder today than yesterday. Your cape offers little protection. Ballas and I must each give you some of our clothing. Otherwise, you will freeze.'

'I am unwell,' said Ballas, scowling. 'I'm *sick*.'

'Laike,' said Heresh, touching the explorer's forearm, 'I shall be fine as I am. A bit of cold air will not harm me—'

'Nonsense! Here: have my coat.' Laike started untying the garment.

'Wait,' said Ballas, angrily. 'Take *my* coat. Go on.' He tore off his furs, then flung them at her. 'Put it on. Stay warm. And my over-trousers.' He tugged off the thick leggings, exposing the thin woollen ones beneath. 'Have them as well!'

Heresh glanced at Laike, uncertain.

'It is not necessary,' said the explorer, 'for you to give up every warm—'

'Have you forgotten what you are, Laike? You're an old man. *You* will freeze if you are not careful. And if you freeze, what happens? Pah!' Ballas hurled the leggings at Heresh. 'Wear them. I will do well enough without. Whisky – that'll warm me.' Snatching a flagon from Laike's rucksack, he stumped outside. The wind swirled over him – yet he hardly felt the cold. His anger warmed him. He uncorked the whisky, and took a sip: it warmed him far more.

With the mountains ice-coated, their progress was slow. Over grassland, they moved at a near-normal pace. But the ledges, looping over gullies and chasms, required caution. Ballas's crampons sank into the ice; as Laike had promised, they improved his grip. Yet they were not perfect. Sometimes, Ballas slipped; sometimes, heaving the spikes from the ice, he overbalanced. Even Laike seemed perturbed. But this, Ballas thought, was Heresh's fault – and Heresh's fault alone. In smooth-soled boots, she found it almost impossible to walk.

Eventually, Laike said, 'This is no use – no use at all. Every slither of your feet is a summons for death to come and bear you to the Forest.'

The explorer suggested a different way of moving. Heresh was to kneel on all fours, and crawl; in her right hand, she would grip a dagger, which she would sink into the ice with every forward motion. To Ballas's ears it seemed preposterous. Yet it worked. They moved faster in this way; and Ballas took a grim amusement at Heresh's predicament – at the way she was forced to plod on, like an animal.

Sometime after midday, on a thin ledge, Heresh slipped. The ledge tilted slightly to its left, towards a gully. Heresh's knees slewed from under her and she fell on to her side. She began sliding, and tried in vain to sink the knife into the ice. As she neared the edge, Ballas sprang forward. Grasping her arm, he hauled her out of danger. She looked up, and their gazes met. It seemed that she might speak – might offer thanks. But she turned away, and continued crawling. Ballas realised she understood him. She was roped to Laike; and it was the explorer's life Ballas had saved, not hers.

More precisely, it was *his own*.

As evening approached, they stopped at a rock face covered with a network of ledges. Its height was impossible to estimate: it slanted slightly backwards from the travellers, thus concealing its higher reaches. As far as Ballas could tell, it could have gone on up as far as the sun.

'We've got to climb it, have we?'

'It is the last great barrier before the summit,' said Laike, touching the rock face.

'Are we almost there?'

Laike nodded. 'Of course, it is not the last barrier *you* will have to cross, if you are to reach Belthirran. There is the rock wall, that—'

'Don't speak of it,' said Ballas, sharply.

'It troubles you?'

'It *bores* me.'

'It seems perverse that a man can be bored by that which might destroy him. Obstacles, like one's enemies, should kindle interest.' Laike paused, frowning. 'If it truly does bore you, that is a bad sign.'

'Oh yes?'

'It means that you have no reason to be interested in it. It means you think it is hardly a threat at all – which, in this case, is supremely arrogant; and failure is the harvest of arrogance. Or . . . or it means that you do not believe you will ever overcome it. It bores you because there is no reason to be interested: no reason to think about it, for no amount of thought will help you. You imagine . . . you believe that the rock wall cannot be overcome. It . . . it is the way, with certain things. If a man knows there is nothing he can do, he loses interest . . .'

The explorer rubbed his palm across his mouth. He breathed heavily, for a moment.

'Come,' he said. 'We must make a start.'

'It'd be wiser,' said Ballas, seeing the first tints of evening in the sky, 'if we pitched camp. Then we'll have all tomorrow to make the climb.'

'You imagine a single day will be enough?'

'It'll take longer?'

'There are places further up,' said Laike, 'where we can make an easy camp. Do we have firewood?'

They didn't; Ballas hacked branches from a couple of rowan trees. Then he killed and gutted another goat, storing the meat inside a leather pouch.

'Is everything ready?' asked Laike as Ballas returned.

Ballas said it was.

'Then let us bring our journey to an end.'

For three days, they climbed the rock face, following the ledges. At first, Ballas found himself surprised by its size – its seemingly never-ending skywards progress. Then he grew bored. The rock face annoyed him: every part of it looked like every other – it was nerve-numbingly monotonous, like sailing eternally upon a sea untroubled by waves. Through the day they walked; at night, they camped in the caves in the rock face. The repetitiveness of their surroundings, as much as the travellers' slowness, made Ballas impatient. He started to feel that Laike had tricked them – had led them, inexplicably, on a journey without end.

Then, on the morning of the third day, tired, still haunted by dreams of stone, Ballas began to find the rock face an unreal place – somewhere dislocated from the world he knew, somewhere governed by different rules and subject to different principles. It was a world of isolation: the lights of Druine couldn't be seen and nothing was visible except other mountains, all immeasurably tall, yet all dwarfed by the rock face. It was a world of dull stone and gleaming ice. And a world of bone-splitting cold: the winds pierced Ballas's flesh, he felt chill-sickened, and he gazed with increasing anger at Heresh, clothed in his furs.

On the third afternoon, clouds crawled into the sky: a few at first, each onyx-black and heavy. Then more came, and soon the sky was a sky no longer: just a ceiling of pulsing blackness. The wind ebbed, the air stilled. Snow began to fall – each flake twisting languidly, then settling on the ledge. They alighted on Ballas's shoulders, and in his hair. Soon the air was full of fluttering white. A breeze blew up, skirling over the ledge, whipping the the snowflakes into a frenetic dance. Then a gust of wind struck, slamming Ballas against the rock face. He cursed; the wind caught Laike and he stumbled but remained upright.

A blizzard had begun.

Everything turned white: the ledge, the air, the rock face, the mountains. Ballas's field of vision shrank to a few feet. Somewhere ahead Laike shouted, 'A hundred paces, and we shall be safe!'

Head bowed, Ballas forced himself onward. The big man had stopped shivering: the snowflakes were so cold that they burned, seeming to singe his flesh like heated cinders.

Following Laike, he ducked into the stillness and shelter of a cave. Upon the floor was a small pile of charred firewood; beside it nestled animal bones. Ballas felt a touch of alarm. Was this the Lectivin's campfire? Had Nu'hkterin somehow overtaken them? Was it ahead somewhere – concealed, waiting?

Then Ballas noticed a pelt of discoloured, moisture-rotted fur. The animal had been slaughtered, and skinned, years ago.

Kneeling, Laike touched the remains of the campfire. 'I know this cave,' he said, smiling. 'This is my fire; this –' he fingered the fur '– was my final meal before reaching the summit. Mountain fox. It had made this cave its home. It was old, and when I arrived it was too slow to run, too weak to fight. I killed it quickly, and ate well.'

'Your final meal,' said Ballas. 'We're almost there, then?'

'Another day's climb, if the weather treats us kindly.'

'When do you reckon the blizzard will stop?'

'Spring,' replied Laike, flatly.

Ballas glowered.

'Only in the new year will the snows recede and a thaw begin,' the explorer continued. 'Before then, there will be lulls. We will have to make do with these. But they ought to be sufficient. Now, let us make a fire, yes? I am cold.'

Ballas did as the explorer asked. While Heresh cooked the goat meat, Ballas took off his thin coat and leggings and put them by the fire to dry. A soft, smoky warmth filled the cave. They ate their meal in silence. To ease the pain of her ribs, Heresh drank a little whisky. Soon after, she went to the back of the cave and fell asleep.

Ballas and Laike remained by the fire. Outside, the blizzard raged, the snowflakes as animated and dense as a locust swarm.

'Is there much whisky left?' asked Laike.

Ballas held the flagon to the firelight. 'This one is three-quarters full.'

'We might as well empty it. At this hour tomorrow we shall be in Belthirran, drinking whatever is favoured there.'

'You don't believe that.'

Laike shook his head. 'No. I do not.'

Laike took a mouthful from the flagon. Ballas watched him closely. In Laike's sightless eyes a contented – almost happy – light flickered. Yet, over the past few days, he had grown distant. As if his thoughts lay not on the climb but on something else . . . something less tangible.

'You are staring, Ballas,' said the explorer.

'How can you tell?'

'Your silence. Your stillness. And –' he lifted his eyebrows '– you are ignoring an offered flagon.' Laike was holding out the receptacle and had been doing so for a few moments. Ballas had not noticed.

'Something troubles you,' said Laike, as Ballas took the flagon.

'I'm part-way up Druine's highest mountain, in a blizzard – of course I am troubled.'

'It is not that,' said Laike.

Ballas was silent a moment. 'Why are you helping me? Days ago, I reckoned you wanted an adventure . . . or something. But now? I don't think so. This isn't an idle pleasure, is it? You could perish here. You knew it would be dangerous. You knew there would be blizzards.'

Laike held his hands out to the fire. 'I have not been honest with you. I said I decided to guide you because I wanted a climbing companion, someone to assist me now and again when things got difficult. I told you no one else was willing to do so.'

'So you did,' murmured Ballas.

'Untrue,' replied Laike. 'There are many foolhardy men, many greedy men, who would have done my bidding. But . . . I was frightened.'

'Frightened?'

'Of the mountains. In my youth, I was reckless. I did not understand my own fragility. Or, rather, I understood but did not care. The pleasures of adventure excited me – so much so that I loathed anything that dulled them. Caution, forethought – these are invaluable, upon the Garsbracks. Yet I shunned them. I treated the mountains as if they were an oak tree, and I was a child scrambling up for fun. But now – now I am old, and blind, and fearful. I loved the mountains; yet they terrified me.'

'On our first evening,' said Ballas, 'you leaped over a gully, on to a ledge. You ran, and hurled yourself into black space. That isn't how a fearful man behaves.'

'What choice did I have? The gully had to be crossed.'

'But you didn't hesitate. You simply sprinted off, without any planning, without making sure you were in exactly the right place.'

'If I had paused,' said Laike, 'I would never have jumped. My nerve would have vanished. I would have found some reason to stay where I was. Then what would have remained but to abandon the journey? And I did not want that.'

'So why are you here? Are you testing yourself? Is this some contest of will?'

'I am here,' said Laike, 'to die. Pass me the whisky, please.'

Ballas did as the explorer asked. Laike took a long gulp, then gasped.

'Last spring, I became unwell. In my guts, there was a pain, a hot pain, a pain like fire upon flesh. It was extraordinary in its severity. My nights were feverish, my days given over to a type of tormented lethargy . . . I am a rich man, Ballas: but I did not wish to see a surgeon. Such men swear an oath of secrecy; yet they also drink, and grow loose-tongued, and speak of their patients' ills. I did not want anyone to know that I was ill. In Dayshadow, I was not well-liked. The quarrymen hated me, for I made them work hard. Those who hold the quarrying rights to the western and eastern parts of the Garsbracks hate me, for I possess the areas of the finest stone, and a few mines, too, from which diamonds can be taken. I did not want them to know that I was suffering, because it would have pleased them. I am a stubborn man, Anhaga Ballas.

'I went to a healer – a dispenser of magical remedies. Living in fear of the Church, they are accustomed to secrecy. Indeed, their lives depend upon it. I could be certain that no one would learn of my condition.

'The healer discovered a growth upon my liver. She described it to me, in some detail: its size, its texture. In a jar, she had something similar, extracted from a horse. Mine, she said, was too large to be removed – by scalpel blade or by spellcraft. This ugly, misshapen sphere of flesh was my death warrant.'

Laike gave the flagon to Ballas.

'The healer reduced its size, to such a degree that I felt – and feel – little pain. But it will grow again, and I will die. Such deaths are unpleasant.

'In such circumstances as mine, everything changes. Death cannot be avoided, that is certain. So one must choose the way that death is met. If I wished, I could die in the lowlands, numbed by drugs, unaware that I was dying, or had ever lived . . . I could fade away, amid the squalor and dirt of humanity.

'Or I could die amid the purity of the mountains. I could die amid rocks, and eagles, and rowan trees.'

'You're going to kill yourself?'

'No. Rather, I shall let the elements take my life. There is a pool, up on the mountain tops, near a rowan grove. I shall settle there, and let the winds blow around me, and the snows pile upon me, until I feel nothing . . . until I *become* nothing. And you, Ballas, have rendered this possible.'

'How so? Surely, you could've hired someone to bring you here . . .'

'What if I became ill during the climb?'

'I don't understand.'

'I crave the mountain-tops and the rowan grove. But if I sickened, no climber – however well paid – would have helped me make the ascent. I would be too great a liability; he would abandon me.'

'You said mountain men were forbidden from—'

'The code of honour is dead,' interrupted Laike. 'In my day, it thrived. But now? The tide of humanity, black and noxious, has drowned it. It exists no more. It has gone.

'You crave the mountain tops as much as I do. When I spoke to you, that much was clear. I knew that no matter how unwell I became, you would help me. Because without me, you won't get there. Without me, you'd never have a chance of finding Belthirran. If needs be, you would have carried me on your back.'

The two men were silent. The fire crackled, shadows crawled.

'Strange, isn't it, how we follow the same path, but for opposite reasons? You wish to live. I wish to die. You want refuge. I, the grave. But perhaps death, for me, will be a type of refuge.' He touched his stomach. 'The pain has returned. Pass me the whisky, Anhaga Ballas.'

Despite the whisky, Ballas's sleep was restless. The stone dream – which still defied all attempts at proper recollection – had filled his slumber, and he woke cold, tired and angry. Yet his mood improved when he found that the blizzard had abated. He stepped out of the cave, into a world of heaped snow crystals. Every rock-face fissure was snow-crammed, the ledge was stacked shin-deep. The air bore a sharp, clean flavour – as if it had been purified by the fierce weather. The sky was clear: the sun burned, and its light glared upward, reflected, from the snow: an eye-searing dazzle that made Ballas squint. It was easy to see how Laike had gone snow-blind.

They ate a quick breakfast of leftover goat meat. Then they set off along the ledge. Ballas and Laike removed their crampons, for they provided no benefit in the snow. No longer in danger of slipping, Heresh walked upright, denying Ballas any more hard, spiteful amusement. And so they moved on, at a reasonable pace and faster than they had done since the frosts had closed in.

Ballas felt contented. For the first time in months, Belthirran seemed truly attainable. Within hours, he would be up on the mountain tops. And then – then there was the rock wall to contend with: the barrier between Druine and Belthirran. Laike thought it impassable – yet this, to Ballas, seemed absurd. He could not say why; he understood that, logically, Laike might be right. Yet Ballas did not *feel* that he was. Instinctively, he knew that the explorer was mistaken.

In early afternoon, snow clouds appeared. After a while, snow began to fall – the pale flakes floating delicately on to the ledge. Ballas licked his lips, tasting the air's cold.

'A blizzard coming, you reckon?' he asked.

'We must hurry,' said Laike.

For some time they moved on, maintaining a brisker pace. Then the winds came. Their arrival was slow, gradual. At first, a breeze swept over the mountains. Then a single hard gust blew, jolting the snowflakes into a sudden dance. It died back, then blew again with doubled strength. Ballas staggered; the wind died down once more, then rose again, so fiercely and suddenly that Ballas was almost knocked off his feet. This time, the wind did not lessen. The gusts became a continual blast.

'Laike!' shouted Ballas. 'We've got . . . got to find shelter!' He peered through the driving snow. The explorer, and Heresh, had dwindled to vague, dark shapes. 'Do you hear? We have to—'

Laike shouted something – but Ballas did not hear: the wind was too loud. Stumbling forward, Ballas grasped the explorer's shoulder.

'We need shelter,' he repeated.

Snowflakes clung to Laike's hair. 'There is no shelter!'

'There must be more caves somewhere . . .'

'*Listen to me! There is no shelter!*'

Something flashed past Ballas's face: a blur of rapid darkness. Startled, Ballas lost his footing. An instant later, he was sprawled face down, his legs hanging over the ledge. Swearing, he clutched at the snow, sinking his fingers into it, trying to haul himself back up. It was a struggle. The snow shifted, breaking apart; and it seemed to Ballas that he had little strength.

Then someone grasped his collar and pulled. Ballas rose, slightly, and this extra help was enough: he managed to drag himself on to the ledge.

He looked up.

Heresh was staring down at him. In her eyes, in their depths, Ballas saw relief. And a type of expectancy. For a few moments, he held her gaze. Then something flickered at the edge of his vision.

On the ledge, twenty paces away, something glowed – glowed with a deep blueness. The light strengthened, so much so that the snowflakes cast grey shadows.

Cursing, Ballas ran over. As he approached he saw, through the blizzard-gloomed space, the outline of a crow. This outline, edged by the blue light, grew larger; it gained height and breadth. By the time Ballas arrived, it had become a Warden.

The Warden sagged against the rock face. Blood poured from the side of his head. His right arm was twisted, badly; a spike of bone pierced his tunic sleeve. The winds had been too strong, Ballas realised. While a crow, he had been dashed against the mountainside.

Ballas halted, watching him.

The Warden raised his head. Then, with his left hand, he unsheathed a small dagger and stumbled towards Ballas. His movements were slow, clumsy. Ballas grasped his wrist, then squeezed. The knife slipped from the Warden's fingers.

'Are there others?' shouted Ballas, moving close.

The Warden did not reply. Ballas seized his broken arm and wrenched it. The Warden shrieked, dropping to his knees.

'*Are there others?*'

The Warden did not reply – he merely groaned. Then Ballas realised how foolish his question was. Of course there would be others. The Warden would not have pursued him alone. He had been the first to find Ballas, true. But soon his companions would arrive. And then?

Grunting, Ballas half pushed, half threw the Warden from the ledge. The wind smothered his cries. He fell, visible only for a moment: a desperate, sprawling figure, disappearing into whiteness.

Ballas ran back to Laike.

'There is trouble,' said the big man.

'The Lectivin?'

'Wardens – those that shapeshift . . . The Church has followed me.'

They hurried along the ledge. Ballas's own words rang through his head, louder than the wind: *The Church has followed me* . . .

It did not make sense. He wasn't threatening the Church – he sought only to avoid them. So why – why were they hunting him? Why, when by now they must know he posed no threat. He was scrambling up the Garsbracks, in a blizzard: the mountain might kill him: so too might the weather. He was taking himself far from Druine, far from anywhere he could threaten the Church and the land it governed. So *why* had they followed him? Why did they demand his death? And why should that cursed Lectivin still be pursuing him?

In his mind's eye, Ballas glimpsed Belthirran – and all such questions faded away. The Church was trying to kill him. Their motives were unimportant. He had to survive. He had to find the Land Beyond the Mountains.

Following Laike, he climbed a small rise – then staggered, as the wind struck him with sudden force. It blew unhindered here, moaning around unseen rocks.

Ballas stood on a plateau of snow-caked stone.

A strange nervousness flickered inside him. Turning to Laike, he opened his mouth to ask if . . . if they had . . .

Laike pulled down his hood and gripped his staff tightly, as if partaking in a ritual, a ceremony. Ballas didn't need to ask his question. The answer seemed to sing upon the air.

They had reached the top of the Garsbracks.

Chapter 20

From Asvirius, the flesh was seared.
Its lungs erupted into flame,
Its bones flared to ash,
Yet in death it promised
A return to life, and vengeance . . .

For a moment Ballas did not move. He felt the wind scrape his skin, the snowflakes whirl around him. He thought, briefly, of the past months: of everything that had led him to this point. Of Papal Square. Of the barge journey. Of the marshes, of Granthaven, of the sewers and Jonas Elsefar's forest home.

He drew in a breath.

What was he supposed to do now? How was he to find Belthirran?

Ahead, there was a darkness – a high patch of grey amid the white. Squinting, he saw that it ran – seemed to run – the full length of the mountain top.

Ballas shrugged out of his rucksack. A grappling hook dangled from the back, fastened by a leather strap. Ballas started to undo the strap's buckle – yet his fingers were numb. And his hands shook.

He was nervous, he realised. And in his guts he felt urgency: a fierce need to hurry, to be quick, for at any moment something might happen – something that might thwart him . . .

Cursing, he ripped the grappling hook from the strap. Then he ran towards the greyness.

The rock wall wasn't truly grey – it was black: as black as snow clouds. Snow lay mounded against the base, curving upward into a long, sharp dune. The top of the wall could not be seen: through the falling snow, Ballas's vision reached only a few feet. He had no idea how high it was. But he could see that the wall was smooth, like a pebble on a stream bed. He touched it, and it felt like bottle glass: he detected no ridges, no fissures. Nothing that could provide a handhold. He had not expected the wall to be like this . . . to be such a perfect barrier.

Ballas hurled the grappling hook upward. The hooked iron claw disappeared from sight. Then hurtled back to the ground, sinking into the snow.

Cursing, Ballas snatched it up.

The wall was higher than he had supposed. He threw the hook again, with doubled effort. This time, it did not fall. Not straight away. Ballas grasped the rope as it hung from the hook, and started to climb. As soon as the rope took his weight, it loosened; Ballas felt the hook slithering from whatever it had found purchase upon. The hook flashed past Ballas's face. The big man uttered a profanity. Then he retrieved the hook and tried again.

The same thing happened: the hook lodged upon something – the top of the wall, presumed Ballas. Then, as he started to climb, it slipped free.

Laike and Heresh approached.

'Laike,' shouted Ballas, striding over. 'You've seen the wall in daylight, haven't you?'

The explorer nodded.

'Where should I throw the hook? There'll be a jagged part, won't there? Somewhere the prongs will catch, and stick?'

'There is no jagged part.'

'There must be!'

'Do you think I did not try a grappling hook, when I was last here? We have spoken of this before.'

'There must be somewhere,' persisted Ballas, 'where the hook will catch. Tell me, Laike: where should I throw the bloody thing? *Where?*'

'Ballas,' said Laike, sadly, 'it is not possible . . .'

'Bastard!' Angered by the words, Ballas drove his fist into Laike's face. The explorer sprawled backwards, on to the snow. His nose was broken: even through his chill-numbed knuckles, Ballas had felt the gristle rupture. Blood poured over the explorer's cheeks and pooled in his eye sockets. Ballas felt surprised for a moment. He hadn't really meant to strike Laike. He had simply lashed out, like a wounded, enraged animal.

But anger persisted. Stooping, he hauled Laike to his feet.

'You said you wanted to die – so die! Go on, you are no use to me! Piss off! Go to your bloody rowan grove and freeze!' He pushed Laike away.

Turning, the big man ran along the bottom of the wall.

'There must be somewhere,' he shouted. 'There must be *some* bloody place where the hook will stick!'

He stopped and threw the hook. It lodged; but when the rope took Ballas's weight, the hook scraped free.

He tried over and over again, at different points. Each time he failed.

He swept up the hook and glared at it. 'You piece of horseshit! You bloody piece of useless horseshit!' He crashed the hook against the wall.

Sparks flared where the steel struck stone. Ballas hit the wall, over and over, until the prongs buckled. He threw down the hook.

Heresh and Laike stood nearby. Whirling, Ballas approached them.

'I told you to piss off, old man! Why are you here, when I told you to go? Does this . . . does it amuse you?' He glared at Heresh. 'You are finding it funny. I can tell – it is in your eyes, you bitch . . .' Clenching his fists, he started towards the woman.

Suddenly, Ballas grew cold, colder than he had been before. He felt as if he had fallen into a frozen pool. His muscles jolted, each one locking in an angry spasm. He staggered, surprised. Then his balance vanished. Swaying, he stumbled – then dropped to his knees. Bile swirled in his throat. His head ached, as if it were being crushed in a carpenter's vice. He clamped his hands over his temples and groaned. From the edges of his vision, darkness encroached. He realised that he was slipping from consciousness. He resisted – yet he felt himself being sucked into oblivion . . .

. . . And as he fell, he remembered . . . he saw again . . . the dream of stone.

Ballas stares at the rock wall – at the smooth blank upthrust of stone. He sees nothing else: the sky and the ground are beyond his vision. And he feels nothing: his flesh is neither warm nor hot, if a wind blows it does not touch him, he cannot tell if the earth beneath his feet is soft or solid. He is aware only of the wall.

Then – he is pacing along the bottom of the wall. He does so without wishing to. He is not trying to walk – but nor is he trying to keep still. Something is making him move, something is working his limbs, and he finds it neither enjoyable nor unpleasant: it is simply happening, and will continue to happen, and it does not trouble or delight him.

He moves at great speed, yet doesn't look where he is going. His gaze is fixed upon the wall. He stares hard at the stone, as if seeking something, as if—

Suddenly, he slows, then halts.

He feels excited – and it is an almost childish sensation: a mixture of urgency, yearning, happiness.

In the wall there is a seam of red stone, running vertically. It ridges out from the darker stone, like a weal; and it glows – glows like a whore's lantern.

Without intending to, Ballas kneels.

The seam delights him, it inspires all manner of joy . . .

. . . And a strangeness – a light-headedness, and a sharpening of desire – sweeps over Ballas. He finds himself remembering something . . . something that does not belong to the dream, yet nonetheless seems unreal . . . something that he

can feel within his mind, yet that he cannot quite coax out . . . something sensed, but not seen . . .

Ballas opened his eyes.

Briefly, he wondered what had happened. Had he fainted?

It did not matter.

Scrambling to his feet, he returned to the rock wall. He placed his hand flat upon it. He groped for the crease, for the weal – yet he could not find it.

Swearing, Ballas stumbled a few paces to his right. He kept his hand against the rock wall. At any second he expected to feel the crease. He took step after step, and found himself running – found himself stumbling through knee-deep snow.

'What are you doing?' cried Heresh.

Ballas glanced back. The young woman had followed him. Laike was with her. Heresh held the explorer's sleeve lightly, so she could guide him.

Ballas continued running. The rock face was so smooth that he could scarcely feel it. He might as well have been touching empty air—

—Until a dull pain shot through his hand. Something tugged at his flesh. He jerked back his hand reflexively. Blood poured from a gash in his palm. Cautiously, he touched the rock wall. His fingertips met a raised strip in the stone. He peered more closely. As in the dream, a weal ran down the wall. A weal of red stone. Through the blizzard it shone, faintly. It extended as high as he could see. Ballas looked down. The weal sank into the snow piled at the wall's base.

For a moment Ballas was numb. He lifted his hand to his mouth. He licked blood from the laceration.

Then urgency seized him.

Dropping to his knees, he dug at the snow. Frantically, he heaved away handful after handful, hurling it behind him.

He did not know what he would find.

Yet he persisted.

Once the snow was cleared, he paused. The uncovered stone seemed ordinary. It was grey, and as smooth as the rest of the wall.

Ballas drew a breath, puzzled.

Then he noticed a patch of dark fungus sprouting from the stone. A cluster of thin, leaf-like growths. Using his knife, he scraped them away.

A marking was etched into the stone. It was simple in design. In the centre of a large circle, there was a smaller circle – about an inch across. Above this circle, and below it, and to its left and its right, there were more circles; each was half the size of the central circle.

Ballas faltered. The marking was familiar.

What now? he wondered.

Without understanding why, he touched the marking. Only with his fingertips, at first. Then he planted his fist against it, and pushed.

Nothing happened.

Cursing, Ballas pondered his next move. The marking was significant – he knew that much. It would lead him to Belthirran – but how?

Suddenly he found himself pressing his thumb upon the topmost circle. He had not willed the action. He did not know what purpose it would serve. Yet he felt he was acting upon some instinct. Some deeply hidden reflex.

Grating softly, the circle sank into the wall.

Ballas raised his eyebrows. He pushed his thumb against the circle on the right. This also sank into the stone. Hurriedly, he repeated the action on the two smaller circles that remained.

Then he pressed the central circle.

There was another grating noise. A harsh scraping of stone upon stone. And, from within the wall, a clashing, rattling sound, as if chains were slithering through iron loops . . . as if counterweights were falling and rising . . . as if an ancient mechanism had been triggered.

The grating noise grew louder.

The wall shook. Ballas wondered at first if *he* was shaking. If he was shivering so violently that it only seemed the wall quaked.

Then he saw a dark line at the wall's base. A slender horizontal opening, growing larger. A panel of rock was sliding upwards. Very slowly, as chains clanked and weights dropped.

'Sweet grief.' Heresh's voice startled Ballas. The young woman had followed him. Athreos Laike stood at her side.

The blind explorer shouted, 'What is happening?'

'I've almost found Belthirran!' Ballas grinned wildly. A powerful ecstasy surged through him. His blood tingled, his heart pounded. 'You don't go *over* this bloody wall! You go *through* it!'

Kneeling, Laike touched the shifting rock. His lips moved noiselessly.

Something flashed at the edge of Ballas's vision. In the distance, a blue light flared – then another. And another.

'Wardens,' muttered Ballas. Rising, he drew his dagger. The grating noise changed. The rock panel was sinking, the gap closing. Cursing, Ballas jammed his fist against the central circle. Chains slithered, weights dipped and lifted. The panel started rising again.

'Laike,' shouted Ballas, snatching the explorer's wrist. 'Keep your hand there, understand? Push at it – go on, push! If you don't, the doorway'll close. D'you hear me?' He pressed Laike's hand to the central circle. The explorer cried out, jerking away from the portal.

'My hand!' he shouted, thrusting it into the snow.

'Pilgrims' blood!' snapped Ballas, seizing Laike's wrist again. 'Do as I tell you, and . . .' His voice trailed off. Laike's palm was burned, the flesh red – and crisp. The explorer trembled.

Three shadows moved closer through the blizzard. They wore black, Scarrendestin-blazoned tunics. Leaping to his feet, Ballas sprinted at the first Warden. The man seemed surprised by the attack. He reached for his sword, but Ballas had already slammed a knife into his stomach. The Warden gaped, his eyes widening. Ballas grasped the man's sword hilt and drew the weapon. A second Warden moved to unsheathe his own sword. But as his fingers closed around the hilt, Ballas swung his sword savagely through the Warden's forearm. The man's hand seemed to cling briefly to the hilt. Then it fell to the snow, resting there like a pale, limp spider. Ballas thrust the blade into the Warden's throat. As he fell, the third Warden ran at Ballas. The big man lurched aside, struggling to keep his footing in the deep snow. The Warden hacked down with his sword, aiming for Ballas's shoulder. Ballas parried, clumsily. Sparks sprang from the clashing blades, gleaming through the falling snow. Grunting, Ballas heaved the Warden's blade aside. Then he smashed his forehead into the Warden's face. The man staggered, dazed. Ballas swung his sword edge down, into the Warden's skull-top. The blade stuck: as the Warden slumped, the weapon was wrenched from Ballas's fingers. Muttering, Ballas snatched up the fallen Warden's sword.

Four more Wardens appeared. Behind them, bursts of light blazed out. One after another, so many that Ballas couldn't count them.

Ballas ran towards the Wardens. The first two fell easily. Ballas half decapitated one with a single blow. He impaled the other on his sword point. The third slashed his sword towards the big man's stomach. Ballas deflected the blow. The Warden tripped, and Ballas slammed his knee into his face. The man's head jerked backwards, vertebrae popped. The fourth Warden took a step forward. Then he hesitated.

Ballas glared at him. 'Lost your nerve, eh?'

The Warden turned to run – but Ballas hurled his sword like a spear through his back.

The big man ran back to Laike. The rock panel had closed completely. Kneeling, Ballas pressed the small outer circles. They sank effortlessly into the stone.

'Why do they burn Laike,' said Heresh, 'yet you—'

'Shut up,' snapped Ballas. He didn't care about the reasons.

He pressed the larger central circle. Within the rock wall, chains rattled, weights rose and dropped. The panel trembled. Then inched slowly upwards.

For a few heartbeats, Ballas watched it rise.

'Sweet grief!' shouted Heresh, pointing.

A dozen Wardens were approaching. They were a quarter of a mile away, but running closer, as fast as the deep snow would permit. At the front there was a shorter figure, garbed in a woollen robe. Under its hood, its face was snow-pale.

Something twisted in Ballas's stomach.

'The Lectivin,' he grunted.

Nu'hkterin ought to have been hindered by the snow. Yet he moved with an animal grace. In his hand, he gripped a white short-bladed sword.

'Be quick!' Heresh urged Ballas.

Ballas pressed harder on the central square. Yet it made no difference. The mechanism ran at only one speed.

He gazed at the panel as it gradually rose.

Then he looked at the Lectivin. It bounded closer, its movements almost pantherish. He could see its eyes now, each one a blood-scarlet pool.

When it was forty yards away, Ballas looked at the panel. The opening beneath was just large enough to squeeze through. Beyond lay darkness.

As if thinking the same thought, Heresh grabbed Laike's shoulder.

'You first,' she said, guiding the explorer towards the opening.

'No,' said Ballas, seizing Laike's arm. He yanked the explorer away from the opening.

Heresh stared at him, wide-eyed. Bracing a hand against her chest, Ballas pushed her away. The woman stumbled, but did not fall.

'What—' she began.

Ignoring her, Ballas half rolled, half dragged himself through the opening.

With the central circle released, the door started to close.

The chains rattled loudly. The shifting counterweights made a noise like dull thunder. Ballas lay in the darkness, watching the opening dwindle.

Heresh stooped, trying to crawl through.

Already the space was too narrow. Soon it was just a two-inch-high horizontal band of snow.

Ballas glimpsed the hem of a brown robe. There was a rasping noise. A noise that Ballas recalled from the sewers. The noise of the Lectivin's thwarted rage.

There came a thin whistling sound – as of a blade cleaving air.
Heresh cried out. Blood splashed the snow.
The panel closed completely.
Ballas was in darkness.

Chapter 21

He swore the world
Would become his plaything, and his people
Would rule, and the human world
Would be naught but a memory . . .

The chains clashed, the counterweights echoed – then fell silent. There was a thud as the panel slammed shut. The air shook, for a moment. Then grew still.

Ballas sat upright, blinking.

He was in a large cave. The cave roof was shot through with veins of red stone, like that which marked the rock wall's face. They glowed, pouring blood-tinted light into the cave. But they were not strong enough to dispel every shadow. At the edges, the cave sank into blackness. The ground – a mass of jagged rocks – was darkness-swamped: it was visible only as a thickening of the general gloom. Ballas couldn't see how large the cave was. Yet every movement conjured a thousand echoes. Even his heart, thudding sullenly, seemed to resonate.

The air was dry, stale. The air of a coffin. Or a mausoleum. Ballas wondered how long it had been, since the panel last opened. How long since daylight, and fresh air, had swept through.

The cave was cold – the type of hard cold found in church buildings. In cathedrals. And also, he realised, in dungeons.

Muttering, he stood.

If the cave *did* connect Druine to Belthirran, there had to be a second panel, in the opposite cave wall. A doorway, leading to Belthirran.

'I am almost there,' he said. 'Pilgrims' balls, but I've almost found Belthirran.' He spoke only in a half-whisper. Yet the words echoed, rustling under the cave roof like a colony of bats. The effect ought to have disturbed him. Instead, he felt utterly at ease. Inside this cave, he was safe. He was beyond the Church's grasp. He laughed – and these echoes rolled wildly, maniacally, through the dark space. He stopped thinking about Belthirran for a moment. Instead, he considered the Pilgrim Church – and the efforts they had made to kill him. He thought of the Penance Oak. Of the Wardens on the river bank. And those in Granthaven – and elsewhere.

He thought, too, of the Decree of Annihilation: of the bloodshed it had caused, and how its failure would anger the Church. He wondered if the citizens of Druine would realise that he had escaped. That he had thwarted both them and the Church. Surely, the Church would not tolerate such speculation. They would claim to have killed the fugitive. To have obliterated him so vigorously that nothing remained – not even his bones.

Ballas started walking, picking his way over the loose stones. The cave's size surprised him: it took him several minutes to reach the far side. Here, the walls slanted to a broad juncture. In the red light, he made out a wall of stone. It bore no markings. No sigil like that outside, on the panel. Nor a vein of red stone. He ran his fingers over it, feeling for any gap or imperfection that might imply a doorway. The wall was uneven: a cluster of dips and edges, all seemingly random. He pressed his ear against it, listening – listening for sounds of wind, of the blizzard blowing . . . blowing, he realised, over Belthirran.

There was nothing.

Swearing, he stepped back. 'What now? How do I get through?'

He wondered if there was a way out at all. Perhaps there was but a single way into the cave. And a single way out. Or perhaps – perhaps there wasn't a way out at all. Maybe he was trapped.

He felt a surge of anger. And frustration.

Then Ballas calmed himself. There *had* to be a way out. The cave was not an accident: someone had built it or, if it had already existed, had chosen to use it for their own purposes. The panel was not a natural feature. Someone had put it there. Surely, those ancient peoples, who had travelled freely from Druine to Belthirran . . . surely it was their doing. The cave was a route from one realm to another. Therefore, there *had* to be a second doorway. Otherwise, the first doorway did not make sense. Otherwise, the sigil-engraved panel had no purpose.

But then – where was this second doorway?

Out of the corner of his eye, he glimpsed something. A square recess had been sunk into the floor, holding what seemed to be a mosaic. Striding over, Ballas saw that a number of stone cubes – sixty or seventy, he guessed – nestled inside the recess. Each was no bigger than a dice. Upon the upper face of each, a rune had been carved, each one a mix of loops, whorls, straight lines and sharp angles. Ballas did not know what each of them represented. Yet they looked vaguely familiar. Plucking out a cube, he found that each of its six faces bore a different marking.

He stared, confused.

What was this? A game? A puzzle?

He returned the cube to the recess. It fitted perfectly among its neighbours. Yet something was wrong. To Ballas's eyes, the overall effect – the general pattern of runes, from one cube to the next – seemed incorrect. Moreover, it jarred his nerves. It gave him feelings of nausea. Frowning, he turned over the cube that he had previously held. A different rune – a vertical line, capped by a diamond shape – was exposed. This seemed better. His queasiness lessened – but only slightly.

Muttering to himself, he turned over another cube. And another. And another.

This new arrangement pleased him. But not much. The configuration of shapes still made him bristle. Earnestly, he turned over a few more – including the first cube: here, inexplicably, he re-exposed the sigil that had irritated him. Now he found it soothing. The effect was strange, yet pleasing. He manipulated cube after cube.

Then he stopped.

'This is a foolishness,' he said. 'I've not got time to be pissing about with this bloody thing . . .'

Yet the compulsion persisted. Ballas worked quickly, rearranging the cubes. He could not understand why; he did not know what purpose it would – or could – serve. Yet it seemed an important task. Some instinct forced him onward. The cubes clattered under his large fingers. He worked dexterously, as if he had performed such an activity many times before.

The cubes *click-click-click*ed, their noise echoing through the cave.

Suddenly there was silence. Reaching out for a cube, Ballas paused. He stared at this cube, and at those around it.

Everything appeared in its proper place. Every rune that had to be visible *was* visible; and every cube was locked into the correct part of the recess. To Ballas's eyes, the runes made no sense. If there was a pattern, he could not see it. Yet he no longer felt agitated, no longer suffered a nervous urge to alter them. It was as if a piece of discordant music had become harmonious.

He got to his feet.

And felt a flash of rage. He stared resentfully at the recess. Why on earth had he wasted time on such a pointless endeavour? He had to get out of the cave! He had to find Belthirran! Yet instead, he had become preoccupied by a jigsaw.

'You are a pissing idiot,' he told himself.

He heard something: a faint rattling noise. He looked down. Inside the recess, the cubes trembled, as if shaken by a hidden hand.

Ballas stepped back, surprised.

The rattling grew louder as the cubes shook with greater ferocity.

Then there came a grating sound – as of stone sliding against stone.

The recess *moved*. Slowly, awkwardly, it split into four sections. Each corner inched diagonally away from the other. Around it, the cave floor quivered, the stones sliding away to make room for the dividing recess.

The shifting parts exposed a hole under the recess. A sphere of smooth, transparent stone, as large as a man's head, nestled inside. It seemed fashioned from glass. Ballas stretched out a hand to touch it—

—Then hesitated.

In the ceiling, the red-stone veins glowed brighter. The change was sudden, unnerving. Their dull light intensified. Shadows shrank as the entire cave became visible: it was big enough, Ballas thought, to hold a village. The walls were irregular; some force had blasted them into a jumble of juts and creases and edges. Ballas sensed that the cave had not been created by a gentle, gradual action – such as millennia upon millennia of spring-water trickling through. Rather, an aggressive, instantaneous force had engendered it: something as brash, as ferocious, as a volcanic eruption.

The light grew painfully bright. Then it tightened into a single shaft, lancing down into the recess . . . into the sphere.

Within the sphere, a tight ball of light appeared. It gradually expanded, seeming to blossom like a rose, until it filled the sphere . . . until the sphere itself blazed red.

The shaft vanished.

Ballas stared numbly. He reached out to touch the sphere; as his hand grew close, the red light shone through it, silhouetting the bones and tendons within. When his fingers were an inch away, a second shaft of light sprang from the globe, surging toward the ceiling.

Ballas looked up.

Something was carved into the dark rock. Something Ballas recognised. Something he had seen, months before – and then he had been there, when his luck had darkened and he had committed the crime for which the Wardens had arrested him.

It was a circle, thirty feet from side to side, crafted from some translucent gleaming stone – pale blue diamond, it seemed. At its top, bottom, left and right points, there were red globes, similar to that inside the recess. In the centre there was a blue gemstone, as large as Ballas himself. Through its depths, golden sparks floated, each a bright, clean splinter of light.

Monument, thought Ballas.

The recess-locked globe's light split into four beams, each sinking into one of the Monument's outer spheres. They pulsed, as red and angry as a summer moon. In the recess, the sphere paled, became translucent. After moments, the sphere was as it had once been: a colourless globe.

Ballas looked up at the Monument—

—Then he staggered as a tremor shook the cave. The ground tilted and there was a far-off roaring sound. And a grating noise, as if stones were being torn in half. Groaning, Ballas fell to his knees. The noise filled his ears, pounded his skull. Slabs of stone dropped from the cave roof. Striking the ground, they burst into shards. Clouds of dust swirled up. The big man swore – then coughed, as dust clogged his throat. The cave trembled, more stone crashed down—

—Then there was stillness. A few loose lumps of stone fell, cracking on the ground. Then a different noise became audible. The muted groan of the wind, blowing some distance away.

Ballas opened his eyes.

He expected to find that the cave roof had crashed down. Yet it was still there. Through the blue gemstone, in the centre of the Monument, he could see the sky. There were stars, glittering. And clouds, hurtling past at absurd speeds: Ballas had witnessed gales, and hurricanes – and he had never seen clouds move at such a rate. As the sky cleared, the moon became visible: full, fat, shining powerfully.

Inside the gemstone, light flared: a tentative blue-silver flash, cut short as a cloud-tatter passed in front of the moon.

Ballas drew in his breath. 'Sweet grief,' he murmured.

The cloud-tatter vanished. The moon shone unhindered. In the gemstone, there was a second flash. This time, it was stronger – so strong that it filled the cave: a blast of hard, eye-scorching light. Crying out, Ballas dropped to his knees. He felt as if a red-hot needle had plunged into his brain. Clutching his head, he squeezed his eyes shut. There was another flash – then darkness.

Ballas opened his eyes. For a long time, he was unable to see: blots of colour floated through his vision. As they lessened, the cave crept into focus.

The light had not vanished. Rather, it had tightened into a single beam, extending from the gemstone to the cave floor. It was the only brightness in the cave. The cave walls were darkness-cloaked. The floor was submerged in blackness – except close to the beam.

Slowly, the beam changed shape. Its base broadened out, and the beam stretched into a cone shape. Around the beam, the air glittered, as tiny ice-shards floated there. The air took on a trace of frost; a breeze blew, gliding cold over Ballas's skin, yet pure, as if it arose from a place untroubled by corruption, decay or disease.

In the centre of the cone, the light altered. At first Ballas could *see* it changing – yet he was unsure precisely what was happening. The bright blue-silver darkened and hung there, like a fog. Then it started to solidify. And to acquire a shape . . .

. . . The shape of a Lectivin.

It had a face similar to Nu'hkterin's. Its eyes were slanted incisions, its nose two perforations under a ridge of gristle. The mouth was lipless – a deft slash, seemingly cut there by a surgeon's knife. Its cheekbones jutted, stark, angular. The skin beneath sagged inward, creating a shadowed hollow. Yet this Lectivin also differed from Nu'hkterin. Nu'hkterin's features were brutal, bestial even; and, despite their apparent resemblance, this Lectivin's had a delicate, tapering quality – they seemed more refined, more minutely sculpted. Nu'hkterin's skull had been bald. This Lectivin sported a long, ponytailed strip of black hair, hanging to the small of its back. Every two or three inches, it was fastened by a piece of silver thread. Though slender, Nu'hkterin had been well-muscled – it had had the sleek muscularity of a hunting dog. This Lectivin was far more slender. It looked weak, almost fragile: a creature of libraries, not forests and fields. Its robe was different to Nu'hkterin's. Nu'hkterin's had been spun from dark wool. This Lectivin's appeared stitched from pale silk. Nu'hkterin had been armed with a curved blade. This Lectivin had a long sword, no thicker than a bamboo cane, worn through a loop in its belt.

And this Lectivin was taller than Nu'hkterin – far taller. Crouching behind a heap of stone, Ballas reckoned it to be eight feet in height. Ballas was himself a tall man – but he found the creature's size difficult to comprehend. It seemed absurd, that a roughly human-shaped entity could have such dimensions.

The Lectivin stood motionless. Then it sank to its knees and bowed its head – as if in prayer.

Its body trembled. The blue-silver hue of its skin turned to a hard, shining white. A glossiness permeated its robe. Moments before, it had been composed of light: now it was a solid thing, *reflecting* light. The Lectivin's sword lost its gleam, growing bone-dull.

The Lectivin threw back its head. Skinning back its lips, it howled. Tendons jerked taut in its neck as it gazed at the Monument . . . at the gemstone.

The cone of light vanished. In the Monument, the red spheres shrank into darkness. The blue gemstone grew dark, inert. Through it, the moon was dimly visible. Stars shone. Clouds drifted across the sky.

The cave sank into blackness. Then: brightness.

A ball of blue light hovered above the Lectivin's palm. The creature got unsteadily to its feet. It breathed loudly, each gulp of air a metallic rasp, like a whetstone upon a sword blade.

Slowly, the creature walked to the far side of the cave.

'*Novasris m'okavin, keldravis evran ma caivis,*' it said, its voice grating like a rusty lock. '*Manvaris vo skallen, miskavrin ecravis . . .*'

In the cave wall, the outline of a doorway appeared, glowing like hot copper.

'*Kavris eldaris, mohavek mustravin fulvarin,*' continued the Lectivin – then thrust its hand forward through empty air. It did not make contact with the wall. Yet the stones in the doorway blasted outward. Beyond the door, Ballas saw the mountain tops: a sprawl of pale, moonlit snow. He heard men shouting, screaming.

The Lectivin took a step forward. Then it halted and turned to Ballas.

Drawing back its hand, it hurled the light-ball. It flashed through the half-lit space towards the cave roof: it struck the gemstone in the centre of the Monument.

Now the roof began to fall.

Ballas curled himself into a ball. He felt stone after heavy, misshapen stone crash upon his body. They struck his legs, arms, shoulders. He cried out, he roared with pain. He felt blood trickle down his face, tasted it upon his lips. The pain grew stronger, and he heard nothing except the thunder of tumbling stone.

When Ballas awoke, the darkness stayed. Now it was a hard darkness: a solid, crushing mix of bone-crumpling weight and flesh-gouging edges. Yet it was broken by a fragment of faint white light . . . moonlight, seeping through the fallen stones that covered him. Groaning, he tried to move. At first he could not be certain that he had succeeded – his body was numb, and he felt the dull, crawling sensation of bruises ripening. Yet he heard stones knocking upon stone – a slithering *crack* as one piece of rubble struck another. He groped with his right hand upwards and outward. There was pain now – much pain: his bones throbbed, his skull ached, his blood itself seemed abrasive, scraping through his veins like lumps of grit. His fingers touched empty air. Grunting, he shifted his arm backwards, pushing away a few stones.

Moonlight washed over him.

Grimacing, he pushed himself on to all fours. Fragments of stone fell from his body, clashing and pattering around him. His limbs shook and he felt sick. He sat back, scarcely capable of lifting his head.

How long had he been under the stones?

Not long enough for the blood seeping down his face to dry. Or for his heart rate to slow.

He wondered if he had broken any bones. He put his hand on his chest, expecting to feel the agony of one rib grating against another. Yet, as his fingers touched his tunic, he paused – and shook his head. What did it matter if he was hurt? He had to find Belthirran. Once he was in the Land Beyond the Mountains . . . once he was there, he would tend his wounds.

A breeze ghosted against his neck.

He lifted his head.

Overhead there were stars, a moon, the blue-black depths of a night sky. There was no cave roof: no cave walls: the light-ball had smashed everything to rubble.

Ballas got to his feet. Blowing from behind, the breeze stirred his hair. It was cold, yet not unpleasant . . . and it blew from Belthirran, Ballas realised. It drifted southwards, and Ballas supposed it was his first encounter with the Land Beyond the Mountains. It was, in a way, Belthirran's greeting . . .

Ballas turned to face Belthirran.

The cave's remains stretched out ahead – a hundred paces of smashed rock. And then – then there would be Belthirran.

There would be sanctuary. Repose.

Strangely, Ballas did not feel excited. For months, he had hungered for Belthirran. But now, when it was only a half-minute's walk away, he felt unconcerned.

He walked over the rubble, towards Belthirran.

As he drew closer, he expected a little tension to pass through him. He *wanted* at least a mild thrill, a flicker of anticipation.

There was nothing.

As he walked, he noticed that the air tasted unusual. Unusual, but still familiar. It took him a few moments to recognise the flavour – the sharp tang of salt. And he heard a dull, booming, roaring crash. This too was familiar.

Now he picked up his pace.

Half stumbling, he left the cave and stepped on to a stone ledge that jutted over empty air.

His gaze dropped . . .

. . . To moonstruck sea water, five hundred feet below. Waves smashed against a jumble of greasy black rocks. With each impact, foam sprayed upwards, glittering like white diamonds; it sprawled over the rocks, then shrank back, returning to the dark water. The sea stretched to the horizon. And there was nothing . . . nothing at all . . . except this sea. No land. No islands.

Only water.

Ballas stood motionless.

He closed his eyes – then wing-beats cracked behind him: the *snick-snick* of a bird flapping its way on to a resting point. The big man did not turn around. Blue light pulsed, tinting the stones around his feet. He ought to have been frightened. Or wary.

Yet he felt as cold, as dispassionate, as the sea.

Only when the blue light faded did he turn.

As he did so, he reached for his dagger. He expected violence. He expected to face a Warden, armed with sword, knife or crossbow. He expected to be attacked once more; and to kill once more.

There was no Warden.

Only a man in a long black cloak that half-concealed the clothing beneath: the scarlet robe and Scarrendestin pendant of a Blessed Master.

Ballas recognised this Master. Recognised him in the way a sculptor recognises his own creations – for Ballas had created this man's form.

Godwin Muirthan's face was scarcely a face at all.

The right side was a block of scar tissue. In the cold, it was a marbled red-pink colour. It surrounded an empty eye socket; inside that cavity the skin shrivelled to a tiny raw hollow. And the Master's face still bled. Trickles of blood seeped from the scars, dripping from his chin, spattering his cape.

Taking out a handkerchief, Muirthan dabbed the trickles away.

'Do you know me?' he asked.

Ballas nodded.

'I have suffered much because of you,' continued the Master. 'By rights, I ought to be dead. Indeed, I often imagined death would be a blessing. I have been tempted by the sin of suicide, Anhaga Ballas. Hemlock, an opened vein . . . these and other methods called to me. But I rejected them. Nu'hkterin healed me. By nature, he is a killer: he is one of the Lectivin hunter caste. His ability to deliver remedies – to dispel cankers and mend flesh – is limited. But he was proficient enough to save me. He is far more competent than any human physician.'

Something distracted the Master. Kneeling, he picked up a shard of transparent stone. For a moment, he examined it.

'There was a *sivis*,' he said, softly. 'I always wondered how it would happen . . .' His voice trailed off and he tossed away the stone. 'You saw the Lectivin?'

Ballas inclined his head in a nod.

'Are you a religious man?'

Ballas shook his head.

'But you know of the Four? And the story of their Melding?'

'Yes,' replied the big man.

'The version delivered by myself – by the Pilgrim Church – is untrue. At least, it is not the entire story. There was a fifth pilgrim – a Lectivin, named Asvirius. It joined the Pilgrims long after their journey had begun. At first, they welcomed it. Then they began to fear it. The purpose of the Melding was to create a single being, capable of leading the souls of the dead through the Eltheryn Forest to heaven. The Melding required vast magical energies – energies that Asvirius would exploit for its own purposes. If it Melded with them, it would exist in the Forest as an entity composed purely of soul, of magick. But it would retain a physical existence. It would have been immeasurably powerful. So . . . so the Pilgrims destroyed it.'

Muirthan shifted slightly.

'Asvirius suspected the Pilgrims might rebel. So it took precautions. It ensured that if it was killed, its death would not be permanent. Indeed, it would turn it to its advantage. In the afterworld, it has learned much about magick. It is powerful, Ballas. And it will not use that power benignly. It intends to resurrect the Lectivin race. There will be another Red War. And this time we shan't win. Asvirius . . . will be too strong.'

Muirthan took a step closer to Ballas. His eyes were lit with pain – and anxiety. The areas of his face that were not discoloured by scars were deathly pale.

'The device you used, in Soriterath – the device Carrande Black tried to take from you – was a *sivis*. Do you know about such things?'

'A priest told me about them,' said Ballas.

'Through the *sivis*, Asvirius made you do its bidding. It brought you here so that you could set in motion the mechanism that would resurrect it.'

'Horseshit!' snapped Ballas. 'I came here because I was seeking Belthirran.'

'Why were you seeking Belthirran?'

'Because you and your pissing Church were trying to kill me.'

'And you sought safety in a myth? In something that didn't even exist?'

'I *believed* it existed,' muttered Ballas.

Muirthan sounded agitated. 'Are you usually given to such . . . such credulity? Do you normally treat fables as fact?'

Ballas opened his mouth to reply. Then he hesitated.

He *had* believed in Belthirran. But now the notion seemed preposterous. Not because he knew the Land Beyond the Mountains did not exist. But because it had been madness ever to believe that there really was such a place. On what had he based such assumptions? What had driven him to pursue such an illusion when all those around him –

clever, learned men like Crask – had decried it as nonsense? Why had he refused to believe Athreos Laike – the only man to have climbed the Garsbracks?

Ballas raised a hand to his forehead.

'Asvirius brought you here,' said Muirthan. 'When you used the *sivis*, it implanted within you the urge to find Belthirran.'

'That is not true!'

'There is a type of magick,' persisted Muirthan, 'that does not force a man into particular actions. But, instead, it kindles passions within him. In the Red War, some human soldiers fell victim to such spells. They became traitors, they murdered their fellows while they slept. The Lectivins did not tell them how to behave. Instead, they gave them a disgust, a hatred, for all things human. The soldiers themselves decided how to act upon those urges, those terrible black lusts. Thus they slaughtered. Thus they butchered not merely their companions but their own families.'

'I came here,' said Ballas slowly, 'to escape the Church.'

'If you hadn't been hunted, you would have found another reason. Perhaps you would have believed treasure lay here, upon the summit of the Garsbracks. Maybe you would have become a religious zealot, making a pilgrimage of your own. Either way, Asvirius would have drawn you here. Either way, it would have compelled you to resurrect it.'

Suddenly, a memory swirled up into Ballas's mind. For the first time, he recalled using the *sivis*. He had been in a lodging room in Soriterath. And he had seen Asvirius. The Lectivin had been in a world of dust. No stars, sun or moon shone. And . . .

. . . The memories seeped back . . .

. . . And it had made a gesture, a strange pressing movement with its hand: and Ballas realised that it indicated the order in which he had pressed the stones in the panel sunken in the rock wall. There had been a tapestry, too: this displayed an arrangement of sigils – an arrangement to which he had matched the cubes in the recess.

And he thought of Belthirran itself: the oft-dreamed-of scene, of fields, cookfires, grazing cattle . . .

Ballas felt as if a parasite had nested within his brain, some vile, thought-corrupting worm . . .

. . . For that scene had been his home. It had been Hearthfall, the valley where he had grown up – a place that he had loved, a place where he had known the kindness, and light, of a family . . .

. . . *And he had not recognised it.*

'No,' he muttered. 'No!'

Spinning round, he strode to the ledge. He gazed at the sea, at the waves grinding over one another, at the luminous spume. He felt a type of longing – for the water's blackness: to be consumed by it, to be utterly smothered by its lightlessness and cold.

'What – what are you doing!' Muirthan sounded alarmed. Bootsteps scraped upon stone. 'Ballas – what are you doing?'

Ballas looked at the waves.

In his mind's eye, he glimpsed Hearthfall. He tried to shake the image away. It was a place of beauty, of all good things – and it filled him with pain. No sword or dagger had ever hurt him so much.

The agony had to end.

He stepped closer to the edge.

'For the Pilgrims' sake – stay where you are! Please, you must listen!' Godwin Muirthan, one of Druine's most powerful men, gabbled like a frightened child. 'Don't move! Step back – I beg you! You must do your duty . . . No: you must . . . Please, please, turn to me! Promise me you won't . . . the waters . . . you are needed!'

'Needed?'

Muirthan moved up beside him. 'Asvirius must be stopped. My Wardens cannot do it. Not even the shapeshifters. And Nu'hkterin – sweet grief, it is a nothingness beside Asvirius.'

'You want me to serve you?'

Muirthan was silent a few moments. 'I want you to serve Druine. Asvirius's magick cannot harm you. The reasons are complex; there is little time to explain but . . . you opened a doorway to enter here, yes?'

Ballas nodded.

'An enchantment lay upon that doorway. Asvirius needed to make certain that only you – only the person who was running his errand – could enter this place. To do so, it placed a spell upon you: when you encounter any device created by a Lectivin – such as the doorway – you are able to manipulate it. Normally, such things repel those who are not Lectivin.'

Ballas recalled Laike's attempt to open the door, and his scorched flesh.

'The Lectivin use of magick is peculiar: one Lectivin cannot cast a spell against another. Perhaps, within their culture, they feared treason and rebellion: and this informed the way magick was taught and practised. Nonetheless: just as the spell placed upon the doorway did not harm you, so you cannot be damaged by any spell Asvirius may launch against you. It used a spell to destroy this cave, did it not?'

'Yes.'

'The falling stones might have killed you, but the spell itself could not have done so.' The Master moved closer. 'Asvirius's greatest strength is magick. Through magick it could defeat every Warden in Druine. But you are immune. Asvirius can harm you only through violence, Ballas.

'And violence . . . well, you have an aptitude for it.' He exhaled. 'We shall be paying out pensions to the families of those Wardens who perished at your hand. We know what you are capable of.'

The Blessed Master shifted uneasily.

'If you do not fight the Lectivin, if you do not kill—'

'All Druine will perish, I suppose.'

Muirthan nodded.

Ballas shrugged. 'Good.'

'What?'

'I don't care for Druine. Nor the people who dwell there. I've had enough. This land has granted me no favours. Nor has your bloody Church.'

'We hunted you because we had to! We knew Asvirius would—'

'So what?' Ballas whirled to face the Master. 'So what if the world is overrun by bloody Lectivins? Why should I care? I've had enough!'

Turning, Ballas stepped to the edge – but then he froze. He stared at the sea. At its grinding, swelling blackness. It delighted him – yet it frightened him too.

He imagined leaping from the overhang. He imagined the moment of commitment when he sprang into the air. Then the split instant of weightlessness before he fell. Then the descent. The moment his destiny would become truly apparent. The downward-hurtling moments in which he would sense, in every nerve, sinew, bone and muscle, his own mortality. He would see death in front of him – and be powerless to fight back. He would be falling; there could be no escape.

For the first time in a long time he felt truly frightened.

He craved the ocean's dark. But to confront the dark, and to see nothing except that dark . . . to comprehend fully, at the moment of death, that he was dying . . .

Ballas shut his eyes, appalled.

He could not take his own life. If he had been capable of such an act, he would have done it long ago.

He did not crave death. Merely oblivion.

Merely a death that did not wear death's real mask.

Ballas opened his eyes. And turned to Godwin Muirthan.

They walked out of the shattered cave on to the snow.

Half a dozen Wardens lay on the pale ground, dead. They had perished, Ballas presumed, by Asvirius's sword. Some were decapitated, their neck stumps blood-wet, their heads close by, the eyes glassy. Others bore slash marks across their chests, their stomachs, their throats. One Warden's ribcage had been hacked open, a neat horizontal gash exposing his lungs and heart. Other Wardens had died by magick. These still stood upright – yet a blast of fire had blackened them. Their eye sockets were burned empty, their hair had crisped to brittle curls. In their charcoal-dark forms, only their teeth shone: each tooth seemingly too long and too broad for their mouths. They maintained their dying-instant postures. One gripped his sword in a gesture of threat. Another was unsheathing his weapon. A third was turning away, as if intending to flee rather than fight.

A hundred yards away there were two more figures.

Athreos Laike was sprawled upon his back. His woollens were blood-soaked and he stared at the stars, the moon – shining clearly, so far from the sky-corrupting lights of cities. Yet they shone unseen by the man who would have most enjoyed their purity.

Beside Laike, Heresh sat back against a rock. Her head was bowed, her hands clamped over her stomach. Her hands were dark, blood-slick.

She looked up, as if sensing Ballas's presence. Their gazes locked – but only fleetingly. Heresh lowered her head, her shoulders sagging.

Ballas drew a breath – then strode over.

'What are you doing?' Godwin Muirthan hurried along behind him. 'There is no time! The longer Asvirius remains in the corporeal world, the stronger it will become. You must fight it while it is weak!'

Ballas continued walking.

Then he halted by Laike's corpse.

A deep incision gaped in the explorer's throat. Within the soft flesh, vertebrae and tendons could be seen – each daubed scarlet, each glinting softly. He had intended to die upon the mountains. But he had craved a placid, introspective death. He had wanted a rowan grove, and numbness. Not butchery. Not terror. But then, it hardly mattered. How many men choose their own deaths? How many actually go to the grave in a manner they desire?

Ballas shifted his gaze to Heresh.

Her hands remained clasped over her belly. Yet through her fingers, through the blood, there was a soft, glistening smoothness – and a hint of grey-blue. Her stomach had been sliced almost completely open. If she were to take her hands away, her innards would slither out. She was shivering and her skin was pale.

She raised her head. Once more, she looked into Ballas's eyes.

'I am dying,' she said. There was no anger in her tone. No accusation. Only loneliness – a loneliness that Ballas recognised. She was slipping from this world. And she knew it. She no longer belonged to the realm of flesh. Of life. And she felt her distance from all living things as a type of intractable isolation . . . It was the sound of black water upon rocks. Of wind groaning around a standing stone.

'You see what wickedness Asvirius commits? You see why it must be stopped?' Muirthan's voice cracked. 'Can you comprehend now what it is capable of?'

'This was *your* Lectivin's doing.' Ballas's voice was dull, flat.

'Then – then I apologise. The Church didn't intend for it to slaughter your companions. This killing does not please me; in truth, it angers me, for we – the Church – will be in your debt, if you destroy Asvirius: yet we have left you bereaved—'

'Heal her.'

'What?'

'Make your Lectivin heal her. It can do that, right?'

'Yes.'

'Heal her, and I'll do as you ask.'

'Such things do not happen quickly! The magick is slow, it takes time – we cannot wait that long. But I swear, if you go now, to Asvirius . . . Nu'hkterin will mend her. It will return her to health. And we will ensure her a safe descent from the mountains.' Muirthan gestured across the mountain tops. Nu'hkterin appeared from behind a rock. As the Lectivin approached, Muirthan said, 'I have never before observed fear in Nu'hkterin. But I see dread now. It believes that if Asvirius finds it, it will be killed – but only after it has suffered the most astonishing tortures. After all, it has betrayed its own people. It is an ally to humans, not Lectivins.'

Nu'hkterin blinked rapidly. Its gaze darted here and there, as if it expected Asvirius to appear at any instant.

Muirthan spoke to it in the Lectivin tongue. It listened, then nodded jerkily.

'It will heal her,' said Muirthan.

Turning to go, Ballas felt a hand on his forearm. The hand was pale, spidery-fingered.

Nu'hkterin said something in Lectivin. Then it proffered a short-bladed dagger and, drawing it from a scabbard, a thin sword. Both weapons were crafted from the same bonelike material as Asvirius's sword.

'Take them,' said Muirthan. 'Lectivin weapons are incredibly sharp – and light, too. You will not believe how . . .' His voice trailed off. Then he touched lightly his scar-scrawled face.

Ballas accepted the weapons.

Slowly, he and Muirthan walked away.

'Destroy Asvirius,' said the Master. 'And you will be rewarded. I will see to it myself. Whatever you request will be yours. What are your tastes, Ballas? Do you like wine? You shall drink only the finest. And women? We shall grant you gold enough for a thousand whores. And, of course, we shall grant you a special dispensation: you will be absolved of all sins. And when you pass away – in old age, I expect – the Four will guide you through the Eltheryn Forest, to heaven, where you shall dwell beside the saints—'

'Visionary's root,' interrupted Ballas.

Muirthan frowned.

'Does it work? You've forbidden it, haven't you? So it must have some use . . .'

'If you want visionary's root,' said Muirthan, 'you can have as much as you wish. We have contacts in the East—'

'Does it bring insight? That's what I want to know.'

'Certain men, who have the proper skills . . . yes, they acquire insight.'

'A root-eater reckoned he dreamed of me. He spoke of three chalices, each holding what he reckoned was the essence of my soul. One held the past, the other the present, the third the future.'

'The Trinity of Chalices. A dream that is difficult to conjure. But of all root-dreams, it is the most reliable. What did the third chalice hold? The chalice concerning your soul's future? Was there velvet, denoting sensuous contentment? Lilies, predicting love? Liquid gold, suggesting wealth? We can provide them all, if you wish—'

'The chalice was empty,' said Ballas.

Muirthan froze. 'Empty?'

Ignoring him, Ballas started down a long slope, following Asvirius's footprints in the snow.

Ballas thought of little as he moved onward.

He felt the wind on his skin, heard the crunch of his feet upon snow. He tasted the brittle air, and for the first time noticed that, as Laike had promised, it was *pure*. Yet it didn't provoke pleasure. Or discomfort. It simply existed, and was neither good nor bad.

He licked his lips. Now, a different taste: blood – his own. The wound above his eyebrow had stopped bleeding. The blood had dried, acquiring a sour taste. A taste he knew well, a taste that – along with ale, whisky and wine – had been with him for ever, it seemed.

So too had a few other sensations. Sensations he felt now: bruised flesh, broken bones, an aching skull. Was it strange, he wondered, to find oneself in extraordinary circumstances – yet feel nothing new? To pursue a Lectivin over a mountain – yet feel as if he were hung-over after a night of revelry and a beating?

He grunted: it did not matter.

For another familiar feeling was with him.

The desire to kill.

Asvirius came into view: a tall, gaunt figure, its robe shining in the moonlight. Despite the snow, it walked with long, sinuous steps. It moved down the slope, six hundred yards away. Even so far off, its height perturbed Ballas: the creature seemed unreal, something that did not exist, *could* not exist.

Ballas cupped his hands to his mouth, intending to shout for it to halt and fight. But he remained silent, and lowered his hands.

There were better ways of issuing a challenge.

He broke into a run, approaching Asvirius from behind. Fifty paces away, he halted. From his belt he drew the short-bladed knife given to him by Nu'hkterin. It was a neat, compact weapon. And very small: in Ballas's large hands, it seemed no more substantial than a dining fork. It was also very light: it weighed as much as a thin strip of wood.

Yet the blade looked sharp. Looked as if it could carve stone.

Drawing back his arm, Ballas hurled the knife. It spun through the air, flickering in the moonlight. It made a murmuring sound as the breeze blew around it. And this alerted Asvirius. The Lectivin halted and turned – but too late to dodge the weapon. The blade pierced hilt-deep into its shoulder. It staggered, raising fingertips to the knife. For a heartbeat it seemed that Asvirius would collapse.

And this filled Ballas with panic. The Lectivin could not – *must* not – be so easily killed. For if it died . . . if no true fight ensued . . .

Asvirius tugged out the knife.

It peered at the blade. It pressed a finger into the blood, then raised it to its lips, tasting it – as if this provided proof that it was no longer in the Eltheryn Forest. As if it showed it had returned to the world of flesh.

Casting the knife aside, it lifted its head. Then it locked gazes with Ballas.

Upon its palm, a ball of light appeared – a floating globe of blue: Asvirius hurled it at Ballas.

Crying out, Ballas covered his face and dropped into a crouch.

The light-ball reached him. Then it exploded in a mountain-engulfing flash.

Ballas expected pain. Expected his skin to blister and his eyes to be searched out of their sockets. But he felt nothing. Not even a faint warmth.

He opened his eyes.

Snow had melted, baring sodden grass, wet stone. A rowan tree yards away smouldered, smoke writhing up from its branches.

Asvirius tilted its head, puzzled. Then it lifted its chin – as if it suddenly understood something.

In a single fluid movement, it drew its sword.

Ballas did the same. Like the knife, this weapon had almost no weight. Ballas swung it back and forth: he might as well have been wielding a bamboo cane. The blade looked sharp – but how sharp? Ballas strode to the rowan tree. He placed the blade against a low branch, and pressed. It sank effortlessly through the burned wood.

Asvirius ran up the slope towards Ballas.

It moved quickly – a flash of white against the different white of the snow. In a few seconds it had reached Ballas—

—And was lunging at him, its sword snaking out.

Swearing, Ballas parried the strike. The Lectivin sprang backwards then advanced, executing a swift downstroke. Raising his sword, Ballas blocked the attack. Asvirius slithered its sword free, then swept the tip horizontally across Ballas's chest. The big man lurched back, the blade point missing him by a fraction.

Breathing heavily, he lifted his sword, ready to deflect another blow.

Asvirius did not attack. It stood several yards away, inhaling lungful after lungful of air. It rocked from foot to foot. And idly flitted its sword back and forth. At first Ballas thought it was toying with him. Then he realised it was getting used to the physical world. The world of sensations. Of flesh, of pain.

Asvirius ran at Ballas. It unleashed a dozen lightning-fast strokes. Ballas parried frantically. The Lectivin's blade moved so fast that it vanished from sight; it seemed less a solid object than a stirring of the air. Ballas felt flickers of pain in his forearms and shoulders. He glimpsed blood. The Lectivin was cutting him. Yet it was impossible to detect which attacks caused the damage. Asvirius appeared to be enjoying itself. To be savouring the violence. There was a near-sensuous delight in its movements. It was taking pleasure from the corporeal world. And this, thought Ballas, was a blessing. If it wished, it could kill Ballas with a few strokes. Yet it treated him like a cat did a mouse: as something with which to sharpen reflexes and hone skills – only when it grew bored of him would it deliver the fatal blow.

That moment came seconds later.

Asvirius made a hissing noise – and its sword swept once, twice, thrice across the big man's chest. Ballas's tunic sagged open. Underneath, a deep cut seeped blood through thick layers of fat. Delicately, surgically, Asvirius sketched a gash across Ballas's forehead. Blood poured into the big man's eyes. Cursing, he turned and sprinted away.

When he halted, he found that Asvirius had not moved. It stood twenty paces away, watching.

Ballas wiped the blood from his eyes. Instantly, fresh blood poured down. Stooping, he snatched up a fistful of snow and pressed it into the wound. There was a moment of pain – then numbness. He threw the snow away: it was bright red. He gathered some more and jammed it against the wound.

He was tired. He felt it now: a dull heaviness in his limbs.

Scowling, he rolled his shoulders, then rubbed snow into his face.

Asvirius approached, walking slowly. Unhurriedly. Then it broke into a run, its sword flickering out. Ballas blocked strike after strike. Yet he was clumsy compared to the Lectivin. Asvirius doubled its efforts. Ballas heard himself roaring. In frustration. And anger. He took step after step backwards to avoid the Lectivin's assault—

—Then the slope steepened and he found himself rolling down it, tumbling head over heels. The sky swung in and out of view. He felt himself gathering speed. Out of the corner of his eye, he glimpsed a yawning blackness: a chasm, sinking deep into the mountain. Swearing, he tried to stop himself. He clutched at the snow. He dug in his heels. He stabbed his sword into the ground, as if it were an ice axe.

Suddenly, he rolled off the edge of the chasm. Briefly, he was airborne, hanging over empty space. Then he fell.

He struck something, he could not tell what. It felt like a thousand dry fingers had clutched at him, then withdrawn. There was a crackling noise – and the scent of wood sap.

A tree – he had struck a tree that sprouted from the chasm's wall.

Thrusting out a hand, he grasped a branch. He held on tightly, but his grip slipped. He fell a few more feet and pain shot through his hand. He grabbed a second branch. And halted his descent.

The rowan creaked softly.

Ballas looked down.

Fifty feet below, there was a jumble of rocks. Ballas looked around. A ledge jutted from the chasm's wall – five feet wide, snow-stacked. He threw his sword on to it. Then, after clambering through the rowan's branches, he jumped down.

He sprinted to a small recess. As he went, he glanced up – and saw Asvirius, peering into the chasm. The Lectivin lingered – then it withdrew.

Something had cut Ballas's right hand. Had *pierced* it: a raw hole gaped in his palm. Blood flowed copiously, making his hand slippery – too slippery to grip his sword. Cursing, Ballas tore off his tunic hem and tied it around the wound.

Taking up his sword, he stepped from the recess.

As Ballas followed the ledge, a thought struck him. It was simple, obvious, something he supposed he had always known . . . but now it carried a certain force.

These past weeks, he had inflicted much death.

He had killed – killed frequently, killed often.

He had killed in self-defence. Wardens had died because *they* wished to kill him. For the same reason, Carrande Black had died. And the young men, the youths, in the Archive Hall in Granthaven.

He had killed for vengeance. He thought of the barge-master, Culgrogan – the arrow lodged between his eyes. And of Jonas Elsefar. True, he had known of Ballas's plans, so Ballas would, one way or another, have been forced to kill him: yet it would have been a swifter death. He wouldn't have abandoned him in the forest. He wouldn't have left him exposed to starvation, to freezing – and to attack by wild animals. Had Elsefar not betrayed Ballas, he would have died without knowing death was at hand. He would not have expired in the jaws of wolves.

Ballas had killed out of practical need. He had murdered Elsefar's employers in exchange for the quill-master's help. He could see them now: one in a pissing yard, a knife in his back. One on his office floor, his throat cut. One sprawled on the paving slabs under his window, his body awash with blood. And he had killed by accident: he recalled the whore in the slab-broken man's bedchamber, a throwing knife protruding from her chest.

And when he did not kill – *others killed*. In Granthaven, Wardens and Under-Wardens had killed because of him. And the populace had murdered those they had mistaken for Ballas. And they had killed Rendeage too – all because he was loyal to the Pilgrims' teachings.

And he had killed, too, as a god might kill: by bringing famine. In Granthaven, many had starved after the city had been sealed.

And people had died simply because they knew him: Lugen Crask, killed by a shapeshifting Warden. Athreos Laike, who had been destined to perish all along but who had been denied the type of death he craved.

'What am I,' murmured Ballas, 'but a bringer of death?'

He took a few steps – then hesitated.

It had not always been so. Once, years before, he had been contented. He had experienced nothing but warmth and security. He had known little of violence, of death . . .

. . . An image of Hearthfall rose unbidden in his memory: a sprawl of green fields, criss-crossed with streams and rivers; cottages, deep trout-crowded tarns, stables and byres and hawthorn bushes, white-blotched by blossom . . .

Something damp touched his face and trickled down his cheek. He reached to touch it. But he paused, shaking his head.

'I'm bleeding again,' he said.

He drew a breath.

'Piss on this. Piss on the whole bloody mess.'

The ledge ended in a heap of boulders. Clambering up, Ballas found himself back on the slope. He had overtaken Asvirius; the Lectivin was a hundred yards behind him. It strode onwards, an elegance in its movements. It had resheathed its sword. And this gesture, this hint of complacency, pleased Ballas.

Ballas stood stock-still, waiting to be noticed.

Asvirius halted, staring.

Suddenly, Ballas felt weak. He looked down at his chest. Blood had soaked his tunic and leggings. How much had flowed from his body? Enough to make him slightly light-headed. To make his limbs shake.

Around his boots, the snow was red.

Ballas grunted: Jonas Elsefar had spoken correctly. Red *was* his colour. For much of his life, it had been the red of others' blood. But now it was his own.

Soon he would have a different colour. One far darker. One that would soothe him.

He looked at Nu'hkterin's sword. At the blade, as long as his forearm. Then he threw it away, into the gully.

From his belt he drew a steel dagger.

He walked towards Asvirius. Snow crunched. A breeze swirled around him. He tasted the purity of mountain air – and now he took pleasure from it.

Asvirius raised its sword, adopting a fighting stance.

Ballas halted, twenty yards away.

Then he ran at the Lectivin, his head low, shoulders forward – he charged like a bull, and roared, and heard those roars echo across the mountains.

Asvirius slashed its sword at Ballas: a clean, sharp, downward stroke. Twisting slightly, Ballas raised a forearm. The blade struck his flesh and slid through it. The cutting edge pierced fat, muscle – then rasped into bone. There was pain: more pain than Ballas had ever known. More, it seemed, than his body could bear.

He ignored it.

Thrusting upward, he sank his knife into Asvirius's stomach. He pushed it harder, deeper – until it was lodged hilt-deep. Then he pushed it further, sinking the handle into the creature's gut. Looping his left arm behind its back, Ballas half lifted, half pushed Asvirius over the snow, moving in a stumbling run. The Lectivin gave a harsh, rasping howl. It struggled wildly against Ballas's grip. Releasing the dagger, Ballas curled his right arm around the Lectivin, squeezing so tightly that he felt its ribs buckle.

He looked past Asvirius, beyond the snow – towards the chasm.

Something stabbed his back, over and over. Asvirius was still using its sword. Perhaps it was trying to sever Ballas's spine – to paralyse him.

Ballas ran on—

—And, suddenly, he was hanging over the chasm – over nothingness.

There was an instant of weightlessness. A delicious instant when Ballas knew that there could be no turning back. Asvirius gave a shrill, hissing shriek – the sound of a vipers' nest set ablaze. Then they started to fall, the wind rushing past them, the rich scents of snow and stone rising around them.

Ballas unsheathed a second dagger and plunged it deep into Asvirius's stomach. The Lectivin's eyes jerked wide. Blood frothed upon its lips as wild spasms shook its body.

They hurtled deeper and deeper.

Ballas looked past the Lectivin. No starlight penetrated the chasm's depths. No moonglow, no pale blue-silver.

Ballas gazed at this blackness . . . and grinned.

Closing his eyes, he conjured a deeper blackness.

And sank gratefully into the dark throat of oblivion.

Out of a chasm, miles away, a flash of blue light erupted, sweeping over the mountains, momentarily enfolding everything: every stone, snowdrift, rowan tree. Uttering a blasphemy, Godwin Muirthan shielded his eyes – then breathed out. His eyes hurt, as if he had stared at the sun. Yet the feeling pleased him. It was the harbinger of fine news. It meant—

Wing-beats sounded, and a crow alighted on the ground nearby. A blue glow – its hue identical to that which had sprung from the gully, but its force far gentler – surrounded the creature. Gradually, it grew larger, the feathers vanishing, the delicate bird-bones thickening.

Blessed Master Hengriste appeared. The old Master opened his mouth to speak – but shivered, and drew his cape tight around him.

'Sweet grief,' he said, 'it is cold. Up here, the very air is ice.'

Muirthan gestured vaguely. 'You saw the light?'

'Of course. A good sign, yes: such brightness – during the Red War, they called it the Magus Glare. When a magicker dies, there is always such a – ah – spectacle.' He fiddled with the clasp at the front of his cape. 'So: let me make sure that I am not harbouring illusions: Asvirius returned, yes? But we destroyed it.'

'*We* didn't,' replied Muirthan.

Hengriste frowned.

'The fugitive . . . Anhaga Ballas: it was his doing.'

'He turned from adversary to ally?'

'At a cost.' Muirthan pointed to Nu'hkterin. The Lectivin kneeled beside the red-haired woman. She was drifting in and out of consciousness – but such things were common, during magical healing. 'He struck a bargain. If we saved her, he would do as we asked. I had no choice but to do as he demanded. And in return . . . in return he killed Asvirius.'

'You sound surprised.'

Muirthan snorted. 'He was a drunk, a thief—'

'He was more than that.'

'What are you talking about?'

'Oh, come, Godwin: could a mere drunk, a mere thief, have eluded us for so long? Every Warden hunted him. Every citizen sought his blood. Yet still he lived . . . And now, it makes a rough sort of sense. It is extraordinary, I grant you – but not unbelievable.'

Muirthan did not understand.

'This morning, I received a package from the archives at Ganterlian. When I first learned that he had used the *sivis*, I requested that all records on Anhaga Ballas should be sent to me—'

'He is a peasant! There can be no records of him.'

'He was a soldier, Godwin.'

'Even so . . .'

'He was a *Hawk*.'

Godwin Muirthan fell silent.

'He was a Hawk,' repeated Hengriste. 'One of the military elite. One of the Rarest. Of course, it was a long time ago: two decades have passed—'

'Two decades? He had a hand in—'

'—The crushing of Cal'Briden. He helped destroy the rebel who would have obliterated the Church. Who would have plunged Druine into chaos.' Hengriste sniffed. 'He had a hand in all the Hawks' major operations. Even the assault on Cal'Briden's mansion—'

'He was there, at the rebel's death?'

Hengriste nodded. 'For three years, he served as a Hawk. Without him . . . Ha! I detect a pattern, Godwin: this is the second time he has saved the Church. As you say, Cal'Briden might have overthrown us. He was rich, he had a private army . . . But Anhaga Ballas was part of the force that defeated him. And now . . . now he has killed a very different adversary.'

'He was a Hawk,' murmured Muirthan, numbly.

Hengriste spat on to the snow. 'They dismissed him, in the end.'

'Oh?'

'The missive from Ganterlian – it included a report by General Standaire.'

'Does he still live?'

'He died years ago. But it was he who dismissed Anhaga Ballas. He was too reckless, said Standaire. Too careless of his own life – and the lives of his comrades. Ballas joined the Hawks when Cal'Briden was on the rise. At that time, such qualities were required. But later on, when rebellions were few . . . ? No. He had outlived his usefulness.' Hengriste sighed. 'Standaire mistrusted Anhaga Ballas. He said he seemed self-destructive. The more dangerous that campaign became the more enthusiastically he got involved. And he was ill-disciplined. He was a great fighter. But as for the rest . . .' Hengriste shook his head. 'He did not obey orders terribly well.'

Hengriste looked towards Nu'hkterin. Muirthan also looked. The Lectivin continued to tend the red-haired woman.

'Tell me Godwin,' said Hengriste, 'do you truly intend to honour the bargain you struck? Anhaga Ballas is dead. He won't ever know what becomes of the woman; he'll never find out if you hold fast to your promise. Ballas is dead,' repeated Hengriste, 'and thus, your bargain is cancelled. That is the way I see it.'

Godwin Muirthan almost spoke – but something occurred to him. 'He is *more* than dead.'

'No man can more be "more than dead".'

'His soul has been destroyed. The blue light – the death of Asvirius – such a force obliterates everything. Is that not what they say about Magus Glare? It obliterates not merely flesh – but the soul? Ballas has gone, gone from existence. He has left this world – and he will not arrive in the next. *His soul has been scrubbed from existence*. He will not be found within the Eltheryn Forest.'

Hengriste stood very still. 'That is true, Godwin. But let us not speak of him with reverence. He was not a saint – not a willing martyr.'

Muirthan wanted, suddenly, to argue with Hengriste. He wanted to mention the visionary's-root dream of the Three Chalices.

But before he could speak, Hengriste said, 'His death will prove useful. In a week's time the Spring Festival will begin. We shall announce that the fugitive has been killed, that he is suffering amid the sulphurous fumes of hell. That will, I think, put fear into the people.'

The aged Master seemed excited.

'We shall say our Wardens were responsible. We shall fashion the entire thing as – as a tale of courage, of pious bravery. No – wait: maybe if Under-Wardens were said to have captured him . . . Then every citizen of Druine will feel as if they were involved. Of course, we must be careful. There are those, still living, who could speak of Ballas's past. His fellow Hawks: I understand that they held him in awe. If they discovered he was the fugitive . . . the sinner . . .' He coughed. 'But they shan't. Within a fortnight, they will all be dead. Precautions are being taken.'

'What of his family? If they know—'

'He has no family. Ballas came from Hearthfall, an agricultural region to the south. It was an area not untroubled by raiders. Once, they attacked the village where Ballas lived, and a terrible slaughter ensued. Standaire suspected, though couldn't be certain, that Ballas's family perished. I have checked the Church records, Godwin – and it seems that the General is correct. The year before Ballas joined the army, there were mass burials in Hearthfall. It seems safe to assume that grief-stricken and orphaned – for he was only fifteen years old when he joined the army, and thus fourteen years old when the raiders struck – he wandered for a year, uncertain what he ought to do. Then, like many aimless young men, he enlisted. Of course, he was three years too youthful to legitimately join the army. But he was twice the size of most recruits, and no one suspected a thing . . . But what does all this matter? These details are petty things. Anhaga Ballas is gone from the world. And history won't remember him.' Hengriste looked toward Nu'hkterin. And then the red-haired girl. 'It would be easier, Godwin, if she died.'

'I made a bargain—'

'Even so. But then – it is your choice, Godwin. I am old, and not long for this world. You reap as you wish. I shan't be twisted by the whirlwind.' He fiddled with his cape. Then he sighed. 'Damn everything. I despise these mountains. I don't care if they are holy, if Scarrendestin once stood here. I shall return to the Sacros. We have suffered a lot, of late – but we have survived, yes? The Pilgrim Church's deathbed has not yet been made. And we are entitled to compensations. I can think of none better than fires and whisky. Yes: I'll return to the Sacros . . . for fires and whisky.'

* * *

Blue light glowed around the Blessed Master. Shrinking, he adopted a crow form. With a dull crack of wings, he skirled away over the mountains.

Nu'hkterin had finished healing the red-haired woman. Now the Lectivin sat upon a rock, its head bowed with exhaustion. The woman gazed blankly across the mountains.

It would be easier if she died – Muirthan heard again the aged Master's words. Their logic was cold, clear. If the woman lived, she could reveal the truth to anyone she chose. She could speak of Asvirius, Nu'hkterin, the Church's secret magick. Most would think she was mad. But some would believe her. Enough, perhaps, to cause problems? Muirthan wondered.

He strode across to the woman. He touched his knife – a fleeting tap of fingertips upon hilt.

Suddenly, Muirthan grew cold. He felt as if every night-breeze was penetrating his robes. He shivered: a single, surprisingly violent spasm. He licked his lips, tasting frost.

He took his fingers from the weapon. Then he held out his hand.

Heresh stared uncomprehendingly.

'There is a contract I must honour,' said the Blessed Master evenly.

Heresh slipped her hand – slender, bloodstained – into his. Her skin was cold. Yet Muirthan felt warm again.

IAN GRAHAM was born in 1971 in the north of England and now lives in a small village on the edge of the West Pennine moors. He works as a bookseller and holds a Masters Degree in British Romanticism. In his free moments, he enjoys fell-walking, folk music, fishing and reading. *Monument* is his first novel.